Praise for the novels of Sara Ackerman

"Brilliantly written...Ackerman's settings blossom with stunning imagery as she brings to life characters that will stay with you long after you've finished the book. A fabulous read that makes me want to drop everything and travel to Hawaii!"
—Madeline Martin, *New York Times* bestselling author of *The Last Bookshop in London*

"*The Codebreaker's Secret* is Sara Ackerman at her best!... Two smart, adventurous women solving a captivating historical mystery, all set against the tropical beauty of Hawai'i during World War II and the 1960s, two fascinating eras. When I finished this book, I was more than ready to book a one-way ticket to the Big Island."
—Elise Hooper, author of *Angels of the Pacific*

"Once again Sara Ackerman delivers with a riveting novel of WWII-era Hawai'i. Her vivid storytelling makes the island come alive around you. A plucky heroine, a decades-old mystery, and a stirring romance make this book positively unputdownable!"
—Amanda Skenandore, author of *The Second Life of Mirielle West*

"Meticulously researched, rich and immersive, *The Codebreaker's Secret* will have you enthralled. A must-read for all fans of the genre. I absolutely loved it."
—Andie Newton, *USA TODAY* bestselling author of *The Girls from the Beach*

"With likable, authentic characters; lush, vivid settings; and secrets galore, the two timelines in *The Codebreaker's Secret* collide in spectacular fashion. Throughout, the book will tug on your heartstrings with its heartfelt depictions of grief, longing, hope, and resilience."
—Addison Armstrong, author of *The War Librarian*

"A wow of a book... A captivating story of friendship, heartbreak and true love. Highly recommend!"
—Karen Robards, *New York Times* bestselling author of *The Black Swan of Paris*, on *Radar Girls*

Also by Sara Ackerman

Island of Sweet Pies and Soldiers
The Lieutenant's Nurse
Red Sky Over Hawaii
Radar Girls

SARA ACKERMAN

The Codebreaker's Secret

ISBN-13: 978-0-7783-8645-2

The Codebreaker's Secret

Recycling programs
for this product may
not exist in your area.

For questions and comments about the quality of this book, please contact us at
CustomerService@Harlequin.com.

Mira
22 Adelaide St. West, 41st Floor
Toronto, Ontario M5H 4E3, Canada
BookClubbish.com

Printed in U.S.A.

For Hawaiʻi, my beautiful home in the middle of the sea.

The
Codebreaker's
Secret

1

THE TIDES

The ocean is far more than water. She swells with the moon, and disappears on the darkest nights. You get to know her moods as you would an old friend, and you respect her movements, her ever-changing ways. Her tides move in and out, bringing coconuts, leaf fragments, dead crabs and old fishing floats onto her shore. There is always an early-morning anticipation of what she has coughed up in the night, and what she has stolen. Those in the know make it down before the rest of the world wakes, leaving only their footprints in the sand.

A lone figure walks on the beach in the dim light of dawn. The high tide line snakes along, marked by small shells and twigs. Farther down, a log or a branch lies twisted and still, halfway up the beach. There is the faint smell of seaweed, pungent and salty. The figure moves leisurely but soon quickens their pace. The log is beginning to look less like a log and more like a body, appendages spreading out like seaweed. The figure stops, bends down as one would inspecting something unusual, something shocking.

If anyone knows death, it's the sea.

2

THE CODEBREAKER

Washington, DC, September 1942

There was perhaps no more tedious work in the world. Sitting at a desk all day staring at numbers or letters and looking for patterns. Taking notes and making charts. Thinking until your brain ached. For days and weeks and years on end. The extreme concentration drove some to the bottle, others to madness, and yet others to a quiet greatness that fewer than ten people in the world might ever know about. You might work for a year on cracking a particular code, only to have nothing to show for it but a tic in your eye and a boil on the back of your thigh. Failure was a given. Accept that and you'd won half the battle.

Isabel sat at her desk staring at a page full of rows and columns of five-letter groups that made no sense whatsoever on this side of the world. But on the other side, in Tokyo where the messages originated, she knew that Japanese officials were discussing war plans. War plans that were on this paper. As her eyes scanned the page, she felt the familiar scratching at the subconscious that meant she was close to seeing some kind of pattern. A prick of excitement traveled up her spine.

Suddenly, a hand waved up and down in front of her face, rudely pulling her out of her thoughts. "Isabel, you gotta put a lid on that noise. No one else can do their jobs," said Lieutenant Rawlings, her new boss.

She forced a smile. "Sorry, sir, most of the time I'm not aware that I'm doing it. I'm—"

"That may be the case, but try harder. I don't want to lose you."

Isabel had a tendency to hum during her moments of deepest focus, which had gotten her in trouble with her supervisors over the past year and a half while at Main Navy. In fact, she'd been transferred on more than one occasion due to the distracting nature of it. She'd worked hard to stop it, but when she went into that otherworldly state of mind, where everything slid away and the images moved around in her head of their own accord, the humming kicked back in. It would be like asking her not to breathe.

Lately, the whole team had reached a level of frustration that had turned the air in the room sour. Though they'd had success with the old Red machine, this complex supercipher seemed impossible to break. Faith was draining fast.

With her dress plastered to her back, and sucking on the second salt tablet of the day, Isabel put her head down, scribbling notes on her giant piece of paper. September in Washington burned hotter than a brick oven. Thoughts of her brother, Walt, kept interfering with her ability to stay on task. He would have turned twenty-five years old today. Would have been flying around somewhere in the Pacific about now, shooting down enemy planes, and hooting and hollering when he landed his plane full of bullet holes on the flattop. Walt loved nothing more than the thrill of the chase. Every time she thought of him, a lump formed in her throat and she had to fight back the tears. No one had ever, or ever would, love her more than Walt had.

More than anything, Isabel wanted to get to Hawai'i and see the spot where his plane plunged into the ocean. To learn more about his final days and hear the story straight from the mouths of his buddies. As if that would somehow make her feel better. She rubbed her eyes. For now, she was stuck here in this hellhole of a building, either sweltering or shivering, depending on what time of year it was.

At 1130, her friend Nora waltzed in from a break, looking like the cat who'd swallowed the canary. Nora had a way of knowing things before everyone else, and Isabel was lucky enough to be stationed at the desk next to hers.

"Spill the beans, lady," Isabel said quietly.

Nora glanced around the room dramatically. "Later."

Most of the team was still out to lunch, save for a couple of girls across the room, and Rawlings behind the glass in his office.

"No one's even here, tell me now."

Nora came over and sat on Isabel's desk, legs crossed. She picked up a manila folder and began fanning herself, then leaned in. "I've heard from a very good source that the brass are tossing around names for the lucky—or unlucky, depending on how you look at it—crypto being sent to Pearl."

Station Hypo at Pearl Harbor was one of the two main codebreaking units in the Pacific. Nora knew how badly Isabel wanted to be there.

Isabel perked up. "Whose names are being tossed?"

"That, I don't know."

"Should I remind Rawlings to remind Feinstein that I'm interested?"

"Absolutely not."

"It couldn't hurt, could it?" Isabel said.

"Sorry, love, but those men would just as soon send a polar bear to Hawai'i as a woman," Nora said.

"You seem to forget that one of the best codebreakers around is female. And the only reason most of our bosses know anything is because she taught them," Isabel said, speaking softly. This was the kind of talk that could get you moved to the basement. And Isabel did not do well in basements.

"Neither of us is Agnes Driscoll, so just get it out of your head. And even Agnes is not in Hawai'i," Nora whispered.

"There has to be a way."

"Maybe if you dug up a cache of Japanese codebooks. Or said yes to Captain Smythe," Nora said with a wink.

Nora and Isabel were a study in opposites. Her short red bob had been curled under and sprayed into place, her lips painted fire-engine red. She had a new man on her arm every weekend and walked around in a cloud of French lilac perfume that permeated their entire floor.

"I have no interest in Captain Smythe," Isabel said.

Hal Smythe was as dull as they came. At least as far as Isabel was concerned. Intelligent and handsome, but sorely lacking any charisma and the ability to make her laugh—one of her main prerequisites in a man. She had no time to waste on uninteresting men. Or men in general, for that matter. There were codes to be cracked and enemies to be defeated.

"Well, then, you'd better pull off something big," Nora said.

3

THE CELLAR

Indiana, March 1925

Five-year-old Isabel Cooper had just discovered a fuzzy cat-erpillar in her backyard, and was bent over inspecting its black-and-yellow pattern when a wall of black blotted the sun from the sky. Always a perceptive child, she looked to the source of the darkness. Clouds had bunched and gathered on the far horizon, the color of gunmetal and cinder and ash. Wind swirled her hair in circles. Isabel ran inside as fast as her scrawny legs would carry her.

"Walter, come look! Something weird is happening to the sky," she yelled, letting the screen door bang behind her.

Walter had just returned home from school, and was stand-ing in the kitchen with two fistfuls of popcorn and more in his mouth. Mom had gone to the grocery store, and Pa worked late every day at the plant, so it was just the two of them home.

Walter wiped his hands on his worn overalls and followed his sister outside. From a young age, Isabel discovered that Walt, three years older, would do just about anything his younger sister asked. By all accounts he was not your average older brother. He never teased, included her on his ramblings in the woods and never shied to put an arm around her when she needed it. Outside, the wind had picked up considerably, bending the old red oak sideways.

Walt stumbled past her and wiped his mouth with the back of his hand, gaping. "Jiminy Christmas!"

Daytime had become night.

"What?" Isabel asked.

"Some kind of bad storm a-brewing. Where's Lady?" Walt asked, looking around.

Their dog, Lady, had been lounging under the tree when Isabel ran inside, but was now nowhere to be seen. "I don't know."

"We better get into the shelter. I don't like the looks of this."

"I need Lady."

The air had been as still as a morning lake, but suddenly a distant boom shook the sky. Moisture collected on their skin, dampening Isabel's shirt.

"Lady!" they cried.

But Lady didn't appear.

Walt held up his arm. "See this? My hair is standing up darn near straight. We gotta get under."

Isabel looked at her arms, which felt tingly and strange. Instead of following her brother to the storm cellar, she ran to the other side of the house.

"Lady!" she yelled again with a kind of wild desperation that tore at the inside of her throat.

A moment later, Walt scooped her up and tucked her under his arm. "Sorry, but we can't wait anymore. She'll have to fend for herself."

Isabel kicked and punched at the air as they moved toward the cellar. "Put me down!"

Walt ignored her and kept running. His skin was sticky, his breath ragged. They had only used the cellar a couple times for storms, but on occasion Isabel helped her mother change out food supplies. The place gave her the creeps.

"What about Mom? We have to wait for her," she said.

"Mom will know where to find us."

In the distance, an eerie whistle rose from the earth. Seconds later, the wind picked up again, this time blowing the tree in the other direction. From the clouds, an ink black *thing* stuck out below. Walt yanked open the door, threw Isabel inside and fumbled around in the dark for a moment before finding the light. Roots crawled through cracks in the brick walls. They went down the steep stairs, Isabel's face wet with tears and snot.

"Come, sit with me," Walt said, pulling her against him on the old bench Pa had built.

Warmth flowed out of him like honey, and she instantly felt better. But then she thought about Lady and her mother, who were out there somewhere. Her whole body started shaking. Soon, a rumble sent vibrations through the wall and into Isabel's teeth. Too scared to cry, she dug her fingers into Walt's arm and hung on for dear life. Suddenly, a frantic scratching came from above.

Isabel jumped up, but Walt stopped her. "You stay down here."

Walt climbed to the top and opened the door. The wind took it and slammed it down hard. A loud barking ensued, and Walt fought with the door again, finally managing to get it open and bring Lady inside. The air possessed a ferocity Isabel had never seen before.

Lady immediately ran down the steps and started licking Isabel's arms and legs, and spinning in circles at her feet. Isabel hugged the big dog with all her might, burying her face in Lady's long golden fur. When Walt came back down, the three of them huddled together as a roar louder than a barreling freight train filled their ears. Soon, Lady began panting.

Walt squeezed Isabel's hand. "It's okay, we're safe down here."

He had to yell to be heard. And then the light went out. Darkness filled every crack and crevice. The earth groaned. The door above rattled so fiercely that she was sure it would fly off at any moment. All Isabel could think about was her mother out there somewhere in this tempest. Soon, her lungs were having a hard time taking air in.

"I can't breathe," she finally said.

"It's just nerves. They act up in times like these."

"How do you know?"

"Because I had it happen before."

She took his word for it, because it was hard to talk above the noise of the storm, and because Walt always knew what he was talking about. Then, directly overhead, they heard a sky-splitting crack and a thundering boom. The cellar door sounded ready to cave. Isabel and Walt and Lady moved to the crawl space under the steps. The three of them barely fit, even with Lady in her lap. Lady kissed the tears from Isabel's face.

Finally, the noise began to recede. When there was no longer any storm sounds, Walt went up the steps with Isabel close behind. He pushed but nothing happened. Pushed again. Still nothing.

"Something must have fallen on it," he said.

"I have to pee."

"You're going to have to wait."

"I can't wait."

Walt banged away on the door with no luck. "Then I guess you have to go in your pants. Sorry, sis."

Isabel began to grow sure that this was where they would

live out the rest of their short lives. That no one had survived the apocalypse outside and they would be left to rot with the earthworms, roots growing through their bodies until they'd been reduced to dirt. Her whole body trembled as Walt spoke consoling words and rubbed her back.

"They'll find us soon, don't you fret."

Lady licked her hand, but Isabel was beyond words, shivering and gulping for air. Every now and then Walt went up to try to push the doors again, but each time, nothing happened. She vowed to herself that she would never, ever be trapped underground again. She'd take her chances with a twister over being entombed any day.

It was more than an hour before someone came to get them. An hour of dark thoughts and silence. In the distance they heard voices, and eventually a pounding on the cellar door. "Are you three in there? It's Pa," said a voice.

"Pa!" they both cried.

"We got a big tree down on the door up here. Hang tight, I'll get you out soon."

When the doors finally opened, a blinding light shone in. Pa reached his hand in and pulled them out, wrapping them in the biggest hug they'd ever had. Never mind that the old truck was upside down and one side of the house was missing.

"Where's your mother?" Pa said.

"She went to the store," Walt said.

Pa's face dropped clear to the ground. "Which store did she say she was goin' to?"

"She didn't say, but she left just as soon as I got home from school," Walt said.

Only half listening, Isabel spun around in disbelief at the chaos of branches and splintered wood and car parts and things that didn't belong in the yard. Sink. Baby carriage. Bookshelf. It appeared as though the edge of the tornado had gone right over their place, leaving half the house intact, and obliterating the rest.

"Son, stay here with your sister. And stay out of the house until I get back. It might be unstable," Pa said, running off to his car.

"Mom will be okay, won't she? The store is safe, isn't it?" Isabel asked.

"Sure she will. Pa will be back with her soon," Walt said.

They wandered around the yard, dazed. This far out on the country road, the nearest neighbor, old Mr. Owens, was a mile away. Drained, Isabel sat down and pulled Lady in for a hug. Pa didn't return for a long time, and when he did, they could tell right away that something was wrong. His eyes were rimmed in red, like he had been crying. And Pa never cried.

"Kids, your mom isn't coming back."

That was the first time Isabel Cooper lost the most important person in her life.

4

THE CRIB

Washington, DC, December 1942

While summer and early fall had scorched, Washington's winter cold bit to the bone. Even more so than back home in Indiana. Isabel was swaddled in a thick pea-colored coat and wool cap, and working on her third cup of coffee. She had been transferred from working on JN-25—the main Japanese naval code—to Magenta, the complex cipher machine that had some of the best minds in the military banging their heads against the wall.

"So far, neither the British nor the Soviets have been able to break it," Rawlings had told her on her first day, in his smooth Southern drawl.

"So what makes you think we will?"

He shrugged. "Just a hunch I have."

In her experience, hunches had no place in cryptanalysis. But she kept her mouth shut. She was the new girl on the team, and that made her almost invisible. Which didn't bother her a bit. She was used to being invisible. Not exactly a wallflower—at five-nine with midnight hair and ice blue eyes—Isabel nonetheless preferred to blend into the background. Growing up with her head in books or out wandering alone through the hemlock and ash trees had shaped her. She wasn't out for fame and glory, never had been.

She just wanted retribution for the enemies who'd shot down her brother, who also had happened to be her best friend.

After a couple weeks on Magenta, Isabel could see why the machine had proved so elusive. Her tiny new team had been forced to construct a similar machine out of thin air. No one had ever seen the machine, not even a blueprint of it, and they were drawing conclusions based on bits and pieces of stolen intercepts. The machine in question resembled a typewriter crossed with a telephone switchboard and was full of wires and knobs and dials. Word was, Magenta was even tougher than Enigma, the German cipher machine. And Enigma was as tough as they came.

On this particular afternoon, Isabel was wishing that, along with Latin and French, she had learned Japanese in school. Sure, you didn't need to know the foreign language in order to break the cipher, but it couldn't hurt. One of the first rules in codebreaking was to understand how the language in question operated. That meant knowing which letters were most common, which letters went together in pairs or triplets, which vowels went with which consonants and so on. But the Japanese language was a far cry from English.

She had been staring at her charts and rows of letters for so long her eyes had begun to cross. Short periods of humming had started up, but she managed to quell them before getting glares from her coworkers. Frustrated, she set down her pencil, the fourth one of the day, and got up to take a break.

At Rawlings's desk, she stopped and said, "Excuse me, sir. May I go outside and take a walk? I need to clear my head."

Tamping down the humming seemed to also dampen her

ability to see patterns, the numbers and letters appearing on the backs of her eyelids, moving and melding and shifting. Whenever she reached a dead end, walking tended to loosen the straps of her mind.

"It's snowing," he said.

"I don't mind. I like the snow."

"Fine, but don't go catching pneumonia on me," he said.

Outside, feathers of snow fell silently on the mall. A thin layer had begun to form on tree branches and all surfaces facing skyward. Isabel pulled her coat tight and headed down Constitution Avenue toward the Potomac, breathing out clouds. Pretty soon, her steps fell into an even rhythm and the letters appeared in her mind. Groups of six and groups of twenty.

While the naval code JN-25 used numbers, Magenta was a diplomatic code and it used letters. It was known that messages that could be pronounced were cheaper to send, and to be pronounceable, even if it was pronounceable gibberish, meant the group needed both vowels and consonants. Six vowels, twenty consonants. Over the past few months, Isabel's team, using knowledge from the old Red machine, which had been cracked, were able to notice a pattern with the six-letter mechanism. They correlated frequencies of vowels quite easily. But how the twenty letters were enciphered still eluded them. Even with the new IBM machines to help.

Shuffling through the snow in a trance, Isabel arrived at the river and headed north along the pathway. A chill rose off the water, carrying scents of fish and boat engine oil. Letters were flashing through her mind at an alarming rate. Encrypting machines used switches or rotors to transpose letters. *B* might become *F*, and then *L*, and finally *X*. Depending on how many cycles, the pattern would eventually repeat. She ran through thousands of possibilities, still nothing materialized.

Rawlings had burst in that morning after a meeting with Admiral Williams, face red, and slammed down a stack of papers. It was unlike him to be so rattled. "Intel says something major is going down between Japan and Germany. We need to get this figured out. Yesterday."

The air was so cold that ice had begun to form on the edges of the river. All the benches were empty, not a soul in sight, which was just how she liked it. The trees and the river didn't mind her humming, and she walked along in a reverie, half-aware of her surroundings, and half-lost in her own mind. Letters swirled around. There had to be a pattern. The cycles had to repeat. Somewhere along the way, a hypothesis began to form in the space beneath her thoughts.

The best way to test this would be to find more than one long message, sent on the same day so that they had the same cipher key. And they needed a crib. Her heart rate ramped up as she turned to hurry back.

As usual, the marine at the door demanded to see her badge. *Specialist Q.*

Cheeks burning and hands numb, she ran into the room in a flurry and tapped on the glass door of Rawlings's small office. "I had a thought," she said to Rawlings, then paused before continuing.

He looked lightly put off. "And?"

"If we can find at least three long messages sent on the same day, and a crib, we might have a chance at unraveling Magenta."

A crib was a string of plain language known to be in a cipher or coded message that offered a way in. The Japanese were famous for their formalities, and these often gave Isabel and her team an entry point. *I am most honored to inform Your Excellency*, and other such phrases, had been handed over by the State Department, who often had the words in English. These proved to be immeasurably valuable.

Rawlings stared at her for a moment, then said, "Well, what are we waiting for?"

Isabel rushed to the file cabinet out in the main room while Rawlings unfolded himself from his desk and announced to the team, "We need to find three long messages sent on the same day, and we need them now."

Nora and the five other gals on watch scurried to the wall of cabinets and began banging drawers, pulling files and riffling through them. Rawlings and Dell, the only other man on the team, huddled together, plotting their approach. Isabel was well aware they'd done this kind of thing before, only to fall flat, and she had to work to keep her excitement in check. For every single success, there were a hundred failures.

"Long messages are fine and dandy, but we really need a crib," Nora said.

Isabel loved how adeptly the women all adopted codebreaking lingo. It made her feel like part of a smart girls' club. Something she had never experienced before. The only club she'd ever been in consisted of an old horse, two goats and a couple of collie dogs.

"One step at a time," Isabel said, fingers black with ink.

Anna, the tall and outspoken blonde in the bunch, said, "You ask me, this is a wild-goose chase. Magenta is unbreakable. The sooner we accept that, the sooner we can get back to working on JN-25."

"Now that's a great attitude to have," Nora said.

"Nothing wrong with being realistic. Someone around here needs to be," Anna said.

Other than being exceptionally bright, Anna was poorly suited for this work. She was always too ready to give up and move on to the next best thing. She lacked patience and perseverance and possibly the dash of insanity that was required in order to be a top-notch cryptanalyst.

Two hours later, the group had lost a bit of steam. Their frantic searching had become more measured, more methodical. But this was how things went here. They all knew that. Still, it was hard to not feel discouraged.

Nora had found one long message dated November 25. Only a few words in the message had been cracked. They still needed two more. Rawlings sent Nora and Anita to Room 1616 to ask for help in finding messages. Not twenty minutes later they burst into the room, flushed.

Nora waved a file. "We got them. November 25, straight out of Tokyo!"

Rawlings smoothed his thin mustache and smiled. "Damn, ladies. Good work. Now, the crib. Does anyone remember a circular or anything else coming through that day?"

"That day is over a month ago, sir," Anna said. "With all due respect, we've had thousands of messages come through since then."

Rawlings responded with a hard glare, and Isabel swore the temperature dropped ten degrees. Everyone scurried to the other side of the room, where cribs were kept.

Speaking softly, so no one else could hear, Nora said, "If we—you—solve this thing, your chances of going to Pearl will go up to about five percent. From zero."

"Thanks, that makes me feel better," Isabel answered.

"But truly, I think it might be the only way to wake them up to seeing your brilliance."

Behind them, Ellen Mary, also known as the most organized woman in the world, was quietly leafing through her own desk drawer and mumbling something to herself. She had a nearly photographic memory.

Isabel walked over. "What is it?"

"I think I recall a circular coming through that same day. It stuck out to me because it was the day before Thanksgiving."

A circular was simply when Tokyo sent messages to the embassies using both the old machine *and* Magenta. These messages were gold, since the old machine had been cracked, and they could thus decipher the messages and then look for correlations with Magenta.

While everyone else was focused on haphazardly searching, Ellen Mary pulled out a slightly crumpled sheet of paper, set it on her desk and smoothed it out with long, pale fingers. Isabel leaned in to get a closer look. Letters and scribbles and more letters with lines through them. And a date: November 25.

"You never cease to amaze me, Em," Isabel said.

Ellen Mary shrugged. "Just doing my job."

Isabel called Rawlings and the group over. "Em here just found a crib."

It was going to be a long night.

5

THE ARRIVAL

Hawai'i Island, July 1965

This was not the kind of place one built a hotel—the land fierce and unforgiving, the sun dangerous. Endless fields of lava flows, some ancient and some as recent as 1859, covered the entire coastline. On much of it, nothing grew but the very occasional kiawe tree or random tuft of grass. Overseeing the whole expanse loomed five massive volcanoes—Mauna Kea, Mauna Loa, Hualālai, Kohala Mountain and Haleakalā across the channel on Maui.

To Lu, it was home.

"Are you sure we're in the right place?" asked the elongated woman sitting next to her in the back of the car.

At the Waimea airport, in howling wind and sideways rain, they had piled into the back seat of a shiny black limousine, sent by Mr. Rockefeller. Lu could barely contain her excitement at being here, but the woman next to her had immediately closed her eyes and passed out. She smelled like jelly beans and caramel syrup, and she snored like a lonely donkey looking for some conversation. But now that they were nearing the bottom of Kawaihae Road, the other woman had woken up and was alert as could be, round eyes taking in the barren landscape.

The driver adjusted his rearview mirror and caught Lu's eye. "No question about it, Miss Diaz."

"You must be kidding me. It feels like we've been duped," the lady said.

Miss Diaz? Lu felt a jolt of adrenaline. She snuck a glance at her neighbor. Long, almost black hair, middle part, button nose. Casual but chic in a white gauzy blouse, jeans and strappy wooden sandals. Of all people, this was *the* Joni Diaz. Somehow she'd missed it in her fuzzy-headed haze back at the airport. It had been a hell of a flight and she'd been stuck in the smoking section next to a man with severe halitosis. Her hair still smelled like the ashtray on her boss's desk.

Joni yawned. "Even the cows look miserable."

A herd of cattle bunched up along a barbed-wire fence. Lu had to agree, they did look forlorn, their long-lashed eyes pleading, *Get me out of here.* When she had first learned of Rockefeller's plan to build a golf course at Kauna'oa, her first thought had been, *He must be insane.* And not only a golf course, but a fancy hotel. Inhospitable, sweltering and in the boonies. But it did have one thing going for it.

"Wait until you see the water," Lu said.

The ocean was the only redeeming quality on this section of the island. The kind of blue heaven that dreams were made of. It was late afternoon, though, and anyone born and bred on the Big Island knew that by this time of day the onshore winds would be whipping.

"No offense, love, but it looks like bloody victory at sea to me," Joni said.

Whitecaps crashed everywhere.

Lu felt defensive of her island. "First thing in the morning, you've never seen anything so pretty. Slick as blue glass and teeming with fish and dolphins and, during the winter months, whales. Give it a chance," Lu said.

Joni turned her way and yawned.

"How do you know so much?" Her tone was more lazy and curious than anything.

"I grew up in Kona."

"Are you a guest at the hotel?"

Lu held up her notebook. "I'm doing a story on Mr. Rockefeller's new hotel for *Sunset* magazine."

Speaking those words would never get old.

Joni looked her up and down. "Come on, you're too young to be a reporter."

Good things come in small packages, Auntie H always said. Small for her age as a child, and with an unruly head of coffee-colored curls, Lu had learned to overcompensate with grown-up words and tall tales.

"Think what you want. And I'm a journalist, not a reporter."

"What's the difference?"

"Reporters report news and facts, journalists go deeper—we tell the stories."

"So what's your name, Miss Journalist from *Sunset* magazine?" Joni asked. She had an innocent feel to her, but there was nothing innocent about her voice.

"Lu."

"Is that short for Lucille or Betty Lou or some kind of Lou?"

"Luana. It's Hawaiian."

"You're Hawaiian?"

"No, I'm Portuguese. On my dad's side. My mom's family is mostly Irish."

Why she felt compelled to elaborate, she had no idea. She'd always been proud of her Hawaiian name, but on the mainland, no one understood, so she shortened it to Lu, which was her nickname, anyway. As a byline it worked well. No one knew she was a woman.

Joni held out her hand. "I'm Joni. Joni Diaz. Might I book you for a morning swim tomorrow? Something tells me you'd be a perfect tour guide."

Lu laughed. "I'd love to swim with you, but I'm no tour guide. This is a work trip, so I'm on the clock the whole time. They sent me last-minute, and I have plenty of catching up to do."

"Don't tell me you've flown all the way across the Pacific to visit the world's most expensive hotel, and you aren't going to have even a wee bit of fun?" Joni said.

That was exactly what she planned on doing. "This is my first big assignment. I got lucky being sent here. It was a fluke, so now I need to take full advantage."

"How old are you, Luana? You don't mind if I call you that, do you—it's such a beautiful name."

"Not at all. I'm twenty-five."

"Let me give you a tip. Don't work so hard that you forget to have fun. I tried that once and it nearly killed me," Joni said, voice trailing off in barely a whisper.

Joni Diaz was not a day over thirty. In the past five years or so, she had shot to fame with her soulful voice and knack for writing songs that made people weep. Women loved her, men wanted her. Old people admired her, and kids wanted to be her. She had always seemed larger than life. But in person, there was a fragility about her that made Lu curious. Not unusual, because Lu was curious about *everything*.

They reached the bottom of the winding road and veered left onto a patchy road heading south. Joni rolled down her window halfway, letting in a blast of hot air, then quickly rolling it back up. "Where are the trees, for chrissakes?"

"Some of these kiawe trees grow quite large. You might know them as mesquite. Or *Prosopis pallida*."

Joni frowned. "Come again?"

"That's their Latin name."

"You speak Latin?"

Lu shrugged. "No, but I know my local plants."

A few minutes later, they turned down toward the ocean, passing a rock wall with a simple orange flower logo and the words *Mauna Kea*. They drove through a row of hala trees and fuchsia bougainvillea bushes, and the barren scrub and crumbly lava gave way to a neon-green golf course. Lu had read about it, and seen photographs, but still had had big doubts that anyone would be able to construct a golf course on a'a lava. Apparently she'd been wrong. They passed through the golf course to the edge of the ocean, where one of the holes perched precariously on the cliff. To reach it, one would have to clear a little cove.

"I don't play golf, but that looks like a losing proposition for just about anyone," Joni said.

Lu had never played golf, either. Golf was for people with money and her family was the opposite of wealthy. They were farmers—rich in macadamia nuts, afternoon rain and spiders. The road swung left toward the hotel, and green sprang up everywhere, dotted with orange and pink flower accents.

"Hey, here are your trees," Lu said with a certain amount of satisfaction.

An assortment of plumeria, royal poinciana, banyan and coconut trees lined the drive. At a roundabout, they pulled up behind a long line of cars—everything from limousines to rusted ranch trucks covered in mud. Lu felt a flurry in her chest. She was actually here! Now she had to manage to write something smart. Something attention grabbing. Something brilliant.

Girls with plumeria lei greeted them, kissing their cheeks and smiling *aloha*. The girls were not much younger than Lu and their coconut and vanilla smells rubbed off on her cheek. A tall, skinny reed of a man swept them into the lobby, where a few stylish guests milled around, holding drinks, talking and leaning on the oiled hardwood railings and looking out over the ocean below.

The lack of outer walls and abundance of plants gave the place a sense of freedom and room to breathe. A huge atrium in the center opened to the floor below, where towering coconut trees stretched toward the sky. There was so much salt in the air you could have bottled and sold it.

Lu was still with Joni, who had put on a pair of oversize shades. A few heads turned, but she paid them no mind. Joni seemed at ease, but Lu felt as though she were in over her head. Then someone behind them latched on to Joni's arm.

"Excuse me, Miss Diaz, can I get a shot?" a man in a khaki suit asked, holding up a pricey Canon that blocked his face.

Joni yanked her arm away. "Not right now, please."

The man clicked, anyway.

"Hey, she said *no*," Lu snapped.

When he lowered the camera, her mouth went dry. Black wavy hair, gap in his teeth. The man in question was none other than Matteo Russi. Legend. Icon. He had been working for *Life* magazine almost as long as she'd been alive. Maybe longer.

"You the bodyguard?" he asked, dark eyes unflinching.

Lu was at a loss for words.

Joni answered for her. "Yes, she is. Now please find someone else to bother."

They veered away before he could respond, Lu reeling from the unexpected interaction. Not a great first impression for the man she had been dying to meet for as long as she could remember. She should have known he would be here. The Mauna Kea Beach Hotel was a photographer's dream, and Mr. Rockefeller would have wanted only the best. She suddenly felt very out of her league.

When Lu opened the door to her room, even though it was on the lowest level and probably the cheapest one on this side, she was dazzled. This was no Holiday Inn. Crisp orange bedspreads, freshly woven lauhala mats, dark hardwood doors and a vase full of pink proteas and ferns. The oceanfront rooms all faced west, and looked down over a crescent-shaped beach and the blue horizon beyond. It was this ocean that she had missed the most. She flopped down on the nearest bed, ready for a nap and yet far too excited to sleep.

Mr. Rockefeller had planned three openings for his grand hotel—an open house for the locals, which had already transpired, one for the upper echelon of Hawai'i, and now a fortunate few were invited to stay the weekend. People were referring to the latter as his House Party. This was reserved for a small group of very important people—politicians and old-money types had come from far and wide for a weekend of golf, horseback riding, fishing and drinking. Lu counted herself lucky to be included. The guest list was closely guarded.

It almost hadn't happened. Two days ago, she had been sitting at her desk punching away at her typewriter with the sticky O, when Rusty Styles, executive editor, came over, smoke pouring from his nostrils.

"Where's your boss?" he said.

"He's at Berkeley in search of nude protesters, I think."

Her boss, Joe, the culture editor, was always pushing limits at the magazine.

"Shit. I need him."

Lu perked up. "Can I help?"

"Sid crashed his bike and broke his collarbone, now he can't go to Napa. I'm sending Joe in his place," he said.

"Joe leaves for Hawai'i tomorrow."

"Not anymore. But now I have to find someone to send to the Mauna Kea and I'm already short-staffed."

Joe would not be pleased, but the opportunity almost knocked Lu out of her chair. "I grew up in Hawai'i. How about sending me?"

"Now, why would I do that?"

"For one, I know the island. My uncle and I used to collect salt along the very rocks the hotel is built on. He works there now, too, so I'm sure he can get me any inside stories. And…" she said, pausing for effect. "I've memorized Mark Twain's book *Roughing It in the Sandwich Islands*, and already have a million ideas for stories."

Partial lie—yes, Mark Twain. No, story ideas. Yet. She was surprised by how badly she suddenly wanted to go. The mainland might have more opportunity, but it still didn't feel like home. As much as she wished it so. The water was cold, the people different, and the air smelled of pine trees and smog and winter. Something about it hollowed her out.

Styles pushed up his black-rimmed glasses and inspected her more closely. "I promised Rockefeller I'd send someone seasoned."

He had her there.

"Mr. Rockefeller hires women whenever he can. He'd more than approve."

"Where'd you hear that?"

By the way he said it, she knew that he knew it to be true.

"I know everything there is to know about him and his new hotel. Joe put me on it to help him prepare."

He rubbed his chin. "No offense, but you look like a sophomore in high school. You won't fit in and you're about as unseasoned as they come," he said.

"You said you needed someone, and I'm someone. I'm a strong writer and I know the island. Give me a chance. Please, Mr. Styles."

"You've never done a feature."

"It doesn't sound as if you have a choice."

Two days later, and here she was, already friends with Joni Diaz and the weekend hadn't even started. The schedule had been placed on the table, and Lu committed it to memory as the onshore winds blew in through the open sliding-glass doors and tickled her skin.

She wished she could talk to Dylan and tell him about her day so far. He would die if he knew that Matteo Russi was here, absolutely flip out and probably embarrass the both of them. Russi had been her friend's idol for as long as she'd known him, which was exactly two years and one month. How she knew that she had no idea. The thought of Dylan filled her with a warm morning sunshine on your skin kind of feeling. Only this was on the inside. Lately, this had been happening more and more, and Lu found it disconcerting.

The first time they'd met, she had been at the beach in Pacifica, getting her ocean fix, and out of the water came Dylan with a Duke Kahanamoku surfboard and kelp wrapped around his neck like a lei. Lu asked him where he got the board, and he told her his dad swam with Duke back in the day. She told him she was from Hawai'i and he started peppering her with questions, as any good journalist would. Soon, they were sipping coffee in a café, listening to Pete Seeger. He was funny and kind and had eyes the color of deep sea. Maybe that was why he felt like home.

Now, Lu was in Hawai'i without him as he got ready for his assignment in Vietnam. It didn't seem fair, but then, when had life ever been fair?

6

THE PATTERN

Washington, DC, 1942

The team retired at midnight, but was at it first thing the next morning. Isabel and Nora walked the five blocks to work in the dark gloom of a frigid morning. At Main Navy something was wrong with the heater and they were forced to keep their coats and hats and mittens on. Nora's teeth chattered as she brewed the first pot of coffee.

"I can't wait to move into the new quarters at Mount Vernon," Nora said.

"Either that or Pearl," Isabel said.

Nora gave her a look and gently rested her hand on Isabel's shoulder. "I understand why you want to go, but he's not coming back, sweetie. And it makes no sense for you to go over there and get yourself killed, too. Hawai'i isn't safe right now."

"I know that. But I feel like I'll never be settled, never be able to move on, until I get over there and see for myself."

"What we are doing here in Washington matters. Sometimes it may feel like we're just part of the machine, but every ship or sub sunk on our watch is a big deal," Nora said.

She was right, of course. Nora had lost a boyfriend in the first month of the war and understood Isabel's burning need to help take down the enemy. But everyone had their own flavor of grief, as the chaplain had said. Everyone moved on, or didn't, in their own way.

With a giant mug of coffee in hand, Isabel sat at her desk and looked down at the paper. Tried to clear her head. Rawlings had copied the messages and the crib on a fresh sheet and doled them out to everyone on the morning watch. Yesterday had been a bust. No patterns had emerged after hours of staring at the letters. But today was a new day.

Sometimes it took a little while to get into the zone. For Isabel, it meant staring loosely for a while and emptying her mind of all thought. Not trying too hard. Not looking for anything in particular. Just looking. The morning passed in a blur of coffee and donuts. And it wasn't until lunchtime that her hands finally warmed up.

Ten groups wide, and running the length of the page, the letters went. JSOUX EXYEP R DETJ GAMPV. Isabel stared and stared, eventually following a pathway of *E*s that struck her as interesting. Halfway down the page, something stood out to her. She flipped to the next page, the next message. Her eyes ran down it, quickly marking off repetitions. Before she knew it, she was humming as if there was no one else in the room.

"Quit that," Anna said.

But Isabel hardly heard her. There was a pattern here. She was sure of it. Her heart kicked against her ribs. With her pencil, she started circling coinciding letters on both the message and the crib. She found a couple more on the next page. And another on the one after that.

Good heavens, this was it!

To be certain, she went over it three more times. A warm

feeling of satisfaction spread through her like fresh maple syrup. She glanced around, suddenly self-conscious and sure that everyone had been able to sense her excitement. But everyone else was deep in concentration, pencils scratching on paper. Rawlings was in his office, leaning back in his chair in that way that always made her think he'd fall backward at any moment. Dell and another guy were in there, too. Who knew what they were talking about, but from the way Dell was laughing, it couldn't be work.

Isabel smoothed down her hair and stood up. She gathered her papers and held them to her chest, moving silently through the room. No one paid her any mind. Instead of knocking, she waved at Rawlings and pointed at her paper.

Rawlings righted his chair and motioned her in. "Whatcha got?"

She tried to maintain composure, but her hands trembled. "I think I may have found something, sir. A pattern."

Isabel stepped in and laid her papers on his desk. A field of electricity sparked across her skin. The physics of excitement. The men must have felt it, too, because for a brief moment the room was so quiet you could have heard a snowflake land. These men had years in the field, even decades. And now they were looking at her with such expectancy her throat caught.

"I'm not sure how it happened, but I noticed something with the *E*s," she said, circling the points where the pattern revealed itself. The men all leaned in. Rawlings tapped his foot like a madman. "I've checked it three times. It works out," she said.

Rawlings leafed through the papers again, flipping them faster and faster, and Isabel watched his face slowly turn red. When he reached the last one, he jumped up, knocking his chair back in the process.

"We're in! We're in! Goddamn, Isabel has done it!" he yelled to the rest of the girls.

Isabel stood still as a coat post, and could not form any words. She had never seen anyone here at Main Navy show such an outward display of emotion. It simply did not happen in this top-secret, classified, somber world. The other men crowded around the papers as the rest of the watch flooded in.

Rawlings roared, "Someone go get Feinstein, tell him it's urgent."

Nora tore off, and Rawlings moved them out to the main table. Then he left and came back with the old bottle of scotch that sat dusty on his top shelf. He set down two glasses. "If anything deserves a toast, this is it."

Minutes later, Lieutenant Commander Feinstein strode in. An intense and bespectacled man with a razor thin mustache, he headed up the decrypt unit here at OP-20-G. The group parted to let him pass. Taciturn and aloof, he nonetheless was responsible for bringing women into the program. Maybe it had something to do with the fact that his own wife was even more brilliant than he was, or just that women had suddenly become more available in the federal job sector. Either way, all the girls worshipped him—and feared him.

"Miss Jenkins here says you have news," Feinstein said curtly.

Isabel was struck by the dark circles under his eyes and the sallowness of his skin. It was well-known that Feinstein was on the verge of a breakdown. Pressures of the job.

"Miss Cooper here has broken the twenties."

Feinstein looked stunned. "You sure about this?"

For the first time, Isabel suddenly faltered. What if she'd made a mistake and there was no pattern? After all, how did Feinstein or his wife, or a hundred others on the case, not solve it? There had been so many conjectures.

But Rawlings answered, "One hundred percent."

"I need to see for myself."

Rawlings nodded to Isabel. "Go on, show him."

Isabel felt weak behind the knees. "Yes, sir."

He came over to the table. Again, she went over the points she had circled and explained the cycles she had discovered. In the quiet of the suddenly warm room, his breathing began picking up speed. By the time she was finished going over the messages, he was nearly hyperventilating. He dropped to his forearms, pressing his forehead to the wood. Nora shot Isabel a concerned look.

After a tense moment, he raised his head and took off his glasses, wiping his eyes. "Miss Cooper, congratulations on a job well done. What we have here is the opening we've been seeking for the past six months. This is huge."

Isabel felt her cheeks go hot. "It wasn't just me, sir. Everyone here had a hand in it," she answered.

Rawlings poured the scotch, handed a glass to Feinstein and said, "To persistence and doggedness and brilliant women. Those Axis bastards won't even know what hit them."

The room erupted in cheers.

Feinstein threw his back and said, "Not a word of this leaves this room. I'll handle passing it on, on a need-to-know basis. Anyone who does otherwise will be hung out to dry—for treason."

Several days later, Rawlings and his team were still hard at work. There had been no big celebration, no party. Only the inner circle knew what had been done. And this was just the beginning, as they still had daily keys to overcome. But everyone knew it was just a matter of time. That was how it was with machines. There was a certain predictability. The group in the room down the hall immediately began working on a new replica of the Magenta machine and were reportedly making good progress.

It felt strange and wondrous to be part of such a huge coup, but Isabel still felt a hollow place in her heart. The war was too far away, too intangible. She wanted to be on the front lines and smell the smoke, taste the fuel. She wanted something she could touch. Something real.

On break, she stepped out for a quick walk along the Potomac. The skies were gray and gloomy, the breeze brisk. From the east, a rain squall blew in, unleashing a torrent of icy rain. She cinched her coat around her neck and reluctantly turned around. On the way back down Constitution, while she was off in a daydream about balmy seas and sunshine, a black sedan pulled up to the curb just in front of her. She paid it no mind until the passenger door opened.

"Care for a ride?" asked the driver, a silver-haired man in a raincoat.

It was common practice in wartime to offer rides to anyone military, so she gratefully accepted. "Thank you, the rain came out of nowhere."

"How long have you been in Washington, Miss...," he said.

Something about him felt familiar, but she couldn't place it.

"Cooper. Isabel Cooper. Almost two years, and I still haven't figured out the weather."

"I've been here a hell of a lot longer and have the same problem. DC weather is its own beast. Tell me, what brings you to this neck of the woods?"

She'd grown used to answering this question, and always kept it simple. "I'm a clerk for the navy."

"You stationed at Main Navy?"

"Yes." He made no move to pull away from the curb, so she added, "And I need to get back soon."

"What exactly do you do in there?" he asked.

"Mostly sharpen pencils and empty ashtrays. But every now and then, on a particularly interesting day, I take out the trash," she said.

The man laughed. "Now you've piqued my interest, Miss Cooper," he said as they finally drove off down the road. "Are you in communications, intelligence or perhaps even crypto?"

Who was this man? His hair was buzzed, his shoulders broad. He had to be military himself, and with those deep creases around his eyes, she would have guessed navy. But any good naval officer knew not to ask too many questions.

"None of the above," she said.

The windows had started to fog and she was beginning to feel claustrophobic. Not to the point of jumping out into the rain, but almost.

"Say, do you know what the Q in Specialist Q stands for?" he said.

A chill spilled through her limbs. Specialist Q was her naval rating, and no one else should know that. She turned to look at him. "Who *are* you?"

As they approached Main Navy, he didn't slow and they passed on by. "Sorry, Miss Cooper, I owe you an explanation," he said. "I wanted to see for myself how quiet you were about the job."

"I don't understand."

Up ahead, he pulled to the curb, under the skeleton branches of a large cherry tree. He unbuttoned his raincoat and pulled it off on one side, revealing the sleeve of his uniform. Isabel's gaze went to the gold stripes, then up to his ruddy face. Her skin prickled.

"I'm Admiral Sutton from Pearl. I head up COMINT in our neck of the Pacific."

"I know who you are, sir. I just didn't place you at first."

Admiral Sutton was legendary. He'd played a major role in

Midway and was known for his risky tactics and doggedness. She could scarcely believe she was sitting here in his presence. There was a weight to him, an air of confidence that filled up the vehicle.

He went on. "Word has it that you got us into Magenta."

She was nervous to say anything, after having the secrecy of their work tacked to their foreheads from day one. "They told us not to talk about it outside the room."

"For God's sake, I'm in charge of all intelligence and communications that pass through Hawai'i. Your secret is safe with me."

Isabel relaxed a little. "All right, then, I helped."

"Rawlings said it was all you. You do realize this is the biggest break we've had since the war started?" he said.

Never one for compliments, she looked down at her shoes. "I do."

"Anyway, I'm on a flight later today back to Hawai'i, so I'll cut to the chase. I want you to come work for us. At Hypo," he said, cracking his window and letting in the arctic air.

She swung her head around. "What?"

"You heard me. We need another codebreaker and you fit the bill. Yours was the name that kept coming up when I asked who was the best in this building." He looked at her and she had the sense that he was sizing her up. "What do you think?"

A rush of emotion washed through her, but Isabel kept her cool. "I'll pack my bags, sir."

He gave her a hard pat on the back. "Good. Now, I will tell you that not everyone there wants a gal on the team. It's not like here, where you have women spilling out of every doorway. You'll be the only one."

"I can handle it."

"Just what I like to hear. Make me proud, Miss Cooper."

7

THE HOTEL

Hawai'i Island, July 1965

After a quick shower, Lu stepped into a sleeveless dress and went down to meet Mr. Rockefeller. He'd written the note himself. *Please meet me on the promenade fronting the Dining Pavilion at five p.m. sharp. LSR.* From everything she'd read, Rockefeller was a hands-on kind of guy in the best sense of the word.

Lu took the side stairs, and worked up her first story in her mind, recalling the opening of *Roughing It in the Sandwich Islands*: "On a certain bright morning the islands hove in sight, lying low on the lonely sea, and everybody climbed to the upper dock to look." To be sure, she would not be able to write like Samuel Clemens, but she could insert her own voice and give it a go. Put a new spin on correspondence coming out of Hawai'i. More real, less offensive.

A low bank of clouds had set up shop along the horizon, toning down the summer heat, but with every step, she felt her hair expanding. Growing up in Kona, she always knew where the wind was coming from. North meant flat and

well-behaved hair. South or west meant wild and frizzy. Just
a byproduct of island life.

On the way down, she passed a giant Buddha—one of the
many priceless art pieces reported to be here—at the top of
a grand staircase leading to the lower deck. Lu admired the
modern, clean lines of the substantial sand-colored pillars.
An "invisible building" had been the goal, and Rockefeller
had succeeded in grand fashion.

When she reached the bottom of the stairs, she saw him
right away. Them, actually. Laurance Rockefeller was standing with Matteo Russi, pointing out something in the water.
Lu took a deep breath. *You can do this.* She pulled her shoulders
back and stood as tall as she could, thanks to her wooden plat-
form sandals. *Promenade,* it turned out, was just a fancy word
for a stone-paved walkway that fronts a hotel. Some of these
new words she'd had to look up in her dictionary. Mrs. Hoapili, her neighbor and *hānai* aunt—Lu called her Auntie H—
had given her the dictionary when she was thirteen and going
into the ninth grade at Konawaena. It was coffee-stained and
missing a few pages, but it was her most trusted ally.

Mr. Rockefeller was dapper in a light blue suit and white
shoes. As soon as he saw her, he held out a hand and gave
her a smile that immediately put her at ease. "Welcome to
the Mauna Kea, Miss Freitas. I understand you know these
parts well."

"Thank you, sir. I feel extremely fortunate to be here.
What you've done is perfect," she answered in her most polite and practiced voice.

He winked. "I'll take that as a compliment. Have you met
Mr. Russi? I thought it would be good to have press from
both coasts. Keep each other honest."

"We haven't met. I'm Lu Freitas, a big admirer of your
work," she said.

Russi, who appeared older in real life than in photos, laughed. "Coulda fooled me. But thanks, kid."

Rockefeller went on. "I think it's brilliant, too, to have both a man and a woman and I'm ashamed I didn't think of it first. We have a host of top-notch women on staff, everything from director of personnel to reservations to waitstaff."

"I'm happy to hear it," Lu said.

Russi was staring out to sea, looking lost in thought. A long pale scar ran down the side of his face, and crow's-feet framed his eyes. But together with his thick head of hair and good bone structure, Lu could see why older women might find him appealing.

"While you're here, I want you to both behave as my guests. The place is yours. You're here to do your job, but also to experience the Mauna Kea and all she has to offer," Mr. Rockefeller said with a sweep of his arm. "But please remember that the other VIPs are here at my invitation and are looking forward to a Hawaiian getaway far from the pressures of the mainland. Write about the hotel, not them. Now, I'd love to show you a few things."

Mr. Rockefeller led them down a stone path, around a swimming pool surrounded with coconut trees and down to sea level. A patio with tables merged with lawn and naupaka bushes crawling onto the beach. Most of the other beaches on the island were black with tiny green olivine sparkles. Not here. This sand was white as sugar.

"I'm betting you like to swim, Miss Freitas. How about you, Mr. Russi?"

Russi's jaw tightened. "Not a big fan."

"A shame, but you may change your tune. The water here has a way of working its magic on even the most ardent non-believers," Rockefeller said.

"I'll stick to the land, but thank you."

Out on the water, the sun slipped beneath the clouds, a red orb of light on the water.

"When I first came here, one of the locals that was showing me around told me that he had never, not once in his life, missed a sunset. And this was not a young man, either. His words struck a chord in me. I want this to be a place where the only thing people have to worry about is missing the sunset. For that reason, we have no televisions and other distractions of civilization."

They stood and watched it slowly disappear.

"How does it feel to be home?" Mr. Rockefeller asked Lu.

"It makes me wonder how I ever left in the first place," she said in all honesty.

"Sometimes we have to leave a place before we understand how much it means to us. And Hawai'i gets under your skin. I know that much."

Russi remained aloof, off in his own world. Maybe he was just jaded to beautiful places, but Lu's gut told her it was something more. He looked to be struggling through this little tour.

Mr. Rockefeller then took them out toward the point, where they turned around and looked back at the hotel, which sank back into the low hillside.

"We started out with nine designs, and this beauty is the winner. She's something, isn't she? We almost went with these small Greek village–style units, but we had one built and then during a tropical storm it was nearly wiped out. I kid you not, it was one thing after another getting to this day. We had a construction collapse, nearly all of our uniforms had to be remade, then half my furniture was stranded on a dock in Hong Kong. I had to charter a plane and send an old Flying Tiger buddy to go rescue it." He chuckled. "If that wasn't bad enough, add in an earthquake, a tsunami warning and a bomb threat. And that's not the half of it."

"Sounds about right. What can go wrong usually does, and then some," Russi said.

He seemed so nonchalant.

"You'd never know it now," Lu added.

"No, you wouldn't. I have fantastic people and my own doggedness to thank for that."

A zillion dollars didn't hurt, either.

When they returned to the lobby, Rockefeller went over to say something to the woman at the front desk. A moment later, the hole over the coconut-tree-filled atrium started sliding closed.

Russi craned his neck. "A hotel with a sunroof. Nice touch," he said.

Even though he was older, and a bit tired-looking, Russi was undeniably handsome. In a rugged, rough-around-the-edges kind of way. And with his dark hair and olive skin, he blended right in.

Rockefeller came back to them, grinning. "So, you two have the schedules. Until tomorrow, you're on your own. I expect you'll want to rest up. It's going to be one hell of a weekend."

With that, he left the two of them standing awkwardly together on the sea-blue tile. Russi began fumbling in his pocket for something. She thought he was going to pull out a pack of cigarettes, but instead it was gum. He held it out to her.

"Doublemint?" he asked.

"Yeah, thanks." Lu felt compelled to speak. "Look, Mr. Russi, I want to apologize for earlier, with Joni Diaz. I had no idea it was you and I kind of just reacted. Long flights, long day."

"More like overreacted."

"Excuse me?"

"You're green, I get it. But if you *had* known it was me, what would you have done?"

"I… Well… I don't know. Probably not have yelled at you, though."

"In this business, you're gonna have to get used to dealing with famous folks, folks in power, folks with money." He paused. "You want my two cents?"

"Please."

"Treat them like you would any old person. The bartender and Mr. Rockefeller are no different. The maid and the senator both eat, breathe and fuck. You can't get googly-eyed over anyone—especially me—or you're screwed. And get used to pissing people off now and then—it comes with the territory."

With that, he left her, gum still unwrapped in her hand and a mouthful of questions.

In her room, armed with a Coke and a tin of macadamia nuts, Lu sat down to compose her first story. Her idea was to do a series of vignettes, much like Twain had. The problem was, while ideas came easily and in large numbers, the act of putting them down on paper had always been a struggle. Letters went backward and words seemed to rearrange themselves before her eyes. Was it *dad* or *bad*? *Dead* or *bead*? The very fact that she was here, on assignment for *Sunset*, was a miracle in and of itself.

Her father, Buster, had balked at the idea of college. Flat out refused to help her pay. "Our family, we're not school people. Don't waste your time." The undercurrent of the message really being, *You're not smart enough*. Lu always wished her mother had been alive to counter that. She'd invent stories of her mother showering her with compliments. *My brilliant girl, tell me about the time you grew wings and flew around the moon. Your stories are spun from golden honey.* Her mother, Sally, had died of a "popped vein in her head," when Lu was just three. Later, Lu learned the medical term for it—aneurysm. Lu mostly remembered her long brown hair and earthy scent, and fragments of her smile.

Not long after Lu's mother died, Donna moved in. Buster and Donna both worked on their small, family macadamia-nut farm. Buster managed and Donna picked and cooked for all the workers. Buster was proud of his farming roots and saw little use for schooling. So it was no wonder they called Donna in one afternoon when Lu was in the second grade, for the teacher to inform her that Lu had mental issues, that her handwriting was illegible and she was obstinate as a mule. But Donna had barely graduated from high school herself, and dealing with a slow child was not in her repertoire. Lu was left to struggle through school on her own, never enjoying it, but compensated by telling stories—mainly to the animals.

The farm was home to cats, dogs, chickens, two cows and a small herd of donkeys, also known as Kona nightingales—for the godawful racket they made if left alone. From a young age, Lu would gather the assortment of cats, a chicken or two and the old donkey, Luna, and tell them elaborate tales. The chickens usually wandered away once the scraps were gone, but the cats stayed and Luna showed her teeth whenever Lu stopped talking. She knew she was onto something.

At school, though, things got worse before they got better. Some teachers were understanding, others oblivious and a few uncool. Her fifth grade teacher was the worst, and repeatedly brought Lu to the chalkboard for grammar practice, as if tormenting her would somehow make her smarter. Jason Hamada, the class nerd, took pity on her and they developed signs and signals that helped some. But she never forgot the burn on her cheeks and the feeling of utter worthlessness as the other kids laughed behind her back.

Everything changed when she met Auntie H, who took Lu under her wing and taught her that smarts came in many flavors. *Book smart, people smart, music smart, art smart, plant smart and so on.* She insisted that Lu was not dumb, just misunderstood. After all, Lu had a bottomless pit of a memory, was blessed with a vivid imagination and made friends easily—both human and animal. "Kindness and compassion make the world go 'round," Auntie H loved to say.

Over the years, Auntie H had slowly transformed from neighbor to tutor to dearly loved aunt, friend and mom, all wrapped up in one. She filled the motherless hole in Lu that Donna never would. It was purely because of her that Lu blossomed, graduated high school and went to college. Lu loved her to the sun and beyond.

The yellow legal pad sat empty on the desk now, save for a few scratched-out words. It would be far more interesting to her if she could write about the people here. Yes, the hotel was gorgeous. Yes, the sea-blue tile on the lobby floor made you feel like you were swimming. But so what? In recent months, she'd had this same vague feeling. Writing about places and events and backyard barbecues wasn't cutting it for her.

On a particularly bright summer day, the hotel appeared out of the lava, a sentinel keeping watch over the lazy blue Pacific. After two thousand miles of air travel, and traversing barren fields of brush, the sight was a most welcome one.

It took her two hours to get those two sentences down, and they were nothing special whatsoever. At some point, she was going to have to go with what she had, so she pulled out her portable typewriter and typed it all up.

★ ★ ★

The next morning, a tapping woke her from a dead sleep. At first she thought it was a bird and pulled the pillow over her head, but the sound grew louder, and she realized it was coming from the door. The sky had just begun to lighten. Why would someone be knocking at this ungodly hour?

"Luana! It's me, Joni."

Lu threw on a robe with an orange flower and went to the door. "What's going on?"

"This is your wake-up call. I thought it would be nice to be the first ones in the water."

Lu rubbed her eyes. "What time is it?"

"Who cares what time it is. Come on!"

"I need coffee. I don't function without it."

"Ah, my friend, the water will wake you right up. You're the one who said early is best."

Joni was holding a glass of something bubbly. It looked like champagne, but Lu didn't want to ask.

"Give me five minutes. I'll meet you at the bottom of the floating steps."

A light periwinkle glow spread in from behind the hotel. Joni was right where Lu had told her to be, looking out over the shadowy beach. Her wavy locks were piled messily on her head. Even at this hour, she looked beautiful.

"It feels like our own private estate. Not a soul is up," she said.

"It used to be so wild, so out of the way."

"It must be strange for you. To have been here before and now see it transformed."

"It's going to take some getting used to."

"Change happens. Sometimes it's a bitch and sometimes it makes your life better. All you can do is roll with it."

"Those sound like song lyrics."

Joni shrugged. "Anything can be a song lyric if you put it to music. Even your stories. I could show you if you want?"

Lu laughed. "I doubt it, but that would be fun, anyway."

On the beach, the water lay silent and still, save for the occasional splash up and down the shore. The familiar smell of kiawe trees added a certain sweetness to the air. They walked to the far end, near the old Parker cottage, which Lu had stayed in with her cousins a couple of times. From there, you had a different vantage point of the hotel and the bay and the sky.

Joni turned to her and said, "Tell me, do you have a man back home? You're so natural and cute and…bronze. You have the most luminous skin."

"That depends on what you mean by *have a man.* I don't have a boyfriend, but I have a good guy friend who I do everything with. His name is Dylan and he's a photojournalist."

Joni chuckled. "I hate to break it to you, but men and women are never just friends. Either you love him, he loves you or you both love each other."

"Dylan is like a brother to me," Lu protested.

"Is he handsome?"

Very, but she knew Joni wouldn't understand. "In his own way."

"A word to the wise," Joni said, downing her champagne. "Men don't hang out with girls they don't like. It's not how they operate. Which means you're in denial. Which means you need to pull your head out of your ass, pronto. Did you know your whole body started smiling when his name came up?"

Beneath the rock-star persona, there was something wise about Joni. She was an odd mix in contradictions. Sultry innocence and happy melancholy. Lu couldn't quite figure her out. And maybe that was her appeal. She felt mysterious, like you could never know her.

"I've just never thought of him like that," Lu said.

Not entirely true.

"Liar."

She came clean. "Until recently."

It hadn't taken long for Dylan to become one of her favorite people. But he'd been fresh out of a breakup, and she, focused on landing the perfect job. Tall and freckly and beachy blond, his eyes were the color of the ocean—deep or shallow depending on his moods. He was a freelancer, and one day early on, he invited her to tag along while he photographed giant sequoias, and after that it became a habit. Dylan captured images of anything from wildfires to wild horses to antigovernment demonstrations, while she fished for stories. He got her out of the city, and for that she was grateful.

For over a year, they lived in the limbo state of slowly getting to know one another, and the unspoken agreement that neither wanted anything from the other. Outings, meetings in obscure coffee shops, late-night phone calls. Lu had been sure—or at least had convinced herself—that she was immune to his earthy charms, until the day he blindsided her with news of his assignment in Vietnam.

He'd shown up at her place unannounced, thrusting sunflowers at her the minute she opened the door. Dylan never gave her flowers.

"Can I come in?" he asked almost shyly.

She moved aside and led him into her tiny kitchen, her heart skipping along at full throttle. Something was surely up.

While she found a milk bottle for the flowers and filled it with water, he sat. After a few moments of awkward silence, he said, "I've landed a gig with AP. They're sending me to 'Nam."

The words hit her like a blow to the gut, and she fought for composure. She'd known he wanted to go, but hadn't really believed he'd follow through. It was the strangest thing: she suddenly found that she could not look him in the eye. Instead, she fiddled with the flowers, cutting their stems and arranging them in various positions in the bottle.

"Lu? Say something," he said.

Get it together.

"This is news."

"Hey, come over here. Sit."

It would be impossible to hide the quiver in her lip, the tears welling in her eyes. "Hang on, I'll be right back."

She ran to the bathroom, splashed water on her face and looked in the mirror. Somewhere, just beneath the surface of her consciousness, was the notion that Dylan meant more to her than just a friend. She'd been stuffing it down for a while now, but feelings had a way of finding their way out, of taking on a life of their own, didn't they?

She went back into the kitchen, standing tall, and said, "I am so proud of you, Dylan, and I'm happy that you're happy. You just caught me off guard, is all."

He smiled, looking much more at ease. "You had me scared for a moment there."

Scared of what?

"So why the flowers?" she asked.

"I don't know, to be honest. They were so bright and sunny and made me think of you. Remember my shoot in the sunflower field last summer? I almost lost you there, they were so tall."

They looked at each other then, and it felt like he knew that she knew and she knew that he knew that maybe what was between them had grown into something deeper. But they carried on as normal, and before she knew it, she was left sitting alone with the sunflowers trying to make sense of it all.

Now, talking about Dylan with Joni felt so natural. As if they were just two girls out for a morning swim, not a superstar and a nobody. Lu wasn't sure why Joni had latched on to her. Maybe it had something to do with wanting to feel like an ordinary person.

Joni pointed to a splash in the water. "Hey, what was that?"

Out near the point, a fin flapped around, then another popped up close by. Lu watched for a second, and knew right away it was not a shark. "It's a manta ray."

"How can you tell?"

"When you see two small fins that flap around like that, it's a manta ray. They hang out around the point in the mornings here. Sharks are hard to mistake—their fins look exactly like you'd imagine them, slicing through the water."

"Do manta rays sting?"

"No, they're gentle and graceful creatures. You're thinking of stingrays. Different animal."

"Can we swim out and see it?"

Before Lu could answer, Joni was beelining for the water. Lu followed and they both dove in at the same time. Clear and salty liquid sunshine, just like she remembered. The sandy shallows extended out a good way, and they bounced along until they could no longer touch. They swam along a ledge, where bright blue and yellow coral heads ran along a wide sand channel.

Halfway out, Joni said, "Are you sure we're safe out here?"

"No guarantees, but we should be."

When they reached the point, the manta was nowhere to be seen. Joni was a splashy swimmer, and probably scared it off.

"Let's float quietly and see if it comes back," Lu said.

Five minutes later, a giant dark shape passed underneath

them, wings lightly waving. The manta was giant, at least ten feet wide.

Joni's eyes grew big. "That better be a manta ray!"

"It is. We're fine"

You could see the animal's white mouth open wide as it collected tiny plankton for breakfast. Neither woman moved, and the manta ray made wide sweeping circles around them, coming within feet. Then more came, at least six.

Pretty soon, Joni teared up. "It's all just so gorgeous I feel like crying and laughing at the same time," she said.

Lu had to agree. There was so much beauty contained in this moment.

"If there ever were a tonic for what ails you, this might be it," Lu said.

"Makes me want to drop everything and move to Hawai'i."

"You wouldn't be the first."

"Why on earth did you leave?"

"If I'd stayed, I would be working on my family's farm picking mac nuts and shoveling chicken shit, but that wasn't my thing. I wanted to tell stories and see the world and make a name for myself."

"You'll be back. It's no accident you came here. Just like me," Joni said.

Lu had been wondering about that, since Joni did not fit the mold of Rockefeller's guests. "How did you end up here? Do you know Mr. Rockefeller personally?"

"No."

Joni didn't elaborate and Lu didn't ask. She probably should have, because any journalist in her position would be clamoring to know more. But there was a line that Lu was not willing to cross. On more than one occasion, her favorite professor had told her not to get attached to her subjects. "Especially when writing obits," he said with a laugh. She knew what he meant. She was a softy.

"Will you be singing?" Lu asked.

"I brought my guitar, should the opportunity arise, but I'm not scheduled to. I'm just here to enjoy the parties and swim in the ocean with you. Promise me we can do this every morning while we're here."

"I would love that."

By the time they reached the shore, the whole place was drenched in sun. Lu had her camera, but decided not to break the spell. They lay in the warm sand and stared up at the sky. If only her father would come up here, to see the hotel, see her. When she'd called to tell him about the assignment, she realized she'd been holding her breath. Waiting to hear him say he was proud, or acknowledging her accomplishment in some way. Or that he would drive up and visit. But he said none of that. His only question was, "Are you going to come down south? See your family?"

It almost seemed like the more she tried to prove her worth, the more he resisted. When she'd been younger and spending more time over at Auntie H's house, soaking up her knowledge like one of those sea sponges, Buster had gone so far as forbidding Lu to go over there. But by then it was too late. She went anyway. And thank goodness Donna had been at least smart enough to see that Lu's teachers were no longer bugging her every week. Buster finally relented, though he somehow took her excelling as a sign of his failures—real or imagined.

Joni seemed to read her mind. "Everything okay?"

"Fine."

"In my experience, when people say *fine*, it means the opposite."

"Really, nothing's wrong. Just wishing my dad would come up to say hi."

"Why won't he?"

"He's too proud, I think."

"Too proud to see his daughter?"

"Too proud to admit that he was wrong about me going off to the mainland. He didn't want me to leave, but I left, anyway. I know he thought I wouldn't be able to cut it, though he never said it outright. He had this thing about me taking over the farm, keeping it in the family."

Joni groaned. "That's better than being a physicist, which is what my father wanted for me. I come from a family of science nerds, if you can believe that. Parents think they know what's best for us. They either want us to become them, or to become a reflection of their broken dreams."

"In my case, he wanted me to become him, or a female version."

"Maybe he just wanted to keep you close to home. There are worse things, babe."

"It's more complicated than that."

Auntie H had said the same thing. *He doesn't want to lose you, too.*

"Life is always complicated. Give him time, sometimes they come around. Speaking of time. We should get back and eat breakfast. All this fresh air has me starved."

Joni pulled her up and they headed back to the hotel. Halfway back, they caught sight of Matteo Russi leaning against a coconut tree. Lu waved. He didn't wave back.

8

THE FRIEND

O'ahu, January 1943

Admiral Sutton must have had some serious pull, because Isabel was able to take a Pan Am Clipper to Honolulu, instead of crossing the country by train and then spending five days on a ship worrying about enemy submarines. Before the war, the Clippers were mostly enjoyed by the wealthy. Now, the military had commandeered the massive flying boats. Getting in the confined space of the plane had caused her palms to sweat, but once they rose above the clouds, she was so taken aback by the fluffy whites and the endless blue above that she forgot to be afraid.

To pass the long hours, she studied one of the Japanese language books that Admiral Sutton had sent, with a note inside that said, "Do your best to learn this before you arrive in Honolulu. And go give 'em hell."

Nora had laughed and Anna scowled, but Ellen Mary raised her eyebrows and said, "You're going to, I just know it."

Isabel wasn't so sure. Language came easily and her memory was strong, but not photographic like Em's. One of the books taught structure, the other vocabulary. Both were a few inches thick and daunting. Every so often, she closed the book and pressed her face against the window. After stopping in San Francisco overnight, they were now bobbing around over the Pacific. She looked down for ships or submarines, but only saw whitecaps.

By the time the pilot announced their approach into Pearl Harbor, the air in the cabin had grown warm and sticky and achingly sad. She thought of Walt for the hundredth time that day. He had been here, in this very sky, above this indigo ocean, in a fight for his life—for everyone's life, really. Once again, her palms heated up. Tears welled in her eyes.

The last time she'd seen her brother he'd been freshly shaved, rattling on about his cushy assignment in Hawai'i, where a sandy beach was always just a few steps away. As far as he was concerned, he had hit the jackpot. He'd only earned his wings two months before, and he was revved up as all get-out.

"And we'll be traveling in style, aboard the *President Johnson!*" he'd said with a huge grin.

His squadron had just returned to Washington from a month of war games in the Carolinas, and now he was off to some speck of sand halfway around the world.

"Any more news on Japan?" she had asked, trying not to show her apprehension.

He shrugged. "Japan is nothing to worry about. Not where we'll be, at least."

It was because of him that she'd taken the position with the navy. Even though he was army air corps. His idealism had been catching, and as always, whatever he did, she followed. "That's not necessarily true, from what I hear," she said.

"What is it you hear?" he wanted to know.

He had no idea what she did, other than that it involved more than answering telephones. He knew better than to press.

"Just that the Japanese have their sights on the whole of the Pacific. And that they're unpredictable," she said.

He checked his watch. "I have to run."

With his calloused hands, he ruffled up her hair and pulled her in for a hug. It was this exact hug that had seen her through the loss of her mother, the unraveling of her father and years of dust and struggle in their hometown. Walt always smelled of baseball gloves and Old Spice and, more recently, cigarettes.

Pulling away, he looked down into her eyes and gave her a quick salute. "See ya, kid."

Now, as she sat looking down over the same blue waters of his grave, those final words played over in her mind. Green as they came, Walt had nevertheless been one of the few air corps pilots to get off the ground on December 7, and one of the only ones not to return.

No, I won't. I won't see you again.

She couldn't wait to locate his friends and find out more about his last days, hours and minutes. Several had written, expressing condolences, and one in particular had caused her to fold in half, sobbing. Only someone who knew loss could have written such a moving letter, and she was determined to meet him and thank him. She had saved the letter, neatly tucked away in her suitcase, from Second Lieutenant Matteo Russi.

The passengers deplaned at a floating dock in the greenish waters of Pearl Harbor. Stepping out, Isabel was hit by a warm burst of air that caught her off guard. Here it was, the middle of winter, and men were milling about in short sleeves and cotton. She had been warned, but until now had not quite believed. The smells were different, too—salt water and mud flats mingled with sweetness.

A husky black man appeared at her side. "Miss Cooper?"

It wouldn't have been hard to guess who she was, seeing that she was the only woman on the plane, and dressed in her blues—a navy coat and skirt with black purse and shoes. "That's me."

"Welcome to Hawai'i, or aloha, as they say here. I'm Chief Petty Officer Jones," he said in a friendly voice.

"Thank you, Chief Jones. I can't believe I'm actually here." The dock rose and fell beneath their feet, uneven as she felt.

"Oh, you'll believe it soon enough when that wool uniform starts roasting you like pig on a stick. But it ain't all bad here. Come on, let's get your bags," he said.

"Bag. I only have one," she corrected him.

He cocked his head and gave her an odd look. "What kind of woman comes to Hawai'i with only one bag?"

"One that's here to work, I guess?"

He saluted her. "Touché."

With so many people around, Jones kept the conversation light, asking about the flight and the weather in DC. Isabel, not in the mood for chitchat, did her best to appease him. She was still taking in the hulking gray ships at what could only be Battleship Row. Where this whole nightmare started. For the past year, the words *Pearl Harbor* had conjured up such violent and twisted images it was hard to reconcile those with the bluest sky she'd ever seen.

"Kinda takes your breath away, doesn't it?" Jones said.

"It's not what I expected."

After retrieving her suitcase, they drove along the waterfront, passing warehouses and buildings and coconut trees. People, mostly men, walked hurriedly down the sidewalks. Everyone looked as though they had a job to do. This was not the Hawai'i of hula dancers and wave riding, rather barbed wire and artillery guns.

Jones slowed as they passed a neat white two-story building. "This is the hub of COM 14. This is where you'll report tomorrow morning at 0700. There's an unmarked door on the far side that you enter through. The only one like it. Your quarters aren't far from here, so you can walk."

Leave it to the navy to be good at keeping secrets. She knew nothing of her housing assignment or transportation or anything, really. Her only instructions had been where and when to catch the flight.

"Can you tell me anything about the job?" she asked.

"I'll save that for Captain Hudson. But I will say this—you are the first woman to join our ranks. Nor are the boys down there your usual suspects. We have what I like to call *a can of mixed nuts*. What I mean by that is there are personalities with a capital *P*. Some are too wrapped up in their own stuff to give you any trouble, but I'm not so sure about others. So, if anyone rubs you the wrong way, you let me know, okay?"

With arms thick as tree trunks, Jones looked like he could handle just about anyone. And he seemed to have an extra helping of confidence to go along with his biceps and triceps.

"Sounds like a deal," she said. "Oh, and what do you mean by *down there?*"

"Combat Intelligence Unit, aka the Dungeon. Our office."

"Why do you call it the Dungeon?" she asked, feeling a chill travel up her spine.

He winked. "You'll see.

Her quarters turned out to be a tiny green house under a feathery tree, in a neighborhood of similar houses under feathery green trees. A hedge of red flowers lined the drive. The place was farther away than Isabel had expected, but as long as there were no snowstorms, she wouldn't mind the walk.

"I suspect they were in a quandary with where to put you.

In the end, Hudson got you bunked with one of the clerks from upstairs. Apparently, a whole new shipment of girls arrived last week. She's been informed to help get you situated," Jones told her.

No one was home, but the door was unlocked, so Isabel said goodbye to Jones and put her things in the empty bedroom. Exhausted, she kicked off her shoes, stripped off her coat and plopped onto the bed. Sunlight slanted in through the window, heating up a patch of skin on her shoulder. The birds outside were chattering and cooing and fluttering around. She was relieved to have the long journey behind her, and excited for the new one to begin. Within minutes, she felt herself drifting off.

She swore she had just closed her eyes when a knocking sound woke her. There in the doorway stood a silhouette of a woman holding a small lantern.

"You must be Isabel. I'm Gloria Moreno, your new roomie. Sorry to wake you, but you've been asleep for hours and I brought you back some food from the mess hall. Thought you may want a bite before going to bed for good, you know? Plus, I wanted to meet you," she said, all in one breath.

Isabel sat up and rubbed her eyes. "Thank you, Gloria. Give me a minute and I'll be right out."

The house was dark, but a thin light shone out from cracks in the kitchen door. Isabel entered and found a dark-haired woman sitting at the table reading a newspaper. She looked up and did a once-over of Isabel.

"Why, we could be sisters! One dark, one light," Gloria said.

Gloria had shoulder-length dark brown hair, eyebrows that curved up as though drawn on, and though her full lips turned down slightly, she radiated goodness. But instead of pale skin and blue eyes like Isabel, her skin was more olive toned and her eyes brown.

"Well, I'll be," said Isabel.

"How tall are you?"

"Five foot nine."

"Me, too!" Gloria said, pulling the chair out and patting it. "Sit. I want to know everything about you. Me, I came from San Diego two weeks ago. I'm single, obviously, and I just finished a course in shorthand. I have nine brothers and sisters and I love to sew and I hate to swim. Coming to Hawai'i is the best thing that's ever happened to me and I plan on landing a husband just as soon as I can. How about you?"

Isabel laughed. "I'm certainly not here to find a husband. I can't sew worth a damn and I love to swim. And let's see, I grew up in Indiana and I studied math and physics at Goucher College." She paused, unsure of whether to say anything about Walt, but decided to get it out in the open. Plus, Gloria seemed so genuine and sweet. "I had a brother, but he died in '41."

Gloria wilted. "Oh, gosh, this breaks my heart. I'm so sorry. Don't tell me he was here at Pearl Harbor?"

Isabel nodded. "Shot down by a Zero. One of the first casualties, from what they told us."

"Those bastards! If it makes you feel any better, they have it coming to them. The Japanese army doesn't stand a chance. Not from what I've seen going on here. I've never seen such determination and heart in the whole of my life. We mean business at Pearl Harbor, yes, we do. Was your brother navy, then?"

"Air corps. Newly minted."

"I'm here if you need a shoulder to cry on, or help with anything on that front. I imagine you'll be wanting to meet up with any of his pilot friends. Count me in on that. I'm good at tracking people down," Gloria said.

"Thanks. Work comes first, but I do have a few names of guys he flew with."

"I'm your gal. Speaking of work, what's your position? With a math and physics degree, you must be smart."

Gloria had more words in her than a dictionary, and just listening to her made Isabel exhausted. "They have me clerking for one of the communications offices," she answered.

"Which one?

"Combat Intelligence Unit."

She'd found that lying was easier when you kept it an inch from the truth.

Gloria frowned. "The one in the basement?"

"That's what I'm told."

"From what I hear, that's no ordinary unit. And you should see the guys that come and go from the back door. They never look you in the eye, all bearded and secretive and plain awkward. A bunch of nuts, if you ask me. What exactly *is* combat intelligence, anyway?"

Isabel shrugged. "I guess I'll find out."

The windows were all blocked with thick black paper and the room was stuffy. A plate full of food sat waiting on the other side of the tiny table, and Isabel eyed it. "Would you mind?"

Gloria put her hands to both sides of her cheek. "Look at me, so rude. Please, I brought this home for you. My brothers say I talk too much, so just butt in if I get tiresome. Fried chicken dripping in fat, and rice with coleslaw and pineapple. Not bad for a mess hall."

They spoke for another hour after dinner, in plenty of run-on sentences, and when they said their good-nights, Gloria told her, "I can tell we're going to be best of friends."

9

THE DUNGEON

Pearl Harbor, Hawai'i, 1943

The next morning, after a dead sleep, Isabel woke to the faint smell of orange blossom. The temperature had dropped in the night, but it was still warm as an early Indiana summer. It took a second to register where she was. Tangled in a thin blanket on a rock-hard bed in Hawai'i. The sound of car engines told her it was probably time to drag herself out of bed.

After showering, she applied her powder, mascara and red lipstick carefully, and then promptly wiped most it off with a tissue. She wanted to make a good first impression, but also wanted to be taken seriously. It was hard to know how to go about that when you had no idea what to expect. And the little she'd heard was not promising. Gloria was already in the kitchen with a box of shredded wheat and a bottle of milk on the counter. She was wearing a short-sleeved blueish gray dress and looking sharp.

"Good morning, sunshine! I'm just out the door. It takes twelve minutes at a good clip to get to the admin building and I pride myself on being punctual. Want to grab a banana and come along? I'll drop you off at your door," Gloria said.

A bunch of bananas hung in the corner from a hook in the ceiling and she plucked one. They were miniature versions of the bananas back home, which showed up in the store once a year and were gone in a day.

"Take two," Gloria said.

Instead of snow on the ground outside, there were coral-colored flower petals, clipped green lawns and an abundance of birds. The trees wore all of their leaves—in mid-January! But despite the wonder of her new surroundings, Isabel felt a growing sense of dread as they approached the building. Her father had called it *hysteria*; the doctor had said she had a *phobia*. An irrational fear of something real or perceived. Whatever it was, Isabel hated the feeling. By the time they stood outside the door, her palms were drenched and her pulse raced along.

"You okay? You look a little peaked," Gloria said.

"Fine. Just the first-day jitters. Nothing to worry about."

Gloria squinted into the sun. "Anyhow, I'm on the second floor, Room 220 if you need me. Good luck."

When Gloria disappeared around the corner, Isabel took a few moments to compose herself. Deep breaths helped, but barely. Now was not the time to have a nervous breakdown. *The longer you stand here, the worse it's going to be.*

She pulled open the door and almost tripped over a couple of burn bags. Papers lay across the steps going down, down and farther down. She picked up one. It was a crypto work-sheet. Lying in the open, for heaven's sake. Heads would roll in Washington for something like this. Her nails dug into her palm as she descended. The air felt soupy, hard to take in. Six steps down, she stopped. This was not going to work. Nope, not at all. Isabel turned around and went back up. When she reached the top, she stopped and chided herself. How could she leave after making it all the way to this point? Walt deserved better.

On the next attempt, she made it more than halfway down the sixteen or so steps before an overwhelming suffocation nearly dropped her. Isabel held a hand to the wall and steadied herself. She was clammy and light-headed and a pathetic mess. *One step at a time.* She debated turning around at least eleven more times, but in the end, the pull of the Dungeon was stronger than her fear.

At the bottom, Isabel paused at a double-wide steel door. This one had no sign, either. With her heart thumping overtime, she pushed on through. A wall of smoke was the first thing to greet her and, beyond that, a murky passageway. It was all underground. How was she going to do this? She turned around, ready to scramble back up the steps, when a voice said. "Miss Cooper? That you?"

This was as wrong as a place could be.

"Yes, it's me," she squeaked.

Jones was by her side in an instant. "Come on, I'll introduce you to the crew."

She was shaking as she followed him into a slightly lighter room that extended in all directions—endlessly, it appeared. Men worked at desks around the room. The two closest to her hovered over a makeshift table on sawhorses and planks of wood. One was in an orange smoking jacket and bed slippers. Very un-navy. Neither even glanced up.

Jones walked her over. "Excuse me, Captain Hudson. I have your newest recruit, ready for service."

Isabel was having a hard time catching her breath, which made her wonder how on earth she'd be able to concentrate in here. Between that and the gauzy layer of smoke. She could hear her mother's voice: *Be careful what you wish for.*

Hudson straightened up and stood a good six inches over

her. "So, you're the girl that everyone at Main Navy is talk-ing about."

"Everyone, sir? I certainly hope not," she said, meeting his gaze.

One side of his mouth lifted. "Everyone with clearance, I should say. Jones, I'm right in the middle of something im-portant. Show her around and get her situated."

Isabel knew of Hudson, had even run into him a few times in Washington. Rumors had swirled when he took over for the legendary Joe Rochefort, who had been transferred back to Washington. But in her mind Norm Denny was the real legend, and she was anxious to meet one of the country's top cryptanalysts.

Jones led her around the massive room. It stretched about a hundred feet one way and fifty or so the other. Desks and file cabinets and mountains of paper were tucked here and there, giving the place a haphazard feel. Still, she had no doubt that what went on in this room could easily win or lose the war in the Pacific. That was made clear with Midway. Eavesdrop-ping on the enemy saved lives. Won battles.

While shaking in her boots, she forced a smile as she met the next cluster of men, the linguists, who were responsible for translating the messages that she would be decoding. One of them had an ashtray with a pile of butts four inches thick. They all acknowledged her, but made no move to get up.

After the linguists, she met the combat intelligence guys and the traffic analysts—or TA guys—who figured out the extraneous parts of the messages. Things like where they orig-inated and who was on the receiving end. Call signs, dates. One of the guys could have been her grandfather, the other looked sixteen, though everyone was a bit hazy. Jones also pointed out what he called the *boiler room*, where IBM machines lived. All Isabel could be sure of was that she would not remember a single name.

Jones brought her to a bank of desks near the boiler room door. "And here we are. The heart of the operation. Our crippies."

Eight desks, six men.

"Where are the rest?"

There were hundreds back in Washington.

"This is it."

A man looked up, then back down at the paper on his desk. He wore round glasses, a Charlie Chaplin mustache and had a handmade sign on his desk that read You Don't Have to Be Crazy to Work Here, But It Helps. It could only be Norm Denny.

Suddenly, Hudson was there at her side. "Lieutenant Commander, greet your new cryptanalyst properly, would you?" he said.

Denny held up a hand, as though he couldn't be interrupted. Isabel knew the feeling. When you were on to something, any distraction could derail the whole train of thought and leave you back at square one. But at the same time, she felt a stab of disappointment.

"No problem. I know how it is," she said.

Being so far back in the room was causing a peculiar vibration under her skin, a gnawing in her stomach. She refrained from scratching by holding her hands behind her back. The only place she might *possibly* be okay was right next to the front door. God willing, her desk could be near Jones's.

Hudson nodded at the empty desk. "Miss, here's your station. Now break some codes," he said in all seriousness, then turned to go. "Oh, wait, you speak any Japanese?"

"A little," she answered. "Two weeks' worth, to be exact."

He laughed. "Almost fluent."

"Almost."

He walked off, leaving her standing between Jones and her new supervisor. Jones pulled out her chair and said, "Hudson has an odd sense of humor. Don't fault him for it, though—the man is a genius. The men love him, and I suspect you will, too. In time."

With that, he was gone. The cold from the floor crept up through her shoes and into her bones. The temperature was lower than inside Main Navy, if that was possible. Not wanting to bother Denny, she sat down at her desk and opened the top drawer. It was empty. So were the others. Fortunately, she had a pen, a pencil and an eraser in her purse. She set them on top of the desk and spent twenty minutes rearranging them. She was at a loss, and the feeling that the roof might collapse at any moment did not help matters. Maybe this whole gig was a huge mistake.

A hoarse voice startled her. "So, you were with Feinstein. I hear he's in the nutter," Denny said, sounding as though he'd swallowed an ashtray.

"He's at Walter Reed, and improving steadily," she said.

A week after the break in Magenta, Feinstein had been hospitalized for exhaustion. You could have seen it coming—the all-nighters, the frantic pace, the mounting pressure—but no one expected a full-blown nervous breakdown.

"Feinstein is why you're here. I wanted him. He sent you," he said.

"Feinstein didn't get us into Magenta," she said in all honesty.

I did.

Denny raised an eyebrow, nodded slightly. "How much you done on JN-25?"

"I spent three months on it when I first started," she said.

"Sounds about the same as your Japanese, then."

"Sir, Feinstein and Rawlings wouldn't have sent me if they didn't have faith. You won't be disappointed, I promise," she said.

"I already am."

Ouch.

The next few days were not much better. Each morning, Isabel had to coax herself down the steps, through the steel door and to her desk. The sense of dread that pressed against her from the inside never left, and often all she could think about was getting up and out and into the light. Going to work had now become *surviving* work.

Hudson handed messages out on a whim, it seemed. Denny this one, Ziegler that and Lipp the other. None of them paid her much attention, though Ziegler at least smiled. Isabel got the scraps, but sometimes scraps turned out to be the most important ones, so it didn't bother her. Plus, getting back into the complexities of JN-25 with its numbers instead of letters, and frequently changed additive books, was difficult enough.

On her fourth day, one of the linguists went up to Hudson and said something in Japanese. Without missing a beat, Hudson answered back effortlessly. Isabel was able to pick up a few words. *Ship, transport, islands.* It struck her then that Hudson—and maybe Denny—was probably the only one in the Dungeon who knew both cryptanalysis and Japanese. Everyone else was only playing with half a deck. If she could get at least a working knowledge, she'd have an edge. At night, she ramped up her studying, which left little time for anything else.

On her first day off, she slept the entire day away, waking now and then to bird chirps and airplane engines overhead. Gloria had invited her to play tennis with a few girls from upstairs, but Isabel politely declined. Her body felt as though it had been through the washing machine a few times over. Neck tense as a lead pipe, eyes bleary from all that smoke. The following day, Sunday, she'd reserved for finding Matteo Russi. She needed her wits about her.

Gloria, bless her heart, had rounded up a rattly gray Buick with a loud exhaust from the daughter of a car salesman in downtown Honolulu. They had it until 1600 sharp. As they tore down Russell Avenue at top speed, Isabel had the thought that maybe she ought to be driving.

"Linda is an absolute doll. All the girls are. You ought to come up for air sometime and join us for lunch. It would do you a world of good to get out of that torture chamber and mingle with the real world," Gloria said as they passed through the main gates.

"I asked for it. I wanted to be stationed here."

"Not down there you didn't. I can ask around and see if they'll move you upstairs."

"No, thank you."

"What harm would it do?"

"I enjoy what I'm doing."

Gloria slapped her knee. "And I'm Bing Crosby. If you call that enjoying, I hope I never *enjoy* another thing in my life. You come home looking more haggard each night. No offense, but that's how I see it."

Isabel tried the half-truth tactic. "When I was little, Walt and I were stuck in the storm cellar after a twister wiped out half our town and killed our mother. It was dark and close, and I was terrified. Now, any time I'm underground it's uncomfortable. But I need to move past it, so maybe this is my chance. A blessing in disguise."

Uncomfortable was putting it mildly.

"Some blessing. And I'm sorry to hear about your momma. What an awful thing to bear. Sounds like you've had your share of tragedy for such a young thing. Let's turn that around and find this fella. I bet he'll do your heart some good."

Isabel pulled out the envelope, which had his address written in neat block print, and set it on her lap.

"You sure you can get us onto base?"

"Have faith."

This was her first foray out of Pearl Harbor, and she couldn't wait to see more of the island. Even if Hickam was only a short drive away. They had to drive out of the naval base and onto the army base. She'd heard so much about Hickam Field and how the bombs fell, killing men and destroying planes and hangars and hearts. Through it all, some men had managed to get airborne and shoot down enemy planes. Same as Walt, though Walt had been at Wheeler.

It started raining. And the rain mixed with sun caused steam to rise from the asphalt, and a golden light surrounded them. Gloria, with her lead foot, seemed in a big hurry to get there. "So, what's our guy's name," she asked.

"Matteo Russi," Isabel said, admiring the glow.

Gloria shifted in her seat, but didn't respond.

"You know him?"

"Nope."

Isabel had the feeling she was withholding information, but let it go. The main gate at Hickam resembled a country club entrance, with white concrete portals and a cabana-like guard shack.

"What's your business, ma'am?" a slim guard asked, bent over at the window. Both women were in uniform, with hats.

"We're dropping off sensitive documents with the command center," Gloria said with a wide smile, holding up her badge.

He studied them for a moment, then said, "You two know where you're going?"

"Sure do, Private. Thank you."

With that, they drove on through.

"See. Easy-peasy. You have to act like you own the place, and pretty soon, you do," Gloria said.

The base was newer than Pearl, and the white paint stood out bright and shiny. Standing above everything was a sky-high water tower of Moorish design looking exceptionally out of place. As an officer, Russi was in the two-story BOQ rather than the hulking barracks building Gloria said was called the "Hickam Hotel." And fortunately, he'd put his room number on the return address.

When Gloria turned off the car, Isabel paused. This was something she'd been wanting for so long, but now the reality of hearing about Walt bore down on her. Emotions were sure to be stirred and she was already feeling vulnerable.

Gloria rested a hand on her thigh. "Feeling nervous?"

"A little."

"You know, you don't have to ask anything you're not ready to hear. And if it's too much for you, we can always leave, come back later," Gloria said.

Isabel knew Russi might not even be there. "You're right, let's go."

Walking around the outside of the building, they turned a few heads before arriving at the correct door. Isabel lifted her arm to knock when the door swung open.

A man stumbled back in surprise. "Whoa," he said, putting his hand over his heart. "You nearly scared the pancakes out of me."

He was Isabel's height, with hair the color of black molasses.

Isabel said, "Sorry. We're trying to find Matteo Russi."

His gaze shifted between the two women before focusing

back on Isabel. For the briefest moment, he seemed ready to bolt. "Do I know you?"

"We haven't met. I'm Isabel Cooper, Walter Cooper's sister."

It was a moment she would always remember, the way he stared through her as though picturing something tragic, and how his eyes reflected back love and pain and something undefinable.

"Isabel?" he said in almost a whisper. "He talked about you all the time."

The words hit her hard. "He always mentioned you, too, in his letters. Russi this, Russi that."

Russi looked over at Gloria and said, "I didn't realize you and Walt had another sister."

"We don't... Gloria is my roommate."

He whistled. "You sure had me fooled. And roommate? Does that mean you're living here now?"

"I've just been transferred to Pearl and thought maybe if you had the time we could talk about Walt...and what happened."

He swallowed hard. "Sorry, but I'm out the door for training," he said, holding up a pair of sneakers. Beads of perspiration broke out above his upper lip in a neat line. "But if you're free later today, I could come by and grab you. Take a drive or something?"

"That would be nice," she said, relieved.

When he smiled, a dimple formed on one side of his mouth. He had a narrow gap between his front teeth that did nothing to detract from the obvious fact that that smile had opened a lot of doors for him.

"If you're anything like Walt, you're going to love it here. War and all," he said.

"I'm not here to enjoy myself, Mr. Russi, so that's really beside the point."

He cocked his head. "I beg to differ. But then that's usually the case, Miss Isabel Cooper." He glanced down at her left hand. "Or have you become a Mrs.?"

"It's Miss."

"Catch you at 1630, then," he said, then he turned and jogged off down the hall.

Whatever she had expected, this was not it.

10

THE LOOKOUT

O'ahu, 1943

Matteo Russi came by at 1630 on the nose in a midnight-blue Ford. Gloria peered out the window when she heard him drive up, and jumped back quickly.

"He has flowers!" she said. Everything that came out of Gloria's mouth deserved an exclamation point after it.

When Isabel opened the door, he handed the blooms to her, fidgeting and looking at his shoes. "I know these are a little late, but no one was flying flowers across the ocean last December. Trust me, I asked."

Isabel took the bouquet and put it in a jar. A mix of red and pink waxy flowers with big dark leaves. They didn't have a scent and were wrapped in smudged newspaper, but they were the most beautiful flowers she'd ever seen. Russi was dressed in slacks and an orange-and-yellow aloha shirt that lit up his eyes. He seemed eager to get back in the car, but once there, he didn't turn it on.

"You been to the Pali lookout yet?" he asked.

"I haven't been anywhere yet."

"Get outta here." He didn't have a thick New York accent, but the *here* came out like *hea*.

"I've been working."

"No time off?" he said.

"I slept yesterday and came to find you today. That's been my only time off so far," she said.

He didn't respond, just sat there, staring off down the road. She said, "So, are we going?"

"Sorry, yeah."

They drove toward downtown Honolulu, with mountains on the left and ocean in the distance to the right. There was a gentleness to the landscape, or maybe it was the soft lighting, and green was in large supply. The trees and flowers and shrubs were different varieties than the ones at home and she didn't recognize any of them.

Russi made small talk along the way about the weather and the island, which was just as well because she wanted to look him in the eye when they talked about Walt. Closer to town, he pointed to a cluster of buildings off to the right. "That there is Chinatown. It's where the boys go to be boys. I don't recommend going there alone, if at all."

"Noted."

They turned up Nu'uanu Valley, lush and narrow, and headed straight for a mist-covered mountain peak. It seemed impossible that there would be any way over, but when they reached the base of a sheer cliff, they followed a thin road up and over a small notch in the mountains. The temperature up there was a good ten degrees cooler than at Pearl, and the air felt crisp against her cheeks.

"You're not afraid of heights, are ya?" he said, glancing over at her.

"Not heights, no."

"Hold on to your skirt," he said with a boyish grin.

The car crested a small hill and the ground fell away before them. They must have been a thousand feet up a sheer cliff, looking across a panorama of half the island, edged by coral reefs and sea beyond, so blue Isabel wished she could bottle some and keep it on her shelf. No wonder Walt had loved it here.

Russi pulled off to one side and turned off the engine. "Takes the breath away, doesn't it? Being up here always reminds me of flying, 'cept here there's no suiting up required and no engine noise, though that wind sure does whip."

They sat in silence for a minute or two after the mention of a plane. Russi was a bridge to Walt, they both knew that. Isabel kept her hands in her lap, and her eyes on the view. This was hard for him, too—she could tell by the way his foot tapped a jitterbug on the floor of the car. And how he kept rubbing a hand through his hair every twenty-two seconds.

Finally, she found her words. "You may or may not know this, but Walt was my life. He was a brother, a friend, a guardian, you name it. When we lost our mother, he stepped in because my father couldn't hack it. I was his little Izzy and he was my big Walt. Everything he did, I wanted to do," she said. "He played baseball, I wanted to play baseball. He studied math, I studied math. Flying was the one thing I stopped at."

"You got somethin' against wings?" he asked, and she could tell he was trying to keep it light.

"The navy wasn't taking female pilots."

"So, what exactly is it you do for the navy, Izzy? Walt always said you were the brains in the family."

She gave him the standard answer. "The usual stuff. Filing, answering phones, emptying ashtrays."

He tapped his fingers on the steering wheel, gave her a sideways glance. "I get the feeling that's not all. Walt said you were crazy smart."

"Sorry to disappoint you," she said.

"Oh, I'm not disappointed. Just seems like a waste of brains and talent. So, what did Walt tell you about me?"

"That you're a P-40 pursuit pilot who flies higher and faster than all the rest. One who doesn't like his picture taken and wears an actual dog tag with your dog Queenie's name punched into it on every flight. My brother thought the world of you, Russi," she said, offering a rare smile.

He shot her a quick glance, then looked out the window. "He told you all that?"

"I have a stack of letters two feet high from him. He signed them all *From Hawai'i, with love.* From day one, he was smitten with these islands. He talked about everything under the Hawaiian sun, and how he wanted to live here when his stint was up, find a gal and buy a coffee farm. He mentioned a couple other guys, Hicks and Rasmussen, but I could tell you were his favorite," she said.

"Yeah, well. That makes two of us, I guess."

Their eyes met and Isabel found she could not look away. An invisible current held her in place, wiping out all thought. His eyes were a burnt ochre, and intense. His nose, bony and slightly crooked. The way his nostrils flared in and out reminded her of a frightened hare and she wondered why.

"What can you tell me about Walt's last days?" she managed to say, breathless and not quite understanding what had just passed between them.

"We came over together on the cruise ship, had a blast, and by the time we hit the shore, we were inseparable," he said, taking a moment. When he closed his eyes, his lashes laid down on his cheekbones. "But you already know that. You want to know about December 7, am I right?"

She nodded.

Russi blew out, as though readying for a race, and began.

"Early Sunday morning, everyone was sound asleep when a loud explosion shook the barracks. Walt was the first one up, as usual, buck naked and running from window to window, yelling. 'What the hell? The sky is full of fucking Japanese airplanes. They're dropping bombs! What the hell?' he kept saying, while throwing on the first pair of pants he could find, which happened to be Hicks's and were four inches too short."

He looked up as if remembering, then went on. "No one believed him at first. Thought it was some prank by the navy boys—that happened now and then, you know? It was Sunday morning when most people were fixing to go to church. Everyone thought it was a drill. But the burning hangar and plume of black smoke said otherwise."

She waited for him to continue, but he didn't. "And then what happened?"

"Walt was one of the first guys up in the air. Most of our planes were destroyed, so guys just started pulling bodies off of the field. Soldiers from Schofield had been tossing the football around getting ready for a scratch game. And then one of the guys started yelling that there were a few intact P-36s. Rasmussen went up in his purple pj's."

"What about you?" she asked.

"I never got airborne that day." His lip twitched as he spoke, and by the way his voice cracked, she wondered if it was wise for him to keep going.

Russi dug into his pocket and pulled out a watch. "Here, Rasmussen gave this to me when he found out you were here. Walt handed it to him before he drove off to Haleiwa and said, 'Give this to Izzy in case I don't come back.'"

The worn leather strap and scuffed-up face were so familiar, so loved. Walt never took the thing off, day or night. She reached out, taking it from him and holding it up to her nose, inhaling. "How come Rasmussen didn't send it?"

"Said he didn't want it to get lost, and planned on hand delivering it when the war ended. Go on, put it on. Walt would have wanted you to."

Though the watch was too big for her wrist, she nonetheless tried. But the last hole was smashed and she couldn't push it in. Russi leaned in and took her wrist in his hand, fiddling with the pin until it slid in. Isabel caught a whiff of spicy aftershave and something salty lifting off his skin. There was something appealing about his closeness.

"I can make another hole if you like? To tighten it," he said.

The watch covered her entire wrist, but she would wear it until the day she died. "Please, and thank you. This means the world to me."

"It's the least I could do, and it suits you," he said.

She spun the watch. "No, it doesn't. But I don't care."

They sat for a while, taking in the sights. Then he pulled out a small photo album and handed it to her. "Go on, have a look. Some real special times."

Isabel opened the album. The first picture was of a pond and a tall waterfall with Walt sitting on a boulder in the foreground. It was a candid shot, no smiling involved. He was looking up at the waterfall with a sense of wonder. It was not a close-up and he looked so small and so happy. A feeling of warmth swam through her. She turned the pages slowly, savoring Walt in this new world, surrounded by beauty and with friends. On a jungly mountaintop, in front of a diner, holding a scruffy puppy, standing next to his plane. Not a bad way to spend the last six months of your life.

Russi opened his door. "Hey, mind if we get out and stretch our legs a little? Talking about that morning always rips me up."

The moment Isabel stepped out of the car, a furious gust of wind took her dress and lifted it clear over her head. A scream escaped her mouth, no doubt drawing attention her way. She clawed at it to pull it down, but they were in some kind of wind funnel and the dress would not cooperate. Horrified, she danced around and finally pressed herself against the car where she got control of the dress. With a mouthful of hair, she looked over at Russi, who was standing near the hood with eyes closed and his hands behind his back.

"You can open your eyes now. For heaven's sake, that was embarrassing," she said, her whole body blushing. Good thing she'd bought new underwear just before the trip, though she wasn't sure why that mattered.

Russi was trying to hide a smile. "Guess I shoulda told you to hang on to your skirt before you got out. Sorry about that, this place is known for its fierce wind."

She wanted to crawl under the car and not come out. "Can we just forget this happened?"

"What happened? I don't recall anything happening," he said with shrug. "If it makes you feel any better I saw guys go up to fight the Japanese wearing nothing but their briefs, I kid you not."

"Be serious."

"I don't joke about that day, miss," he said with his hand over his heart.

He seemed so earnest she couldn't help but smile. "They have me beat, then."

"And anyway, you'll be running around in a swimsuit in no time—not much difference."

"I doubt that. Aren't the beaches closed?"

"There's barbed wire, but you can still get on 'em." He pointed toward the ocean. "Out there is the Kāneʻohe Naval Air Station. It was hit pretty bad by the Japanese and four of our guys flew over from Wheeler to help. They ran into a line of Zeros and managed to take a few out, but they had already blasted the crap out of the place. Hangars blown up, planes destroyed, men killed."

It was impossible to imagine an attack of such magnitude taking place right in front of where she stood, in such calm skies. Her brain would simply not register it. "It must be hard for you to come here," she said.

He went on. "Only three made it back to Wheeler that day, and Rasmussen, the lucky fuck, came in with five hundred bullet holes, no rudder and no brakes. Sterling wasn't so lucky and ended up in the water. Makes you wonder why some died and others lived," he said, pulling out a pack of gum and offering her one.

Like Walt. She'd thought the same thing no less than a thousand times. Without any answers, she stood there next to him looking out at the rolling hills of green below and the misty cliffs to the left. His presence loomed large next to her, and she tried to ignore it.

A few minutes later, he turned to her and said, "Normally, I don't talk about this with anyone, so thanks for being a good ear."

She still had so many questions, but couldn't bring herself to ask right now. "Anytime. It was hard for me to be so removed. Your stories are like a gift."

"Hey, would you be up for something?"

"That depends."

There was a new excitement in his voice. "Walt and I went all over creation before the war started—beaches, waterfalls, weird places to eat. Well, you saw in the pics. He specialized in finding the most out of the way holes in the wall. What if I took you to see those spots? Kind of retrace his steps, and I could tell you stories along the way. How does that sound?"

It was the very reason she'd come.

"Sounds perfect."

★ ★ ★

On Monday, the Dungeon seemed even more oppressive than the previous week. Between the smoke and the sheer amount of earth and concrete between Isabel and the blue sky above, she found herself perspiring even though everyone else was layered in sweaters and jackets. Hudson kept handing out messages, and she kept failing miserably at decoding them. Every now and then, she would get a word or two, but that was it. Maybe the Japanese naval code was not her cup of tea.

JN-25 was a codebook of five-digit numbers divisible by three, and there were several versions of it in use. Each set of numbers was assigned a meaning, be it a phrase, a word, a letter or a number. The intimidating part was that there were 33,333 code groups in there. The fact that some were assigned more than one meaning complicated matters greatly. Between the guys in the Dungeon, her friends back at OP-20-G and an overseas team who was now operating out of Melbourne, they'd recovered only a small percentage of the codes. Those IBM machines helped, but there was no replacement for the human eye.

The worst part for Isabel was not the codes, but something called an additive. Japanese intelligence had created another book of five-digit numbers—three hundred pages' worth— that were meant to disguise the real code group numbers. While they didn't change the main codebook often, they did switch up the additive books, which meant starting from scratch in a lot of ways. Isabel found herself staring at the numbers until her eyes burned. Nothing happened.

Denny and two of the other cryptanalysts, Ziegler and Lipp, talked over her as though she wasn't there. She worked to the sound of pencils on paper, scuffing chairs and voices conferring with Hudson. She was miserable. The few times she even came close to getting into her flow, and felt the humming coming on, she stood up and fetched more coffee. The last thing she needed was to draw any attention to herself.

After her fourth cup, Ziegler looked up and said, "I'm surprised you're not on your desk doing jumping jacks—the coffee here is three point five strength. Anyone warn you of that?"

"No, but I do feel a bit jittery. And thanks for the tip."

She wanted to ask how he knew it was three point five and not just three or three point six, but knew better. And to be honest, she felt as though a hive of bees had taken up residence in her chest. Jumping jacks sounded pretty good about now.

This was the first time any of the boys had so much as acknowledged her, and she took the opening. "I'm having trouble with the additives. Do you have any tricks to share?"

He fingered his nonexistent mustache. "You gotta make sure you're on the right book, and there are loads of them. Fourteen as of last count. But sometimes they use the old ones," he said.

Ziegler was thinner than a wire and wore a pencil behind each ear, with several more in his jacket pocket. He seemed to work in furious bursts, get up and pace for ten minutes and then sit back down.

Isabel looked down at her message. "No wonder the numbers aren't adding up," she said with a spark of understanding.

The so-called additives were ciphers, meaning they involved an operation that transcribed one thing to another. In this case, numbers. So, on top of having the five-digit codes that replaced words or other information, those codes were then added, using false arithmetic, to another five-number group, and that was the number group sent.

"How come no one told me this before?" she said.

"Dunno. Guess you never asked. And I'll tell you something else, too. The Japanese are their own worst enemy."

"Why is that?"

"Because the code clerks are lazy. You'll find that instead of using number groups from the middle of the book, they use the same ones again and again. It's easy to see the pattern, if you're looking."

That made sense. "I see," she said.

Clearly excited about the subject, he held a finger up as if he were conducting an orchestra. "And…they have such a fondness for their own highfalutin rigamarole that they've practically handed us the key. Every time."

This, Isabel knew well. It was the same with the diplomatic code. The Japanese military loved their formalities, and those formalities were a codebreaker's dream.

"Does this mean I can ask you anything? I mean, in the future, about JN-25? Denny sometimes seems unapproachable."

His shoulders went up to his ears. "Why not?"

As quirky as he seemed, at least she now felt like she had an ally. A small victory. And in this business, small victories were a big deal.

11

THE OPENING

Hawai'i Island, July 1965

Lu felt jittery as she got ready. The air was abuzz with what people were deeming a momentous day on the Big Island. Nothing like this had ever been constructed in Hawai'i, and the whole world was watching. In Lu's book, Rockefeller was the perfect man for the job because of his love for the wilderness. Having money was one thing, but having money and doing good things with it, something else entirely. Especially when it came to one of her favorite beaches on the island.

She was happy to be a part of opening weekend, and yet still felt intimidated by all the big names and money. This was not a study on how to prune your lemon tree or the best sourdough in the west. This felt big-time in a way that nothing else had before. For her, at least. If only Dylan were here with his calming presence. *Worry not, little one,* he would say. He could be a dork when he wanted to, but that only made her love him all the more.

She dressed in a slim orange skirt and a white sleeveless blouse, grabbed her yellow notepad, slung her camera over her shoulder and headed down to the lobby where chaos ensued. A happy kind of chaos.

Then she saw Russi. He was standing next to Mr. Rockefeller and friends in a loose circle of powerful men. Crisp suits, pressed aloha shirts, shiny shoes and not a dress among them. Russi must have been telling a joke or some kind of funny story because, soon, all the men broke out laughing. Lu observed from the far railing. For some reason, seeing his nonchalance and ability to blend in made her wonder what she was even doing here. She tried to shake it off, and turned her attention to the growing crowd.

Guests were arriving in droves, hotel staff scrambled to make sure everything was impeccable and the sky seemed unable to make up its mind. Rain had fallen off and on all morning. Lu meandered through the crowd, observing. She recognized some faces from Kona, greeted a few old friends from high school and appreciated the vibrancy of the morning. Hawai'i was a land of colors, something she often missed. She jotted down notes, but mostly took photographs of art pieces, the hotel itself and the guests.

At lunchtime, Mr. Rockefeller—looking dapper in a suit, oval-shaped glasses and a beautiful lei—gave a welcome speech on the promenade near the Dining Pavilion, under the watchful eye of two dog-size bronze carp.

Reverend Abraham Akaka, a well-known Hawaiian clergyman, performed a blessing. *Let no evil have claim upon this place. Let thy spirit of Aloha ever be its spirit, that Mauna Kea Beach Hotel may bring refreshment and renewal, joy and gladness to all who come here—a place in which all may find deliverance from emptiness, deliverance from lack of relatedness to nature and neighbor and meaning and self and Thee.*

When he finished speaking, Lu felt his words ringing through her body. As though her entire morning experience had been prescribed by God. The water had certainly brought joy and gladness and renewal, and it seemed hard to imagine that any kind of evil might have claim here.

Throughout the whole thing, part of her was paying attention to these moving speeches and half was scanning the audience trying to pick out Mr. Rockefeller's special guests. In the front row alone sat Bobby Dean Dixon and his wife, Mina, of *Readers Monthly*, oil magnate Joe Wallace, June and Leonard Cosgrove, big philanthropists of Manhattan, and Senator Richard Fuchs of Pennsylvania and his wife, Lynette. Joni was also up there, looking sunny in a turquoise dress and suede boots. Among all the suits and upper crust, she stood out.

Spread out around them, seated and standing, were notable Hawai'i families—the Smarts, Perry-Fiskes, Dillinghams, Baldwins, Sextons—decked out in their best aloha attire and flower lei. A good portion of the guests wore red and yellow lehua lei. Not an easy task for the lei makers, since there were rumored to be seven hundred guests.

Matteo Russi was there, too, but every time Lu looked, he was in a different place. Changing vantage points like a real pro. She decided she better do the same and moved around so her back was to the ocean and rather than seeing Mr. Rockefeller—or LSR, as people here referred to him—she saw the faces of the guests. They were all watching him intently, hanging on his every word. LSR was a magnetic character. When he spoke, you listened. Though not if you were Senator Fuchs, apparently.

The man could not take his eyes off Joni. Though maybe not old enough to be her father, he was old enough to know better—especially sitting next to his wife, a well-manicured brunette with a bob and a string of pearls big as marbles. What was it with politicians and pretty girls? Lu moved again, following Russi, but taking care not to get too close. This time, she had a better view of Joni, whose dark hair shone in the sun.

Lu had always been drawn to the stories behind the stories. Rather than headlines and big bangs, she was more interested in the psychology of it all. The who and the why and, even better, the why not. People and their motivations fascinated her. Which was why the thrill of landing a job at *Sunset* magazine was beginning to wear off. There were only so many backyard barbecues and wine tastings she could attend.

Lu lifted her camera and aimed. When she did, she saw Joni look down at the ground and then casually glance around. She stopped when she reached Fuchs. Her lashes fluttered. Hard to tell in the glare, but it almost looked like she smiled, then quickly looked away. Lu forgot all about taking a picture.

When the hoopla ended midafternoon, and people dispersed to their rooms, Lu went to the beach bar in search of Uncle Jerry, her father's younger brother. When Lu was a young girl, Jerry used to tell her that he had been born with gills. That he was part fish and so was she. She believed him, since most of his time was spent in or on the ocean—fishing, diving, surfing, paddling, you name it. He was the one who would bring them up along this coast to gather salt and to dive for *he'e*—octopus. Even when things went rocky with her dad, Jerry had always been there. Dark skinned and bald with a glowing white smile, half the women in Kona wished they could snag him. But Jerry was a bachelor through and through, married to the sea.

It was midafternoon, a steady onshore wind blowing in and ruffling up the fronds on the thatched roof of the bar. Out front, bodies slick with suntan oil lay prostrate on beach chairs set up in neat rows on the sand. Some of them would end up with second-degree burns, especially those who sun-bathed drunk.

Lu approached from the side and slid onto an open bar stool. "Give me a triple shot of tequila, please," she said.

Jerry spun around, face lighting up when he saw her. "Luana! My favorite little fish." He came around and gave her a big hug. "When Donna told me you were invited by LSR himself, I was so proud. Sit down. I'll make you a drink."

She knew there was no use arguing. A drink sounded good about now. He made her a pineapple and citrus drink in a cocktail glass with a sugared rim, fancy and refreshing, and it went down much too easily. While Jerry peppered her with questions in between serving guests, she started constructing today's story in her mind. It had been a heartfelt and touch-ing dedication, but where was the angle? Everything had a story, sometimes it was just harder to find. She scribbled a few notes on her legal pad, in what might appear to someone else as hieroglyphics.

Next to her, a bar stool slid back. "Mind if I join you?" She was surprised to see Russi.

"Not at all," she said, covering her writing with her hand.

"Aloha, what can I get for you, sir?" Jerry said.

"Whatever she's having."

A protective look came over her uncle's face and Lu was quick to say, "Uncle Jerry, this is Matteo Russi with *Life*. We know each other."

"Yeah, me and the kid go way back. A pleasure, Jerry. Tell me, how did you land this gig?" Russi said.

"I met Mr. Rockefeller on the beach one day when I came in from diving. We got to talking and one thing led to an-other."

"Looks like you won the prize for best job on the island. And did I hear her say uncle?" Russi said, looking back and forth between the two of them. "Yep, the resemblance is plain as day—those green eyes are hard to miss."

Lu blushed. People noticed her light eyes often. She didn't like attention focused her way, so changed the subject. "Is this your first time to Hawai'i?"

Russi took a big swig. "Nope."

No elaboration.

"Were you chasing a story?" she prodded.

He ran his finger along the rim of his glass, coming away with sugar. "More like chasing a dream. I joined the army air corps and they shipped us to Hawai'i, early 1941."

Lu had known he was a WWII veteran, but for some reason, she'd assumed Europe. "So, you were here during the attack?"

She'd been just a wee thing when Pearl Harbor was bombed and they had holed up in a lava tube on the farm. She had no memory of it, but her mind conjured up images of water dripping down the roots that hung from the rocky ceiling, waiting for another attack. Maybe her father had told that story.

"Not here. On O'ahu," he said.

"That's what I meant. Were you up in the air?"

"Shoulda been." Russi downed his drink, and she swore his hand was quivering. "How about we talk about something else? Like what you two ladies were swimming with this morning. Looked like a herd of sharks. I was thinking I might need to call in the coast guard."

Lu laughed. "It's called a shiver. A shiver of sharks. But those weren't sharks, they were manta rays, which are harmless. You should come tomorrow. We'll be doing it again."

"I don't swim."

"As in, you don't know how to swim or you don't like to swim?"

"As in, it's a long story—one I don't tell strangers."

"Sorry, I wasn't trying to be nosy. But Rockefeller is the one who suggested we immerse ourselves fully in the Hawaiian experience, and the ocean is at the top of that list."

Russi asked Jerry for some peanuts, then said, "Don't waste your time trying to change my mind. I'm not the story here, remember that. You got heaps of other things to write about."

"That's the thing. It seems like I would, but everything I've written just feels like a laundry list of descriptions. The mountains of Mexican flagstone, miles of narra wood and art from all corners of the Pacific."

Why she was telling him this, she had no idea.

"Those aren't story," he said.

"I know that."

"So, what are you asking *me* for?"

"I wasn't asking you. I was just stating a fact."

He gave her a hard look, then surprised her. "Maybe try getting out of your head and just be here at this bar eating peanuts and drinking your fancy drink." He tapped a finger to his temple. "Observe the subjects in their natural habitat."

Lu laughed. "You sound like a zoologist."

"I think you mean anthropologist, kid."

"Either way."

"Have you looked into the lives of the employees? Elije Junte is a sommelier, for chrissakes. How many women in this country can say that?"

He was throwing her a bone, and she wasn't sure why.

"I suppose I could."

"This hotel and its people have their stories to tell, and I guarantee they are more interesting than the guests. All you gotta do is listen," Russi said, looking down at her oversize notepad. "You could start with your uncle."

It wasn't actually a bad idea.

"Would you mind?" she asked Jerry, who had been listening in.

"Ask away."

She felt self-conscious with Russi breathing over her shoulder. "You mentioned meeting Mr. Rockefeller on the beach one day. Tell us more."

"Like I said, he was on the beach. We'd had a big storm a few days back and Billy Santos and I came down the coast in his boat looking for glass fishing balls. Just off Ka'aha Point, we hit the mother lode. They were still in nets, big ones, little ones, long ones, green ones. Some even had Japanese characters still visible. There were too many to fit in the boat, so we drove in and dragged a bunch up the beach and hid 'em in the bushes. Then along comes this *haole*, out of nowhere. He wanted to know what we were doing, and Billy Santos, you know him, he wanted to know what a *haole* in a suit and tie was doing down there in the middle of nowhere. He got a little territorial, but Mr. Rockefeller seemed to know a lot about the area and had so many questions for us. This was before they'd even broken ground on the golf course. After talking story, he finally told us who he was and what he had planned and gave us his business card. Said to call him in a few years if we wanted jobs, and here I am," he said with a smile.

Click. Russi had pulled out his camera without her even noticing.

She went on. "Did he remember you when you called him?"

"Oh, yeah. I was sure he wouldn't, but he did. We gave him one of the glass balls and he has it in his office. Told me he'd been hoping I would call."

"And how has it been so far? Working here."

"So far so good. One thing he got right was hiring the locals. Only a handful not from here, and it already feels like *'ohana*."

Family.

Russi added, "The man is no dummy."

A couple came up to the bar, the woman wearing a kukui nut lei, and Jerry turned his attention to them. Lu could ask him more later, but it was a good start. Maybe Russi was onto something.

"See? And do yourself a favor, lose the big notepad. You want to blend in," he said.

"I need to take notes."

"Relax, kid. Train your brain." He tapped his temple. "When you're taking notes, you're missing out on half the information and most of the experience. This isn't some big investigative job...it's culture, lifestyle."

"Accuracy is important to me, and I haven't been doing this for a hundred years like some people."

Russi laughed. "Easy there. I've been at it awhile, but maybe not that long."

"You know what I mean."

"Affirmative. Now, tell me how you managed to get in with Joni Diaz?"

A gust of wind fluffed up her hair, and she twisted it in a big knot on her head. "She found out I'm from Kona and I was telling her about the ocean and she asked if I'd take her swimming. For all that fame, she seems pretty genuine."

"She can be sweet, but she has her demons." Russi threw down some bills and said, "See you at the lū'au."

Lu barely had time to brush out her hair, change into a long fitted *mu'umu'u* and apply her favorite coral lipstick. She rarely wore lipstick, but the splash of color on her coffee-toned skin made her feel more sophisticated, less like someone's kid sister tagging along. She'd taken Russi's advice and left her notebook in the room. She hoped she'd be able to commit all the details about the night to memory. Walking down the floating staircase, she felt empty-handed.

Out near the point, in a wide grassy lawn, tables had been set up for a much smaller group than the earlier ceremony. Right away, she realized this was no ordinary lū'au. It wasn't overdone, and reminded her of a Matson steamer menu, with the low tables, red and orange hibiscus, koa bowls full of poi and ripe pineapples.

Women wore *mu'umu'u*, and the men appeared as a rainbow of aloha shirts and linen pants. Many of them were old enough to be her grandparents, but they were well preserved. Money had that tendency. Russi stood out all in black, looking like he was attending a funeral. The one thing that tied everyone together was the sheen of tropical sweat on their skin. Clothes should have been optional, especially at this time of year.

Waitresses in orange were floating around, offering cold drinks, and Lu took a ginger ale. She wanted her wits about her when she sat down to write later. Mr. Rockefeller graciously came over and pointed out who was who. Most she recognized, but a few she didn't. When it came time to sit, she and Russi were on the end of a table with Joni, her manager, Stanley, Senator Fuchs and his wife and the Dixons. They were all in various degrees of comfort and discomfort, sitting cross-legged on lauhala mats.

The ocean had glassed off and waited patiently for the sun to set. Lu wished she could slip away and take a swim. People were feeling good—it was hard not to here—and chattering about the beauty of the place and what a fine job Mr. Rockefeller had done. *Outstanding. Groundbreaking. Mind-blowing.*

Mrs. Dixon and Mrs. Fuchs obviously knew each other and started up a conversation, and Stanley began picking Mr. Dixon's brain about the media and how to use it to Joni's advantage, which left the senator to turn his attention toward Russi and Lu.

"I'll wager getting assigned here sure beats 'Nam," he said with that famous smile.

Russi answered coolly, "I did my time, so, yeah, it does."

A moment of awkwardness fell around the table, and Lu jumped in. "I was born and raised on the island, so this assignment is special to me."

Fuchs ignored her and zeroed in on Russi. "Maybe with a reputation like yours, you pick and choose?"

"Something like that," Russi said.

A look of annoyance flashed over Fuchs's face. Wasn't it usually the reporter questioning the politician?

Russi shoved a handful of mac nuts in his mouth, chewed them slowly, then turned to Fuchs. "What are your thoughts on the hotel, Senator? Is it everything you expected?"

"To tell the truth, I was leery when I heard the plans. If it had been anyone else, I would have tried to talk him out of it. But Laurance is a visionary, and I knew that if anyone could pull something off in this remote of a location, it would be him."

"So, you've been to Hawai'i?" Russi asked.

"Once or twice."

Joni leaned in. "The more remote, the better. When I first went to his Caneel Bay, I thought I'd died and gone to heaven. No annoying press to hide from, no television, no nothing. Just sand and water and cocktails," she said, before covering her mouth with her hand. "You don't fall into the annoying press category, Luana, so please don't take offense."

Lu looked to Russi, who only seemed amused.

"And how about that Hawaiian temple that Mr. Rockefeller helped restore. Impressive feat of engineering if I do say so," Fuchs said.

Russi shrugged. "Haven't seen it yet."

Lu couldn't help but jump in. "Puʻukoholā Heiau. It stands over Pelekane Bay, just up the coast. Rumor had it that the heiau overlooked a smaller heiau, now underwater, that had once been dedicated to the shark gods."

"Don't ask any of us to repeat that name," Fuchs said.

Joni eyed Lu. "I think my favorite tour guide forgot to mention a shark temple in the vicinity."

The white tip sharks were still there; Lu had seen them, fins cutting through the water. "They're nothing to worry about. Sharks were believed to be protectors of certain Hawaiian families. Every family had—or has—what was called an *'aumakua*, a guardian animal, and that animal would protect the people, and in turn the people would protect the animal. In Kawaihae, the king had his own special sharks."

Bobby Dean Dixon, who was now listening in, chuckled. "Makes a good case for sticking to golf."

"Reef sharks are generally harmless to humans."

"Still, Rockefeller was wise to leave that out of the brochures," Russi said.

The music started up then, a loud drumbeat, and mountainous plates of food appeared on the table. Glasses were topped off every few minutes. Joni, Lu noted, was throwing them down fast.

"Slow down there, Jo," she heard Stanley say.

"Don't call me that. I've told you," she said.

His nostrils flared, and for a split second Lu thought he might snap back, but instead he carefully unwrapped his steaming *laulau* leaf. It had been far too long since she'd eaten Hawaiian food and her mouth had been watering just thinking about it. *Chicken long rice, lomi lomi salmon, squid luʻau.*

"Hey, Luana, what's the brown paste in the bowl?" Joni asked.

"It's poi. Mashed taro root. The staple of the Hawaiian diet."

Joni tried a tiny spoonful and made a face, but Russi was eating his with both fingers, the way it was meant to be eaten. She tried to picture him on O'ahu twenty years ago, young and cocky and unaware that, in just a few months' time, his life would be changed forever. Lu was well aware of his reputation with the ladies, but she didn't get that vibe from him at all. The fact that he called her *kid* said everything.

Hula dancers came on, wearing red cloth tops and green ti leaf skirts, hair loose and flowing. They danced Hawaiian and Tahitian and knew their stuff. It made Lu homesick to see, even though she was already home. The guests sat transfixed. When they finished, Mrs. Rockefeller came up and asked the crowd for any volunteers. Everyone glanced around at everyone else. *You go. No, you go.* Husbands nudged wives and wives nudged friends.

"Get up there," Lu said to Russi.

He made a face. "I'd rather go swimming."

The next thing she knew, Joni was gliding across the grass. A tall woman with strong hands positioned her next to a few other women and an old guy in a cowboy hat and wrapped hula skirts around their waists. Even Mrs. Rockefeller joined in. The dancer demonstrated how to move their hips. The cowboy and two of the older women had trouble getting the moves, but Joni surprised her by being pretty good. She reminded Lu of a little girl playing dress-up. Then, when the hula was over, someone yelled out for Joni to sing a song. Someone else whistled, and a moment later she was behind the mic.

She swayed and then caught herself, almost as though she was trying not to tip over. But her soulful, husky voice still hit each note and the song sounded just like it was meant to.

Lu had to admit that Joni was innocent and sexy and mysterious all at once. The men had all put down their forks and
were watching.

The next song was one Lu hadn't heard before. Halfway
through the first verse, Joni tripped on the words. *On the top
of the mountain, looking down on the sea—um.*

"Excuse me," she said, obviously drunk.

Lu glanced over at Stanley, who was perched on the edge
of his chair. This was not the kind of crowd you wanted to
embarrass yourself in. Joni tried to make it through a couple
more lines, before bursting into tears. She handed the mic to
Mrs. Rockefeller and said, "Sorry, everyone, I can't do this."

A hush fell as Joni ran off into the night.

12

THE EXPEDITION

O'ahu, 1943

Isabel and Gloria readied themselves for an outing with Matteo Russi. Isabel had begged Gloria to come along for moral support. When asked where they were going, all he'd said was, "Wear a swimsuit, shoes you don't mind getting muddy, and bring some bug juice."

"Bug juice?" she'd asked.

"Mosquito repellent. You're going to need it where we're going."

Isabel did not own a swimsuit that wasn't ten years old, but thankfully Gloria had lent her an extra. No matter she looked like a ghost in it. Gloria had set her hair the night before, and she was unrolling the wide curlers at the kitchen table, setting them in a bowl. "Do you think he'll bring a friend?"

"Who knows. But didn't you tell me yesterday that you have no interest in dating a pilot? I would venture a guess that all his friends fly airplanes," Isabel said.

"I said I don't want to marry a pilot. Marry and date are two different things."

Isabel's logical mind sometimes got her into trouble. "In

order to marry, you have to date. And after a certain amount of dating, you fall in love. It's the being in love part that could break your heart if he leaves or dies. So, maybe it's that you don't want to fall in love with a pilot?"

Gloria twirled a lock of hair in her fingers. "That is far too much supposing for me."

Russi arrived right on time, with a back seat full of coconuts and a wicked grin. "Dang, looks like double trouble," he said, jumping out. He moved the coconuts into the trunk so Gloria had room to sit.

They set out on the same route they'd taken to the Pali lookout, but they kept on going, snaking down the side of the cliff on the most hair-raising road Isabel had ever been on. Gloria suddenly quieted, and when Isabel turned around to check on her, she was bone white.

Russi turned around, too, and she yelled, "Keep your eyes on the road!"

He laughed. "You know, Walt and I said this should be a prerequisite for flight school. If you could handle this road, you were in." He glanced over at Isabel, who was enjoying the fresh air and the view. "I guess you'da passed," he said, causing just the tiniest flitter along her skin.

The weather was different today, with mounds of gray clouds hanging out along the horizon. The air was warm and sticky and Isabel was now wishing she'd worn shorts instead of long pants. Gloria had warned her that it took time to figure out how to dress here, and boy, was she right.

As soon as they reached the bottom of the mountain, Gloria became her usual chatty self. "What were the Solomons like? I've heard a few horror stories about the snakes and crocodiles and man-eating sharks. My friend's husband, Bob, came back half his usual size and full of some kind of parasite. And on top of all that, you had the enemy lurking in the jungle and flying night raids every night. It sounds like my version of hell."

Russi nodded. "That they were. But they were also heaven on earth. Sandy blue lagoons with a heck of a lot more coral than here, colorful birds you've never seen the likes of and sand the color of snow. Half the time I was terrified out of my mind, and the other half, in love."

"Well, that's a new perspective," Gloria said.

Isabel rather appreciated his optimism.

"Just because there's a war going on doesn't mean beauty disappears. I take my camera everywhere I go for that reason. I can show you my albums one of these days," he said.

"Walt said you don't like your picture taken. Why is that?" Isabel said.

"I like to be behind the camera, not in front of it. Oh, and I brought her along, hope you ladies don't mind."

"Brought who along?" Gloria said.

"My camera."

Where the land began to level out, they turned off the main road and followed a rutted dirt road through vine-draped trees and mud puddles. Light shone through in thin crisscrosses. The forest was so thick you'd need a machete to get through.

"Are there snakes here?" Isabel asked, a creep running up her spine.

"No snakes, no crocs, no big cats. Hawai'i is as benign a place as they come—if you don't count man," he said.

"How did you and Walt find this place?" she asked.

"You know Walt, he made friends with everyone. A group of girls from Shafter came down here one day and we tagged along. A few of them were locals, and they knew all the ins and outs," he said.

"In all his letters, Walt never mentioned any girls. Was he seeing anyone?"

He shook his head. "We were too busy training and exploring and being boys. He went on a date now and then, but nothing serious."

"How about you?" she asked, wanting to get it out in the open and not have any awkwardness between them. Russi was Walt's friend, and that made him family.

"How about me what?" he said, looking out the window.

"Are you seeing anyone?"

A nervous laugh. "Me? Sure, I've taken a few girls out, but I'm not looking to get attached. Winning this war is my one and only."

Isabel could relate.

The trail was not really a trail at all, and she and Gloria had to follow close on his heels to avoid sinking into deep boggy mud. Russi wore combat boots and fatigues, and a tight-fitting olive-green T-shirt that stretched thin over his broad shoulders. He looked the part of a soldier, and it wasn't hard to imagine that they were in some far-off jungle evading the enemy. At any moment, bombs could fall. They clambered up rocks, through groves of banyans, and crossed small streams. Isabel quickly came to realize that despite her frequent walks, she was not in top physical condition. Russi, on the other hand, never once seemed winded. He gave off a quiet power.

He also turned out to be a good guide, whistling along with an adorable orange-breasted bird and picking passion fruit from a vine. Whenever the trail grew steep or rough, he always offered a calloused hand. At one point, they scaled a vertical embankment, hanging on to branches and roots to pull themselves up.

Gloria laughed, but you could tell she was having second thoughts about coming. "You weren't kidding when you said we'd get muddy. Not that I mind, but do you think we'll be there soon?"

"It's just around the next bend," he said.

But there was no waterfall around the next bend. Or the next. With the sun overhead now, mosquitoes swarmed in the steamy air, especially around Isabel. She had to walk with her arms in perpetual motion, swatting them away. This was not her idea of fun at all. But in honor of her brother, she didn't complain. Then Russi turned around and gave her a large fern that he'd broken off.

"Use this as a fan," he said, stopping to pull the bug juice out from his backpack.

"How come they're only after me?" she asked.

"Seems like they like people fresh off the boat. New blood," he said with a hint of a grin.

Red welts had begun popping up wherever skin was exposed. He handed her the bottle and she rubbed it down her arms. Gloria followed suit. They continued on, and just when she had convinced herself they were lost, she heard the roar of rushing water.

Just beyond a curve in the trail, a waterfall several times taller than the tallest tree spilled into an enormous green pond. Sunlight dappled the surface, moss-covered rocks lined the edge. The spray from the falling water created its own wind.

Russi looked at her like an expectant dog, hoping for a bone. "Welcome to paradise, ladies. What do you think?"

Despite being caked in mud and covered in bites, Isabel felt a warmth on the inside she hadn't felt in over a year. And the strangest thing was, she didn't even know why.

"It's straight out of one of those slick travel advertisements they used to distribute in the middle of winter," Gloria said, slipping off her shoes and dipping her feet in.

Isabel was about to answer when the first raindrop fell, big as a guppy, on her shoulder.

Russi looked up at the sky and then quickly pulled his shirt off. "You know what they say about the last one in."

It was impossible not to notice his smooth and toned body. Each muscle was perfectly delineated, and when he bent down to pull off his long pants, Isabel was forced to notice the notches in his side. He could have been carved out of wood.

Russi stood back up, caught her looking and said, "Whatcha waiting for?"

"I'm not a swimmer. I'll just wait on the rocks," Gloria said.

He nodded to Isabel. "I know you swim, Izzy. Race you to the falls?"

Izzy. Only Walt called her Izzy. With that, he was in the water and swimming as fast as he could. Even though she knew she had no chance, she tore off her clothes and jumped in. The water was cool but not cold, and despite feeling weary from the long hike, she put her head down and swam for the falls, rain tickling her arms. As she got closer, the moving water began pushing her back until she was swimming in place. The water tasted of mountaintop and clouds.

"Come to this side," yelled a voice.

Russi was standing on a small ledge ten feet or so above the pond, on the right side of the falls, half-submerged in a white curtain of water. Isabel made it over but had trouble climbing out onto the slippery rock. Finally, she grabbed a clump of grass and pulled herself out like a seal. When she got to him, he reached out and held her forearms.

"This here is God's own shower. If you stand here long enough, you forget everything about the outside world. It just washes everything away," he said, pulling her closer.

They inched into the waterfall, which was pelting them

so hard Isabel could hardly open her eyes. But suddenly, they were in a space behind the water.

"Walt called this the green room. When we came here, he was the one who found it. He disappeared behind the falls and did not come out. It was funny, because back home I had always been the first one to do everything. First to jump, first to take the shot, you name it. And then I met Walt, and it was like we were the same person. It made us both push even harder," he said, yelling over the roar.

"Sounds familiar."

"I miss the hell out of that man," he said.

"So do I."

They stood there for a few more moments, his hand still clutching her arm, warm and strong. Then he stepped through the falling water and she followed. Back outside, rain was coming down so hard Gloria was just a shape across the pond. Isabel should have been shivering from cold, but she felt oddly fine. Only in part because of the lukewarm water.

Russi grabbed her hand. "Now we jump. On three," he said.

Isabel squeezed her eyes shut. *One. Two.* As soon as the word *three* lifted off his tongue, she leaped up and as far out into the pond as she could. A rush of freedom blew through her and for a flash she felt like a kid again. A squeal escaped her lips. Next to her, Russi must have cannonballed, because she heard a huge *kerplunk*. They both came up laughing. He spit water at her face and she dove under and made for the other side, long legs kicking hard. Still, Russi beat her back.

When they got out, Gloria was huddled against a nearby boulder, drenched. The skies had gone black as night. "I thought you two were drowned and I'd have to find my way back in this godforsaken storm to bring help," she said.

"I had something to show Izzy," Russi said, pulling out a stringy towel from his backpack and offering it to her.

"About Walt," Isabel added.

Gloria's voice softened. "Oh, right. Sorry."

"I was hoping to get some photographs. I guess that'll have to wait until the rain lets up. Or next time."

"As long as next time we go to a sunny beach instead," Gloria said, trying to put her shoes on while Isabel dressed in her soaked clothing.

"Aw, you gotta love the rain. You know what they say. No rain, no waterfalls," he said.

Gloria frowned. "I thought it was no rain, no rainbows."

"It can be whatever you want it to be."

Later, after Russi dropped them off and they were hosing the muck off themselves and their clothing, Gloria said, "He's different than I expected."

Isabel turned. "I thought you said you didn't know him."

Gloria took a step back. "Well, I don't know him. But to tell the truth, I know a little bit about him. Through the grapevine."

"Why didn't you tell me?"

"Because it wasn't my place. Whatever I know of Matteo Russi, it's all secondhand. And he was your brother's dear friend. I didn't want you to judge him before you'd even met the poor fellow."

"What have you heard, then?"

"He dated a girl I work with, Malia, a while back, and he has, well…he has a bit of a reputation."

"What kind of reputation?"

"The girls all say he's a real ladies' man. A love 'em and leave 'em kind of guy, and very full of himself, too. Of course, women still lined up knowing that."

Isabel had witnessed this phenomenon often back in DC. "The less they want you, the more you want them. Is that it?"

"That was the impression I had, until I actually met him."

"He seemed perfectly nice to me."

On this side of the island, it was sunny as could be. Gloria sat down in the grass and turned her face to the bright sky. "Maybe that was it. Since neither of us had any interest in him *that* way, he let his guard down and acted natural."

"He reminds me a lot of Walt, but with more of an edge." *And that smile.*

"He seems to really fancy you."

"He loved Walt, and I'm Walt's sister."

Gloria got a mischievous look. "I got the sense it was more than that. Almost like I wasn't even there. Sure, he was polite to me, but he was awfully attentive to you. I caught him watching you a few times when you weren't looking. And—"

Isabel held up her hand. "Please, stop. I don't want those kinds of thoughts anywhere near me. Not with this guy, okay?"

She could tell Gloria was dying to say something else, but refrained. They stretched out in the sun and compared childhood stories and hopes for the future.

13

THE TAVERN

O'ahu, 1943

On Wednesday after work, on a freshly squeezed sunshiny day, Gloria invited Isabel to join a few of the girls for a quick round of drinks in Honolulu. Drained from the extra energy it took working underground, Isabel wasn't in the mood and politely declined.

"I won't take no for an answer, young lady. You can't just hole up with those kooky men downstairs and never interact with the rest of the human race," Gloria said with her hands on her hips.

"I don't have anything to wear."

"Oh, please. I have just the perfect thing for you. And then you and I are going shopping first chance we get. All those navy blues and blacks are not meant for a tropical climate. You look like you're going to a funeral every single day."

"Fine, but I'm on a budget."

"We all are."

Isabel was coming to see that Gloria could talk people into almost anything. She always did it with a smile on her face, but there was a hidden power behind her words.

Linda, a freckled beauty with a shock of red hair, picked them up and drove them to a restaurant at the edge of downtown Honolulu called the Peacock Tavern. The place looked a little suspect, but unlike the Black Cat Café several blocks down, there wasn't a line of sailors halfway down the street waiting to get in.

Malia was already there, saving a booth near a jukebox. Her warm smile put Isabel at ease right away, even though Isabel had come not wanting to like her. Though that was more than unfair, she knew. Gloria had filled her in about the two girls, both raised in the islands, and swore that they were the kind of people you wanted on your team.

They were all a-chatter about the latest news. "Have you heard they've begun to ration shoes? Three pairs a year is all we get," Linda said.

"Shoes I can do without, it's not having butter that's killing me," Gloria said.

"I go through three pairs a month just walking back and forth to the filing cabinet. There are so many official documents it makes my head spin," Malia said.

Speaking of her head, Isabel couldn't help but admire the thick waves of sun-streaked hair that cascaded nearly to her hips. She and Russi would have made a fine pair.

Soon, a round of whipped coconut and rum drinks showed up, along with a bowl of boiled peanuts, and a plate of small rice patties wrapped in seaweed and a thin slice of meat on top. Spam musubi.

Halfway through the drink, Malia said, "Gloria tells me you two went hiking with Matteo Russi the other day."

Here it comes.

"We did. He was friends with my late brother, Walt," Isabel said.

"She mentioned that, too. What a devastating loss."

"Thank you, it's been hard."

"No one should have to go through that. And that's why I feel obligated to warn you about Matteo. He's a nice guy, but the last thing you need is any more heartache, which is precisely what you're in for if you keep seeing him."

Isabel shot Gloria a look. "I'm not seeing him. He's just being a good friend to Walt. No one needs to be concerned."

"Us girls need to stick together, and you seem really nice. I only wish someone had warned me," Malia said. Her big eyes and unusually long lashes gave her a certain innocence.

Linda joined in. "Not only will he drop you as soon as someone else strikes his fancy, that man has a death wish."

"What do you mean?" Isabel asked.

"Madge, who works with us, is married to one of his pilot friends. He says that Matteo is always the first to volunteer for the most dangerous job, the most impossible mission, and he takes risks that no one in their right mind ought to," Malia said.

Isabel sipped the rum drink, which was going down in record time. "That's his business, I suppose. And why does it seem so impossible for a man and a woman to simply be friends?"

"Some men, yes. Not men like him. He was no doubt flirting with the nanny when he was still in diapers. And the nanny fell for him."

Despite herself, Isabel asked, "How long did you two see each other?"

"About a month. Which is longer than most, from what I hear. This was last year, right before Midway. Things were hot and heavy and then he left and I missed him and worried the whole time he was away. But when he got home, we went out once and he drank himself silly and never called me again," Malia said, cheeks flushed.

Gloria said, "Sounds like he needs a taste of his own medicine. That usually cures them."

"I appreciate you looking out for me, but like I said, I have no interest in dating him," Isabel said, holding up her glass and ready to change the subject. "Cheers, ladies."

Malia held up her glass. "To new friends."

"To victory."

"To victory!" everyone said in unison. Two men at a nearby table raised their glasses, too, and before Isabel knew it, they had pulled their chairs up and had become part of the group. One sat close by her side, knobby knee bumping hers, the other next to Malia. Vern and Dickie were their names.

Gloria honed in on Dickie right away. "Where are you fellas stationed?"

"Here and there."

"I'm surprised I haven't seen you before," Gloria said, pressing.

Blond and tan, Dickie smelled strongly of aftershave. "They keep us busy," he said with a wink. "I thought I was seeing a mirage when I walked in. You don't happen upon a table of four beautiful broads every day around here. What's the occasion?" Dickie said.

Isabel could tell Malia was not impressed. "No occasion, just *pau hana* cocktails with the girlfriends," she said, emphasizing *friends*.

He smiled. "You lost me there for a moment. Come again?"

"Pau hana. It means 'after work.'"

He didn't miss a beat. "Oh, right. So, where do you gals report?"

"Pearl. Admin," Gloria said.

"Dang, how come we don't have secretaries that look like you? Ours grow mustaches and wear pants."

Broads. Gals. Secretaries. Isabel was about to excuse herself to use the restroom for a breather when she noticed Malia staring in the direction of the door. She turned. Russi had entered, with a girl hanging on his arm. Three seconds later he noticed Malia, and promptly steered wide. Then he locked eyes with Isabel. Feebly waved.

Gloria spotted him and waved back. "Hey, Russi, come say hello!"

He stepped closer, as if moving through tar. "Ladies, gentlemen. A pleasure to see you all."

It was so obviously not a pleasure that Isabel felt for him. She held up the watch, which she now wore on her wrist. "We added another hole on the strap. Fits like a charm now. Walt would be happy."

He looked relieved. "Glad to hear it. Speaking of Walt, this was one of our haunts." He gestured to the back wall covered in photographs. "You'll find a picture of him up there, holding a surfboard on Waikiki Beach looking like a champ."

Isabel perked up. "I was about to use the ladies' room. Would you mind showing me?"

The girl on his arm twirled one of her curls and cleared her throat.

Russi fumbled for a moment, then said, "Izzy, meet Alice. A friend from work."

A frown crossed over Alice's face, but she graciously shook Isabel's hand. Russi led them over to the photograph, larger than most of the others and right at eye level. Walt stood casually, leaning up against a wooden board twice his height, with Diamond Head rising up in the background. His expression said, *I'm up for anything, how about you?*

"He was a natural. Me, I had to work at it," Russi said.

"I doubt that."

"No really. I love the water, but I'm no fish."

"Must have been all that time in the old quarries. We

went every chance we could. But there are no waves in Indiana," she said.

"Just you wait. We'll go this weekend if you're free," he
said.

The tiniest flutter.

Isabel felt bad for Alice, but hopefully Alice knew the situation with her and Russi. "Do you surf, Alice?" she asked.

Alice rolled her eyes. "Heavens, no. I never even learned
to swim. You wouldn't catch me dead out there. But I enjoy
watching from the beach."

For some reason, the thought of tagging along with Alice
and Russi was far less appealing than having Russi to herself.
The feeling unsettled her. "I may have to work, but we'll see."

He thrust his hands into his pockets. "Rumor has it we
may be shipping out soon, so I'd love to take you before I go."

Time pressed in on them. It was foolish to believe that a
person could have a normal life here, but that was exactly
how she'd felt on her brief outings with Russi. War was all
around them, and yet the intricacies of daily life remained.
Waterfalls fell, wind blew skirts up and waves rolled in.

"It's not up to me," she said.

He nodded toward the table. "Either of those fellas your
boss? Maybe it would help if I asked for you. Say I need you
for an important operation."

Isabel was flattered. "My boss rarely leaves the office, and
when he does, he sleeps. Those two just pulled up their chairs
and invited themselves in."

Russi glanced over, assessing the two men. He was about
to say something else when Alice grabbed on to his elbow
and said, "Sugar, I'm thirsty and we're running out of daylight, come *on*."

"I'll let you know. Enjoy your drinks," Isabel said.

"'Night, Izzy," Russi said, standing there like he didn't want to go.

In all honesty, Isabel felt the same way. She forced herself to turn away, feeling a burn on the back of her neck as she walked to the restroom.

At the table, Dickie turned out to be smooth as coconut syrup, while Vern remained almost mute. Gloria hung on every word Dickie said as he talked about repairing ships, which was apparently what he did. Poor Malia kept glancing behind them, where Russi and Alice were sitting, even though he had strategically placed himself out of their line of sight.

Just after sunset, Dickie and Vern walked the women to their car. The clouds lit up like orange honeycomb, lighting the sky on fire. While most people were trying to figure out ways to stay out after dark, Isabel was thankful for the curfew. It meant no late nights out, no pressure to socialize when she'd rather be home reading a book or playing chess. Gloria and Dickie hung back, heads close together and speaking in low tones, even when Linda and Isabel had already climbed in the car.

"Hurry up, slowpoke. I don't want to get arrested," Linda finally called out the window.

Gloria tore herself away and hopped into the back seat with a dazed smile. Isabel knew that look. She'd seen it a number of times on girls back in Washington. It usually meant that they were goners. Something she had never experienced herself, which was fine by her. Wherever men went, trouble seemed to follow.

14

THE CHARTER

Hawai'i Island, July 1965

Joni never showed up for the swim, so Lu went on her own. There were no mantas so she walked to the end of the beach and swam back. Water clear and silky, without a ripple. Same as yesterday, Russi was under the coconut tree, sitting with his back against the trunk. Lu looked up. Fortunately, the coconuts had been trimmed off.

"Don't worry, I checked," he said. "Where's your pal?"

"Hungover, I'm guessing. She was pretty wobbly last night."

"Too much fame, too young. And the woman can't handle her alcohol."

"You seem to know a lot about her."

He shrugged. "I know a lot about a lot of things. It comes with the territory. Speaking of knowing a lot, you sound like you know a thing or two about this place. Could be a valuable asset."

"How do you mean?"

"Dunno. But those kinds of details are what people want. Local knowledge. Keep that in mind."

She saluted him. "Will do. So, are you going fishing?"

Three boats had been chartered for the group today. Out of Kawaihae.

"Nah. They don't need me out there."

"It's part of the experience, isn't it? You should come."

"I got a bad stomach for that kind of thing."

Russi's hair stuck out in all directions, dark like seaweed. Almost as tousled as her own. The bags under his eyes were the size of small duffels. Something about the way his gaze danced around told her there was more to the story. Lu wasn't sure why, but for some reason she wanted him there.

She pressed. "The water's calm today, and if you keep your eyes on the horizon, you'll be fine. I really could use a friend."

"You're a big girl, Miss Freitas, you don't need me out there."

"You and I are the only outsiders, the only regular folk, so it sort of feels like we're a team."

He chuckled. "Most journalists aren't team players."

"There's no rule that they can't be."

"Fair enough. How long have you been with *Sunset*?"

"Less than a year."

"And how's it going?" he asked.

His question almost felt like a challenge.

"It's a great magazine. The offices in Menlo Park are beautiful and I enjoy the people I work with. I'm just getting started, but I know I'm going to love it."

"You hate it."

It felt like a slap in the face.

"I do not."

"Your body says otherwise."

"Sorry, but you're mistaken," she said.

"I'm good at reading people. My sense tells me you're

there because you feel like you should be, not because you want to be."

"Well, your sense is wrong. I busted my butt to get there, and I love everything about my job. I have a great boss and a great editor and I'm going to make a name for myself."

"Making a name for yourself isn't all it's cracked up to be."

"Says the man with a big name."

The side of his mouth curved up. "It's less about the name than about doing what fires you up inside, and I'm just saying that maybe you're not fired up by where you're at."

"We all have to start somewhere."

"But it's not here. Not home."

"And your point is?"

"You have *Hawai'i* written all over you," Russi said.

No, it wasn't home. He was right about that. His words felt like a small kiawe thorn in her foot, one that she had never been able to get out all the way. Had she been so driven to prove herself that she missed the cues along the way?

She shook it off. "*Sunset* is where I need to be right now. What about you? You've been at *Life* forever. How is that going? Might it be time to get a fresh perspective, Mr. Russi? When people do something for so long, they can wind up getting a little too comfortable. Maybe even lose their edge," she said.

"You think I've lost my edge?"

"Not at all. But it's just a thought I had," she said.

"To answer your question, I've just left *Life*. I'm freelancing now. This is my first gig. Rockefeller asked for me personally."

This was a shock. "Seriously?"

"It was time."

"Come fishing. You don't want to let Mr. Rockefeller down."

"I'm not going fishing."

It was plain to see that beneath the tough-guy facade lived a fear as wide as the ocean.

"If you weren't scared of the water, would you want to go?" she challenged.

"Who says I'm scared of the water?"

"You sit here staring at it like a long-lost lover or something." Maybe she was being too forward, but she couldn't help herself. "Why are you really here?"

Russi started flicking the tiny baby coconuts that lay around his feet. "Unfinished business. Now go do your job and forget about me."

"Does it have to do with a woman?"

He blinked in rapid succession. "None of your business."

There had been pictures of him in the papers over the years with numerous beautiful women, from actresses to artists to heiresses. Yet as far as she knew, he had never married. He wore no ring.

"I'm a good listener."

He sighed. "Here's the thing, even if I wanted to, I can't go back and do things differently. So talking about it now is a moot point."

"The more you avoid it, the worse it gets, have you noticed that?" she said.

"Who are you, Freud?"

She sat down under the next coconut tree, wrapping herself in her damp pareo. "No, but I know from experience. I'm sure whatever happened to you is on a different scale, but when I was little, I was so freaked out about writing that I'd ask to go to the bathroom, and then hide in the dumpster when it came time to write. And later, I found other ways to avoid it. But the more I avoided it, the larger it loomed. Fears are like that."

"Thanks, doc. You do realize I'm old enough to be your dad. I've been around the block a few times."

She shook her head. "It doesn't matter. What I'm saying is God's own truth. It's so much easier to run away than to face your fears, so most people run. Just answer my first question and then I'll leave you alone. Promise."

Russi stood up and wiped off the seat of his shorts. "Sometimes you gotta know when to quit, kid," he said before walking away.

An hour later, Lu and the group piled into limos and were driven up to Kawaihae, a dry, dusty place that fell somewhere between town and a few old houses along the water. Kawaihae had once been a quaint Hawaiian fishing village, but in the fifties, the government decided to dredge the ocean out front and turn it into a shipping harbor. Then the village was no more. Lu tried to remember it the way it was when she was little, because to do otherwise broke her heart.

At the dock, there were four boats waiting, so Mr. Rockefeller divided the group into four parties. Couples were broken up, though not all wives had chosen to come, and Lu ended up with Big Joe Wallace, Joni, Merrill Carlsmith, a prominent local judge, and Senator Fuchs. Their boat was the *Leesa Jo*, captained by Max Macadangdang, and first mate Lala Chun. Both men were sun-worn and full of toothy smiles.

"The main thing is to catch fish, have fun and, for Pete's sake, stay in the boat," Rockefeller said as they boarded.

"Tally ho!" Big Joe said.

Standing next to him in her rubber slippers, Lu could see why they called him Big Joe. He was at least six foot five and had arms as big as tree limbs. He dwarfed everyone on the dock, even the senator, who was tall and slim with a tennis player physique. With his aviator shades, Fuchs reminded her of Steve McQueen. More leading man than politician.

While Max and Lala gave them a quick safety tour, a speeding Jeep came skidding around the shipping containers and slammed on the breaks, kicking up dust. Everyone turned. Matteo Russi climbed out of the passenger door, dressed in an orange T-shirt and plaid shorts.

Cool as ever, he called, "Got room for one more?"

"We're the lightest. Come with us," Max said.

As he walked onto the boat, Russi never once looked down at the water.

"You know anything about fishing?" Lala asked.

"A thing or two. But it's been a while."

"I'm glad you came, Mr. Russi," Lu said.

"Wish I could say the same," he said, holding tight to the rails.

The boats headed out through the buoys and toward Māhukona, the old sugarcane port. Between the cool air off the water and being surrounded by blue, Lu experienced an old familiar lightening of being. Anyone born and bred in Kona knew the feeling. There was still no wind line, but by the looks of the clouds—small and puffy, like a field of cottontails—that might change.

Out on the sea, you usually encountered two types of people: *those who thrive and those who dive*, as her uncle used to say. Lu surveyed the group and placed bets on who would thrive and who would dive. Big Joe, Bobby Dean and Merrill Carlsmith would thrive, while Joni—who already looked pale as the side of the boat—and the senator would dive. Russi was still to be determined.

Between Kawaihae and Upolu Point, it got deep fast. At night, you could hear the whale song drifting up out of the water. Uncle Jerry always raved about the *aku* and the *'ōpelu* in these parts, and how just before dark, the *'ōpelu* would congregate. That was when you came out to fish for them.

She still remembered the old landmarks: Black Point, Red Hill, Honokoa Gulch.

Lala set up the fishing lines, with help from Mr. Carlsmith, who by the looks of it knew exactly what he was doing. Max played tour guide, explaining the lay of the land and sharing a mixture of old Hawaiian, ranching and sugarcane history.

Lu couldn't help but add, "Kawaihae used to be famous for its salt pans, too. As a fishing village and a port, as well as being below Waimea with all its cattle, that made it the best place on the island to buy fish. Salt was used to preserve everything, and it was a hot commodity back then. If you hike out along the coast, you'll still find pools of salt dried all along the lava."

Being home was opening the floodgates of all this information she'd been storing in her head. The kind you acquired by osmosis just from living in a place and loving it. On the mainland, no one cared, but here, it felt weighty and important and meaningful.

The farther out they went, the more of the island you could see. Big, sloping shield volcanoes patched with shades of green and brown. Rock walls, roads and fences divided up the land. She tried to imagine how it must be for someone who had never been here before, and how stunning the views were.

Once the lines were out, Lala opened a big ice chest and started offering drinks. "Passion Orange? Coke? Beer?"

It was eleven o'clock in the morning. Big Joe took a beer and so did Joni, who said, "Will we see sharks? I have a strange fascination with the creatures."

"Possible, but I doubt it. If anywhere, they hang out near the mouth of the harbor, waiting for leftovers," Lala said.

Senator Fuchs said, "I thought they were top predators."

"They are, but the ones around here have gone lazy. Why hunt when you don't have to?" Lala said.

"When I was here last, we were a hell of a lot more worried about enemy subs than sharks," Fuchs said.

"Were you military?" Lu asked.

"I was."

Lu glanced over at Russi. "Did you two ever meet?"

Russi shook his head, eyes glazed over. Fuchs answered for him. "I spent every waking hour in the shipyard, so that's a negative."

"Please keep an eye out and let me know if any of you see one—a shark, that is," Joni said, holding up her beer and clinking it with Big Joe. "Cheers!"

Fuchs grabbed one from the cooler and joined the toast. "To a beautiful day—and crew."

Once again, he seemed to have his eye on Joni. It would be hard not to, in her halter top and purple paisley shorts. Legs for miles. She'd braided her hair into two long ropes that hung down to the bottom of each breast. Her naturally gold skin had browned even more in the last day, giving her a freshly toasted glow.

"Thank you, Senator. I'm feeling particularly beautiful today. You want to know why?" Joni said.

It was hard to tell who she was talking to and Lu was about to respond when Fuchs said, "No, but I'd like to."

"Because I'm happy. And happiness makes you shine from the inside out. I'd even venture to say that happiness and beauty are one and the same," Joni said.

"What are you so happy about?" Lu asked.

"Oh, just everything."

How could you argue with that? Russi, however, did not look happy—or beautiful. He was standing nearby, but not paying attention. His shirt was already sticking to his back and he looked a thousand miles away. Lu left them all and went to the back of the boat to see what was happening. Lala, Big Joe and Judge Carlsmith were discussing the intricacies of fishing lures and which ones worked best with *ono*. Joe claimed it was the minnow, hands down, while the judge claimed a bullet head with a trolling skirt was the only way to go.

Lu hung back with them for a while, but she was worried about Russi, who told her to leave him be every time she came near. He had gone inside the cabin, where Fuchs and Joni had posted up, and then come back outside. He couldn't seem to find a place to settle.

"Why don't you have a beer? Take the edge off," Lu suggested.

"Fine. Bring me one."

She brought two. One for her and one for him. He downed his in one pour, then handed her the bottle. "Maybe I should have another."

In the back, a bell rang and Lu heard the high-pitched whine of fishing line running out. Someone hooted. They all ran to the stern, but just as soon as Big Joe was seated and strapped in, the line broke.

"Son of a gun," he yelled.

"Sharp teeth those buggahs get," Lala said.

The boat continued for another hour with no bites. It was unusual but not unheard of. Lala served tuna salad sandwiches and snacks, and as they went, Joni kept up with Big Joe, beer for beer. She bounced around between the back, the front, the flybridge and the cabin, like a wayward butterfly, and Lu wondered if she was on something other than alcohol. Wherever she went, Fuchs followed.

"Make sure you drink some water, too," Lu told her, knowing all too well how people got dehydrated all the time out here.

A few minutes later, the weather took a turn. The slick blue turned into black chop, and ten minutes after that, whitecaps. A gray cloud bank bulked up in the west, slowly closing in. Captain Max turned the boat around, and the island suddenly felt very far away. Lu wasn't worried, but she could see concern on some of the other faces.

"I need to go up front," Russi said, turning.

Lu grabbed his arm, which was surprisingly hard. "That's the worst place to be."

His teeth were chattering, but it wasn't cold. Not yet. They were still dry.

"This was a dumb idea. I shoulda never come," he said, letting her lead him portside.

"You've done great up until now. See that mountain? Just keep your eyes on that. It's going to be bumpy, but these guys do this all the time. This is typical for up here," she said, looking toward the Kohala Mountains, which were now half-covered in mist.

Russi closed his eyes, and Lu worried he was going to pass out. "Mr. Russi?"

"Just Russi, okay? Cut the *Mr.*"

"Don't forget to breathe. Big, slow, deep breaths. Our neighbor's husband was in the war and he used to have…episodes. I remember his wife would talk him down and count out inhalations and exhalations. Want me to do that?"

She could still hear Auntie H's smooth voice: *Long breath in…one two three four five, long breath out, one two three four five. All is well.*

"I want you to leave me alone," he said breathlessly.

He looked like a frightened rabbit, so vulnerable, so afraid. It pained her heart. Whatever he'd been through had nearly broken him.

"Listen to me. You can get through this." Lu grabbed his hand. He didn't resist. She started counting. "You are safe, Russi."

Soon, the boat was cresting the waves and crashing into the trough, spray dousing them. Lala herded everyone else into the cabin. Both Joni and Fuchs had turned green. Lu moved Russi toward the back, where it was more stable, and Captain Max handed them rain jackets.

"Seasick?" he asked.

"Yeah," Lu said.

This was all her fault. "I'm sorry for getting you into this. I just had the sense that you yearned to be in the water, and I thought it would be a good idea to push you a little. I had no idea how serious your situation was."

He shrugged. "I used to be fearless. I flew to the ends of the earth doing all kinds of crazy shit and never once worried about whether I lived or died. And now here I am, wuss of all wusses," he said.

Keep him talking.

"You were brave back then and you're even braver now. Sometimes the smallest fears are the most terrifying. They might even seem irrational, but that doesn't make them not real."

"Here you go again with the Freud talk," he said.

"Call it what you want, it's the truth. You can't just will your troubles away."

"What does the doctor recommend?"

"Have you ever talked to anyone about what happened back then?" Lu had to raise her voice to be heard above the motor and the angry seas. Behind them, the rain line was moving faster than they were. She could taste the metal on her tongue as it closed in.

"Nope."

"Have you ever written about it?"

"Nope."

"That would be my prescription. Talk. If you can't talk, write."

As the words left her mouth, a wave broadsided the boat, knocking it precariously horizontal. Someone inside the cabin screamed.

"This is fucked up," he growled.

"If you want to talk, I'm here. I know you hardly know me, but maybe that's a good thing. I'm a champion listener."

Lala opened the cabin door and insisted they come inside, but Russi wouldn't budge. "I'm not going in there. If this boat goes down, I don't want to be trapped like some caged rat."

"We not goin' down, bruddah. This is *manini*—just a small kine storm," Lala said in thick pidgin.

Lu backed him up. "These guys are out here every day, Russi. If they aren't worried, there's no need for us to be."

"I don't care. I'm not going in," Russi said, more forcefully this time.

Lala looked back and forth between them.

"We're okay out here. I grew up in Kona—I'll keep an eye on him."

"Shoots."

They lurched and plunged and crashed their way back to shore. Russi held fast to the rail and kept his eye on the mountain, just as she told him. Every so often she reminded him to breathe, and spoke words of encouragement. Lu was thankful for the foul-weather gear, because they were drenched with rain and salt water. A part of her felt guilty, because she loved this weather. Loved being back on the water.

When they finally pulled into Kawaihae, the harbor itself was whipped in whitecaps. Two 'iwa birds—harbinger of storms—hovered overhead, low enough so you could see their forked tail feathers. When they docked, the rest of the group filed out of the cabin, Joni first.

"I'm never setting foot on a fucking boat again. Never," Joni announced, bleary-eyed and marching toward land without a glance at anyone.

So much for happiness and beauty. Lu and Russi disembarked last. She was proud of him for holding it together. Despite everything, there was an undercurrent of strength running through him.

By the car, he pulled Lu aside. "I'll tell you what," he said quietly. "That's the first time I've had salt water on my skin since 1945. Thank you."

15

THE SURF

Oʻahu, 1943

On the codebreaking front, over a month in, and Isabel had little to show for being in Hawaiʻi. Working with the crew in the Dungeon was not much different than working by herself. She was coming to badly miss the girls back at Main Navy. There, at least, she was part of a team. Even though much of the time she had been in her own head, people had been rooting for her. Nora, Ellen Mary, even Anna. Not so here.

Her nerves had subsided slightly, but only because she had discovered that by going outside every hour or so, it was like letting the lid off a steaming kettle.

Jones, at his desk by the door, had asked, "Is everything okay, Miss Cooper?"

"Just female issues," she answered, effectively preventing any further questioning. In her experience, it was the quickest way to get a man off your back.

JN-25 was a beast of a code, and she plugged away at nonurgent messages as best she could. Which was not saying much. There were still so few code groups recovered that it felt like sifting sand through a colander—most of it got through except for a few particles in between the holes.

Denny and the boys rarely gave her anything of importance. There had been mention of her having to prove herself, and yet how could she prove herself with weeks' old messages about a small fishing vessel near the Kuriles or a missing minesweeper in the Solomons? Hadn't she proved herself with Magenta? It made no sense.

For the most part, Denny flat out ignored her. He was too wrapped up in solving Ultra messages—Ultra was the code name for top-secret decrypted messages, either German or Japanese—and meeting with Hudson and the brass. Ziegler spoke to her in small bursts, just like he did everything else. Out of nowhere, he might say, "Try the previous additive book" or "that code group has two meanings." Every little bit helped.

On Sunday morning, Russi picked her up just after sunrise, with a long wooden plank of a surfboard sticking out of the trunk of his car. Isabel had invited her roommate, but Gloria had plans with Dickie, so it was just the two of them. They rode with the sun in their eyes, talking about everything but the other night. He didn't mention Alice and she didn't ask.

"I consider wave riding a form of Mass, but don't tell my pops that," Russi informed her as they drove down Kalakaua Avenue.

"Were you raised Catholic?"

"My dad was Catholic, my mom Protestant. So I was raised confused," he said with a laugh. "But seriously, they loved each other so much none of that mattered. My mother could have been from Timbuktu and he would have moved there to be with her. Warms the heart to see the two of them."

Isabel wondered how he'd turned out so apparently different. "What about you? Don't you want that for yourself?"

His thumb started tapping on the steering wheel. "Just haven't found the right one yet. And anyway, there's a good chance I'm not coming out of this alive, so why put someone through that, you know?"

She did know. Had lived through it, in fact. On Christmas Eve 1941, a telegram arrived in a letter postmarked December 12. Isabel was home for Christmas, just her and Pa and the dog. Pa was sipping on his fifth Budweiser in his recliner, listening to the radio for any scrap of news, while Isabel mashed potatoes in the kitchen. Neither was in any mood to celebrate, but Isabel was doing her best to put on a good front for her father's sake.

As soon as the mail came, she hurried out the back door to fetch it before her father did. A part of her had an ominous feeling this was coming, the way animals know a storm. Even though communication had gone down around the country, Walt would have found a way to let them know he was okay. Losing their mother had nearly ruined Pa, and losing Walt would finish off the job. Bile rose in her throat as she tore open the letter.

The US Army deeply regrets to inform you that your son, Walter Cooper, was killed in action. Isabel stopped reading. Fell to her knees on the hard wooden floor, trying to catch a breath. She felt the need to climb out of her own skin, if that were somehow possible. In her fist, the crumpled letter scorched. No matter how much she'd dreaded the possibility of this moment, and tried to fight it off by hoping and praying and carrying on as normal, the truth was: nothing could ever prepare you for the death of a loved one.

"Your folks must worry about you, out here," she said, shaking off the memory.

"It's killing them. Especially my dad, knowing Italy is on the other side. This is one fucked-up war, you know that?

Families on both sides of the ocean, pitted against each other. Everyone just praying for it to end," he said.

"I pray all day long."

"You and me both."

They rode in silence for a while after that.

They passed the Royal Hawaiian Hotel, pink and pretty, surrounded by manicured grounds, coconut trees and barbed wire. Every time she forgot for a few seconds there was a war going on, something like that woke her back up. From what she'd heard, the navy had taken it over at the start of the war as a place for sailors to rest and recuperate. It was strange to think that amid such beauty, there could be such heartbreak.

Farther on, they drove by the Waikiki Theater, where the marquee read Tyrone Power & Maureen O'Hara, *The Black Swan* and *The March of Time*. People milled about on the streets wearing less clothing than was legal in Indiana.

"Consider yourself lucky because I'm taking you to a secret spot. Waikiki is great and all, but there can be a *lotta* people on the waves," he said, drawing out the *o* in *lot*.

Beyond the hotels and beach clubs they came to a giant park lined with tall long-needled trees. It looked to Isabel as though they were going to drive right up Diamond Head, but he slowed as they went past a long wall-like arched structure. *The War Memorial.*

"Walt and a few of us came down here one day for a little friendly swim competition with some navy boys, and while we were here we spotted a nice break out front," he said. "Now the navy uses the natatorium for training, took it over like a lot of places here."

"Who won?" she asked.

He looked offended. "Who do you think won?"

"Something tells me you flyboys had it in the bag."

One side of his mouth went up. "Damn straight we did."

A minute on down the road, they pulled over near a tree with a trunk as wide as a house. Nothing moved. There wasn't a stitch of wind on the water and the air smelled of salt and sunshine. It felt like a moment in a postcard, surreal as it was beautiful.

"Here we are," he said, turning to her and suddenly looking serious. "Now, I need to warn you about something before we go out."

"Sharks?" she asked.

The thought had crossed her mind on more than one occasion.

He laughed. "Not sharks, but you oughta know that surfing can be addicting, and you might fall in love."

"That's a bold claim," she said.

He shrugged. "You'll see."

It took the two of them to hoist the board out and walk it down a bushy pathway to the beach. The wood was smooth as a coffee bean. To the right was a small cottage, dwarfed by trees and fronted by a long pier.

"My friend Tony's mom owns the place. He said he'd leave a board out for me," Russi said, scanning the area.

But there were no boards around, and aside from a couple young kids on the pier fishing, not a soul in sight.

"Maybe it's too early?" she said.

"Coulda been a late one for him. He plays Hawaiian music around town, and is even more in demand since this war started, if you could believe it. Hang tight, I'll have a look around."

Isabel dipped her feet in the water, expecting an early-morning chill. But the water was pleasant as it swirled around her ankles. Russi came back a few minutes later, empty-handed.

"Looks like we might have to go tandem. You game?"

"The both of us on that one board?"

He held up his hands. "I won't bite."

She'd seen photos of men riding waves, women on their shoulders, or holding them up like dolls in fantastic positions.

"No, thank you. I doubt you could lift me, anyway."

"I don't need to lift you. We both just stand up on the board. You're thinking of the surfing competitions—the newspapers love those. Way above my pay grade," he said. "And for the record, I could lift you with my left pinky."

"I weigh more than you think."

"We'll see about that."

Out beyond the reef, neat lines of white water lined up one after another.

"You don't think the waves are too big?" she asked.

"Nah. The waves on this side only get big in the summertime. Think about Walt. Would he have gone out?"

That did it. Somewhat self-consciously, she slid out of her dress and stood pale as an ivory statue under the warm Hawaiian sun. Russi bent down to grab something out of his backpack and came back up holding his camera. When he caught sight of her, his eyes moved down her body, causing a rush of heat across her skin. She could have sworn he whistled.

"Damn, that suit sure suits you. We need to get a shot of you standing with the board, ocean in the back, just like Walt. The light is perfect now," he said.

The blue-and-white floral one-piece crossed in the back and came down low in the front, but not too low. Despite feeling seminude, she liked how it fit, and how it accentuated her long legs. He set her up in front of the ocean, arranged her with the board, which probably weighed fifty pounds or more, and moved back to get the picture. For some reason, she found it hard to look at him.

"You're gonna have to try a little harder than that, Miss Cooper. Gimme some teeth," he said, kneeling in the sand.

She gave him her best smile, just so they could get on with it.

He whistled. Camera clicked. "Whoa. Okay. Beautiful."

"Can we go out now?" she said, mainly because she felt so exposed, as though he could see right through her.

"A minute ago, you were hemming and hawing. What gives?"

"Says the man who refuses to have his picture taken."

"From purely a photographer's standpoint, you've got this quality about you. The blue eyes..." he said, shaking his head and standing up. "Hard to explain."

After tucking their belongings under a hedge near a co-conut tree, Russi took off his shirt and gave her a brief dem-onstration of where to lie on the board, how to paddle, what to do when the white water hit them, how to catch a wave. His shorts came up midwaist and fit tight against his hard stomach. He swung the board around as if it weighed noth-ing, and set it on the water.

"Go on. You're in front," he said.

That meant he would be behind her—almost on top of her. For some reason the paddling part of tandem surfing had not occurred to her. "I'm happy to go in the back."

"That's not how it works. The person in control is in the back."

There was nothing to do but climb on. A second later, his hands were on her waist, sliding her forward just a hair. Strong and sure. And then he hopped on, sliding his way up so his chest was up against her rear. Her legs parted slightly to make room. Suddenly, they were gliding ahead and the inside of his arms rubbed against her thighs.

"Just paddle and I'll keep time with you," he said, as if this were the most natural thing in the world, his chin hovering over her low back, her rear literally a pillow for him.

Isabel did as instructed, trying to block out the unfavorable positioning. *Pay attention to the water*, she ordered herself. Indeed, the water was a dazzling blue, and made a soft splash each time her hands disappeared into it. They sailed along, Russi keeping good time and providing most of the muscle. In no time, they had passed through a coral-lined channel and reached a deeper blue. They paddled out beyond the surf, which had now vanished, and waited. The quiet was something Isabel could get used to. Surfing, she thought, could be the perfect companion for codebreaking.

Russi held a finger to his lips and said, "You hear that?"

She listened. Soon, a distant low rumble filled the air.

"Pursuits coming in from patrol on the east side," he said.

A moment later, the calm was shattered by a line of warplanes rounding Diamond Head, flying low over the water. When they approached, nearly overhead, Russi stood up on the board and started waving madly. One of the planes dipped a wing. Then the board wobbled and he dove off into the water, nearly knocking her off in the process.

The planes passed by directly overhead, so close she could feel the vibration in her teeth. She swallowed hard. Something about seeing those planes and their painted-on stars, all in formation, caused a welling-up of emotion.

"Those are the new guys. Sunday morning patrols always go to them," he said.

"Seems more like a reward than a punishment, being up there on a day like this," she said, coming back to the moment.

"Good point," he said, swimming up to the board and draping his arms over it. "You know what really gets me? The fact that, on that Sunday morning, we were still on Number

1 Alert. Only the navy had a few planes on patrol that day, out looking for subs. We had zilch. In my book there shoulda been a sky full of planes out on patrol. We shoulda been at Number 3 Alert."

"What's your take on it?"

"The brass was worried about alarming the civilian population. Of all the messed-up things. They knew the Japanese were up to something, but underestimated them by a long shot," he said.

The *what-ifs* haunted her, too, especially in the early-morning hours, in that quiet time when her darkest thoughts took on a life of their own. "I've lost months of sleep imagining how things could have turned out differently."

"I have this dream where I'm flying along in the clouds, almost blind. Then they part and there's a whole line of carriers as far as the eye can see. It's just me up there, and I dive down and shoot and shoot but nothing happens. My guns are full of blanks," he said.

"I expect that's normal."

He bit his lip. "I want that shot. I want to take down something big."

"A carrier would be nice."

Everyone knew the carriers were the top prize.

"And I'm more than happy to sacrifice myself. If those Japanese pilots can do it, so can I," he said.

"I'm not sure your folks would feel the same way. But I know how you feel. Some of the girls back at Main Navy thought I was crazy to want to come out here. But being out here meant being closer—" She stopped, realizing that for the first time ever, she had almost alluded to being other than a secretary.

He tilted his head up at her. "Go on."

"Closer to the front lines...the action... Walt."

"One of these days, you'll tell me what you're really doing down there. Why not now?"

"Russi, enough with that."

"Just wait and see, I have my ways," he said with a dangerous smile.

Before she could respond, he dove under and disappeared. A minute lapsed. And then another. When at least two had passed, and he still hadn't surfaced, she spun around, scanning the water. There was no sign of him. Concern coursed through her. Had he somehow gotten wedged in between two coral heads? Carried off by a shark? Then, without warning, Russi erupted out of the water with a gasp and set a large brown squishy thing on the board in front of her.

She recoiled. "What is this thing?"

"Lunch."

She tried to discern if he was serious, but his expression was unreadable. "Tell me you're kidding. Please?"

"When Walt and I came out here with old man Makua, one of the beach boys in Waikiki, he brought one in after our session and cut it up, poured a little salt on and laid it out on his surfboard for us all neat like in a restaurant, I kid you not. Not wanting to be rude, Walt took a bite. I watched his eyes water and he gagged a few times before swallowing."

Isabel almost gagged just thinking about it.

Russi went on, "I could hardly believe my eyes when he reached for a second piece. 'This is great, thanks, mate,' he said with that goofy smile of his. That right there earned us respect from the old man. He said Walt was the first *haole* he knew who had ever gone for a second one."

Isabel had recently learned that *haole* was what Caucasians were called here in Hawai'i.

"What about you?" she asked.

"I forced one down. Nearly died in the process. I'm not as

brave as Walt," he said, looking out to sea. "Hey, here comes a wave!" He jumped on behind her and swung the board around so they were facing the shore. "Paddle hard. I'll tell you when to stand up."

It all happened so fast. The feeling of him half on top of her paddling like mad, the back of the board lifting up and shooting down the face of the wave. Water sprayed up in her face.

"Slide back a little," he yelled.

She did as instructed, and the spray died down.

"Okay, stand up!"

Now that they were moving, the board was no longer wobbly and she kneeled and then stood with both her arms out. They raced along the face of the water. Isabel imagined she was a low-flying seagull. Then the board wavered for a moment and Russi was up. He grabbed her waist from behind and pressed his whole body close against hers.

"Hang on," he said, mouth an inch from her ear.

There was nothing to hang on to but air, so she leaned into him. Right away, the board turned and they shot along sideways, away from the breaking white water. They passed over coral formations and patches of sand and she felt like a kid again, wild and free. A small squeal escaped from her mouth. Russi held her firmly. A few seconds later, the nose of the board went under and Isabel flew headfirst into the water. After an underwater drag and tumble, she came up slightly disoriented with all body parts intact. Russi was nearby, but the board was nowhere to be seen.

"You all right?" he asked.

"I think so?"

"Atta girl," he said, swimming over to her with an ear-to-ear smile.

"What's so funny?" she asked.

"You seem so serious a lot of the time. It was nice to hear

you let loose a little. But was that an *I'm having fun* scream or a *get me outta here* scream?"

People had always accused her of being serious. Her father even went as far as saying she should *lighten up, men want to see a lady smile once in a while.* But early on, she realized that you can't change who you are, no matter how badly others may want you to.

"A little of both, I think. And for the record, I'm not always serious."

Russi's eyes suddenly widened. "Uh-oh, here comes another one. Just before it hits, take a big breath and dive down with me," he said, grabbing hold of her hand.

Isabel turned to see a wave double the size as the one they'd caught coming their way. This was certainly no lake and she was wondering if coming out here had been wise. Russi might know what he was doing, but she sure didn't. They dove down as swirls of moving water rushed along her back. Russi's hand pulled her down, and then up once the wave had passed. They broke the surface together, Isabel on the verge of panic.

"You okay?" he asked again, hand still holding tight to hers.

She nodded, trying to maintain her cool. Their eyes met and for a few seconds neither spoke, neither looked away. A charge passed between them, sending tingles up and down her spine, along her skin and out through her toes. This was not part of the plan. She closed her eyes, pulled her hand away.

Walt's best friend.

Off-limits.

Trouble.

Heartache.

"Fine. Just a bit shaken up. I wasn't expecting that," she said, risking another look.

He was still staring at her. "Me neither. Not one bit." He

shook his head slightly, the way you shake off a scare, then glanced in toward the reef. "Listen, I need to go get the board. Do you want to wait here or come with me?"

"Go with you."

They swam in, fortunately not too far, since the board got stopped up by a coral head. She stayed close on his heels. When they climbed back on, she was acutely aware of his chest rubbing against her and his hot breath on her skin, warmer than the rays of the sun. They paddled back out, caught a few more waves, wiping out on every single one and crashing into the water with limbs tangled.

"The wipeouts are part of the fun," he said, coming up and spitting water in her face.

She laughed, splashed him right back. As long as they kept moving, Isabel was fine. The intimate feeling from earlier began to fade. There was nothing unusual about what they were doing. Surf lessons happened all the time in these parts. And Russi was a patient teacher. He told her where to stand, when to bend her knees, exactly when to start paddling for the wave.

Finally, he said, "I think you're ready."

"Ready for what?"

"To catch one on your own." He slid off and swam a few feet away, then held his hands up, framing her. "Wow. This is the money shot, right here. You, Diamond Head. Eyes blue as the sea."

Isabel was lying on the board, hands on her chin. Something about being in the ocean covered in salt water made her feel appealing in a clean-scrubbed way. Nature's beauty school. "You're just drunk on ocean," she said.

"The best kind of drunk to be. Look, here comes your wave," he said, nodding behind her.

The wave looked big, but Isabel turned and started paddling, anyway. Without Russi, the board moved at half the speed.

"Harder!" he yelled.

She paddled harder, then felt the wave lift her up, up and up.

"Move back!"

Suddenly, she found herself at the top of a steep face, staring down a blue wall. She slid back on the board but it was too late, even she could tell. The board skipped along the surface, gaining speed, then plowed into the water. Isabel was catapulted off as the board shot back up into the air somewhere nearby. Instinctively, she covered her head and ducked underwater. When she came up, Russi was by her side, looking like a concerned mother.

"Can I try that again?" she said.

He broke into a huge smile. "You betcha."

It took three more tries, but she finally rode a wave on her own for fifty yards or so. When the swell petered out, Russi was hooting and hollering from a coral head nearby. And for the first time in a long time, she had completely forgotten about the war and why she was here.

16

THE MARU CODE

O'ahu, 1943

That evening, Isabel and Gloria compared stories. There was something so endearing about the way that Gloria wanted to know every detail about Isabel's life, no matter how large or small. It was imperative to know who her first kiss had been, what her favorite foods were and whether she preferred Humphrey Bogart or James Stewart. *Peter Weldon. Spaghetti and meatballs. Bogart all the way.* These were details she rarely gave much thought to, but she appreciated the feeling of normalcy they brought. Perhaps Russi was right. She was too serious.

They were in the midst of some kind of heat wave, in the middle of winter, mind you, and Gloria pulled an old sheet out of the closet and set it up in the backyard. Isabel's entire body had been toasted pink from the sun, which might have been part of the problem. Sweat pooled at every crease of her limbs. They watched the sunset, wearing Hawaiian pareos and holding cold Primo beers in their hands.

"So, I have an announcement to make," Gloria said.

Isabel had sensed a simmering excitement in her friend all afternoon. "And?"

"Dickie and I are an item."

Not news.

"That was obvious from the start."

"No, I mean, he asked me to be his girl, which means we are exclusively seeing each other," she said, beaming. "After tennis we took a drive up Tantalus and he pulled over at the lookout and told me he's never fallen for someone so quick and that I'm all he thinks about. He even talked about after the war, which means he's thinking long-term. Oh, Izzy, I feel so lucky!"

"That's wonderful, Glory. I'm not surprised. But don't you forget that he's the lucky one," Isabel said.

"You think so?"

"I know so."

Isabel wished she could feel more joy for her friend, but truth be told, she didn't think he deserved Gloria. It was more a feeling than anything, and to be fair, she hardly knew the guy. Maybe that would change if they became better acquainted.

"I haven't had a chance to tell you, but the weirdest thing happened the other night when I stayed over at his place. It was middle of the night and I was woken by this godawful croaking outside. I think it was the cane toads, the kinds with the warts on their backs? Anyway, then next to me Dickie started mumbling. At first I thought he was talking to me, but his eyes were closed. And then he started carrying on a conversation in what sounded a lot like German, all guttural and lively, like he was extremely animated."

"Are you sure it wasn't just gibberish?"

"That's what he said when I asked him in the morning. He said his father was German but he never learned the language. Is it possible he somehow picked it up as a baby without knowing it?" Gloria said.

Isabel had never heard of that, but nothing was impossible. She knew that brains and language had interesting circuits. "I'm not sure. But why would he lie?"

Gloria shrugged. "He wouldn't. Say, one of his friends has a house at some beach on the other side of the island with a long name. He's invited me out there next weekend if he can get away. Do you want to come?" Gloria said, crunching into her pickle.

"Who else is going?"

"Just us, but you could invite Russi. I bet he'd jump at the chance."

"Sounds fun, but I don't want him to get the wrong idea," Isabel said.

A family of sparrows landed on the grass and started hopping around them, waiting for crumbs. She tossed them part of a cracker.

"You two spent *all* day together, a good portion of it with him on top of you while you were both scantily clothed. You don't think that gives him an idea?" Gloria said.

"I told you. We're retracing Walt's steps, and now I have another photo of me standing in the exact spot he was, holding the same board. I can't explain why it matters to me, but it does."

Gloria's expression softened. "That may be true, honey, but sometimes nature takes over and we no longer have a say in the matter. Can you look me in the eye and tell me there is no spark between the two of you?"

Immediately, Isabel remembered being half-submerged with her hand in his, and how when they came up, his eyes were searching hers for Lord knew what. And how by the end of the day, every little touch and smile had added a layer of healing over the crack in her heart. So much so that she hadn't wanted to say goodbye.

Gloria threw a peanut at her. "See, you can't even answer me. Where were you just now?"

"Remembering."

"With stars in your eyes."

"Oh, please. I just don't see any point in trying to analyze it. Whatever happened today was thoroughly enjoyable. The perfect antidote for work and the war, and I appreciate that," Isabel said.

"I know he's gotten a bad rap, but for what it's worth, I really like him."

"So do I."

The Dungeon operated seven days a week and twenty-four hours a day. On Friday and Saturday nights, Isabel was assigned her first night shifts. She had napped during the day in preparation. Walking from her house to the admin building, the mild temperature still surprised her. The lemony sweet scent of plumeria filled the night, and a cricket chirped someplace close. She felt a strange mix of melancholy and hope.

For some reason, going down when it was already dark made her less anxious. Denny was still at his desk. She'd learned early on from the degree of grease in his hair that he stayed at work for days on end. He was doing what needed to be done, pure and simple. War didn't care a damn about sleep.

She set her purse down quietly. "Good evening, sir."

He was leaning back in his chair, reading a paper, and his eyes peered over the top. "We just received two messages marked urgent. Take the second one."

The place felt deserted without the regular crew milling about, but the air conditioner still blew at full force. Settling in with her blanket on her lap, she looked at the rows of code on the paper. Something looked off.

"Why are there only four numbers per group?" she asked.

"This is the Maru code, for merchant tankers and freighters and transports. The Brits figured it out, and now we get our subs on their convoys when we can, like money in the bank. That man you see every morning at 0900? That's Commander Vogt. He meets with Huckleberry, our ship-plotting wizard, and they review the latest Ultra information."

The most closely guarded intelligence in the military.

"Am I cleared for Ultra?" she asked, since in Washington not everyone was.

"You're in here, aren't you?"

A thrill ran up her spine.

"Yes, sir."

He tossed her a booklet. "This might help."

It was filled with substitution tables needed to decipher the code. She scanned the booklet cover to cover. This time, she found she was able to focus, and before long, she started humming. Numbers moved around in her mind, shifting and transposing and rearranging themselves, one on top of another. That sense of calm had returned, with beauty in order and rightness.

A loud tapping snapped her back to the room. "Would you mind? This isn't a church," Denny said, flicking his pencil on the desk.

"Sorry, sir," she said apologetically.

He pushed his glasses back up his nose and frowned, then went back to his paper. Several more times, Isabel fell into her reverie, started humming. Each time, Denny tapped his pencil and drew her out of it.

Frustrated, she said, "Do you mind if I walk around?"

He didn't look up but nodded.

There was only one man at each station, and no one near the plotting table. Huckleberry was mostly a one-man show, aside from his assistant, so she slid past his plotting table and walked back and forth down a corridor that went to a back room no one was using. She held the paper close to her face in the dim light, using a piece of cardboard as a backer, and hummed to her heart's content. The tune was never anything in particular, and she often wondered if it coincided somehow with the numbers. A hidden melody of sorts.

Despite her unfamiliarity with the Maru code, having four numbers instead of five made the task easier. Her heels clicked on the cold concrete. Though only Denny seemed to be smoking, the air still smelled thickly of smoke. In fact, in the shower each night after work, she'd had to wash her hair twice to get the stench out.

Half an hour later, she had a thought, and hurried back to her desk. She flipped through the pages and saw what she was looking for. The code group for *submarine* caught her eye. There were certain words you memorized first, and *submarine* was one of them.

She sat up straight. "Excuse me, sir, but I think I may have found something," she said.

Denny held a sandwich in one hand and was midbite. He stopped chewing and swallowed. "What is it?"

"Could it be possible a transport ship mistook their own submarine for one of ours?" she asked, pulse speeding up.

"Possible, yes. Likely, no." Still, he stood up and came around to her desk, smelling of mustard. "Why?"

"Because after *submarine sighted*, the line below says, *torpedo attack, submarine down*."

His face was unreadable. "What else does it say?"

She hadn't deciphered all of it yet. "The message originated from the Solomons. I don't know what this word is, but isn't this one *waters*?"

Japanese codes were in kana, a form of syllabic writing that used the Latin alphabet, which added another layer to learn. But for Isabel, new language unfolded easily, like an unspooling thread.

Denny rushed over to the plotting table, meanwhile yelling to Bird, the linguist, to get over here. "What does this mean?" he asked, pointing to the word in question.

"Shallow."

"And this?"

"Corvette," Bird said, his finger passing over the deciphered code groups. "It looks like the submarine was hit by two New Zealand corvettes, who then turned their guns on the transport."

Denny went white. "Hence the single *I am sinking*. A Japanese sub down in shallow waters. Fucking A, we need to get on this ASAP."

At about the same time, the secure line near Huckleberry's desk rang loud into the room. Denny ran over and picked it up. Isabel could only make out a few words—*codebooks, maps, anything, divers*—but his arms were flailing around like a puppet as he spoke. She sat at her desk quietly, even though her insides were all revved up. No need to get overly excited until they were sure about things. She had to work to keep her cool, though.

He came back, red-faced and wheezing. "That was ComSubPac—it's confirmed. Japanese sub was chased in near Kamimbo Bay and ran aground on the reef. Reports are that her bow is above water. Some survivors, but dear God, if we can get ahold of any of their books, it would change everything."

Bird was more subdued. "The Japanese won't let that happen. They'll die first."

"If there's one thing we can count on, it's human error. Let's just hope it's in our favor this time," Denny said to Bird, not even glancing her way.

Isabel, it seemed, had faded into the background, but she was used to that.

17

THE INCIDENT

O'ahu, 1943

After such a mind-bending week, Isabel had never felt more ready for a break. Her shoulders ached from hunching over and she felt about a hundred years old, with scratchy eyes and throat from all the smoke. It couldn't be healthy. A room full of men had an entirely different feel than a room full of women. No one brought flowers or gifts or cake, and there was a certain exclusivity in the air. Nothing but the cream of the crop here. The top minds in the country, and they knew it.

Not only that, but the level of urgency to the messages felt double that of Washington. Maybe it was the proximity to the enemy.

Russi had called the night before, asking if Isabel was up for another adventure. "You have no idea how ready I am. What should I bring?" she asked.

"A swimsuit and an open mind."

Just hearing his voice soothed her. When he picked her up midmorning, he still refused to say where they were headed. This time, they took the same route as to the waterfall, but at the bottom of the cliff, he turned left and they drove through several small towns with quaint storefronts and mostly empty streets. Farther along, a few scruffy horses were tied up to a tree next to a woman selling dry *aku* and shells. Russi pulled over.

"What are you stopping for?"

"Lunch," he said.

"What's *aku*?"

"Fish."

"I hate to disappoint you, but I'm not a big fan of fish."

He smiled. "Didn't I say to bring an open mind?"

"Fine. You get fish and I'll look at the shells."

On the table, there was a bag of fish on one side, and a sprinkling of rings with cowrie shells bordered by dotted silver on the other. They were beautiful. Two in particular caught her eye. While all the other shells were a glossy brown, these had worn down their outer coat and were a pale purple.

"Did you make these?" Isabel asked.

The woman held up both hands, revealing silver rings on all ten of her long fingers. "My husband fishes and finds the shells. I weld."

Isabel had never met a woman welder, and she admired her craftiness. "I'll take two, this one and that one," she said.

Not one for spontaneous purchases, she was struck by the fine work and felt an overwhelming need to have one. And she knew that the minute Gloria saw hers, she'd want one for herself. A perfect Hawai'i memento. She slipped one in her purse and one on her finger. Back in the car, she held out her hand to show the ring off to Russi.

As they drove off, he said, "I always stop for this kind of stuff. Seems like you end up finding what you least expect, and maybe something you never thought you needed until it randomly appeared in your life."

He was a good driver and an even better tour guide. He also seemed comfortable rattling off Hawaiian names, which she found impressive. *Kailua, Kāneʻohe, Kahaluʻu.* The language was simple and beautiful, and one she wanted to learn someday. In another life.

"I think this is the drive that made Walt fall in love. Me, too," he said.

It was easy to see why. Green cliffs on one side, turquoise ocean on the other. No road she'd ever been on had come close to the stark beauty. They passed a sand-swept airfield, tin roof shacks on the beach and deep and lonesome valleys all under a cloudless sky. Isabel could have kept driving forever, but eventually they drove down a rutted unpaved road and stopped in a grove of ironwood trees on the beach.

"Here we are. Goat Island," he said.

Out front was a low-lying island a couple hundred yards offshore. "How will we get there?" she asked.

"Walk and swim. I brought an extra pair of tabis for your feet. The fishermen all wear them here." He must have sensed her hesitancy, because he jumped out and opened the trunk, returning holding two black inner tubes. "Just in case."

As they made their way to the water, she asked, "How on earth did you two manage to find this place? It feels like the end of the world."

"Believe it or not there's an army base and an airfield not far from here, up at Kahuku Point. They were working on the field before the war broke out, and we went out to have a look. Along the way, we saw this island and the rest is history. Came back the first chance we got," he said.

They tied the backpack, a canister of food and a canteen

to one of the tubes. "The tide is rock bottom, so we oughta be able to walk most of the way," he said.

There was no swell to speak of, thank goodness. Isabel was wearing a swimsuit and the black tabis, which were a combination of socks, shoes and slippers. Gloria would have laughed at how ridiculous she looked, but in this case she would take function over beauty any day. She'd seen the spiny sea urchin—*wana*, in Hawaiian—and they looked dangerous.

They set off from the point into a calm and silky ocean, not a stitch of wind. Russi pushed the tube with their stuff and Isabel held on to the empty one. He navigated them through sandy channels where he could, the water coming to her waist.

"Just be careful not to step in any holes if you can help it. Eels," he said, almost as an afterthought.

"Eels bite, don't they?"

"If you bother them they do."

"Can't we just swim, then?"

"There may be a current when we get farther out. Just follow me and you'll be fine."

From then on, she paid close attention to staying in his footsteps, forget the scenery. As with each of their adventures, she felt a tingle of anticipation that bordered on fear of the unknown. It reminded her of being a teenager again, when everything was fresh and new and you were exploring the unexplored, be it discovering the laws of gravity or the sweet softness of a first kiss.

Halfway to the island, the water came up to her armpits, and Russi had been right—there was a current. But they pushed on through. Their goal was a crescent-shaped white sand beach lined with small clumps of trees.

After nearly half an hour, without ever having to swim, they finally washed into shore on small breakers, set their gear in the shade and stretched out to thaw on the warm sand. Her fingertips looked like pale pink raisins and she had a small chill going, despite the warm water and sunshine.

"I'm glad you're game for all this. A lot of girls wouldn't be caught dead walking out here with me," he said, rolling onto his side and facing her.

They were several feet apart, but now it felt like inches. The left side of her face started heating up, and not from the sun. She kept her gaze on the thin layer of hazy clouds out to sea.

"Somehow I find that hard to believe," she said.

He motioned over his chest. "Cross my heart."

"Russi, you are aware that you have a reputation, aren't you? Among women here. And even after breaking their hearts, a good number of them would follow you to the moon if they could."

"I never mislead any of them, you know that?"

"I haven't paid much attention to the talk. Since I'm not trying to date you, it doesn't matter. Not my business," she said in all honesty.

He laughed. "I like your style. No BS."

"Why would I need to BS?"

"No reason. But some girls do."

Isabel turned to look at him. "I promise you that the only reason I'm here is because of your friendship with Walt. And now, your friendship with me. Nothing more. You know that, don't you?"

There. She said it out loud. It was the truth.

Wasn't it?

"Sure as eggs is eggs," he said, sounding not so sure at all.

Warmth from the afternoon sun spread across her entire body—thighs, abdomen, cheeks, forehead. Isabel let herself sink deeper into the sand and soaked it in from above and below. The gentle wash of the water lulled her, and within minutes she was half dreaming of someone rubbing warm coconut oil across her skin, working her sore muscles with big, strong hands.

Something warm fell softly on her stomach, waking her up instantly. She felt it. A piece of coral. Russi was looking at her upside down. "You seem to know so much about my love life. What about you? You got a man waiting in the wings back at home?" he said.

"No one."

"Now, I find *that* hard to believe."

There was no point in telling him about the few boyfriends she'd had, and explaining that she had quite probably never been in love. Jimmy Polanski in high school with his giant ears and narrow mind, or Yates Buttonfield, college chess champion and the only man in the school better in math than she was.

"I haven't dated anyone since the war broke out. Between losing Walt and committing to the war effort, I've been more than occupied."

"What if you met someone you took a fancy to?" he asked.

"I guess I'll cross that bridge when I get there," she said, feeling more than a little disarmed by his intimate questioning.

Russi chewed on that for a few moments, then stood and looked down on her, casting a shadow across her face. "Don't move," he said.

She froze. "What is it?"

"Nothing, just stay where you are."

A minute later, he returned with his camera. "No offense to Walt, but you are much easier to photograph. And right now, with you in the sand looking so natural and gorgeous— makes it hard to resist using up the entire roll of film."

His words knocked the wind right out of her. *Gorgeous?*

She lay there as instructed, mind flitting about like the tiny green birds in the trees, as Russi knelt about ten feet away in the sand. He lowered the camera down and set it on a towel. *Click.* He moved a few feet up the beach. *Click.*

"Perfect," he said, sitting back down again on the towel.

"How did you get into photography?" she asked, squinting up into the sun at his outline.

"I worked my way through school at the local paper as a copy boy. One of the fellas there taught me the ropes and now I can't get it out of my system."

"I've always wanted to learn."

"In my mind, a picture tells a hell of a lot more than a thousand words. Words can't capture an expression or a mood or a feeling. When all this is over, maybe I can teach you," he said.

"Is that what you want to do when the war is over?"

He picked up a twig and started drawing in the sand with it. "I told you. There's a good chance I won't be around after the war."

Isabel sat up, irritated. "That's just plain horseshit. If you keep talking like that, you won't be. Why not hope for the best?"

He broke the stick. "Because I don't care what happens to me."

"Now you're talking crazy," she said.

He shrugged. "I have a pact with God. It's just how it is."

The thought of losing Russi suddenly felt suffocating.

"Would it change your mind if I said I don't want to lose you? I've already lost one brother," she said.

"This is the exact thing I want to avoid, hurting anyone I leave behind."

"Matteo. Look at me."

She wasn't sure why she switched to his first name. Maybe it would have more impact. Or maybe calling him Russi made her feel like a guy. Either way, he stared out to sea and ignored her.

"Please?" she asked.

Still, he wouldn't meet her gaze.

"Being human involves allowing yourself to get close to others. Otherwise, what's the point?" she said.

"Only my mama calls me Matteo," he said.

"Oh, for heaven's sake. You have a thick skull, don't you?"

"I guess you can call me Matteo, too. Sounds kinda nice coming off your tongue."

"That's not what I'm talking about, but I think I will."

The deep ochre flecks in his eyes glistened. He shook his head side to side, ever so slightly, then grabbed her hand, pulled her up and said, "I didn't bring you out here to argue. Can we pretend for the rest of the day that there's no war? Would you do that for me?"

Here she was, dishing out advice as though she was some expert, when he was the one putting his life on the line. "Of course," she said, feeling bad for pushing him.

Without another word, he took off toward the water at high speed. Isabel was left standing to make sense of what had just transpired between them. In her palm, the coral he'd placed on her stomach still felt warm. She opened her fist. A perfect, white heart.

"The ocean will make a kid out of anyone," Matteo said after riding a wave in on his stomach, arms by his side, reminding her of a seal.

He explained the mechanics of it, and Isabel soon discovered that bodysurfing wasn't as easy as it looked. Only the larger ones were easy to get onto, but those lifted her up and slammed her into the sand. On more than one occasion, she came up white from head to toe. Sand on every surface and in every crack and crevice, embedded in her scalp and coming out of her nose. The sand here was fine as powder, unlike the coarse Waikiki sand.

Matteo warned her, "It'll be weeks before all the sand comes out. That happened to us last time. Just think of it as a souvenir from the island."

Waterlogged and surfed out, they eventually ended up on the beach again. Matteo moved the towel up under a tree and produced an interesting assortment of snacks from his canister. Dried *aku*, a can of sardines, dill pickles, Saloon pilot crackers, boiled peanuts and rice balls covered in black seaweed. Famished, Isabel was looking at having crackers and pickles for lunch.

"Sorry, it never crossed my mind you might not eat fish. Guess I should have asked," he said, taking a rice ball and layering it with sardines and aku. When he took a bite, he closed his eyes and groaned. "Damn. This right here is God's food."

He made another and held it out to her.

Isabel didn't take it. "You eat it. I'm fine with crackers."

"Crackers? You can't survive on crackers and expect to have any juice left for the rest of the day."

"Maybe a pickle, then. And some peanuts."

"Have it your way, but you're missing out."

After eating, lounging and discussing the finer points of island life, Matteo led her on a narrow trail out to the far point. As Isabel walked behind him, it was impossible not to notice the smooth skin of his broad back, and how he moved easily across the rocks.

"We named this Whale Point because when we came, there was a whole school of whales spouting and breaching and having some kind of whale party out there. You ever seen a whale?"

"We don't have whales in Indiana," she said.

Matteo turned and she nearly bumped into him. "Do I detect some sass, Miss Cooper?"

She gave him a small salute. "No, sir."

They were standing two feet apart, and his eyes ran across her shoulders, down her torso, then her legs, and back up, hovering. This time, he made no move to hide the fact that he had just taken a tour of her body with his eyes. Isabel felt her cheeks flush. A swoosh in her lower abdomen. The breeze suddenly picked up, whipping her hair across her face. Whatever it was between them had just intensified tenfold. She willed the sensation away.

Nothing good can come of this.

Matteo must have felt it, too, because he turned and picked up the pace. Isabel found herself almost running to keep up with him. They passed through low grass and leafy shrubs, over patches of rough and sharp coral, eroded from years of weather and waves, and alongside tide pools full of seaweed and sand. When they reached the point, they stood side by side and watched the ocean, which had turned bumpy in the onshore wind. His shoulder was not touching hers, but she still felt it.

"Every now and then, I fly over a whale. Right now they have babies and there's something magic about seeing a mama and baby whale cruising along in the blue, spouting in unison. I just need to figure out how to get a photo," he said.

"That would be something."

"I wish you could see one. You'd be smitten."

Out where the water went from light blue to dark blue, there was a big, table-shaped rock. White water crashed and boiled around it. She turned to Matteo, who was watching it intently.

"Let's head back," he said.

Isabel wanted to keep going. "I haven't seen a whale yet. And what about my island tour?"

"It's getting late, we should go."

On the way back to the beach, many of the same rocks they'd crossed over were now wet. The waves seemed to have picked up and sprayed them as they passed along the rocky edge. Fine mist cool and salty against her skin. Matteo moved swiftly.

"Is everything okay?" she asked.

"Good. Fine. Nothing to worry about," he said stiffly.

When they rounded the bend to the beach, she saw why he was uneasy. The whole bay had turned white and frothy. Water tumbled this way and that. The roar deafened.

"What the—" she said.

He cut her off. "A winter swell. It can pick up fast."

"I'll say."

Along with the surf, a band of slate gray clouds had slid in behind them, blotting out the late-afternoon sun. Matteo began gathering their things and stuffing them into the canister. Isabel helped him lash it to the tube, and then tied both tubes together, all the while wondering how they were going to get through the surf. They ran down the beach to the point closest to O'ahu.

Matteo stopped her just as they were about to jump in. "I need you to kick like hell, and whatever you do, do not let go of this tube."

"Could we just stay here until it calms? It would certainly beat drowning," she said.

He looked her in the eye. "I have training tomorrow at 0600. I can't miss it."

"You might have to."

He squeezed her hand. "Don't worry, I've got you."

There was something in his voice, his look, that made her

trust him. She realized then that there was a distinct possibility that she would follow him anywhere, just like other girls whose hearts he'd broken. They plunged in, diving under mountainous waves that pulled her swimsuit around her knees. The force was furious and angry, dragging her down into darkness. She kicked and kicked, and pretty soon they were through the shore break, floating in a churned-up sea. Waves broke from all directions. Clinging to the tube with everything she had, she spit up water.

"This is where we need to push," he yelled.

Isabel pushed with everything she had. A few minutes later, they fell into a current that swept them sideways rather than toward the shore. Every so often a wave broke on their heads. Not used to this kind of exertion, Isabel began to tire. Her shoulders burned. The land seemed so far away and only showed itself in glimpses—a treetop, a patch of beach.

"I'm tired," she said, trembling and coughing.

"Hang on."

Whenever things get unbearable, just let go. Suddenly, Walt was talking to her in that reassuring voice of his. *Stop trying to fight it, instead relax.* Fear opened its grip, and in its place came grief as deep as the sea that swallowed him. Walt was out here somewhere, in the vast blue Pacific. He was part of the ocean now.

"Walt!" she cried.

"Izzy, stay with me!"

Then a wave ripped her hands from the tube. Her head went under and she reached up and felt around for the slippery rubber. Only water. How easy it would be to listen to her brother, and just let go. Is that what he had done? Or had he been dead before he hit the water? A searching hand found her arm, and yanked her back up to the surface. Or was it pulling her down, into the depths?

"Walt?"

"It's Matteo, hang on!"

He tucked her under one arm and began frog swimming with all his might. Once she had caught her breath, Isabel managed to kick some, too, but her limbs felt sluggish, uncooperative. Eventually, by some miracle, they washed in over a coral reef into a fishpond of some kind. The land looked unfamiliar. Matteo helped her up onto the beach, where they both collapsed. Isabel kissed the sand and then slowly dragged herself to sitting. She looked around. The sun had gone behind the mountains, leaving them in the shadow of ironwood trees. A chill set in, turning her entire body into a trembling mess—whether from cold or a close brush with death, she couldn't be sure. Teeth chattered, arms shook, stomach clenched uncontrollably.

"I don't know what's wrong with me," she said.

"It's a response to fear. Happens to the best of us."

Matteo opened the canister, which had stayed lashed, pulled out the towel and set it over her shoulders. He then moved in behind her, wrapping his whole body around hers and hugging tight. Warmth poured out of his chest and melted into her back, like honey under the noonday sun. She could hear him breathing hard in her ear. Feel the thud of his heart.

"I should have never taken you out there," he finally said, the stubble on his jaw chafing on her shoulder. "I'm an idiot."

"How were you to know?"

"I've been around enough to know the surf can pick up unexpectedly."

"Don't worry about it. We're sitting here alive on the beach, aren't we?" she said.

With one hand, he smoothed down her hair and slid it behind her ear. It was matted in sand, as was everything else. In any other circumstances, sitting in his arms like this would have felt taboo, but now it just felt natural.

Perfect.

They sat in silence for a while, soaking in the safety and comfort of dry land, and the closeness of another human who you'd just nearly died with. Slowly, her trembling stopped and life came back to her fingers and her toes. Still, Matteo made no move to separate. Nor did she. She found that she couldn't. Having his arms wrapped around her felt better than a blanket and a hot cup of cocoa. Better than a hot shower. Better than anything, really.

"You think you can make it to the car?" he finally asked.

"Sure."

"Honestly, I could sit here all night, but that wouldn't be a good idea, so we need to get moving," he said, scooting back.

I could, too.

It dawned on her that she was in up to her teeth. Matteo was trouble. The kind that attaches itself to your heart and follows you to the ends of the earth kind of trouble. It wasn't as though she hadn't been warned. But at that moment, he also seemed inevitable. So much for carefully laid plans.

18

THE GAME

Hawaiʻi Island, July 1965

The storm that roughed up their fishing trip blew away almost as quickly as it had come, and by late afternoon the water was smooth but with swell, and you could see strips of blue showing between the clouds. Lu sat on her lānai and watched guests begin trickling down to the beach like small ants. From up here, you could see the kaunaʻoa, an orangey twining vine, sprawling around at the edge of the beach.

A knock came on her door, starting off soft and ramping up to pounding. "Open up, Luana babe, I need you." When Lu opened the door, Joni stepped inside, looking fresh as sunshine—a bottle of champagne in one hand and a cigarette in the other. "Time to get groovy!"

"Aren't you singing tonight?" Lu asked, though she knew the answer.

"Yeah. So what?"

"Don't you want a clear head?" *After last night's fiasco,* she wanted to add.

Joni set the bottle down and started unwrapping the top with shaky hands. "I don't even know what that is anymore.

Besides, I threw up everything I ate and drank earlier, so I have a clean slate. Humor me, will you?" She went outside to pop the cork, then poured them both a glass. "Here's wishing for a world without men in it."

Lu almost laughed, but the look on Joni's face made her pause. "Did something happen?"

"No...maybe... I can't talk about it," she said, flopping down in the chair and putting her feet up on the desk.

"Is your manager being weird?" Lu asked.

"Yes, he's a pig, but it's not that." Joni took a long drag on her cig, and blew a perfect smoke ring. She'd obviously had practice.

"You can talk to me as a friend. I swear I won't breathe a word of whatever you want to tell me."

Joni smiled wistfully. "I envy you, you know that?"

"Says the woman who has everything."

"Not everything. Your life seems so real. Mine feels manufactured. I travel around and bare my soul to everyone and then always go back to an empty hotel room, an empty home. Any guy I meet along the way is not interested in me, Joni. They're interested in all the trimmings that go along with me. At least you have Dylan. People always say that the best relationships are those that start out as a friendship."

"Dylan is leaving and who knows when or if I'll see him again."

Joni sighed. "You haven't called him yet?"

"Not yet."

"Promise me you will. Soon."

"Promise."

Lu had to ask. "Is there any man in your life? Someone you want to be with?"

Joni filled their glasses again. "There is someone, but I'm sworn to secrecy. At first I wasn't into him—he's not my type—but he was persistent and good in bed and got me hooked and now I'm a goner, babe. I think I might love him."

"What's wrong with that?"

Joni stood and walked to the railing, holding out her arms like fine-boned wings. "Everything," was all she said.

Tonight's dinner was more formal, and Lu wore a gold halter dress that had cost nearly a month's salary. It was her one ritzy outfit, but in this business you had to be prepared to blend in anywhere. She hadn't worn it since the night Dylan asked her to accompany him to the War Memorial for a shoot. He had grown quiet when he saw her, and she saw something in his eyes she'd never seen before—desire. Sure, there had been jokes and innuendos, but neither had ever crossed that line of making things uncomfortable. Neither wanted to ruin the rock-solid friendship they'd cultivated.

On the promenade, she found the Rockefellers and guests decked out in linen, silk and chiffon. Men were snappy, if sweating, and from the looks of it, the wives had been to the salon. Senator Fuchs's wife had a beehive big as a coconut. To their credit, none looked worse for wear after a stormy day at sea. These were hardy people, used to pushing the limit. They didn't get to where they were by being weak. The only person missing was Joni.

The smell of kerosene and kiawe floated up from the beach, and Lu went to the edge and looked down. From this vantage, she could make out the wingtips of a big manta, circling around in the water, swallowing plankton. What a view. Not just the mantas, but the beach, the blue expanse and Hualālai rising in the distance, topped in clouds. That was one thing about the Big Island that she loved. The wide-open space and *bigness* of it all.

Just when Lu started wondering if she should go check

on her new friend, Joni slid into the mix as unobtrusively as possible, in a beige crocheted minidress and knee-high suede lace-up boots. Tanned arms covered in turquoise bangles. When Lu got closer, she could see that Joni's eyes were bloodshot. When Joni caught her looking, Joni blew a kiss, but didn't come over. Instead, she went and stood by Stanley, clinging to his arm.

That was when Lu noticed Sunny Dawson, standing in the shadows, watching. Part Hawaiian, with almond eyes and a dimpled smile, she had a reputation as a beautiful hula dancer.

Lu walked over. "What a perfect night."

"Every night is perfect here—in its own way."

"I'm Lu Freitas, with *Sunset* magazine. Would you mind if I ask you a few questions?"

"Jerry's niece, right?"

Lu nodded. "My dad is his brother."

"I only have a minute, but fire away."

"Were you surprised when Mr. Rockefeller offered you a management position?"

Sunny laughed. "Not a bit. From the get-go, this place has felt different from other hotels. Mr. Rockefeller is way ahead of his time. He knows the value of hiring the best person for the job, whether they wear pants or a skirt."

She spoke with her hands, as any good hula dancer tended to do.

"How did you two meet?" Lu asked.

"I applied the good old-fashioned way, but it didn't hurt that I already knew half the staff. You know how it is."

She certainly did. It always helped to know someone's sister's uncle's cousin's son. They talked more about the hotel and the job and Mr. Rockefeller before Sunny excused herself to fix a downed tiki torch. Lu imagined ways of working her into her story.

Dinner passed in a blur of gorging on mac-nut-crusted *ono* that Mr. Rockefeller himself had reeled in. Lu had somehow ended up surrounded by guys and the talk was all fishing tales. As though being out on the fishing boat together had somehow bonded them.

As the evening progressed, the stories grew more and more outlandish. *The marlin that got away was at least a thousand-pounder. That was a great white following the boat, I'm sure of it.* And of course, Big Joe's fish that got away was *longer than the boat.* But unlike Lu's boat, all others had caught at least one fish before the storm arrived.

After dinner but before dessert, Joni got up with her guitar and tuned and strummed and tested the mic. Her eyes had cleared some, and she looked at ease.

"Good evening, all you gorgeous friends. How's everyone doing on this balmy Hawaiian night?" Joni said.

Great. Blessed. Fat and happy.

"You know, I have a confession to make," she said, pausing as her eyes swung around the room. "I invited myself on this trip. Unlike all of you, I didn't receive the gilded invite in the mail. I knew Mr. Rockefeller from Caneel Bay, and when I heard about his new hotel, I called him and begged him to let me come."

A few murmurs rose.

"In typical LSR fashion, he told me I was more than welcome, on one condition. That I come as a guest and not to perform. He said the Mauna Kea would soothe my soul—he knew I'd been burning the candle at both ends. How sweet was that? But for me, music is like air. I need it. So, here I am, sharing that need with you. Whether you like it or not," she said, one side of her mouth turning up.

She didn't sound drunk or manic or weepy. When she started up, conversations ceased and everyone sat motionless in their chairs. A breeze rustled. It was the opposite of last night. Joni was an accomplished guitar player. Lu had never heard a woman play so fluidly. She was as good or better than any man, fingers flying along, plucking up a storm. But what really stood out was the emotion pouring out of her. The music cut into you, bringing up feelings Lu never knew she had. Something about it made her think of Dylan.

Down by the water, you told me you never loved me. You denied me forever, now let the sky fall. Oooh, let the sky fall. That was the day I knew my old story was true. The stars had always known, but I refused to listen.

Dessert came. Guava sorbet and a five-layered chocolate cake with 'akala berries on top. Lu eyed the cart afterward, to see if there was any leftover. The whole experience felt magical. The warm island air, the familiar food, the soul-cutting music. Rockefeller had succeeded in picking up where nature left off.

The night was too beautiful, and Lu too full, to go straight to her room, so she decided to take the long way back. She followed the promenade past the illuminated pool and up a few flights of stairs. The hotel was a maze of hidden alcoves and rooms, and she passed a frame of old bells and fish-shaped gongs, a gold dragon from Thailand and a series of Hawaiian quilts and tapa cloth encased in glass. None were locked up. Rockefeller wanted the place to feel like a home. Though no home Lu had ever been in had art like that.

When she passed the lounge, she noticed Russi setting up a chessboard. He looked so intent and in his own world that she kept walking. But he must have spotted her, because he said, "Don't think I didn't see you, kid. Come back here."

Lu slunk back, half-hidden by a heliconia leaf. "I need to

get back and work on my notes, and try to pull my story together."

"That can wait. I need a partner. Do you play?" he said.

"It's been a while."

"No matter. As long as you know the difference between a pawn and a king, you're in," he said, showing for the first time the full magnitude of his smile.

She came over and pulled up a chair across the table. "So, you've forgiven me?" she asked.

"That remains to be seen. I had to hold on to the wall in the shower and I'm still rocking and rolling."

"I had a bit of that, too."

He studied her for a moment. "Today was hell, I'm not gonna lie, but sometimes it takes being in hell to recognize heaven. Maybe you're too young to even know what I'm talking about."

"I do know," she said.

"When I was your age, during the war, there was this immediacy to everything. Like you wanted to cram your whole life into one day. Only thing was, my priorities were all messed up. I thought getting back at the enemy was the only thing that mattered. And proving myself," he said, setting the last pawn in place. Lu thought he was going to go on, but he spun the board around so white was on her side. "You're up."

While it had been some time since Lu played, that didn't mean she didn't know how. When she made her first move, he immediately countered. She did the same. They went back and forth a few times. The marble felt cool against her palm. It was nice to play again.

He looked up. "Don't tell me you're some secret chess whiz," he said, leaning back and cradling his hands in his head. "That might be too much for me to take right now."

She laughed. "How long have you been playing?"

"I learned during the war. Had a friend who used to play. I knew I'd never be able to beat her, but I had to at least try."

"Her?" Lu said.

"Yeah. Her."

She sensed a story here. "Did you?"

"Did I what?"

"Beat her."

It was his turn. He had his hand on the queen, and was about to make a move that would prove deadly for him. "I only had one chance. And I blew it," he said, biting his lip.

It felt to Lu like he was talking about more than just chess. She remained quiet, waiting for him to move so she could finish him off. But he realized his mistake before he made it, and moved the rook instead.

"Good move," she said.

Chess had always come easily to her. The intuitive nature of it, and how it required nothing but time and an open mind. Two commodities that she regarded as essential to everything she did. It was through patience and perseverance that she'd made it this far.

"You know that neighbor of yours you mentioned before. The shell-shocked one. What happened to him?" Russi asked out of the blue.

She almost lied, but that wouldn't be fair. "He hit the bottle pretty hard and eventually his wife had to kick him out. He got ugly a few times and she gave him an ultimatum. Last I heard he was in and out of hospitals on the mainland and had married and divorced again."

"Do you know where he served?"

"Tarawa and later Saipan. I always liked him, but every now and then he got this really heavy vibe. He turned white and quiet and you could tell he was somewhere else. I always left the house when he got like that."

Russi nodded. "Tough tours. But no one came out unscathed, I don't care where they were. Some just deal with it better than others."

"You seem to have coped pretty well," she said, knowing so much of the pain happened behind closed doors.

"I've managed to stay out of the looney bin, if that's what you mean. I have the work to thank for that—it keeps me on my toes."

He turned his attention back to the board and assessed his next move. Lu had predicted he'd do one of two things and she was right. So she was ready. Russi seemed to sense her closing in on him.

"What the hell?" he said.

His playfulness was endearing. And though he guarded his king valiantly, in the end, she cornered him. "Checkmate," she said, unable to hold back a smile.

Russi smacked himself in the forehead, pretending to make a big fuss, but she could tell he was impressed. "We're gonna need a rematch."

"Anytime."

After the game, Lu was wide-awake, so she took the path down to the beach. Arcturus shone brightly, high in the summer sky. The sand felt cool on her feet. She walked along the water's edge, counting stars and feeling lucky. Being home felt even better than she'd imagined. The swell washed higher up the beach and the low rumble of it stirred up the air, filling it with salt. With the moon already set, the night was black as lava rock. Half-tempted to go back and grab a blanket so she could sleep out here, she instead moved up the beach into dry sand and lay down on her back, breathing in the sea.

Her head swam a little, leftover effects from the boat ride, but soon subsided. She thought about Dylan and how much he would love it here. With the shock of blue and black and green, he would never want to put down his camera. He would be following Russi around like a puppy dog, too. And then she thought of Dylan flying off to Vietnam and what Joni had said. Had they come down the road of friendship too far to make a switch? She'd been wondering that lately. And what if she said something, but he didn't feel the same way?

Call him, said a voice inside.

Sometime later, Lu woke with a start. It took a moment to register that she was lying in the soft sand, hair tangled in a patch of beach morning-glory vines. She opened her eyes and was about to sit up when she heard voices nearby—a man and a woman, speaking just above a whisper. She remained in place, trying to get her bearings.

The temperature had dropped, cool air from the mountains filling in. The stars were now hidden by clouds, tiki torches blown out. Everything was ink black, but she sensed movement down by the water. Then she heard a splash, and another. She strained to hear their voices, but whoever it was grew quiet. A few moments later, the man groaned.

Not wanting to hear any more, Lu hopped up, dusted herself off and backed up to the bushes, following their uneven edge back to the hotel. Stealthy as a panther. Along the way, she felt a prick of envy. Deserted beach, balmy ocean, endless sky. Whoever was out there had picked the perfect night for romance.

19

THE SCORE

O'ahu, 1943

Other than the success with the Maru code—and even that had been coming to them, anyway—Isabel was growing nervous that she hadn't produced any significant results. She blamed part of it on being underground and part of it on the complexity of the ever-changing code. Most messages that they successfully translated had been sent in minor codes, interisland codes or diplomatic codes. Denny and the boys were able to piece together some messages using JN-25, but only through sheer doggedness. She was starting to get the feeling that she was excess baggage with a skirt on.

But on the first day after the trip to Goat Island, a curious thing happened. When Isabel approached the steps into the Dungeon, the usual feeling of dread was absent. Upon entering, the strangling sensation that always wrapped around her chest and snaked up her throat didn't have the same tight grip. She inhaled deeply as she passed Jones.

"Morning," she said cheerfully.

Jones gave her a questioning glance. "Had a good weekend, did you, Miss Cooper?"

Was it that obvious?

"It was lovely—if you don't count the near drowning and the third-degree sunburn," she said. Every square mile of her body was a bright tomato red, especially the backs of her thighs, which hurt to sit on. Gloria had suggested she bring a pillow, which had been a brilliant idea.

"Sounds like my first time in the ocean, minus the sunburn. Turns out my arms and legs are made of lead," he said.

Inside, the Dungeon itself looked different. Lighter, more spacious, less ominous. The scent of coffee and the hum of the IBM machines were almost like old friends, and instead of putting her head down and making a beeline for her desk, Isabel said a hello to the traffic analysts and waved to the linguists. Hudson was on a call, so she didn't bother him. Something about the underwater experience had slung her fear out of orbit. She felt positively giddy, as though she could conquer the world. Or at least the Japanese naval codes.

Bring them on!

Five minutes after she had sat down, Hudson called her to his desk. He motioned for her to sit without even glancing up from his paper.

She eyed the chair. "Mind if I get my pillow? I have a terrible sunburn."

He set down his pencil slowly and looked up at her. "This should be quick."

Isabel's cheery mood drained away in an instant. She sat, gingerly. Leaning his tall frame in and speaking low, he said, "I'm going to get right to the point, Miss Cooper. A few of the boys have commented that you aren't pulling your weight around here. I was willing to take a woman on because Admiral Sutton pulled some strings, but I'm running a tight operation. If you can't hack it, I'm going to be forced to send you back to DC."

Isabel was gobsmacked. "Sir, I don't know what to say."

"I don't expect you to say anything, just do your job. And knock off that humming if you can help it. It's driving everyone nuts," he said, opening his notebook as though the conversation was finished.

She sat there in shock, swallowing tears and finding it difficult to breathe. "For the record, I did determine that the I1 had been hit. I haven't been a complete dud," she said, feeling compelled to defend herself.

"That was Denny, from what I understand."

What?

She lowered her voice. "No offense to Denny, sir, but I was working on that message. I recognized a few of the words and brought it to him for advice."

"One of the reasons we work so well here is that no one cares who gets credit. It's us against the enemy, not us against each other," he said.

"I know—"

He cut her off. "Look. I know you're a smart girl, but CIU may not be the best fit for you. Prove I'm wrong and I'm happy to keep you," he said.

"I'll do that, sir," she said, tapping her temple in a salute.

Being sent back to Washington was an impossibility. She had work to do here, and still so many places to see with Matteo Russi.

Isabel did not eat lunch; she ignored the fact that the back of her crisp thighs were sticking to her dress, and for the first time, she was actually able to focus on the messages coming across her desk. Little did Hudson know that threats against her intellect were her secret weapon. Challenge accepted.

The latest message was a short one but labeled Ultra. Denny had handed it off to her while he rushed off to consult with the linguists on another apparently more important message.

As usual, he looked like he hadn't slept in days, and Isabel felt guilty. While she'd been off frolicking with Matteo, Denny had probably slept here. She decided then and there that she needed to put in more time. Take a step back from Matteo, who had lately become an affliction. More and more on her mind. This was not like her.

Recent intelligence had come in that a Japanese floatplane had been spotted near Rabaul in Papua New Guinea. Floatplanes often patrolled ahead of IJN convoys to spot enemy submarines. Then aerial photographs from a US reconnaissance plane showed a stocking-up of ships in port at Rabaul. Something big was in the works. But no one could say what it was.

With this particular message, the TA guys had determined it was from the 11th Air Fleet to headquarters in Rabaul. The paper itself contained a certain static electricity, which often happened when she'd encountered an important message. One of those *feelings* that came when you held enough encrypted messages in your hand. A crackle that hopped from paper to hand.

Isabel took her time in going through the code groups. One stood out to her as familiar, and she checked the book. *Convoy*. She sat up straighter, tapped her pencil on the desk. Anything to avoid humming. Another of the five-letter groups looked familiar, but she couldn't place it, so she got up and walked over to Ziegler.

"This one is eluding me, though it looks familiar. Do you recognize it?" she asked him.

Ziegler was hunched over a half-decrypted message and eating sunflower seeds, but he quickly shoved his work aside to help her. "Hmm," he said, staring at it for a few moments. "I believe it's *destroyer*. Hang on, lemme check."

He leafed through a notebook filled with illegible writing. Isabel held her breath.

"Yep. *Destroyer*, it is," he said looking up at her as the implication dawned on them both. "As Denny would say, fucking A!"

A destroyer would bolster the convoy theory.

Isabel's pulse sped up. "Do you want to decrypt this one together? I could use the help."

"Hell, yes, pull up your chair," he said, swiping notebooks, papers and debris from the desk.

They split up the message. Something about Ziegler put her at ease. Whip smart and the fastest crippie of the bunch, he nonetheless reminded her of a clumsy puppy. Within minutes of starting, he had his pencil between his teeth and was gnawing on it like a bone.

Ten minutes later, Ziegler pounded a fist on the desk. "This one is March and that is five. Something's going down on March 5. You got anything?"

"Not yet," she said self-consciously.

"My gut tells me this is big. Keep at it, you're doing great," he said, then spoke under his breath. "Don't worry about Hudson. Sometimes he gets a hair up his ass. He's under so much pressure right now. We all are. Just do the best you can."

His encouragement was just what she needed. They plugged away for a while longer when Isabel got a hunch. Messages often followed a similar format, and the way this one was organized, she hypothesized that the last code groups were locations. She pulled up the book with place names and began scanning through it for a match. Now that the Japanese were out of Guadalcanal, they had to be mobilizing to go somewhere. Activity had been bumping up in the Southwest Pacific, so she searched there first. A few minutes later, bingo. One name lined, up, then another.

"I've got it!" she said, a little louder than she meant.

Hudson raised his head and glanced over.

"Wewak, Madang and Lae. The convoy is headed for Papua New Guinea. Have a look," she said to Ziegler.

Ziegler checked the codebook, but she knew she was right. That was the beauty of numbers. They never lied.

He jumped up, limbs flailing around. "Oh, boy. Hudson needs to see this!"

She remained in her seat. He motioned for her to come along. Reluctantly, she did.

"Sir, Miss Cooper and I might have just discovered where all those ships in Rabaul intend to go," he said, shoving the paper under Hudson's nose.

Isabel stood quietly with her hands behind her back.

"You sure about this? What did the linguists say?" Hudson asked, taking a puff on his pipe and blowing it off to the side.

"I'm on my way there now. But we have *Rabaul, convoy, destroyer, March 5* and the three islands. I think it's safe to say that's what's cooking," Ziegler said.

Just then, Denny returned. "What's up?"

Ziegler told him.

Denny looked at Isabel. "Not bad, Cooper," he said.

Her cheeks burned.

"Thank you."

For the rest of the week, she worked longer hours in the Dungeon, and at night spent time beating Gloria at chess and studying Japanese language and characters. Gloria was a good sport at losing.

"You sure this ring isn't a consolation prize rather than a friendship ring?" she said.

Isabel laughed. "I got the ring before I beat you, so that doesn't hold up."

"I never stood a chance, and you know that. But the funny thing is, I don't mind losing to you. After all these years being the only girl in my family, it feels like I finally have a sister."

Isabel had always thought it would be neat to have a sister. Another girl in the house, especially after her mom died. But having Walt for a brother made up for it and then some. Now with Walt gone, it was nice to have someone who was beginning to feel like family.

When Gloria tired of losing, Isabel turned to the Japanese language books. Sure, the kana was easier, because it was romanized and they needed that in order to transmit via Morse code, but the calligraphy was far more interesting to Isabel—each one a tiny work of art. It didn't take long for her to memorize many of the characters. They stuck in her mind like stamps. In her dictionary, rather than alphabetically, they were arranged by meaning. It made perfect sense.

But there was a problem. Namely, Matteo Russi. While at work she'd been able to concentrate better, at home her mind continuously wandered to the past Saturday at Goat Island. The way his eyes traveled up and down her body. The feel of the coral heart on her skin. Hot breath against her neck. Friendship was fine, but the realization came that friendship might not be enough.

Not with him.

She was off in a daydream trying to convince herself that she had not in fact fallen for him when Gloria came out to fetch a glass of tonic. "Looks like someone is distracted."

"Just giving my eyes a break."

"You aren't fooling me. I know that look. Ever since this weekend, you've had your head in the clouds. You have a thing for Matteo Russi. Why not admit it?" Gloria said, with her hands on her hips.

"Because there are so many reasons not to."

"The heart doesn't care about reasons."

"Well, I do."

"Tell me the main one."

Isabel thought for a moment. "Matteo himself has said many times that he is not looking for anything serious. He has this belief that he's not coming out of this war alive. And I can't lose anyone else. It would do me in."

"In case you haven't noticed, it's much too late for that. What else?"

Cracking JN-25 was a big reason, but she couldn't mention that to Gloria.

"I refuse to date a known womanizer."

Gloria nodded. "Okay, that's fair. But even known womanizers can change their stripes with the right person. I say you see what happens. There's no need to make any big decisions at this point in the game, but don't rule Matteo out. You obviously have feelings for the man."

She could at least admit that. "A little."

"Lord, you're insufferable! For the past few weeks, it's been Russi this, Matteo that. I wasn't born yesterday, I know love when I see it."

"Love?"

"You heard me," Gloria said, marching off to bed.

Was that what this was?

Lord help her.

Good fortune came on a Friday morning. Isabel was working on decrypting a message when Hudson strode in from his morning meeting at fleet headquarters. He was moving at a faster pace than usual, dropped a thick manila folder on his desk, then came straight to their area. A few heads across the room turned, but then went back to their own business.

"We got the books," he said in his typical understated fashion.

Denny set down his pencil and looked up. "What books?"

"Divers at Guadalcanal recovered five books from the sub that went aground. The boys there claim one is a superceded JN-25 codebook," he said.

Denny sat for a moment with his mouth open, then said, "Fucking A."

Isabel felt as though she were in a movie theater, watching a major drama unfold. Every cryptanalyst dreamed of recovering enemy codebooks.

"This calls for a drink," Ziegler said, pulling out a flask and taking a swig.

Hudson didn't bat an eye.

"We have a courier bringing them in next week, flying in on a transport. Say your prayers, fellas," he said.

No one corrected him and Isabel wasn't about to. Being lumped in with the fellas was standard procedure around here. You just swallowed it.

"I guess this means we'll be sleeping here for a while," Denny said.

Ziegler pulled out four shot glasses from a messy drawer, even though it was still early. "This could be the best thing that's ever happened to us. Other than the invention of Spam," he said with a chuckle.

He poured everyone a glass, then held his up. "To taking these bastards down."

"To the bottom of the fucking ocean," Denny added with a clink of his glass.

Isabel could certainly drink to that.

20

THE PARTY

O'ahu, 1943

A man can smell a desperate woman a mile away. Which was why Isabel was annoyed with herself for waiting for a phone call that never came. Matteo had mentioned early-morning flight training, so she told herself that was the reason for radio silence all week. Gloria, on the other hand, had spent nearly every waking moment aside from work with Dickie. In fact, she'd only spent two nights out of the last seven in her own bed. She was nose over toes in love, and happy to let everyone in on it.

Isabel envied her carefree attitude and gumption. Gloria knew herself and made no apologies. A man was what she'd wanted, and now that she'd found one, she was going all-in. Isabel knew what she wanted in regards to the war, but everything else had fallen to the wayside. Love and life had taken a back seat. She wasn't sure if that was normal, but that's the way it was.

It was a cool and crisp Saturday morning. With nothing planned for the whole weekend, she brewed a cup of coffee and sat down with her Japanese dictionary. The coffee here was so rich that she'd doubled her intake since coming to Hawai'i. It helped that it wasn't rationed in the islands.

A few minutes later, Gloria waltzed in. "No Matteo today?"

"Nope. Which is just as well, because how am I going to learn Japanese if I don't have time to study?"

Gloria made a face. "It beats me why you're so hell-bent on learning Japanese. The writing looks like a cross between finger painting and chicken scratch. Our brains aren't made for that kind of thing, Isabel," she said, as if she really had any idea. "How about you come with Dickie and me to Kailua. One of the girls from work has a family house there and a bunch of friends are coming out to barbecue and play horseshoes. It would be fun!"

"I should stay here and catch up on things."

"Don't tell me you want to be here in case Matteo calls."

"Absolutely not."

Maybe a little.

"Nothing will make a man want you more than you being unavailable. If he does call or come by and you aren't here, that'll wake him up," Gloria said, snapping her fingers.

Isabel looked out the window. Nothing but blue sky. "You sure you want me as a third wheel?"

"Go pack your bag, you're coming."

Dickie picked them up an hour later and they went over the Pali again, this time to Kailua. He was dressed in swim trunks, an aloha shirt and a straw hat—the perfect image of a tourist to the islands—and he spent ninety-four percent of the drive talking about himself. By the time they pulled up to the house, Isabel knew that he had been high school class president, had built his first car from scratch, was the club chess champ and voted most likely to succeed by his classmates. He had a penchant for machinery and could assemble anything he set his mind to. Boat, car, radio, you name it.

The interesting part of it all was how the more he boasted, the more Gloria beamed at him. Any time Isabel tried to get a word in, he maneuvered the conversation back to himself. The moment the engine stopped, Isabel hopped out of the car. She couldn't take another word. Sure, he was handsome, but good looks could not compensate for lack of character.

"Can you believe this place?" Gloria said, slamming the door and twirling around in the grass.

The house was board and batten, one story and green as a forest. The lawn went on for miles and was only interrupted by the odd coconut tree here and there. A few cars were strewn about haphazardly. When they walked around front, they were greeted by a cluster of men playing croquet and several women lounging on towels in the grass, cheering them on.

Isabel immediately regretted coming. Social affairs like this were not her strong suit. More comfortable with her nose in a book, she never knew quite how to join in a conversation and more often than not ended up hanging out with the dog or the cat. Gloria seemed to know most of the girls, and they said their hellos. They all seemed friendly, but after her bad sunburn, Isabel had no desire to sit in the sun roasting herself.

Instead, she went for a short walk on the beach, which was littered with blue bubbles with long tentacles. Portuguese man-of-war, someone had said. She wore a wide brimmed straw hat she'd borrowed from the house, and draped a Hawaiian piece of material over her shoulders. With each step, a layer of the outside world lifted off her. Grief over Walt, worry about her lack of success at CIU, mental strain from thinking so hard, confusion over her feelings for Matteo. All of that slowly evaporated. Peace moved in. And for a time, the tang of salt water and fish was all she knew.

When she returned to the house, more people had arrived. A game of horseshoe had been set up and, off to the side, Dickie and another man were standing over a smoking barbecue pit. Gloria was there with them, saw her and waved. Isabel made a beeline for them.

"Izzy, this is Wayne," she said, grabbing Wayne by the arm and pushing him toward her.

Wayne turned and his eyes went wide. "This your blue-eyed sister?"

"Sisters in crime," Gloria said teasingly.

"I told you," Dickie said to Wayne.

He gave her a once-over and said, "Wanna be my partner in the next horseshoe match?"

"I'm not very good," Isabel said, which was a flat-out lie. She and Walt used to play for hours on end, and when it got too cold outside, they went in and played chess. Horseshoes was his game, chess hers.

"You just stand there and look pretty," he said with a wink.

When their turn came up, she allowed Wayne to show her how to toss the horseshoe and explain the rules of the game. He was friendly and nice, but he never once asked if she had played before. She let him assume. In her experience, assumption was a good indicator of ignorance.

When their opponents came up, Isabel recognized the man right away. Lieutenant Clark Spencer, linguist in the Dungeon. Their eyes met and a look of acknowledgment passed over his face. Isabel gave an imperceptible nod. Eva, his wife, was a nurse at Tripler. The two touched every chance they could. A hand on the waist. Shoulder rubbing shoulder. A light kiss. The sweetness gave Isabel a sense of longing.

Clark and Eva went first, both touching the stake right off

the bat. Wayne, however, missed it entirely. He seemed more interested in showing off his slabby arms as he tossed than anything else. Above all, horseshoes was a game of concentration. Isabel blocked out everything and tossed. *Clink.* Tossed again. *Clink. Both* horseshoes hugged the stake.

Wayne whistled. "Looks like we have a ringer."

She held up her hands in mock surprise. The game continued much the same, with Isabel landing ringers and leaners, until she heard a very familiar voice in the crowd at her back. She casually turned to see Matteo standing with some of the pilots. Malia was by his side, looking sun-kissed and gorgeous. Matteo hadn't noticed her yet, but Malia waved. Isabel smiled, then turned away as quickly as she could.

She blew the next shot, and the next, but managed to hit the stake on the last one, holding on to their lead by a grain of sand. Wayne grabbed her hand and held her arm up, spinning her around like a trophy. The group around them cheered, drawing attention their way. Matteo glanced up and caught her eye. His expression was unreadable. It could have been surprise or disappointment or a bit of both. He smiled, but the smile didn't reach his eyes.

Once she was able to tear herself away from Wayne, she went to the ladies' room to splash some water on her face. Looking into the mirror, she gave herself a pep talk. *You have bigger things to worry about than Matteo Russi. He's just a small diversion along the way. Stay strong and stay true to the cause. Do not let him get you down. He means nothing.* But if that was true, why did she feel like a fish dragging on the line?

Back outside, wherever Matteo was, Isabel made sure she wasn't. She forced herself to mingle, not even caring if she had anything smart to say. She even grabbed a cold Primo beer from the cooler. Not like her at all. The only saving grace was that someone had brought a giant black Labrador named

Captain, and the dog seemed to sense her unease, following her around like a nanny would a child. Eventually, she ended up sitting under a tree rubbing his stomach and looking out at the ocean, which had gone from deep blue to gray.

Gloria finally came over and kneeled down next to her. "What's gotten into you? I've watched you run away from Matteo like he has VD. The poor man is probably wondering what the dickens happened. Last weekend you were best friends and now you won't even look at him."

"That's not true. I looked at him once."

Gloria rolled her eyes. "Oh, for heaven's sake."

"Why didn't you tell me he and Malia were together again? Here I was telling you that I might be falling for him."

"Malia never said a word to me. Besides, I doubt they're together—" Gloria stopped midsentence, then smiled sweetly at someone behind Isabel. "Hello, Lieutenant."

Isabel froze.

"Hey." Matteo smiled down at her.

"Hey."

Gloria stood. "Excuse me, I'd better move our stuff inside. Looks like rain."

Matteo jammed his hands into his shorts pockets. "Nice place, huh?

"Very nice."

"You been here long?"

The air around them felt thick as mud.

"A couple hours."

Why was it suddenly so hard to hold a conversation?

He knelt down and began rubbing behind Captain's ears. "Sorry I didn't call this week. We had night training and they put us through the wringer. I'm still recovering."

Captain groaned.

Up close, she could see the dark shadows under his eyes, almost like bruises. "No apology needed. I've been busy, too."

"Work?"

"Mostly."

"Are you here with Gloria or with Wayne?" he asked, trying to seem casual, but his jaw did something funny. In fact, his whole demeanor seemed funny.

"With Gloria. Dickie drove us."

She didn't bother to ask him who he came with.

Matteo fingered his dog tag. "I have something for you, Izzy. Are you free this week? Maybe I can give it to you one of these nights?"

"Don't feel like you owe me anything, Matteo. That's the last thing I want," she said.

A raindrop landed on her shoulder.

He frowned. "Why are you acting so weird? Did I do something? Are you mad at me for almost getting us killed?"

"No, I'm not mad at you."

She was mad at herself. For being foolish—and jealous—and unable to control her emotions. This was new territory. A sheet of rain moved in. Captain sat up.

"Time to move inside," he said, holding his hand out.

Isabel was afraid to touch him, but didn't want to be rude. She let him pull her up. His hand was as warm and rough as she remembered. They rushed to the covered lānai along with everyone else. Isabel blended in with the huddled crowd, weaving away from Matteo. The lānai had obviously been built with rainy afternoons in mind and was set up with two long wooden tables, and enough chairs for half the army. Isabel noticed two guys playing chess at the far end of the table. Beer bottles lined up in front of them, as though they'd been playing awhile. She wandered over and looked at the board. The dark-haired guy was two moves away from a checkmate.

"Mind if I watch?" she asked.

Neither looked up.

"Be my guest," said the other, a big guy with a mop of curls.

On the dark-haired guy's turn, instead of moving the rook into position for the win, he moved a pawn. Isabel held back a sigh. Or at least she thought she did, because the dark-haired man glared at her.

"Would you have done something different, Miss—"

"Cooper. Now that you ask, I would have."

Curly made a face. "Too late, mate. Nor do we need any advice from the peanut gallery."

The rush of rain on the metal roof almost drowned out his words. Isabel stepped away. All along the table, cribbage games had started up, and Gloria was watching Wayne and Dickie play a game of chess. Isabel went over and joined them. It took all of five minutes for Dickie to beat Wayne. They played again and the same thing happened.

Then that buzzing again on the back of her neck. A moment later, Matteo and two other men sat in the empty chairs next to them.

"Want to join in on our cribbage game?" Matteo asked Isabel.

"I've never played."

Before he could respond, Malia appeared. She pulled out the chair on the other side of him and sat. "I'd love to play."

Matteo said, "Izzy—"

At the same time, his friend said, "You and I can be partners, Malia. I need an old hand."

"Do you mind, Isabel?" Malia leaned over and asked.

"Not at all."

Acutely aware of Matteo's voice and movement at all times, she kept her back to the cribbage and eye on the chess. Dickie soon tired of Wayne, and others cycled through. Never once

did he ask Gloria or Isabel to play. While Dickie was a de-
cent player, his opponents were not. Which made him appear unbeatable.

"You all are a very uncivilized lot. Any other takers?" he
called down the table with a smug look on his face.

Matteo leaned into Isabel, held his cards over his mouth
and whispered. "Take the guy down."

Isabel smiled in surprise. "What makes you think I can?"

He tapped his head. "I know everything about you. Remember?"

"Walt—"

"Was a proud big brother."

Across the table, Gloria said, "How about Isabel? She beats
me every time."

Isabel looked at Dickie expectantly.

"Fine by me. I'll even let you be white," he said.

"Actually, I prefer black."

He raised an eyebrow. "Black, it is."

She knew from watching the past games that he always
started with e4—the queen's pawn moving forward two
squares. He did the same with her.

Boring.

She wasted no time in moving her king's pawn two squares
forward. E5 was a riskier play, but likely to lead to a faster
game. Already her mind was working out scenarios. Dickie
moved his knight to f3. A popular opening. She countered
with her knight to c6. The feel of the cool marble felt familiar under her hand.

Dickie rested his chin on two fingers and stared at the
board for a while, then slowly raised his steel-blue eyes. "Miss
Cooper, I do believe you know a thing or two."

"I've played."

"A civilized woman. I appreciate that."

She smiled. "Not always, but most of the time."

That got a laugh. As the game progressed, people moved in to watch. A sphere of intensity surrounded them. Dickie knew his moves, but he was predictable, a common downfall of players who were good but not great. He backed her into a corner a few times, but she found her way out. For the first time since being in Hawai'i, she felt completely in her element. A game of chess with a worthy opponent required utter concentration, something she knew a thing or two about.

Matteo ended his cribbage match and took up watching theirs. A line of perspiration formed over Dickie's upper lip. His mouth pinched. Every time he moved, she countered him.

"Not only are you good, but you're fast," Dickie said.

"I don't believe in wasting time."

"I don't believe in losing."

This time, she laughed.

The wind picked up fury, blowing sideways rain in on them. No one seemed to notice or care. Primo beer and some rotten-sock-smelling spirit called ōkolehao were flowing freely and suddenly everyone on the lānai was riveted by their game. In recent months, Dickie apparently had earned a reputation as the resident chess expert. No one had beat him yet.

"Where did you learn to play?" he asked.

"I taught myself. How about you?"

"My father played in the Berlin chess cafés. I learned from him before I left, before he died."

"I'm so sorry."

He shrugged. "It came with the territory."

Isabel pulled the pareo up around her shoulders, shivering as she waited for him to make his next move.

Matteo nudged her. "Are you cold?"

"A little."

Without hesitating, he pulled a towel from behind his

chair and set it on her shoulders. His touch felt brotherly and possessive and downright sexy, and she wished it were just the two of them sitting here, weathering the storm. Those warm arms around her, stubble grazing her neck. She shook her head to clear the thought. Dickie finally made his move and Isabel felt a rush of knowing. He was done. Though her heart was pounding, she moved her knight in the most nonchalant manner she could muster.

Dickie searched the board for escape routes. But they both knew there were none. More time passed as he sat there in a state of near panic. Maybe he couldn't admit defeat, or maybe he wanted to save face. Either way, Isabel was used to it. Most men hated losing to a girl.

Matteo popped a beer and handed it to him. "Here you go, buddy, you might be needing this."

Dickie did not take the beer. Instead, Gloria did and set it down in front of him.

"Zugzwang," Isabel finally said.

"Miss Cooper, you played me. Nice work," he said.

His face flashed anger despite his attempt at a smile.

"I played the game, not you, Mr. Thompson."

She waited for him to lay down his king. Instead, he grabbed the beer, stood up and knocked the king over with the bottle as he walked away. The crowd parted around him, no one quite sure how to react. Isabel was stunned. Next to her, Matteo started clapping. Soon, whistles and cheers went around the lānai. The two drunk chess players from down the table came up and shook her hand.

"Spectacular game," said the mop-headed one.

"Come play with us anytime," said the other.

Isabel smiled graciously.

It was late afternoon now. The rain had settled to a light drizzle, and people began to trickle out. Driving in the rain

SARA ACKERMAN
202

was bad enough, but rain plus dark plus headlight covers was over the top dangerous. Gloria was off somewhere consoling Dickie, and Isabel was more than ready to leave. She was in the kitchen pouring a glass of water when Matteo walked in.

"I'd offer you a ride, but I hitched a ride with Manny and he's got a full car," he said.

"I thought you came with Malia."

"She rode with us, too. With all of us," he said, emphasis on the *all of us*.

He took a step closer.

Isabel's feet grew roots in the linoleum.

Another step.

He spoke softly. "I don't know what's happening here, but I can't seem to—"

"Russi, we're out!" yelled a man who appeared behind them, silent as a cat.

Matteo jumped a foot in the air. "Damn it, Toots, you scared the crap out of me."

"Didn't mean to interrupt, but everyone's waiting. Come on, man."

Isabel wanted to reach out and take his hand. Keep him there with her, to finish whatever it was he meant to say. But maybe it was for the best. If she kept him as a friend, she wouldn't lose him.

At least that was what she told herself.

21

THE DEPARTURE

O'ahu, 1943

In the Dungeon, they waited. The recovered codebooks were to be brought in that afternoon, and for once, Isabel was not the only one having a hard time focusing. The bad news was, the Japanese had changed the codes. They weren't stupid.

But they hadn't changed the additives.

By midafternoon, Denny had finished his third sandwich and Ziegler was pacing every five minutes instead of ten. Hudson had been making the rounds from station to station, checking in for any signs that the Japanese were onto them. Isabel stared at the same message she'd been working on all day with no success whatsoever. There were more pencil marks than code.

And then the door opened. Jones stood up and greeted Admiral Lawton himself. Though not a Dungeon inhabitant, Lawton had been a key player in the Battle of Midway, and he had a direct line to Hudson. It was no secret that everyone down here worshipped him. Trim and dapper, he carried a large briefcase in each hand, and set them on Hudson's desk.

The entire room went silent and only the deep thrum of the machines could be heard in the background.

"Gentlemen, what we have here are codebooks, maps, charts, diaries and the ship's log. As you know, the IJN tried their damnedest to destroy that sub over the last few days, everything from strapping depth charges to shooting torpedoes to dive-bombing with Vals. But we stopped them. I know you were hoping for a cipher machine, but these will have to do," he said with a sly smile.

Hudson called out to everyone in the room, "Get your butts over here, stat."

Lawton snapped open the first case with a loud click. Isabel stood on the outskirts and watched with the kind of anticipation you'd have waiting for a baby to be delivered. Not that she'd ever seen one, but still.

"Some of this stuff is for the crippies, and some for the linguists. The diaries could be gold and need to be translated yesterday. I'm told some of the codebooks are for future versions so those are priority, too. Hell, all of it is priority. They had to dry them out on the radio receiver on the island, so they're brittle. I don't need to tell you to treat them as if your life depends on it. Because it could," he said.

He carefully set each piece on a folding table Jones had set up. Isabel could scarcely believe what lay in front of them. A large red hardbound book with not only the current Japanese naval codes but also reserve editions slated to go into effect in the near future. A slew of thinner folders and pamphlets full of additives tables and call signs. Grid charts, area designators. Even diaries of several of the sailors aboard. She felt her heartbeat in her ears. No one spoke a word as they stared at the goods. A fatal error on the part of Japanese submariners. She wondered if she would have had the wherewithal to save the codebooks—or save herself.

"Chance of a lifetime, right here," Hudson said, rolling up his sleeves.

Ziegler looked to be drooling. "God bless those Kiwis."

Lawton slowly swung his head around the room, making eye contact with everyone in the group. "Get to it."

When he reached Isabel, his green eyes leveled her. "Miss Cooper, here's your opportunity to shine."

He knew her name?

"Absolutely, sir," was what came out.

Lawton then said, "Oh, and, Bird, we captured one of their men on the sub. Be ready to help with the interrogation."

Once Lawton left, Hudson and Denny sorted through the material, handling it like fine china. Hudson gave the diaries to Bird for translating, the charts to the TA guys. Much like Christmas morning, there was something for everyone.

Bird leafed through one of the diaries. "Fuck, this whole thing is in sosho." He picked up another. "Same with this."

"There a problem with that?" Hudson asked.

"No one here reads sosho."

Isabel perked up. Sosho was what she had been studying all these months. The cursive writing.

She held up a hand. "I do. Some, at least."

"How in hell do you know sosho?" Bird asked.

"I've been learning it, along with kana," she said. "For fun."

He laughed. "No one I know has ever said learning Japanese characters is fun. But okay, I'll take it. How about you work your way through this and see what we get."

Denny cut in. "Hang on, we need all hands on deck with the codebooks. Even though they've changed it, we can still cross-reference all our old messages. Those are number one."

Isabel felt more in demand than she had since arriving. "I can look at the diaries at night."

Hudson spoke in that calm voice he was known for. "It's all number one. Right now, we all just work until we're done. You know the drill."

And so they did. For the next few days, Isabel lived in the Dungeon, coming up only to sleep for a few hours at night. By day, there were many *ooh* and *aah* moments, where they were able to look back and see where they'd been right with past messages, and where they'd gone wrong.

Thoughts of Matteo temporarily faded into the background, but did not disappear. She kept telling herself maybe she'd imagined the whole thing. She was also happy she didn't have to explain her long hours to Gloria, because Gloria was hardly home. Thanks to Dickie.

On a particularly balmy evening, Isabel decided to take an actual break for a few hours, and she had the radio on loud, playing Hawaiian music. She was lying on the couch, half in a dream about thick vines and sunken submarines, when a knock came at the door. She bolted upright. It was almost nine, the witching hour when everyone had to be in their homes.

"Who is it?" she called.

"It's me, Matteo," he said, sounding impatient.

Her heart dropped to her knees. "What are you doing here?" she said.

"If you let me in, I'll tell you."

Wearing only underwear and bra, she slipped on a robe and went to the door, smoothing out her smooshed hair. Matteo was on the step, outlined in moonlight.

"Hi," she said, rubbing her eyes.

"Sorry if I woke you."

"No, it's fine. I was just unwinding."

Matteo made no move to enter. "I came by yesterday—no one was around."

"Work has been busy."

"Emptying all those ashtrays, huh?"

"You'd be surprised."

He chuckled. "I bet I would. So, you gonna invite me in? I wanted to give you this before we leave," he said, holding something up.

Leave?

Still dazed from her dream, Isabel stepped aside. "Come in, sorry. Let me put the drapes down so I can switch on the light."

He brushed past her, smelling of his own particular brand of man—salty, with notes of airplane and sky. He remained by the door until the light was on, and only then did she see he was in uniform. Normally, uniforms didn't do much for her, but he looked so sharp and dignified. More handsome than he had a right to.

"You're leaving?" she asked.

"We ship out tomorrow. Wish I could say where we're going, but I don't even know."

She felt it between her shoulder blades. A Hawai'i without Matteo would not be the same. "Nor would you tell me if you did," she said.

"True. But I'd want to tell you. Just like I know you want to tell me what you do," he said, fixing her in place with his gaze.

"Please. You know I can't," she whispered.

That same strange electricity buzzed about the room, hovering between them like radio static. She rubbed her arms to diffuse it but nothing happened.

He held out an album. "Here. I assembled this for you," he said, voice strangely shy.

Isabel took it and sat on the couch. He joined her, keeping a safe distance, an arm's length away. On the cover, he'd written in neat block print, *Walt & Izzy*. And below that, *From Hawai'i, With Love*. She had no words, and her throat tightened as she opened the book.

The light was dim, but there would be plenty of time to view it more closely in the daylight. On the first page was a large photo of Walt at the Pali lookout, standing with his arms up as though holding up the sky, his whole life ahead. Or so he thought. On the other side, a photo of Isabel clamping down her dress and looking horrified, but also laughing.

"The look on your face is priceless," he said.

"Wait a sec. I can't believe you got a picture of that."

A wicked grin crossed his face. "You oughta see the other one."

"Please don't tell me—"

He squeezed above her knee. "Just kidding, just kidding. We'd just met and I knew you'd be mighty embarrassed if you saw my camera out. I was pointing to shoot before the gust came. Scout's honor," he said, staring down at the shot.

His palm print left a warm patch on her leg. She flipped the pages. Photos of her and Walt on the beach before their surfing escapades. There was something surreal about seeing the two of them in the same place, but not in the same time. As though she might walk out of one picture frame and into another with her brother. Matteo had added in some keepsakes, too. A napkin from the Peacock Tavern. A Primo beer label.

When she reached the Goat Island page, she slowed. There she was, smiling into the camera, sand on her cheeks, hair this way and that. The ocean spanned out behind her. This was not one of the candid shots. Matteo had moved in close and said something to make her laugh, she couldn't remember. Isabel examined her expression. Pure joy, contentment and something far bigger.

Matteo cleared his throat. "That's my favorite."

She was afraid to look at him. "None of Walt on the island?"

"I didn't bring my camera. Thought it might be too risky. But with you, I had no choice."

She squirmed. Outside, a cane toad croaked.

"Here you are leaving and there's not even one picture of you in here. How is that fair?" she said, trying to lighten the moment.

"You know that saying, *all is fair in love and war*? It's horseshit. There's nothing fair about war—or love." He looked at his watch. "I should get going. I still have to pack."

Stay, she wanted to say, but what good would that do? Isabel turned off the light. And in the time it took for them to get to the door, she already missed him. Matteo had told her he was terrible at goodbyes. Well, so was she. Especially when there was so obviously something powerful hanging between them on a ledge. In fact, *goodbye* was her least favorite word in the English language.

"Will you write?" she asked.

He stopped abruptly and she bumped into his back, steadying herself on his arm. His hand reached out and felt for her, pulling her in for a hug. Isabel rested her chin on his shoulder, looking out at a deep yellow moon, low in the sky. It dawned on her then that no matter what happened, the moon would still rise and set. The world would go on spinning its ethereal beauty, flowers would still open and close and birds would sing.

Matteo rubbed her back and spoke quietly into her hair. "You bet I will."

"Just promise me one thing," she said.

"You know I'm not good with promises."

"This one's easy. When you come back, you'll let me take a picture of you."

He pulled her in tighter, if that were possible. "We'll take it as it comes."

They stood there for what felt like hours. Isabel did her best to memorize the feeling of his strong arms and his heartbeat. The sound of his breath. Then he tilted up her chin and dusted her lips with a kiss, his breath hot. She froze in place, ready for another. But Matteo was already down the steps. Isabel ran her tongue over the spot he'd touched, trying to make sense of what had just happened. Halfway to the car, he slowed and then stopped in his tracks. *Come back*, she willed.

Matteo turned, saw her watching and called out, "You'll be on my mind."

Isabel was on the verge of breaking down, but wanted to be strong for him. "Same."

He waved and then was gone.

22

THE MYSTERY

Hawai'i Island, July 1965

The surf rose in the night. Lu could tell the minute she woke up and heard the roar. Summer surf favored the south side of the island, but every now and then, if there was enough west in it, a swell snuck through. Probably a result of yesterday's storm. Lu and Joni had plans to swim early, before heading up mauka to Parker Ranch for horseback riding and a barbecue. It had been forever since Lu had been to Waimea and she could hardly wait.

"Lovey dove, if I don't show up at your door at six o'clock, come drag my lazy ass out of bed," Joni had said.

Lu put on her suit and braided her thick hair down her back. She looked in the mirror at her puffy eyes and noticed a swollen red bite on her forehead, possibly from a scorpion. Scorpions thrived in the dry terrain here, making homes in coconut fronds or rock walls. You always checked your shoes or hat or whatever before putting them on. Served her right for falling asleep in the sand.

Joni was late, and Lu went onto the lānai to wait. With waves like this, they wouldn't be able to swim out and look

for manta rays, but they could at least dip. Maybe even body-
surf if it wasn't too big. After about ten minutes, she decided
to follow Joni's orders. She climbed the steps to the top floor
and knocked softly. There was no answer. Not wanting to
wake the whole floor, she eventually gave up and made her
way to the beach.

A thick blanket of clouds brought dead calm to the air. It
was already sticky and warm. No sign of the sun. Lu didn't
find Joni on the beach, either. She swam in the middle of the
bay. The water had come halfway up the beach in the night.
Something about the morning felt off-kilter, but she couldn't
put a finger on it.

Back in the room, she sat down and tried to write. Nothing
at all wanted to come out and it felt like wringing water from
a stone. While her Kona coffee percolated, she willed ideas to
pour forth. She read through her notes on the fishing fiasco,
and wrote two sentences. Scratched those out and wrote another. Pretty soon, the page was covered in black lines.

The hotel was a brilliant feat of imagination. An Oceanic
art museum. A staff full of aloha. Even the leaves and the
flowers welcomed you. Wealthy people would flock here
for years to come. The current guest list was proof of that.
But what Lu realized was that maybe Russi had been right;
it was the people behind the hotel who she was most interested in. She thought about Jerry and Sunny. But even more
than that, she was drawn to Matteo Russi himself. American
icon, shell-shocked veteran with a complicated story waiting
to be told. War heroes had been celebrated for their bravery,
but what about twenty years later? How were they faring?
Sunset magazine was not the place for that kind of story. But
that was what she wanted to write.

The phone rang, startling her.

"Hello?"

"Miss Freitas, it's Stanley. Is Joni there with you by any chance?"

"No. We were supposed to swim, but she never showed up. I came up and knocked on her door, but she didn't answer, so I went without her."

Again.

"So, you haven't seen her this morning?" he repeated.

"Nope."

The line went dead. Twenty minutes later, it rang again. It was Russi. "Meet me in the lobby."

Lu looked at the clock. In half an hour, they were supposed to leave for Waimea. She wanted to flesh out this story more. "I'll be down at ten."

"You might want to come now."

She threw on her jeans, a plaid shirt and cowboy boots and ran down the stairs. Russi was leaning on the railing eating a banana and watching two women in swimsuits and heels stroll by below.

"What's up?" she said.

He turned. "Whoa, cowboy. What happened to your face?"

"I fell asleep on the beach after our game," she said, fighting the urge to scratch.

He glanced around, but no one was paying them any attention. "So, I was down here getting the paper and I heard Stanley Welch arguing with the front desk lady about getting a key to Joni's room. When she told him they don't give out keys, he got all worked up, saying she's missing. The lady said she'd send someone up to check on Joni."

Lu's immediate thoughts were about Joni, but a part of her also wondered why Russi would let her in on this. The more time she spent with him, the more he surprised her.

He went on. "I waited down here. When the bellman came

back, I heard him tell the lady that Joni's stuff was there and to let Rockefeller know."

"She's probably out for a walk," Lu said, while at the same time feeling a thread of apprehension loop around her.

"Stanley said he looked everywhere."

"On the whole property? I doubt that. She could have hiked down to Hapuna, or up toward Spencer."

"Joni's not the kind of girl to go off hiking by herself. She needs people around her. Haven't you noticed that?" he said.

"How do you suddenly know so much about Joni?" Lu asked.

He looked down at blue tile. "We go back a ways."

"What does *that* mean?"

"It means I know her enough to know that," he said.

An understanding came over Lu. "You and Joni dated, didn't you?" With looks like his, it was no surprise women threw themselves his way, but somehow Joni did not seem his type. Way too young and moody. But what did she know?

"*Date* is not the right word."

"Screwed?"

He flinched. "I took her out a few times when she came to New York. We met at a dinner and she and I were the only two single people there."

A moment later, Mr. Rockefeller came down the steps. He, too, was dressed in his finest *paniolo* attire—faded jeans, blue checkered shirt and a tall Stetson. He beelined to a woman at the front desk and exchanged a few words. Russi approached, Lu right behind him.

"Excuse me, I couldn't help but overhear Stanley earlier. Has Miss Diaz been located yet?" Russi asked.

LSR looked pained. "I think the man might be making a mountain out of a molehill. He seems a bit—how should

I say it—overbearing. But to be sure, I'll alert Mr. Button-wood to put out feelers."

He was right about Stanley, but Lu still felt uneasy. "I know she was looking forward to going up the mountain. She told me she loves horses. She knows to be here at ten," she said.

"We'll regroup then," Mr. Rockefeller said, waving to one of his security guards.

She thought about the couple in the water. Could the woman have been Joni? Maybe she was holed up in the room with some unknown male guest. It wouldn't be out of the question. Though, so far, Lu hadn't seen any solo men. Not that she went around looking, but as an unattached woman, you noticed these things.

Russi seemed to share her concern, because he said, "Let's do a sweep before we go. You take the point and the beach, and I'll take the hotel."

They split up, and Lu passed the Dining Pavilion and walked down the long path toward the point, which then hairpinned back down to the north end of the bay. She scanned the rocks, the beach and the water. Only a couple people were standing in the shore break, looking unsure about jumping in. A strong rip tore up the middle of the bay.

On the beach, she rolled up her jeans and hurried across the sand, scanning for towels or shoes or some kind of sign that Joni might have been there. But there was nothing, only scattered coral, a small cowrie and a few twisted pieces of driftwood. Coming back from the far end, she walked along the berm. Sandy grass and trees went back from the beach to a cliffy area covered in kiawe. Nothing.

Russi was waiting for her in front of the Dining Pavilion. "If she's here, she's in one of the rooms. Possibly passed out from an all-nighter," he said.

"What if she left without telling anyone?"

"With all her stuff in the room? I doubt it. If you haven't noticed, Joni is bright and charming, but she's a lost soul," he said.

"I sensed something."

"I felt for her, you know? Fame like she had couldn't be easy, especially at her age. She told me what a messed-up childhood she had. She immigrated from Tijuana—drunk mom, and a bunch of brothers who lived on the wild side. She dropped out of school and hit the road just to escape. Her and her guitar."

"Wow, so you did spend some time with her," Lu said.

"Joni was high as a kite the first night I met her. Told me her whole life story under an Ansel Adams photograph. More than I wanted to know, really. She was lucky I didn't print any of it, but she told me I could if I wanted to."

So he did have a heart.

"I know. I had the same feeling with her. Like I wanted to protect her," she said.

"Seems like she was on a path of self-destruction," Russi said.

"Do you think she would have done something stupid?" Lu said, looking at the beach again and half expecting to see Joni appear.

"I don't know, but I have a bad feeling," he said, lifting up his camera and snapping a shot of Lu, right in her face.

"What was that for?" she said.

"Documenting what I'm guessing is going to be a big story."

"Why me?"

"Your expression says it all. I don't know that I can explain it. Years of studying people. That's what it takes. And when the moment moves me, I shoot away."

In the lobby, the group assembled. Big Joe and the senator both had the same cowboy hat on, and the wives had not a hair out of place. Mrs. Carlsmith was the only one in a dress.

"I leave the hard stuff to the men. Give me a beach towel and a book any day. I'm just going along for the ride," she said with a sweet smile.

Somehow, word had spread that Joni Diaz was missing. Mrs. Rockefeller milled about, assuring them that LSR had it handled. Someone was going door to door to all the rooms inquiring. Trucks were lined up outside to take the group up the hill, but they were waiting on Mr. Rockefeller. Some on wooden benches in the circle, others in the lobby. You could sense the impatience as the time went by. Joni was infringing on their adventure. How rude of her.

"It feels wrong to leave when a member of our group is missing," Lu said to Russi, off to the side.

"It's gonna be interesting to see how this all plays out."

Ten minutes later, Mr. Buttonwood came around and informed them that Mr. Rockefeller would not be accompanying the group to Parker Ranch. "Miss Diaz's whereabouts are still unknown and he needs to tend to the situation."

Lu turned to Russi. "I'm staying."

He seemed to be weighing what to do, then said, "We'll stay here and do what we can to help."

Lu wanted to hug him.

"I'm afraid there's not much any of you can do right now. I suggest you all go to the ranch. If she's still missing when you come back, then we'll sound the alarms."

Mrs. Rockefeller, bless her heart, said, "I should think that those who want to go should go, and those who want to stay, stay. Laurance will be here."

No one else knew Joni personally, so though they expressed concern, they all piled into the trucks and left.

"Now what?" Lu asked.

"We go find her manager, and get his take."

Though it was still morning, they found Stanley down at

the beach bar gesturing wildly as he spoke to Jerry. "Theoretically, how far could someone go up and down this coast by foot?"

Jerry, who was slicing chilled lemons, calmly said, "There are old Hawaiian trails that go pretty much around the whole island—or used to, at least. But it's not easy going. Between the lava, the kiawe thorns and the sun, most people don't get too far."

Jerry greeted them, but Stanley kept talking. You could hear the desperation in his voice. "What about the water? If you got swept out, where would you end up? Joni could swim, but she was no Olympian."

Jerry looked out at the water. "Right now, it's running straight out to sea. After that, it all depends on the tide and the wind and the current. Every day is different out there."

Stanley seemed to just notice Lu and Russi. "How come you two are still here?"

"We wanted to see if we could help," Lu said.

Russi pulled out a stool and sat. "Where do *you* think Miss Diaz is?"

"If I knew that, I wouldn't be down here picking this guy's brain, would I now?" Stanley said, blowing a greasy lock of hair off his forehead.

"You knew her better than any of us. Do you think she'd have just left without telling anyone?" Lu asked.

"You never know with Joni, but I saw her last night before she went to bed. We had a glass of brandy together in her room. She was already in her robe. Said she was tired from the long day, and I left. We had plans for coffee this morning after her swim with you," he said, eyeing Lu.

"So, let me rephrase my question. Are you worried that Miss Diaz has accidentally gotten into trouble—maybe out in the water? Do you think she left the premises on purpose, or do you think she may have done something stupid?" Russi said.

Stanley looked pissed all of the sudden. "Now hang on. The last bloody thing we need is the press all over this. I'm talking to you two as friends of Miss Diaz. You don't have my permission to print any of this. Not a word."

Lu had never been in a position like this, where she was actually part of the story, not just the one writing about it.

"No one here is going to jump the gun, so don't worry about that. Miss Freitas and I just want to help. But if Joni is genuinely missing, a story will come out whether you like it or not. So, prepare yourself," Russi said.

Stanley sat on the stool next to Russi, looking thin and deflated. "You two had a thing. You weren't together last night, were you?" He was a small man with a thin mustache and a big nose. He wore bell-bottoms and gold-rimmed glasses. He also worshipped Joni to a fault.

"Negative. I was playing chess with Miss Freitas here."

Lu figured it was time to mention the couple in the water. "After we played, I went for a walk on the beach. It was such a nice night I lay down to look at the stars and ended up falling asleep. When I woke up, I heard a man and a woman's voices. They were in the water."

Stanley glared at Russi. "Maybe that's why she wanted me out. You sure you two didn't go for a midnight swim?"

"Look, man, I took Joni out a couple years ago, a couple of times. That's it."

Lu stuck up for him. "Mr. Russi does not swim. So, it wouldn't have been him. It was probably just some young newlyweds, but I figured I'd mention it, in case."

In case what?

"We should see what's missing from her room. Shoes,

purse, that kind of thing. That would help determine where we should look," Russi said.

Stanley looked doubtful. "If they'll let us."

Uncle Jerry chimed in. "If I were you, I'd send a team out to search up and down the coast. If you get off the trail in places, it can be easy to get turned around, especially if you're in the kiawe."

Lu remembered crawling around with her cousins hunting for petroglyphs. There were a whole bunch scattered up and down the coast, old Hawaiian carvings in the *pahoehoe*—the smooth lava. Canoes and fishhooks and men holding paddles, or geometric patterns and dots and circles that were said to commemorate births and other life events. The petroglyph field near Puako was hard to find and she recalled it being sweltering and full of bees. Kiawe thorns had poked through her shoes in many places, and once there, all she'd wanted to do was go jump in the ocean. Pretty soon, they realized they were going in circles, and it felt like hours before they found their way out.

LSR was in his office with Mr. Buttonwood and Keith Kanuha, head of security. As soon as he saw Lu, he waved them all in.

"Folks, I heard you had stayed behind. That's good of you. I need you keep this all private until we either find Miss Diaz or have to call in the police. Preferably the former," he said.

"She'll turn up. They always do," said Mr. Buttonwood, looking smug.

Lu felt like hitting him. "We can't assume that."

"Have you checked the airport? In case she decided to hightail it out of here for some reason," Russi said.

"We did. They haven't seen her. Nor did she book a flight."

Stanley crossed his arms over his chest. "We need to send out a search party ASAP."

"Do any of you have insight into what may have caused her to disappear? It would be helpful to know what kind of frame of mind she was in," Mr. Rockefeller asked.

"Do we think she'd try and off herself? That's what you mean, isn't it?" Stanley said.

"I didn't say that, but we may as well put everything on the table."

They all looked to Stanley, who suddenly seemed jumpy and twitchy. "I'm not getting into her personal stuff, but I would not put it past her to do something rash. Joni could be impulsive, especially when under the influence."

Under the influence of what, was the question.

LSR stood up and walked over to a big aerial photo on the wall of the whole area. "Do you want to search first and then call the police if we don't find her? Or call the police now? I'd rather be safe than sorry, but it's your call."

"Search, then call," Stanley said.

23

THE NEWS

Oʻahu, 1943

Matteo's absence had left an indent in her heart. Every night, Isabel leafed through the photo album and revisited their outings. As much as she appreciated the pictures of her and Walt, she craved one of Matteo. Only in her mind could she conjure up that sly smile that went up on just one side, the soul-searching eyes, the kindness that radiated off him. Gloria came and went, but Isabel didn't feel like doing much other than working and translating.

"You have that whole album and not one photograph of Matteo?" Gloria said one night, curling up next to her and sipping a gin and tonic, her favorite drink—when she could get ahold of a bottle of gin. They were hard to come by.

"He doesn't like his picture taken."

"Why not?"

"He says it's bad luck. A pilot superstition, I guess."

"Go figure. Jean Aubrey's husband is a pilot and he sticks a ratty stuffed owl behind his seat on every single flight. Believes with every ounce of his being that he needs that owl to keep him alive. As if a stuffed owl has any real effect," Gloria said, downing the rest of her drink and wiping her mouth. "Men do the darnedest things."

Isabel laughed. "And they call us the weaker sex."

"Smarter sex is what we are. Speaking of," Gloria said, lowering her voice. "Can I run something by you?"

"Of course."

"I know it's probably nothing, but last night when I was at Dickie's I read something that I wasn't supposed to and now wish I hadn't. You know me, I like to stick my nose in other people's business. In this case, I saw a letter on his desk and my eyes honed in. I didn't mean to read it, but I couldn't stop—it was clearly a woman's handwriting. The letter was from someone named Nancy Kuehn and she mentioned ship locations and photographs and something about the Japanese consulate. At first, I skimmed over that, looking for signs of who this Nancy person was, worried that Dickie might be two-timing me. He was in the shower and my heart was hammering like mad. In the end, Nancy told him she loved him and couldn't wait to see him at the Lanikai overlook and she'd give him the envelope then. I wanted to go back and read the first part, but the shower turned off," Gloria said, all in one breath.

Isabel was not entirely surprised about the girl, but the bit about the Japanese consulate, now that was interesting. "Did you get to read the rest?"

"No, because Dickie was coming out. But the letter was dated November 1941. So whoever this Nancy person was, was in the past."

"I'd be less worried about Nancy than the other part."

"Do you think he could be a spy?" Gloria said.

"If he were a spy, they'd have rounded him up already. But it does sound suspicious."

That seemed to appease Gloria. "That's what I thought. But Dickie is a die-hard patriot, he would never."

"Remember you thought he was talking German in his sleep?"

"I can't be sure it was German, though."

"You seemed pretty sure the other night."

Gloria looked nervous. "You can never trust things that you think happen in the middle of the night, it's a proven fact. I could have been dreaming for all I know."

Isabel doubted that, but didn't press. "I'd ask around if I were you, see if anyone knows who this Nancy person is."

"In the meantime, please don't mention this to anyone."

"Who am I going to mention it to? You and Matteo are my only real friends here."

"It's just that I love Dickie and don't want anything to ruin it."

"Wouldn't you rather find out now that he's possibly shady, or having an affair? Better than five years down the road when you have three kids and a German shepherd," Isabel said.

"Not funny."

"Sorry, I didn't mean that. A poodle, then. The point is, just dig a little before you give him your whole heart."

"Too late, I already have."

Gloria poured another drink.

At work, Isabel was tiring of breathing in smoky air. Not only did her eyes burn, but the alveoli in her lungs were starting to feel stuffy. Short of breath. In her walks around the Dungeon, while pacing and thinking in an unused hallway, she had come across a handle in the wall. Unable to resist, she pulled the handle. It didn't budge. But handles did not exist for no reason, so she tried again, leveraging her whole weight. When it finally gave, a vent opened and a gust of fresh air swooped in. She couldn't wait to inform Hudson.

"Excuse me, sir, but think I've found a vent to the outside," she said.

He looked at her as though she were crazy. "There are no vents to the outside down here. You must be dreaming."

"I don't think I am. When I opened it, fresh air whooshed in."

"Miss Cooper, stick to the work at hand," he said dismissively.

She went back to her desk, but slowly over the course of the morning, the stale air began to thin out and freshen. She could see the TA guys and the maps on the walls.

Ziegler noticed. "Someone leave the door open?"

"Negative. I just checked it."

"I opened a vent," Isabel said.

"What vent?" Denny asked.

Pretty soon, Hudson came over. "Show me the vent you were talking about."

She walked him to the dim hallway, where the air was now scrubbed clean. Denny had followed, as had Huckleberry, Jones and some of the others. She demonstrated opening it. It certainly wasn't cryptanalysis. But they all seemed dumbfounded. Leave it to a group of men to ignore what was right in front of their faces.

Isabel summoned courage and said, "This is why you need me. A man and a woman's mind think differently. I see things from another angle and that could come in useful someday."

Hudson looked put on the spot, but surprised her by saying, "You just might be right about that."

Denny mumbled under his breath, "Fucking A."

One point for the females.

★ ★ ★

For the next two days, radio traffic had picked up and they were spending every waking hour either trying to decode messages or working on the I1 materials. Isabel stayed late in the Dungeon, and when she returned, Gloria was either out with Dickie or asleep. Truth be told, she was thankful for the work, which kept her mind occupied. On Friday evening after work, Isabel found a note on the table, slid under the bowl of bananas.

Izzy,

Dickie is taking me with him to the Big Island! Lucky thing he has a general friend who is well connected. I know no other details other than I am bursting with excitement at the prospect of a whole weekend on a remote beach, war be damned! P.S. I did find out something curious. Tell you when I get back.

G

The weekend dragged. Skies spewed down a drizzly rain, and Isabel only left the house to grab dinners in the mess hall. She thought about Dickie and the letter and wondered what Gloria had discovered. Probably not much, if she was still willing to fly away with him. The dilemma for Isabel was that as much as she wanted to like Dickie, she still didn't. Especially after the chess game and how he'd been such a sore loser, knocking down her king like that. Then on the drive home, acting as though nothing had happened. Maybe it was all in her head.

Sunday night, she waited up as late as she could, playing chess against herself and analyzing moves. Gloria never arrived. She finally went to sleep telling herself that Gloria had probably stayed with Dickie. In the morning, Isabel left for work with an uneasy feeling. It was not like Gloria to miss work. But then, maybe she'd packed her uniform.

Isabel felt jumpy. Not hungry. She downed two cups of coffee, which made things worse. At twenty past nine, the door swung open and a policeman came in. Jones was up in a flash, exchanged a few words with the man, then pointed toward Isabel. Denny was lost in his work, but Ziegler looked up.

"Everything all right?"

Isabel shivered. "I don't think so."

Jones waved her over. Isabel dropped her pencil and rushed over. "Miss Cooper, this is Detective Lopes. He wants to speak to you about your roommate."

Her mouth went dry. "Is Gloria okay?"

Lopes motioned toward the door. "Let's go outside, shall we?"

She skipped every other step and at the top followed him to a nearby bench under a yellow shower tree. They didn't speak, but from the quiet way he moved, and his solemn face, she already knew something terrible had happened to Gloria.

Isabel sat on the sun-split wood. "Tell me," she said.

"Miss Moreno was swept out to sea on the Big Island and is presumed dead. I'm sorry," he said.

The way he spoke reminded her of one of those Hawaiian radio announcers, and Isabel felt as if she were listening to a detective show. The kind that Gloria often had playing in the background. She felt the all-too-familiar pain spread through her body like spilled fuel, lit by a tossed match. Gloria was too young and too beautifully alive to be gone. There were already enough people dying in the war. Drowning while on holiday was not part of the deal.

"*Presumed* means you aren't sure, doesn't it?"

"Unfortunately, in the case of Miss Moreno, we are sure. She was last seen being sucked out a channel into huge surf, waving for help. That was yesterday morning."

Isabel vividly remembered the channel at Goat Island and how the ocean had tossed her around like a hollow stick, lifting and rolling and slamming. Water cared not who or what you were. If it hadn't been for Matteo, she wouldn't be here now. Still, her mind refused to accept the news.

"How do you know she's not washed up on some beach, stranded?"

He placed a big, brown hand on hers. "That coastline that side is jagged lava, cliffs. And the few beaches were checked—will still be checked—for her body. I'm sorry, Miss Cooper."

Body.

Such an awful word. They used it for her mother, they used it for Walt. As if somehow you could separate the body from the person. She already felt like a girl with only half a heart, and now this would leave her with even less of one. People just kept dropping out of her life, and it wasn't fair.

Rage swept over her. "Can you tell me the circumstances that led to this? Why was Gloria out in huge surf to begin with? She was a timid swimmer. And what does Dickie have to say?"

"The two of them were in the shallows, where it was calm. A rogue set came out of nowhere and held him down. When he came up, she was already halfway out the channel," he said.

"Did he try to rescue her, for heaven's sake?"

"He did."

"What about others? Surely someone could have."

"There was no one else around."

She wanted to keep probing, keep him talking, as if that would somehow delay the finality of the news. But that would be futile. Death was as final as it came. Isabel put her face in her hands and cried. Jagged sobs tore into her body. Tears wet her cheeks. Lopes handed her a handkerchief and sat next to her quietly. He'd obviously done this before.

"Was Dickie hurt at all?" she asked.

"A few bad scrapes, and he's pretty shaken up. You may want to check on him. Were you two friends?" he said.

Isabel hesitated. "Just through Gloria. I haven't spent much time with him."

"How long had Miss Moreno been dating Major Thompson?"

The passage of time had blurred, but when she thought back, it had only been about two months since the Peacock Tavern. "Not long, since mid-January. But she was with him every chance she got."

"Any trouble between the two of them?"

His question caught her off guard, knocking loose the edgy feeling that had been circling around her consciousness.

"Not that I know of. Why?"

Should she mention the letter?

"Just procedure."

The house was hollow as one of those empty cone shells they'd found on the beach. Feeling the effects of the one-two punch of Matteo leaving and now the unimaginable loss of Gloria, Isabel was at a complete loss for what to do. She pulled out the chessboard and rotely moved the pieces around, while her mind replayed her own near drowning over and over again. But instead of her own eyes, she was looking out through Gloria's.

A little while later, Linda and Malia and a few other women from Gloria's work showed up, red-faced and puffy-eyed and bearing flower lei. They hugged, they cried, and Malia set up a smiling photograph of Gloria on the table, and hung the lei over it.

"Give me your hands," Malia said.

They all obliged and Isabel found a small measure of comfort in the soft skin of Linda's and Madge's hands. Malia chanted something in Hawaiian, then switched over to English. *Dear Heavenly Father, we pray that our dear friend went swiftly into Your arms, and that she is now resting peacefully and without fear or pain. We ask that You provide her family and Dickie the strength they will need to get through this devastating time. And we thank You for blessing us all with her presence in her short time on earth. Our dear Glory was special and we will never forget her. Amen.*

"Have any of you spoken to Dickie?" Isabel asked after wiping the tears from her eyes.

"No, but I asked Vern if we could visit. He told me maybe in a day or two. Dickie's a real mess. Banged up and unable to eat or sleep," said Linda, who had struck up a friendship with Vern after their night at the bar.

"I'd like to think he would come by the house when he's ready," Isabel said.

Malia agreed. "One would hope."

"I can't even imagine what that poor man is going through. Grief does strange things to people, remember that when you see him," Linda said.

Wasn't that the truth.

The sadness came in waves and dredged up the old pain of losing her mother and Walt. She felt unhinged, alone and breakable. Hadn't she already reached her quota of loss for a lifetime? She felt like running outside and standing in the yard, screaming up into the heavens. *Enough! You hear me? How much can one heart take?*

Four days later, Isabel tired of waiting. She needed to hear what happened from his own mouth. Dickie and Vern lived together in a cottage on the other side of Pearl and she headed over as soon as she was done with work. She walked along the waterfront where she could, shoulders toasting in the late-afternoon sun. If you didn't count all the warships, the place was as pretty as they came. Dickie's cottage was set back from the road, painted crispy white and tucked under a shower tree. His Buick was parked out front.

Isabel called hello as she walked up a paved pathway to the house, and stepped loudly on the wooden steps, so as not to surprise anyone. It was quiet inside, no voice and no radio. She knocked on the side of the screen door. There was no sign of life, but she thought she heard the faint thud of footsteps.

"Dickie, are you here? It's Isabel," she said.

No one answered.

"Vern?"

Still, nothing. It wasn't out of the question here to leave your house wide-open when you weren't home, but his car was out front. She got a bee in her bonnet. If Dickie was in there and ignoring her, that was plain wrong. Yes, he was the one who witnessed the drowning, but Gloria was her roommate and Isabel's heart was broken, too.

"I loved Gloria, too, you know. Please talk to me."

A gust of wind opened the door and then banged it shut. Dust scattered in her face. She was just about to leave when a shadow moved in the house. Dickie was suddenly at the door. He looked like hell. A big gash on his cheekbone and dark purple bags under his eyes, the kind that show up after months of missed sleep or sickness. But it was his expression that fixed Isabel to the step. He didn't look sad, he looked angry. Furious even.

Grief does strange things to people, she reminded herself.

"What do you want?" he said in a dead voice.

"All of us girls are heartbroken over this. Devastated." Her voice went higher, quavering. "I just wanted to see how you're doing, and if there was anything you needed."

His voice cut right through her. "Gloria was my girl and she drowned on my watch—how do you think I feel?"

Isabel was stunned. "I—well—gosh, it must be really hard on you, I'm so sorry. But from what it sounds like, there wasn't a lot you could have done."

Except not have taken her swimming in the first place when the waves were up.

"I swam out after her, if that's what you mean. But once she went under, she never came up again. I was out there flailing around, almost drowned myself, except I made it to the rocks and dragged myself up, urchins and all." He held up his forearms, covered in cuts and scratches and black spots, which she knew to be *wana* spines.

"How did you get back to shore?" Isabel said.

"I had to scale the lava barefoot back to the beach, then hike a half mile to where the Jeep was. By the time I reached the authorities there was no chance in finding her alive."

"No news about her body?"

"Not a word. They told me not to expect anything. When people go missing here, they rarely find them. Too much current or caves or whatever," he said, looking down at his feet.

Isabel shuddered. "Oh, heavens."

The anger in his voice had lessened some, and he said, "How much did Gloria tell you about us? I mean, did she share things with you? Girl-talk kind of stuff?"

Her mind blanked for a moment, trying to make sense of what he was asking. *And why.* "Not a lot. In fact, I hardly saw her at all since you two started dating. You know that."

His eyes bore into her. "She didn't say anything before she left?"

P.S. I did find out something curious. Tell you when I get back.

"Nothing. Why?" she asked, faking casual.

Dickie stepped closer, and she caught a whiff of liquor. "Just curious. I was planning on asking her to marry me, and I think she may have overheard Vern and I discussing it. Now, I guess we'll never know."

"No, she never mentioned it."

Surely Gloria would have mentioned overhearing *that*. Ninety-six percent of what came out her mouth pertained to Dickie. He was her sun and moon and everything in between.

Looking peaked, he began rubbing his forehead with two swollen fingers. "Miss Cooper, I feel like hell, so if you don't mind, I'm going to go lie down."

Something primal tugged at the fringes of her mind. This all felt amiss. She still had so many questions, but the strangeness of the interaction kept her quiet. Dickie closed the door and disappeared into the dark house.

24

THE LETTER

O'ahu, 1943

The diary translation was slow going, and while interesting and somewhat sad, none of the information contained inside was of much use. Isabel could only translate about two-thirds of the characters, and had suggested on more than one occasion that they bring in a Nisei to do the work. The first class had graduated almost a year ago in San Francisco, and these were men who had been raised hearing their parents speak the language. But for whatever reason, that never happened.

The more time she spent on the diary, the more conflicted she became, developing almost a fondness for the writer, whose name was Sho Ishikawa. Young and observant, the man spoke of missing the seasons back home, and how much he longed to walk in the woods with his sweetheart among the falling maple leaves and sunlight. He also wrote a lot about food and described in great detail his favorite types of seaweed. He seemed so unlike many of the accounts she'd heard of the war-minded Japanese sailors. Sho was a sensitive soul.

One entry in particular struck her, and though she couldn't

make out every stroke, the gist was there was no escaping the darkness and water, and that every night when he laid his head on his pillow, he was fully aware that the submarine could very well end up being his tomb. One torpedo was all it would take. He also noted that lately the whole ocean seemed to be crawling with American subs, full of *kichiku*. Ogres.

"That's because we're on to your codes, mate. They aren't as unbreakable as you thought they were," Ziegler had said when Isabel read him the entry.

As the diary went on, Shu mentioned dreams of the dead, being unable to sleep and feeling unlike himself. Isabel could only imagine. Being on a submarine would be the death of her.

All through this, she was grateful to be doing her own thing for the moment, as she was numb with pain and memories of Gloria. Getting lost in another person's life was strangely transporting. It took her out of her own sorrow. Weeks passed, and instead of the days getting lighter, they seemed to grow darker.

Meanwhile, Denny and the boys had been unspooling codes from the recovered codebook and plugging them into the IBM machine. Which meant that intercepted messages were being translated in half the time it had taken before. And yet more messages than ever were being intercepted. Everyone was in a good mood, except for Isabel, who must have been putting off a keep-away scent, because they all steered clear. She even began thinking that maybe Hudson had been right. Maybe she ought to go back to DC. Hawai'i meant nothing but heartache.

April arrived with a splash, bringing monsoon rains, spores of mold and a letter from the Pacific, addressed to

Miss Isabel Cooper. It could only be from one person. Her hands trembled as she opened it.

Dear Izzy,

As I write this, you're probably sleeping with that sweet breeze blowing in your window. We made it to our first destination, which I'm happy about. The seas were hell for a few days, with swells high as buildings. Half the guys were sick as dogs. One thing I know you would have loved were the albatross we saw along the way. Great hovering creatures full of grace. If only I should fly with such ease.

I hope you are having a little fun, aside from all that Dungeon work. Letting off steam is important, doctors' orders! Get those friends of yours to take you out and about. You'll never guess what else I've been up to. Johnny Delmonte brought a chessboard and we played the whole way here and now I'm hooked. Will you save a game for me?

So, here's the part where I make a confession: I've been thinking about you a lot, remembering our time together fondly. I've never met a girl quite like you, honest to God. Smart and kind and bold and lovely as the night sky. I hope you don't mind me saying that. I wanted to tell you before I left, but I was feeling tongue-tied. Anyway, it's getting late now. I should try and get some sleep. We'll be heading out on our first mission in the morning. More soon.

With love,
MR

Isabel read the letter slowly the first time, savoring every speck of ink. Matteo, tongue-tied? It was hard to imagine. His script was surprisingly delicate, with loops and swirls, and she could almost feel his heartbeat between the lines. She read it again and again, and finally turned off the light, the sound of his voice loud and clear. *Smart and kind and bold and lovely as the night.*

In the Pacific, radio traffic had been brisk in the Solomons. Isabel had studied a few of the maps and charts that Huckleberry had up, and memorized the important ports on each of the islands that spanned west from Papua New Guinea. Some had English names, like New Britain and New Ireland, while others retained their native names, like Vangunu or Chouiseul. No matter the island, fighting between the Allies and the Japanese had been fierce and ugly. Isabel wondered how the local inhabitants felt—if there were any —and what they thought of someone else's war in their small corner of the world.

Hudson burst in one morning, after meeting with Lawton and the brass, with news that Guadalcanal was now *Condition Very Red*, a rare status. The Japanese apparently were going on the offense again in a last-ditch attempt to capture the airstrip.

"Our ships in Ironbottom Sound have fled to safer waters, and coast-watchers are reporting swarms of enemy aircraft overhead. Little do they know that we've got every fighter plane on the island waiting to greet them," he said.

Though Matteo could have gone anywhere, chances were good he was somewhere in the vicinity. Knowing he was part of the fighting gave a new urgency to every bit of news, every message.

Huckleberry was hopeful. "They're signing their own death warrant. Without troops on the ground, even if they did control the airspace, it won't be enough."

It was a tense several days, with news coming in about fierce dogfights, a sunken destroyer, a US tanker and a half dozen lost fighters. Isabel felt sick to her stomach and shaky. Being this close to all the intel was not a good thing in this case. She'd rather not know the ins and the outs. But every time she thought she was about to completely fall apart, an invisible hand propped her up.

She still had work to do.

Every night, before drifting off to sleep, Isabel's mind returned to her discussion with Gloria about the letter on Dickie's desk. She had tried to convince herself that it was nothing, just old romantic correspondence. But the mention of the Japanese consulate gnawed at her. Was there enough to go to the police and ask them to look into Dickie? Would they blow smoke in her face and laugh? She should have said something that first day, but was so stunned she hadn't been thinking clearly. In the morning paper, however, she read something that turned her blue.

AXIS SPY OTTO KUEHN SENTENCE COMMUTED

The German national was convicted of unlawfully obtaining information affecting the national defenses and disclosing such information to the Japanese Consulate in Honolulu. Originally, Kuehn was to be shot by firing squad, but his sentence has been commuted to fifty years of hard labor. He will be transferred to the US Penitentiary at Leavenworth, Kansas. Kuehn is a member of the Nazi party, and had been in Hawai'i since 1935. The FBI had been keeping an eye on him due to lavish lifestyle with no real job, and his apparent interest in befriending US military personnel. He was arrested two days after the attack on Pearl Harbor.

Nancy Kuehn was the name Gloria had mentioned in the letter. There were hardly German nationals crawling the streets of Honolulu. Kuehn could not be a common name here. Isabel decided to visit Detective Lopes first thing, whether he took her seriously or not. In the meantime, she called Linda and Malia and asked if Gloria had mentioned anything about a Nancy Kuehn. Both said no.

At half past eight, Isabel drove Linda's car, which was big as a boat, to the Honolulu Police Department building on Merchant Street, a white building that looked more country club than police station. Ever since martial law had been declared, the police fell under the military. Either way, she was anxious.

Lopes seemed surprised to see her, and escorted her back to his office, a tiny green-floored space overlooking the street. They were eye level with the top of a coconut tree.

"What's this about, Miss Cooper?" he said as soon as they sat down.

Unsure of where to begin, she said, "I know I should have mentioned this when you came to the house, but I didn't think anything of it until I read the paper yesterday and connected the name."

"What name?"

She told him about the letter and Gloria's note about finding something curious, and then reading about Otto Kuehn. True, Gloria hadn't mentioned what the curious something related to, but Isabel knew. The suspicion about Dickie felt like an itch in the middle of her spine, one she couldn't quite reach.

Lopes swigged his coffee. "You got a copy of this letter?"

She shook her head. "It was on his desk. She didn't take it. But I'm betting that Nancy Kuehn is Otto's daughter or relative."

"Accusing someone of being a spy is a serious offense. You sure you want to go down this road?" he asked.

"I have no idea if Major Thompson is a spy. I just want you to look into it."

"Thompson has already been investigated. Like I said the other day, it's procedure. His story checks out," he said, opening a file and leafing through the pages.

"But this is new information."

"Bring me the letter and then we'll talk."

Isabel felt her cheeks heat up. "You asked me the other day if there was any trouble between Gloria and Dickie. If she approached him with this, there could have been."

He stood and tugged up his belt. "I'll make a note in the file."

"Can't you at least search his house?"

"This is a simple drowning. I'm sorry for the loss of your friend, but the case is closed."

"This case will never be closed. Not in my book," she said before storming out.

On the eve of April 13, a storm blew in from the south, rattling windows and sending the trees into a frenzy. Isabel had been trying to catnap before her graveyard shift, but sleep would not come. As she had so many times, she unfolded the letter from Matteo and read it. If Gloria had been here, Isabel knew she'd never hear the end of it. But Gloria was not here, and all Isabel had were letters to keep her company.

She pulled her hair into a tight ponytail at the base of her neck, stepped into her uniform and started out. Branches were scattered across the ground. Halfway to the admin building, a clap of thunder sent her two feet into the air, followed immediately by raindrops as big as fish. Isabel put her coat over her head and ran the rest of the way, but still ended up drenched. It seemed to be a common occurrence in Hawai'i.

Ziegler was already there, leafing through papers with his long grasshopper legs sticking out in both directions. Under the fluorescent lights, his skin looked sickly yellow. Three stacks piled up in front of him, and Isabel knew from experience he was grouping them according to importance. At least a hundred messages came through on any given shift, but only a handful were usually worth anything.

He didn't look up, but said, "So you know, they changed the additives again."

Isabel slid into her chair, already feeling defeated. "Thanks for the good news."

"My pleasure."

"Any more news out of the Solomons?" she asked.

"Things have quieted down south, but they're still gunning for New Guinea, from the looks of things. I don't need to tell you this, but treat anything out of Rabaul as urgent. Also, Yamamoto has his eye on some airfields on Bougainville, so that's another hot spot. Here, help me sort through these," he said, shoving a stack her way.

The messages had already been run though the IBM machine, and she started in on unknown code groups. Even with the recovery of the books on the I1 sub, they still had to piece together and infer meaning on most messages. Isabel's brain shifted into that in-between space, and she hummed quietly to herself. Ziegler never seemed to mind, thank goodness. Before she knew it, hours had passed. Neither had uncovered much of interest. Only a message about recent battle losses in the air attack, which were always embarrassingly exaggerated. Propaganda.

Near midnight, Ziegler got up and stalked off down the hallway, returning with the whole pot of coffee. The smell woke her right up. He filled her mug to the brim, then hovered over her for a second longer. "For what it's worth, I'm glad you stuck it out after Hudson's little talk with you. It shows gumption."

"It's not as though I had a lot of choice, but I appreciate you saying it."

For all his quirks, Ziegler was a good man.

He shrugged and handed her some new papers. "These just came."

They both returned to the papers on the desk, sipping coffee and blocking out everything else in the world. The first one was nothing more than a storm warning, but the second made her sit up straight. C–IN–C COMBINED FLEET. She did a double take and scanned through to make sure that wasn't on the From line. But the message was from C–IN–C, 8TH FLEET, SOUTHEASTERN AREA FLEET. A cold rush swam through her, causing the entire surface of her body to tingle. CINC was shorthand for Commander in Chief of the Combined Fleet of the Imperial Japanese Navy.

Admiral Isoroku Yamamoto.

The man responsible for Pearl Harbor.

For killing Walt.

Her eyes raced down the message, picking up a numbered list of times and codes for military bases—RXZ, RXE and RXP. The words *inspect* and *bomber* also popped up on a few lines. The rest still needed to be decrypted.

"Ziegler, you need to see this," she said.

Ziegler had a Do Not Disturb sign in his desk drawer that he prominently displayed while decoding messages. And even though it was just the two of them now, the sign was up.

He lifted his palm and mumbled, "Give me a minute, will you?"

"Trust me, whatever you're working on can wait," she said with more force this time.

He set his pencil down and looked over at her. "What is it?"

"It looks like a flight plan," she said, words sticking in her throat. "For Admiral Yamamoto."

His face slackened. "Come again?"

"The title of this message is CINC Combined Fleet, and it has dates and times and places, as far as I can tell. It was sent out to commanders of various air bases."

Isabel handed him the paper and his eyes danced up and down the words and code groups. He was silent for a few moments, then said, "By God, Miss Cooper, this might be the mother of all jackpots!"

"Should we call someone?" she asked.

"Call Hudson and Denny and help me get the rest."

Isabel made the calls, though couldn't say anything other than, "Sir, you need to get down here, on the double."

Most Americans knew Yamamoto as the evil face behind the war machine. The man responsible for pulling off the most daring attack in recent memory. Killing thousands. But Pearl Harbor was only the beginning, and as the months marched by, more and more blood had been shed, on his orders. There was also the poster on a wall upstairs with his picture on it that said, *I am looking forward to dictating peace to the United States in the White House at Washington.* Isabel knew that the story was likely more complicated than that, but Yamamoto represented all that she wanted gone from this world.

Not ten minutes later, Hudson burst in, with Denny on his heels. "This better be good," he said.

Denny's hair stuck up in all directions, and his shirt wasn't tucked in.

"This could be the single most important message that's

ever come through these doors. That good enough?" Ziegler said, waving the paper.

Hudson went white. "What does it say?"

Ziegler nodded to Isabel. "You caught it, why don't you do the honors?"

"Well, we're still working on it, but the message contains a detailed flight plan, with dates, times and places." She hesitated for a moment, mouth dry. "For Admiral Yamamoto, sir."

The room went blank around them. Silent as snow.

Hudson shook his head. "They'd never put that out over radio. You must be mistaken, Miss Cooper."

Ziegler cut in. "She's not mistaken, boss. The message is titled CINC Combined Fleet and there's enough there to know that this is no joke."

Denny flopped down in his chair. "Fucking A!"

"You're sure?" Hudson asked.

"As sure as I'm standing here."

They spent the next few hours, until an invisible dawn broke outside, trying to decrypt the rest of the message. Hudson wanted it as bombproof as possible when he called Lawton on the secure line. With Denny helping, they made good headway, inferring several of the code groups. The book of locations recovered from the submarine helped.

"Do you think we'll actually go through with nailing Yamamoto?" Ziegler said to no one in particular.

There had always been talk of hunting Yamamoto and taking him down. Now, the opportunity had presented itself loud and clear.

"Nimitz will do what needs to be done. The man is as sharp as they come," Denny said.

"You know if we nab Yamamoto, it'll tip them off that we're listening in. It could ruin us going forward."

"It's not up to us."

"Can you stress that, Hudson, when you talk to Lawton?" Ziegler asked.

Hudson chimed in from one of the nearby desks, where he'd planted himself. "Noted. But I can tell you this—Yamamoto will not be dictating peace from the White House anytime soon."

Isabel felt a big welling-up of emotion as she decrypted the last line. They all looked at her expectantly when she set down her pencil and slowly raised her eyes. She read the line aloud. *"In case of bad weather, it will be postponed for one day. Let's pray for good weather."*

In its entirety, the message laid out the whole day: Yamamoto leaving RR at 0600 on CHUKO, a land-based bomber, with six fighter escorts, arriving at 0800, then taking a sub-chaser to RXE, arriving at 0840. At 0940, leaving RXE by same subchaser...and on and on until 1540 arriving back at RR, aka Rabaul. Headquarters. The date was April 18. Four short days from now.

"The man is nothing if not punctual," Ziegler said.

"I still find it hard to believe they broadcast this. What are the chances?" Denny said.

Hudson took the paper and called Lawton. He then came back and said, "Miss Cooper, would you like to walk this down there with me to CINCPAC headquarters? This needs to be hand delivered."

She glanced over at Ziegler, who gave a small nod.

"It would be my honor, sir."

25

THE CALL

O'ahu, 1943

Everyone had been keeping an eye on the black secure telephone, the one to Lawton's office. So, when Hudson hung up, all he had to do was nod.

"It's on."

The whole room was watching. Excitement rippled out into the room, so thick it coated everything in the entire Dungeon. But there was a somber feel, too. Ziegler was still shaking his head about the codes, while Huckleberry high-fived Hudson and Denny and even Isabel. They all knew that this had the potential to be a decisive moment in the war with Japan.

The beginning of the end.

Once home, she collapsed into a dream-swamped sleep. In one, Isabel was flying a plane with no top on it. Wind blasted her face. Bullets whizzed past. She flew through columns of smoke so thick she tasted ash on her tongue. When she turned to check her tail, the sky was gray with enemy fighters. She was their target, and there was no escape. Nothing but water below. She woke in a sweat, drank a glass of water and fell back into a fitful sleep.

Matteo, where are you?

A letter had come two days ago, and she had already memorized his words. She went there now, in her mind.

Dear Izzy,

We're on an island now, which is all I can really say. Me and the boys spend a lot of time training and tossing the football around, and I'm still managing a few games of chess. These past few days were pretty dull, but last night we had a plane come through shooting and tearing up the trees around us. It woke everybody up lightning fast. Scared the shit out of us, but no one was hit. These enemy pilots are something else. No damns given if they live or die. Which I suppose I understand, you know?

The heat here is almost unbearable. By 0800 you're sweating your tail off and by 1000, well, you may as well call it a day. But I'm hanging in there. All that time out with Walt and with you, those are the memories that keep coming up in my head. Some days, they're like moving pictures and I watch them again and again. Those were good times, some of the best of my life.

Can I tell you something? I know this sounds crazy, but I have this feeling that something huge is right around the corner. Like the calm before the storm. I want to be ready for anything, and I want you to know that you mean a lot to me, Isabel. A real lot. Take good care of yourself.

With love,
MR

Isabel walked into work on April 17 feeling proud but anxious. Hawai'i was three hours ahead of the Solomons. Actually, it was twenty-one hours behind, but that only mattered to the clocks. Today was Yamamoto's inspection day. The Dungeon was on red alert. So far, nothing had been picked up to indicate any changes in the scheduled plan.

The other morning, Hudson had gone as far as apologizing on the walk over to Lawton's office. "I was wrong about you, Miss Cooper. Sometimes, us men, we get a little territorial about things. I'll admit I had my doubts when you first came down the chute, but I'm going to personally call Admiral Sutton and thank him for sending you."

Praise from Hudson felt good, but she wasn't here for praise. She was here for retribution. And they were so close. In regards to the ambush, word had circulated that something was afoot, but Huckleberry and a few of the boys who knew the map and knew planes were saying that it would be damn near impossible to get anywhere near Yamamoto undetected. Most everyone in the room had congregated around Huckleberry's giant map table, speculating.

"I don't know of any navy aircraft that has that range. Guadalcanal, which would be the most likely launch point—the only launch point, really—is almost four hundred and fifty miles from Ballale," Huckleberry said.

RXZ, they knew to be the airfield on Ballale Island. Yamamoto's first stop.

"What about a carrier?" asked Denny.

"None in the area."

One of the ex-pilots said, "Maybe not navy, but army. The P-38, if you added an extra tank, could do the job."

"They'd have to fly far from any islands in order not to be detected. The Japanese have eyes on almost every single one of them," said Huckleberry.

"Then they'll have to fly wide."

"I guess we'll know soon enough," Denny said.

Hudson rubbed his chin. "Sounds like a suicide mission to me. Godspeed to whoever is on this, they're going to need it."

A chill ran through Isabel. All she could think about were Matteo's words: *I have this feeling something huge is right around the corner.* Matteo was army. And he would leap at the chance for something like this. If he was in the area, he was their man. No doubt about it.

By lunchtime, she had no fingernails left. Not that she had any to begin with, but still. The extra cups of coffee didn't help, nor did Hudson's pacing and Denny mumbling curse words left and right. Isabel went back to the diary of Sho. Strangely, something about him reminded her of Walt. Just a young man, in the spring of existence, missing home and pondering life's deeper questions. Doing his best to be honorable. At the mercy of the moon and of men in high places. Lawton showed up at the door that afternoon, with a faint quiver of a smile. He marched straight to Hudson's desk and handed him a paper. Isabel watched Hudson's eyes grow wide as he read. He set it down gently, and turned to the room. "Fucking A. We got him!"

P-38s LED BY MAJOR J. WILLIAM MITCHELL USAAF VISITED KAHILI AREA. ABOUT 0930. 18 SHOT DOWN TWO BOMBERS ESCORTED BY 6 ZEROS FLYING CLOSE FORMATION. 1 OTHER BOMBER SHOT DOWN BELIEVED ON TEST FLIGHT. 3 ZEROS ADDED TO THE SCORE SUMS TOTAL 6. 1 P-38 FAILED RETURN. APRIL 18 SEEMS TO BE OUR DAY.

The whole room went crazy. Codebreakers were usually a quiet bunch, but not at that moment. At that moment, they were cheering and hooting and celebrating. The bottle of whiskey came out and toasts were made.

Victory!

God bless our boys!

Hallelujah!

Amid the party atmosphere, Lawton and Hudson stressed the utmost secrecy of this knowledge. Japan could never know. Isabel thought she would feel happier, but the weight of a man's death, no matter how reviled, pressed down on her. Yamamoto might be dead. But so was an American pilot. A life for a life. Soon, two families on both sides of the globe would receive news that would break them.

Please don't let it be me, again.

Because Isabel was not family and because there was no way to go around asking about a mission that no one even knew about, she could do nothing but wait to hear from Matteo.

It was bedtime. The moon was nearly full and crickets chirped outside her window, reminding her of home and a time before the world turned upside down. A banging on the door startled her out of her book, *The Hobbit*. She opened the door, and went to peek out, but before she could utter a word, Dickie stepped past her. She pressed back against the door, startled.

"Miss Cooper, we need to talk," he said, clomping into the middle of the room and spinning around.

For a split second, she thought maybe the impossible had happened. "Have they found Gloria?"

"No, they haven't," he said, glaring at her. "But I heard it on good authority that you were at the police department spewing nonsense about me. Is that true?"

"I went there with information I thought might be valuable to the case."

"The case? There is no case. Gloria drowned," he said, spittle on the sides of his mouth.

Isabel stayed near the door. "My understanding is that there *is* a case. There's always a case when someone dies under mysterious circumstance. Lopes asked me if there was any trouble between the two of you. And I told him what I knew."

"And what exactly is that?"

If he wanted to play mean, she would not give him a thing.

"That is none of your business."

"Don't give me that crap. When you go around telling the police I'm a goddamn spy, that is my business," he said, moving closer, then very slowly saying, "Tell me what Gloria said to you. I know she must have said something, or you wouldn't have gone to Lopes."

A twitch started up on one side of his mouth, like half of him was trying to smile. It gave her the willies. She wanted him out.

"Gloria happened upon a letter from your German friend, and she approached me about it. That's all I told Lopes. I figured he ought to know."

"So, you think I killed her, is that it?" he asked.

Isabel was trying to appear calm, but inside she was close to panic. While before, the thought that Dickie might do something violent had seemed too outlandish, now she wasn't so sure. He was staring through her, as though looking at someone on the far end of the room.

"I never implied that whatsoever. I was merely providing the detective with what he asked for."

For a moment, neither of them moved an inch. He was dog panting and perspiring and looking peaked. Isabel could not read his expression, but got the feeling that he was battling for control of his own emotions.

"Tell you what, Miss Izzy," he said, drawing out the *z*'s.

"That letter that Gloria *thought* she might have seen from Nancy was nothing more than conjecture. The FBI knows I used to work at Kuehns furniture store and I had no part in whatever he was doing on the side. Nor was it my fault that his nutty daughter took a liking to me and fancied us a couple. I never even gave her the time of day. But she was persistent."

Isabel stumbled backward, but he slid toward her, coming within an inch or two. So close she could smell the garlic on his breath. And the fear. "So do yourself a favor and stay the fuck out of this. I know people, and I know what you do down there in the Dungeon, so if you want your job and you want to stay out of trouble, you'll keep your trap shut."

Isabel stood her ground, just barely, hiding her shaking hands behind her. "Please leave, this moment, before I scream so that every neighbor within a mile can hear me."

His eyes were like wolf eyes. Wild, almost frantic. Without looking away, Dickie backed toward the door, and then slipped away into the moonlit night.

26

THE DISCOVERY

Hawai'i Island, July 1965

Lu and Russi went toward Kawaihae. They took a golf cart to the far end of the course and set off on foot through the kiawe. It was almost lunchtime, and even with the sun blocked by clouds, heat shimmered off the lava. Not far away, jagged rocks crumbled into the sea. Small coves and inlets swirled with coral heads and crashing waves. When the water sucked out, you could see the red pencil urchins, bright like flowers. There wasn't a hint of breeze. Thankfully, LSR had outfitted them with wide straw hats, canteens full of water and instructions to drink plenty or face sunstroke. Lu knew the drill.

"I don't see Joni making it more than ten feet in this," Russi said.

Before they'd left, Lu had kept expecting Joni to walk up with a towel in hand, flutter her eyelashes and say, "What's all the fuss about?" But a bellman had gone door to door knocking, and the maids checked empty rooms. The hotel had been effectively combed.

Ten minutes in and they were drenched in sweat. Twenty minutes, Lu felt her mouth turning to cotton.

"Ouch! Dammit!" Russi yelled, hopping around on one foot and lifting his other to examine the bottom of his shoe. As expected, a kiawe branch was lodged in the sole. "I remember this stuff from Pearl days. My buddy nearly lost his foot to an infection he got while hiking out from his downed plane. The Japanese didn't kill him, but a one-inch thorn almost did," he said.

"Were you there during the attack?" she asked.

He didn't answer immediately, pulling out the stick and whipping it away. "I was."

"Were you up in the air?"

"Unfortunately, not."

"I'd think it would be the other way around," Lu said.

"Not when your friends are up there getting their tails shot up by the enemy. There's no more helpless feeling in the world, I can promise you that."

"I'm sorry, that must have been hard."

"The worst. All of my flying in Hawai'i was just training for the real thing. For me, that was at Guadalcanal and in the Solomons. And...well..." His voice trailed off.

Lu knew about the Solomons and Guadalcanal, everyone did. The numerous battles, countless dead. A few Pulitzer Prizes had come out of it, as well as the book and recent film, *The Thin Red Line*. "A lot of people talk about Midway as a defining moment in the war, but I've heard that Guadalcanal was just as important," she said.

"It was the first time we were on the offensive, and boy, were we ever. You always hear about how tough the Japanese pilots were and how cunning. Course, they had their nutjobs, but that's another story. Our guys had more heart and more balls by a long shot," he said with conviction.

"I can't believe you were actually there," she said.

"You and me both, kid."

She was hoping he'd say more, but he didn't. He stood there, expectantly, waiting for her to keep walking. With the lava and ocean behind him, she realized it would make the perfect shot. Lu pulled up her camera and aimed it his way.

"Whoa," he said, reaching out and pushing the lens away from his face.

She frowned. "What was that for?"

"I don't do pictures."

"What do you mean?"

"I mean I don't have my picture taken."

"You come with a lot of rules and requirements, you know that?" she said, not even bothering to ask why.

"Yeah, well, I have my reasons."

"Sometimes it's good to reexamine your reasons. You may just find that they're outdated and no longer serve a purpose."

He marched past her and said, "I'll keep that in mind."

Soon, they reached an area where they could barely make out a trail. Toward the ocean was a steep drop, so they veered inland slightly. The clearest way was through the kiawe. With the taller trees, the air cooled. There was a desolate, stark beauty to the place. Lu felt it, and she sensed that Russi did, too, because he stopped complaining. Ten minutes later, they reached a tiny salt-and-pepper sand beach, not more than thirty feet wide.

Lu rushed down to splash some water on her face, and run her wet hands along the back of her neck and her arms. Russi hung back.

"You want some?" she asked.

"What do you think?" he said, taking off his hat.

She cupped some in her hands and walked up to him. He closed his eyes and let her splash it on his face. The moment felt oddly intimate. They drank hot water out of their canteens and discussed the next route to take. One trail, which was just a series of smooth stones, went close to the water, the other inland.

"Should we split up?" she asked.

"Nah, I don't want to have to come rescue you, too. Let's go up through the trees and come back along the water," he said.

So they did. Lu led, Russi followed.

She tried another approach to get him talking. "Did you meet any women while you were stationed in Hawai'i?"

He groaned. "I should have taken the low road."

"I'm just curious. There were so many wartime romances, it's a natural question."

"Sure, I met a lot of fine ladies."

"Anyone special?"

"As a matter of fact, yes. She was my buddy's sister and she was the smartest person I ever knew, and the most down-to-earth. A real stunner." Russi went silent for a bit, and she only heard the crunch of his boots on the lava. "We had a good time," he said quietly.

"What was her name?" Lu asked.

"Izzy."

"What happened? Why aren't you still with her?"

"Sorry, kid, you've passed your allotted questions for the day," he said.

"Oh, please. It wouldn't be a bad thing to get some of this off your chest. Think of it as practice for telling your story," she said, half turning and giving him a pleading look.

"There you go again. You ever hear the word *finesse*? It works wonders when you're trying to get information out of people. Right now, let's concentrate on our mission out here." He stopped and looked around. "Do you even know where you're going?"

"I do."

Five minutes later, they were ducking through kiawe, going in circles. Sweat dripped off the tip of her nose.

"If Joni came out here, this same thing could have happened to her," she said, then called out into the thicket. "Joni! Hello?"

Russi's T-shirt was dripping wet and clung to his arms and chest. For an old guy, he sure kept himself in shape. "If this is some cockamamie plan to get me in the water, you may just succeed," he said, fanning himself with the bottom half of his shirt.

They were all turned around, and Lu was mad at herself for letting this happen. She listened for the sound of the ocean and would have headed toward it, but a wall of gnarled trees stood in their way. Instead, they climbed down a small crack in the lava and followed it a ways until it ended at a large opening. By the time they reached it, Lu was covered in old spiderwebs.

Russi stopped. "What do we have here?" he said.

Lu stepped into the mouth of the cave and felt a burst of cooler air. "Lava tube. They're all over the place on this island. Some go on for miles."

The tunnel was almost high enough to stand in, and thirty or so yards in, the top had collapsed, creating a natural skylight.

"Joni, you in there, girl?" Russi called, his voice swallowed by rock.

The possibility of Joni making it into this off-the-beaten-path lava tube were almost nil, but something drew Lu in, anyway. "You wait here, I just want to walk to the skylight and look around."

"What's the point? Let's get out of this godforsaken forest before we cook."

"I'll be fast."

The bottom of the lava tube was mostly smooth, but she had to watch the top, where chunks of lava and root clusters hung down. The faint scent of animal poop filled the tunnel. Mongoose, probably. But there was another, older smell, one of decay and darkness. Goose bumps formed on her arms. As Lu neared the pool of light, her foot kicked something hollow. Definitely not a rock. At first she thought it was a coconut, but when she looked down, she saw the white.

She jumped back. "Oh my God!"

"What is it?" Russi yelled.

"Bones."

Her first thought was pig, but the skull, which was what she kicked, looked round. Lu had seen enough wild-boar skulls to know that they were angular and more jaw than anything. Her uncle was a big hunter and helped eradicate them from the farm now and then. She also knew that there were Hawaiian burial caves in the area, but those had been closed up with rock to preserve their contents. Crouching down, her eyes adjusted enough to see the form of a skeleton splayed out around her.

"What kind of bones?" he asked.

"Human, possibly," she said, moving carefully backward to avoid stepping on anything.

His voice grew louder. "Are we talking new bones or old bones?"

"Old. But how old it's hard to tell."

The next thing she knew, Russi was beside her. "You weren't kidding, were you? Jesus. Is this one of those Hawaiian burial caves?"

"I doubt it. There would be other things in here with the bones. Like lauhala mats or wooden bowls or even canoes. And probably more skeletons."

Russi shivered. "I got a bad case of the heebie-jeebies, like we don't belong here. We oughta split. Now we have two mysteries on our hands."

Lu walked over to the skylight and checked for a way beyond. But the rockfall blocked any chance of seeing what else might be there. "If there are more, Mother Nature has closed their tomb permanently. But this one doesn't seem that old, does it?" she said.

"I'm no expert, but no, it doesn't."

There was something unnerving about standing in a dark cave with an unknown dead person. Lu looked around for signs of clothes or jewelry or other human artifacts, and then realized that under the pile of ribs there was a reddish piece of material. She stepped away.

"This is creepy—let's go back," she said.

"What about Joni?"

"You were right, I don't think Joni would have made it ten steps off the golf course."

They somehow managed to find their way out of the thicket, and Lu tied her bandanna on a kiawe tree. Every tree and rock on this stretch of coast looked the same, and she wanted to be sure they could find the cave again. They were quiet as they stayed close to the water's edge on the way back to the hotel, Lu lost in thought about who the bones might have once been. What kind of person would be so far off the beaten path? Lost sailor? Fisherman?

When they passed the orange trees, near the Buddha statue, Russi picked one and peeled it in ten seconds flat, handing her a juicy piece of flesh. They found Mr. Rockefeller outside the Dining Pavilion talking to Mr. Buttonwood.

Russi leaned into Lu and spoke quietly. "Don't mention anything about the skeleton until we have Rockefeller alone.

We don't want to get people worked up for no reason, and skeletons have that tendency."

They approached the men. "Good afternoon, gentlemen," Russi said. "I'm sorry to report that there was no sign of Miss Diaz up north. Any luck on this end?"

"One of our guys found a pair of women's shoes on the rocks out toward the point. Stanley wasn't sure but thinks they may belong to Joni. I've called in the police."

Up until this moment, she'd been holding out hope that this was all just a big mistake. That surely Joni had taken off on a whim and would come strolling back from wherever she'd gone in time for a sunset cocktail and the green flash.

"Until we know for sure, let's not jump to conclusions," Rockefeller said.

Mr. Buttonwood excused himself, and when they told Mr. Rockefeller of their find, his face pinched up in concern. "We surveyed every square inch of this place before breaking ground. My team would have found a skeleton," he said.

She doubted it was that new.

"It's possible we were beyond the resort boundaries. We passed over an old rock wall, and got ourselves lost, which is the only reason we stumbled upon it," Lu told him.

Rockefeller shook his head, looking out on the water. "One lost, another found. Not exactly what I had planned for the weekend."

"We plan, God laughs," Russi said.

27

THE DANCE

O'ahu, 1943

Something about the interaction with Dickie dislodged something in Isabel. All that pain now reared up and leveled her. She was sick for days, feverish and nauseated, and for the first time since arriving, she told Hudson she couldn't come into work. He sounded understanding, concerned even. She had made herself more than useful, and had helped decipher one of the biggest messages of the war. But the victory felt hollow in the shadow of losing Gloria in such an unfair manner. Helplessness swarmed all around her. Death, it seemed, had been following her. Creeping in and plucking loved ones from her life at the very moment she started feeling comfortable again. *Mom, Walt, Glory.*

What was the point of everything, anyway? Living and loving meant dying and losing. The two went hand in hand. And the pain from the losing rattled your bones, squeezed the blood from your heart and turned your world dark. Matteo might be onto something—avoid love at all costs. She was done with it, quite frankly.

In desperation to block all thoughts and feelings, she read.

The Hobbit was an unusual book about a little hairy man who unexpectedly embarks on big adventures. The book belonged to Gloria, but Isabel had picked it up after running out of her own. As she turned the pages, fresh and magical words began to seep from the paper, wrapping her in their wisdom. Urging her on. There was only one thing to do: go forward and honor those who no longer could.

When she returned to work, Isabel asked the guys to ask around and see if anyone knew the name of the pilot lost in the Yamamoto mission, which they'd learned had been called Operation Vengeance. No one knew a thing. At lunchtime, she risked a visit to the mess hall to chat with the girls upstairs, and see if any of them had news. But none did.

The following day, Isabel was sitting at her desk at half past three when Jones brought her a handwritten note, folded in quarters. Her name was scrawled across the front. *Miss Cooper.* She recognized the writing right away.

"Where did you get this?" she asked.

"Some guy delivered it."

"Why didn't you come get me?"

"He said not to bother you."

"Did he say his name?"

"Negative."

"Tell me what he looked like," she demanded.

"Olive skin, about this tall," he said, holding his hand up.

"Was he in uniform?"

Jones nodded. "Army whites."

Isabel felt light-headed, breathless. She waited for Jones to go back to his desk, but now Ziegler and Denny were watching her as though she had a bird nesting on her head.

"Carry on. This is none of your business," she said.

"Everything okay?" Ziegler asked.

No one here knew a thing about her private life. It wasn't like DC, with the girls, where even in the thickest of circumstances they talked about men and intimate things.

"Fine. It's just a note from a friend."

Unable to wait another second, she opened the note.

Do you feel like dancing tonight?
If so, be ready at 1800 hours on the nose.
MR

She stared at the words. But it wasn't the words so much as the writing itself and the calloused hand that had held the pen. That hand was back on Hawaiian soil, alive and in one piece. Her whole body went slack, casting off layers of worry—and longing.

"Must be some friend," Denny said.

Her eyes filled with tears. "It is."

Isabel wore the new dress that Gloria had picked out for her on the one occasion they'd made it to the department store. Orange with pink flowers, it was the polar opposite from anything she would have chosen for herself. And that was precisely why she loved it. The dress would always make her think of Gloria, and she'd wear it until she was an old lady, if she should be so lucky.

Matteo drove up at two minutes past six, in a cloud of sandy dust. The second he turned off the motor, Isabel had no idea how to proceed. She wavered between standing in the kitchen pretending to casually notice his knock at the door, or sprinting outside and throwing her arms around him the minute he set foot on the pavement. Yes, something was definitely wrong with her.

Matteo climbed out. "Hooey!" he called, doing double time toward the house.

At the sound of his voice, all questions disappeared and she rushed to the door and tore down the steps toward him. He opened his arms and she fell into them. A strong force held them together and little by little the fear and hurt siphoned away.

"You made it," she said, speaking into his neck.

"By the skin of my teeth, but yeah, here I am."

She pulled away and looked into his eyes. "Your letter—"

He cut her off. "Turns out I had some kind of premonition, because wouldn't you know it, something big did go down."

"Can you talk about it?"

"I'm not sure you have clearance," he said, breaking into a sly grin.

She could guarantee her clearance was higher than his, but said nothing. There would be time for more talk later.

Rays of afternoon sunlight slanted around them. Trees turned golden and doves cooed softly to their mates. For now, she was content to have him here by her side.

The officers' club on the beach in Waikiki was known as Halekai: sea house. A grand white mansion with pillars and columns, decks and fancy railings and lime-green manicured lawns. Like so many other places, the military had taken it over. As soon as they parked, Matteo pulled her by the hand and did not let go. They made it onto the beach just in time to catch the sunset. A few other couples and groups had the same thing in mind.

"I swear the beach and the water and even the sunset have never been so sweet," he said, looking out at the blue glass ocean.

A coconut tree rustled behind them.

He went on. "Guadalcanal was some mad version of a dream. On one hand, the place beautiful as they come— lush jungle, fruit everywhere, blue lagoons—but on the flip side you had a well-trained enemy messing with your head, mozzies just as dangerous and, in the water, crocs longer than the boat and man-eating sharks just waiting for someone to fall in. Seemed like the whole island was designed to kill you."

"I had a feeling you were on Guadalcanal," she said.

It was his first mention of where he'd been. On the drive over, they'd spent the whole time talking about Gloria.

"Did some island hopping, but yeah, mostly. Do you know what the marines call it down there?"

"What?"

"The Green Hell."

He seemed subdued, altered in some undefinable way. The things those men saw were not something anyone should ever have to witness. They stood shoulder to shoulder and watched the sun lay down a yellow path on the water. Neither spoke. Neither needed to. Whatever was going to happen would happen.

"Come on, let's go get a cocktail," he said.

On the patio, uniformed men and decked-out women sipped drinks, talking and laughing. It was not Isabel's scene and she didn't recognize a soul. They moved past a trio of musicians playing Hawaiian music, and up to a long wooden bar. A few couples slow danced and you could feel the love drifting through the balmy air.

"What are you having?" Matteo asked.

"Surprise me?"

"Two Honolulu Number Ones," he said to the bartender.

Isabel watched the man pour copious amounts of gin, with a splash of orange and a dash of pineapple juice, into a shaker with ice, and then martini glasses. One would be plenty.

Matteo turned to her and held up his glass. "To ending this damn war."

She clinked. "I'll drink to that."

His eyes shimmered. "And to Walt. Best man I ever knew," he said.

"To Walt. Lord how I miss him. And to you coming home, Matteo. We can't forget that."

He nodded. "And to those who didn't."

It felt like they were just getting started.

"To Gloria."

There were so many people and reasons to toast, she could have kept going until her arm gave in. Or until Matteo kissed her. That was coming, she felt it in the marrow of her bones.

"To you," he said, finally taking a drink.

Isabel did the same.

Lounge chairs and coffee tables were scattered around the patio. Most of them were taken, and clusters of men played gin rummy and backgammon and chess. Women sat aside them, smoking cigarettes and talking. Their glamorous dresses and feathered hats made Isabel feel underdressed.

"You wanna play? I know you already have it in the bag, but I learned a thing or two while I was away," Matteo said.

He set up the board, and she let him go first. White. He was going to need all the help he could get, but of course she didn't tell him that. There was only one way to get better, and that was by playing people better than you. People often got a false sense of confidence with chess and stuck to playing their own level or below. Matteo would never be that kind of player. He'd lose until his hands bled if it meant winning down the road.

"Don't go easy on me, either. Swear?" he said after opening with the bishop's pawn moving two spaces.

Isabel glanced up, surprised. It wasn't a usual opening for beginners. "Swear," she said.

In defense, she played the symmetrical pawn. Matteo's eyes flickered and he made his next move swiftly. But as they went back and forth, he began to take longer pauses. He absentmindedly chewed on his pineapple as he frowned in concentration. Isabel already knew exactly where the game was headed, but kept a poker face to spare him. His tenacity was admirable. And adorable.

When she captured his queen, he shook his head slowly and shot her that killer smile. "I'm toast, aren't I?"

"You might be."

On the next move, she called checkmate.

"You ruined me. I knew you would," Matteo said.

Isabel got the distinct feeling that he wasn't just talking about the chess game.

When darkness fell, everyone made their way upstairs to a blacked-out ballroom where the music was blaring. The dance floor was already full of bodies. Matteo set their glasses on a table and pulled her onto the black-and-white tile. The song was slow, and he held her close. Isabel was acutely aware of his hip against hers and the heat of his hand on her back. The liquor had gone to her head, making her woozy and a little clumsy.

Matteo danced with confidence and a bit of swagger, and when the music picked up pace, he spun her and dipped her back. The man knew how to move. But even through the dancing, he never loosened up to his predeparture self. He seemed restless and agitated, and on more than one occasion Isabel caught him watching her. She'd thought he was going to say something, but each time he turned away.

The room was stuffy, and they danced until dripping.

When Isabel asked to take a break, Matteo led her down to the bar again.

"None for me, thanks," she said.

But he ordered her one, anyway, and gulped his down as though it were lemonade on a hot summer day. They went onto the lānai and leaned on the railing overlooking the beach. Matteo plucked a flower from the tree and slipped it behind her ear. His hand traced a line of heat down her cheek.

"I'm beat. You ready to call it a night?" he said.

"Sure," she said, swallowing disappointment.

Isabel had gone through a hundred scenarios of how things would turn out tonight, but this was not one of them. In one imagining, he'd kiss her on the dance floor; another, on the beach under starlight, and yet another on the hood of the car. But maybe she'd been sorely mistaken and reading into things. Lord knew she wouldn't be the first girl to fall for his charms.

Driving with headlight covers was not much different than driving in the dark, and Matteo had to focus on the road. Still, he seemed unnaturally quiet.

"Can I ask you a question?" she finally said.

"Shoot."

"What if I told you that I know about what happened on Bougainville."

She thought she heard him swallow.

"That's not a question," he said.

"Did you have anything to do with it?"

"For a secretary, you must have some pretty high clearance." He ran a hand through his hair. "What if I told you I did?"

They were treading on treasonous ground, and yet she knew that he already knew and now he knew that she knew. No one would be any the wiser.

"Was it you?" she asked.

"I don't think we'll ever really know. There were clouds and chaos and one guy says this and another says that. I shot up both of the Bettys, at least I thought I did. Even saw a line of smoke coming up from the jungle after it went down. But our lead guy says he made the kill, so I'm scratching my head. But I'm just thankful we completed the mission."

"Did they tell you beforehand who it was?"

"Not at first. We knew it was something big, and all Mitchell told us was to have our planes ready at 0500 and it was gonna be a long day. They'd outfitted them with extra fuel tanks and the birds were loaded with as much ammo as they could carry. He told us who we were going after that morning, and that four of us would be the attack team. He said this would be the most important mission of our lives."

He paused, and Isabel let his story sink in.

"He also gave us an out. Said none of us had to go, it was pure volunteer. We knew what we were getting into. But wouldn't you know it, every pilot on that island was gunning for the chance, and none of us was willing to give up our seat."

"Were you afraid?" she asked.

"I'd be lying if I said I wasn't. We knew our chances were a million to one. We had to loop out over open water, flying low and under strict radio silence. We had our course laid out, with airspeed, fuel and weather predictions all specified with no room for error. And if we were lucky enough to make it there and do the job, we still had to fly back. But Mitchell anticipated every possible detail. That man is my hero."

The car rolled to a stop in front of her house, and he killed the engine. Even in the dim light, Isabel could tell that his hands were gripping the wheel. She reached over and placed her hand on his shoulder.

"You guys are all heroes."

Isabel might have had a hand in it, but the pilots were the ones with their lives on the line. Matteo's sacrifice meant everything.

"Yeah, that's not what the brass says."

"What do you mean?"

"You ever heard the term *shit flows downhill*? What you probably don't know is that one of our guys broke radio silence at the end of the mission, and then two of them spilled all to a reporter at the AP. Our censors stopped the story, but now all of us are in hot water."

"For completing your mission?"

"The leaks on this mission were all over the place. Truth be told, I don't blame Nimitz and King for being pissed."

"I'm sorry."

A dense silence fell between them. She could have tried to think of something smart or comforting to say, but instead she slid toward him, moving so their faces were almost touching. Before she knew it, Matteo reached up and ran the side of his hand along her cheek, tender as moonlight. Heat swirled around her navel, weakening her limbs.

"You sure you want this?" he asked.

"Very."

He kissed her with sure lips and hot breath, holding softly the back of her head. Her heart beat madly. Matteo moved his tongue lazily, exploring and testing and sending sparks along her spine. His breath tasted of liquor and peppermint. Isabel rested her hand on his chest. When they finally broke apart, they looked at each other, almost surprised. Neither spoke.

He grabbed her hand and pulled her out of the car. At the front door, he had her pinned to the wall and was kissing her as if his life depended on it. Isabel fumbled to unlock it, and they fell through. With her eyes closed, her head felt a little swimmy, so she kept them open. She'd had too much to drink. Maybe he had, too.

"I thought about you while I was gone. Did I mention that?" he said.

"You did."

"About every other second or so."

They were in the bedroom now, on the bed. Window shades down. A candle lit. Matteo on top of her, holding himself up with one arm. Hair tangled in his fingers. His other hand ran down her ribs, slowly circling her breasts and then, light as a feather, tracing over her lower abdomen. He reached beneath her and cupped her rear. Squeezed her toward him. Her heart felt raw and open and full.

He kissed her deeply. Rough with want. Isabel savored his touch. Shivered. He ran his hand slowly up her forearm, stopping abruptly when he got to the watch. His mouth went slack. He rolled off her, laying his head back on the pillow and sighing.

"What is it?" she said.

"Shit," he mumbled.

"What's wrong?"

"I can't do this."

Isabel sat up, confused. "Do what? Kiss me?"

He put his face in his hands, then rubbed his head vigorously until his hair stood on end. "There's something I haven't told you and it's been eating a hole in me. Wouldn't you know it, I promised myself I'd tell you that first day at the Pali, and then every time after that, but whenever I saw you the words just froze up in my mouth. I knew if I told you, you wouldn't have any interest in getting to know me."

A feeling of dread snaked through her. "Please tell me what you're talking about," she said.

"It's my fault Walt died."

"I don't understand," she heard herself saying.

There were tears in his eyes, and he stared at the wall as he spoke, remembering. "On the night of December 6, we went to a dance at the officers' club. There was no shortage of booze, and no shortage of girls. After the dance, Walt and most of the guys went and played cards, but me and Jimmy Ortiz went to Waikiki with two of the girls."

Of course he did.

He stopped, looked at her. "I know what you're thinking."

"Just keep going," she said.

"We ended up staying over at one of the girls' houses, a big place on Diamond Head. We were so impressed with ourselves, dumbasses. I woke up to the sound of engines and gunfire and I knew we had blown it. We raced to Wheeler doing ninety and change. Pearl was burning when we passed, you could see the black smoke rising up in columns. When we got to Wheeler, same thing. Hangars and planes destroyed, men down," he said.

His face had paled. His hands twisted together, fiddling with an invisible thread on the bedspread. Meanwhile, Isabel tried to process this new chunk of information. Still wondering how he was to blame.

"Right away, I went looking for Walt. One of the guys on the field told me they'd gone off to Haleiwa. It was too late to try and catch up, and we needed to save the planes. This all was between the two attacks, mind you. The skies were quiet but you got the feeling something big was coming. No one understood what was happening, where they'd come from. It was spooky as hell."

He stopped talking, trying to compose himself.

She waited.

"A little while later, we saw two planes shoot by overhead. P-40s. American. They dipped their wings in a flyover and

I knew it was Walt. But wouldn't you know it, that's when the Zeros came back, those bastards. See, Walt was my wingman, he always had my back. And when it mattered the most, I let him down."

Isabel felt for him.

Matteo stood. "I should get going."

"You understand that your logic is faulty, though, don't you?" she said.

"How do you figure?"

"It was the Japanese that killed Walt, not you."

Sure, she didn't like that he'd lied. But had he? Maybe it was more a case of omission. He'd left out a key detail. When she thought back, his account of that morning had been secondhand. How he'd said, *I never got airborne that day.* She'd never thought to ask why.

"Those other pilots came looking for *me* that morning, not Walt. They needed one more guy and I was the lead pilot. The one with the most kills, the most experience. I should have been there. If I had been, Walt would never have gone up."

The guilt had been gnawing away at him, that much was obvious. Now she understood why he'd been so uncomfortable that first day at the Pali, fidgeting and avoiding eye contact as he relived the morning. And tonight, he'd seemed on edge.

"Do I wish you'd told me? Yes. But that doesn't make it your fault."

Did it? How might things have turned out had Matteo not been chasing girls around Waikiki?

He looked at her sadly. "Do yourself a favor and forget about me."

"Isn't that my decision to make?" she said.

"Actually, it's not," he said, voice cracking as he stood. "You're a good woman, Isabel, and you deserve a better man."

She was suddenly fuming, and hurt. "You mean to tell me that all those kisses meant nothing? Why would you do that to me?"

"Must have been the gin. And I do care about you, a lot. You're a good friend."

Friend? Even he didn't sound convinced.

"I'm sorry, but I don't believe you."

It was human nature to be afraid. And Lord knew he had his reasons. But they had become so close. She loved him, that much was plain as day now. How could things have gone so wrong?

He backed away. "Believe it."

"Fine. But if you leave now, don't bother coming back. Ever!" Her voice rose into a fury. "I don't need any more friends and I have no use for cowards," she said, whipping her pillow at him.

Matteo dodged it and walked out the door, shoulders slouched, all of his swagger gone. The guilt was going to pull him down and ruin him. Isabel lay back, half expecting him to come running back in, saying he had made a bad mistake. But the motor started up, idled for a few minutes, and he drove off. She curled into a ball and let the tears come.

28

THE SURPRISE

Hawai'i Island, July 1965

Lu and Russi were in the lounge distracting themselves with a game of chess, waiting for everyone else to return and the cops to come. Lu had already won one game, and was about to checkmate again. She felt bad for Russi, but not that bad.

When she moved her queen into position, Russi threw up his hands and fell back on the couch. "And here I was, getting ready to make a deal with you, but now I'm not feeling so generous," he said.

"A deal?"

"Yeah, but forget it."

"Tell me."

"I was thinkin' maybe you can help me get in the water again, and I'll answer some questions for you."

Lu raised her eyes. "Are we talking war questions? You would do that?"

He shrugged as if it was no big deal. "It couldn't hurt."

She heard the vulnerability in his voice and knew that, for him, this really was a big deal. "I promise I'll stop when you tell me to."

"Fair enough."

Just then, a dark-haired man with a dog as big as a horse entered the lounge. He scanned the room and came over. Even with a pronounced limp, he moved with a good amount of power. After introducing himself as Sheriff Rapoza, and his dog, Bull, he said, "Mind if I ask you two some questions?"

"Have at it," Russi said.

Dressed in jeans and a blue palaka shirt, he looked more like a cowboy than a sheriff. The dog sat obediently by his side, all paws and jowls. Rapoza picked up a napkin and wiped a line of sweat from his forehead. "Sounds like we have two possible incidents, one old, one new. I'm most concerned about Miss Diaz right now, but will also need to know everything you can tell me about what you saw in that cave," he said.

They filled him in on what they knew about Joni, and how she was supposed to meet Lu this morning for a swim. Lu went first and Russi filled in the blanks. She also mentioned the couple in the water.

"How long had you both been acquainted with Miss Diaz?" the sheriff asked, lighting a cigarette with an old pineapple grenade lighter.

"I met her on the ride down from the airport," Lu said.

Russi hesitated. "I've known her for several years."

"Business or personal?"

"Both. I met her on business, but took her out a few times. Nothing serious, ended amicably, if that's what you're after."

Rapoza blew smoke out in slow bursts. "Until we know what we're dealing with, I'm not ruling anything—or anyone—out."

Was Russi now a suspect?

"Fair enough," he said.

"Anyone else here, aside from her manager, who knew Miss Diaz? Or maybe you saw interacting with her?"

Lu remembered Joni talking about Mr. Rockefeller. "She knew the Rockefellers from Caneel Bay. And it sounded like she maybe knew the senator and his wife a little. But don't quote me on that."

He asked them about their whereabouts last night and then, when he'd gotten all he could, he moved on to the skeleton. Lu went over every detail, then said, "I think we could find it. I tied a bandanna to a big kiawe tree down by the water in line with where the entrance was."

"Have there been any missing persons around these parts in recent years or decades?" Russi asked the sheriff.

Rapoza looked to be around the same age as Russi. Possibly late forties or around there. Old enough to have been in the field a while.

"Hmm," he mused. "Not off the top of my head."

"Mr. Rockefeller said they found shoes down by the water. Did they belong to Miss Diaz?" Russi asked.

"That we haven't determined yet. I was thinking maybe one of you might recognize them. Want to come up to the office with me and have a look?"

"Was there anything else out there with the shoes? Or any sign of trouble?" Lu asked.

"That I can't say."

Back in the office, the minute Lu saw the strappy wooden sandals, all the blood left her head. "Joni was wearing those in the limo. Those are hers."

She looked for the nearest chair and sank down into it. Her beautiful new friend, out to sea.

Gone.

Later that afternoon, Lu was scribbling down notes when Russi came knocking on her door. When she opened it, he walked in without waiting for an invite. "Did you hear? Rapoza said no one can leave until further notice."

"No, but that makes sense. Not a bad place to be stuck, though."

The best, in fact.

"Makes me wonder if they know something we don't," he said.

"Are you going to write it?" she asked.

He scratched the silver stubble on his chin. "Journalism 101. Never turn down a good lead, even if it's not what you came to write. But I'm not feeling it. With Joni, it's almost too personal."

It did feel personal. Crushing, in fact.

"Did Rapoza say anything about keeping quiet?" she asked.

"He asked me to at least wait until tomorrow. But someone's bound to talk," he said.

"The workers here will listen to Rapoza, and I think they respect Mr. Rockefeller enough to keep it under wraps. You should have a little wiggle room."

"Makes me uneasy, though. It's not my usual MO."

"What would you normally do?"

"State the obvious. Joni Diaz is missing. Nothing wrong with that. And if she turns up, no harm done."

"What do *you* think happened to her?" Lu asked.

Russi was leaning against the wall looking very James Dean–ish in a white T-shirt and jeans. His casual cool was part of his appeal. She half expected him to pull out a cigarette at any moment, but she knew he didn't smoke. *Death sticks*, he'd called them.

"It doesn't surprise me that she went for a swim. But why not from the beach? Why would she go out on the rocks at night?" he said.

"That's what I was wondering," Lu said.

"But Joni thought differently than most of us mere mortals, so she could have had her reasons."

"Do you think she's dead?" Lu asked with a shiver.

"I have a sense that she is. You?"

"I'm having a hard time fathoming it—" Her voice broke as she said it.

Russi stepped over and wrapped her in a hug, patting her back tenderly as he might a young child. "I know, it's rough. There's a saying in life that the good die young and the rest of us remain. Sure seems true."

She absorbed the comfort as best she could. "You seem pretty hard on yourself."

He pulled away. "The war took the best friend I ever had. On day one. So, yeah, I'm allowed."

A small crack had seemed to open, and story fragments were slipping out. But Lu wanted it all.

"I'm sorry. I'm here if you ever want to talk about it," she said.

Instead of brushing her off, he met her gaze and said, "Thanks, kid, I'll keep that in mind."

While Rapoza, with Bull at his side, was taking statements from guests and staff, Lu and Russl went to the bar to talk to Uncle Jerry, who was back on duty after a long day in the sun. They told him about their find in the lava tube.

"Do you remember anyone going missing in these parts?" Russi asked.

"What's our time frame?"

"Hard to tell. The police are going out tomorrow to get a better look. Not too old, though. Maybe a couple decades at the most."

"Hmm. Give me a minute to think on that," Jerry said.

Lu watched him throw pineapple, coconut milk and ice in

a blender and pour it into two tall glasses. His brow creased in concentration. "Piña coladas, on the house. You two look like you could use some cooling off."

"You're not kidding. Feels like someone cranked my thermostat on high," Russi said.

"So," Jerry said. "I remember one scientist type disappearing down near Anaehoʻomalu about ten or twelve years ago. He was out surveying the petroglyphs and just vanished. It was in all the papers, and people searched, but never found a trace. There were rumors that he'd maybe staged his disappearance to get out of a lawsuit of some kind, but who knows? I doubt he would have been this far up the coast, though. You remember that, Lu?"

Now that he mentioned it, the story sounded vaguely familiar. He went on. "And then during the war—I think it was '43 or '44—an Oʻahu lady was swept out to sea up at Mauʻumae. The surf was big and they never found her body."

Russi sat up and snapped to attention. "Hang on, that was near here?"

"Yeah, just up the way," Jerry said.

"Close to the lava tube. Why?" Lu added.

"My friend Izzy knew that woman, if it's the same one. Gloria something or other. Just before I left Pearl in '43, I remember Izzy being crushed about her roommate drowning on the Big Island. Apparently she and her guy had come up here for the weekend and she never came home," he said.

"Weird. But if she drowned, then that's not her," Lu said.

Jerry shrugged. "That's all I got."

Even in times of trouble, people still need to eat. Mr. Buttonwood had the barbecue moved from up mauka down to the hotel and on the same grounds where the lūʻau had been. The mood had soured some, but life went on. Worn-out and emotionally drained, Lu hung back and watched the crowd. Tiki torches and steel guitar reminded her of little-kid times, when the adults would talk story and drink into the night. She'd curl up on a towel and fall asleep, sun-kissed and content from a day at the beach.

The next thing she knew, Senator Fuchs wandered over and said, "Hard to swallow, isn't it?" He looked very solemn, with his hands in his pockets and his head down.

"Very," she said, surprised that he had singled her out, of all people.

"You two seemed close. Did you know Joni well?" he asked.

"Not really. I just met her, but we clicked right away."

"I saw you two swimming that first morning, all the way out to the mouth of the bay. That takes guts," he said.

"Not really. I grew up here, so I'm just as comfortable in the water as on land, if not more so," she said.

He smiled. "I envy you that. Was Miss Diaz a good swimmer, like you?"

"Good enough. What about you, Senator, did you know her personally?" she said.

"We've run into each other a few times over the years. In fact, she sang at one of my fundraisers. She seemed like a nice young lady."

"Did anyone else in your group know her? Or have any ideas about what might have happened?" Lu asked. "You guys must have talked about it today at the ranch."

"We were speculating, but no one saw anything. You know us geriatric folks, we like to hit the hay early. How about you, you learn anything?" he said.

"Nothing other than that they found her shoes out by the point. But Russi and I came across something else of interest out there," she said, then added, "Unrelated."

"Oh? Do tell."

"Sorry, I can't say."

"Now you have my curiosity piqued. Is there something going on the rest of us need to be concerned about?" he asked.

"No, nothing like that."

"I'll be meeting with the police first thing in the morning to make sure they're doing all they can. I guess they'll let me in on it," he said.

"Yeah, they probably will."

His polish faltered. "Don't forget I'm a US senator, Miss…"

She was probably overreacting, but she didn't like his tone and the way he waved his power in her face like a baseball bat.

She filled in the blank for him. "Miss Freitas. And yes, I'm aware of that."

"Hey, there you are," Russi said, coming up from behind and startling her. He nodded at Fuchs. "Senator."

"I was just leaving. Good evening," Fuchs said, stepping away.

Russi frowned. "What was that all about?"

She waited until he was out of earshot. "He was just throwing his weight around. I mentioned we found something, but wouldn't tell him what it was and he got pushy. My fault for mentioning it in the first place."

"Dumb move. You should always hold your cards close."

Lu thought about the way she'd seen Fuchs watch Joni. "Did you ever notice him staring at Joni?" she asked.

Russi's mouth went up on one side. "Every guy stared at Joni."

"This felt different. Spooky, almost."

They both looked over at him. Fuchs was backlit, standing with his wife under the shimmer of hanging lights. When he went to touch her waist, her whole body leaned away from him. He stepped closer and pulled her in firmly, but her arms remained at her side, stiffly.

"Hmm. He's a dodgy man from what I hear. Years back, a buddy doing a story on US ties to Nazi Germany told me Fuchs was one they were looking at. But nothing ever came of it. I wouldn't trust him," he said.

Lu was struck with a terrible thought. "Joni told me she was involved with someone, but was sworn to secrecy. And now that I think about it, the two were pretty chummy on the boat. What if she and the senator were having an affair?" The hairs on the back of her neck bristled. "What if it was them in the water that night?"

"I'd say that's a whole lotta *what-ifs*."

29

THE FIND

Hawai'i Island, July 1965

All night long, Lu rolled around in her bed, tangling in her sheets. Her mind had taken on a life of its own, following every thought down dark crab holes. All thoughts became fair game, things that in the light of day seemed implausible now made perfect sense. *A bad case of the night furies*, her grandma would have said. She became convinced that Joni and Senator Fuchs were having an affair, and could not shake the feeling. Eventually, she moved outside to the lounge chair and watched the night sky.

Before dawn, when she couldn't take it anymore, she picked up the phone and called Dylan. He was three hours ahead.

"Dylan Hall," he answered.

The sound of his voice made her feel better already.

"Hey, it's me."

"Lu? Is everything okay?" It wasn't like her to call while away, so he was probably wondering what was up. She heard him rustling around, and imagined his tousled hair, freckles, green eyes. The way his mouth puckered up when he said her name.

"I'm fine, but things aren't really going as planned. It's been a crazy last two days."

Anything she told Dylan was one hundred percent safe. Another thing she loved about him. "Tell me everything," he said.

She didn't know where to start. "For one thing, I've somehow become good friends with Matteo Russi, which was unexpected. He reminds me of you, or maybe you remind me of him. But that's not the thing. The thing is that Joni Diaz has disappeared, possibly drowned, but they haven't found a body yet. And then when Russi and I went searching for her yesterday, we found a skeleton in a lava tube. An older one. Then, on top of all that, I can't seem to get it out of my head that she was having an affair with Senator Fuchs. Before she disappeared, she confided in me she was in love with a mystery guy, but sworn to secrecy."

There was silence on the other end.

"Dylan?"

"Holy shit, are you for real?" he said.

"I know it sounds wild. The senator part is pure conjecture at this point, though. I've been up since two a.m. with the night furies driving me insane."

"And you were worried about finding a story."

"That's the weird part. I feel like I've written a bunch of fluff. The hotel is amazing, but all I really want to do is a feature on Matteo Russi. To be honest, until this happened, all I've been trying to do is get his story from the war. Something big happened to him, I can tell. And he's still hurting. He's the most interesting person here if you ask me. Or was, until Joni up and vanished."

"Classic Lu. Going for the human element. Haven't I told you *Sunset* is not your thing? I see your byline in *Life*."

"It's even got me thinking about doing a whole series on

World War II veterans. These men need to tell their stories—
they're just festering inside, eating away at their psyches.
Maybe I can do them on the side, freelance."

"Damn, I wish I was there with you," he said with a softness to his voice.

"Me, too. You would love everything about this place. It's
rugged but refined, and fancy in an island way. But the best
part is that it's surrounded by the bluest ocean you've ever
seen. Every which way you look is a photograph waiting to
be taken. I wish you could meet Russi, too. You'd love him."

"I'm leaving next weekend, Lu. I have my ticket and everything."

Her heart swayed. "What?"

"Yep. Saturday. Will you be back by then?"

"I'm supposed to visit my Auntie H and my dad at the end
of the week and fly home Saturday, but the police said no one
can leave right now, so I don't know. Weren't you supposed
to leave next month?" she said.

"Things changed." After an awkward silence, he said, "I'd
sure love to see you before I go. In case, well, you know."

In that moment, she knew that whatever happened here,
she'd figure out a way. She *had* to see him. "I'll do my best to
be there. I want to see you, too. And don't think bad thoughts
like that, please?"

"Just being real."

Losing Dylan would break her. "The only outcome I'll
accept is you coming back in one piece. With a heartbeat."

"I'll do my best."

"I know you will," she said. "Look, I know this is bad timing, but I need a favor."

"No promises, but shoot."

"Can you find out everything you can about Senator

Fuchs? Past history, history with women, indiscretions, that kind of thing. And be discreet."

"Consider it done."

"I knew I loved you for a reason," she said, wishing she could give him a big hug and get lost in the smell of developing solution.

In the past, they threw around the word *love* casually, as one would an old football on a lazy Sunday afternoon. But suddenly, she felt self-conscious about having uttered the word.

"I love you, too, but I can't remember why," he said.

She could picture the lopsided grin on his face. Lu didn't want to hang up, but felt a burning need to swim before she took on the day. "I have to go, but call me as soon as you find out anything. And wait for me, I need to see you before you go," she said.

"I need to see you, too."

Wingbeats in her heart.

"Bye."

"Bye."

The phone did not want to leave her ear, and she finally understood the meaning of *a long goodbye*.

After hanging up, Lu went straight to the beach. The sky was still dusky and the occasional dove cooed. If only she could feel so peaceful. This time, instead of leaning against a coconut tree, Russi was down at the far end of the beach doing push-ups in the sand. Shirtless. He didn't acknowledge her until she was upon him.

"Hey," she said.

He jumped up and dusted off his hands. "How'd you sleep?"

"Terrible. You?"

"I was up all night writing and thinking and remembering. Felt like I'd had ten gallons of coffee before lying down," he said.

A thick layer of sweat made his skin shine.

"How long have you been out here?" she asked.

"Long enough to almost want to get in the water," he said, out of breath.

"Seriously?"

"I said *almost*."

"Oh, Russi. I wish I could help you."

"Now is not the time."

"What about just getting your feet wet. Little by little, expose yourself to what scares you. When I was younger and first started being tutored, I was terrified of books," she said, laughing at the thought. "Can you believe that? Who's scared of books? But I was. I know it's because reading was so hard for me, and because I'd been embarrassed so many times reading in front of the class. Each time I opened a book, my hands got all clammy and I felt like throwing up. Our neighbor Auntie H had me carry around the book for a week, but I wasn't allowed to open it. Then, the week after that, I could open it, but I had to keep my eyes closed. I was supposed to just feel the pages, and smell them."

Russi put his hands on his hips. "She sounds like a real piece of work."

"I remember thinking it was dumb, but after those first two weeks, I got really comfortable with the book. Suddenly, there was no pressure and it was this inert object that lost its power. Then the next week, Auntie H sat with me and she opened the book and read me the first line. Then we read it together, only a couple lines at a time. Little by little, I ended up dying to know what happened next. And by the end of the book, I was hooked."

"What book?"

"The Lion, the Witch and the Wardrobe."

"A good choice."

"That book turned my life around. And if I hadn't had someone there by my side, holding my hand very firmly, and guiding me along, I wouldn't be here today. It takes guts, but it's doable. Especially with help. I guess that's my point. You don't seem like the kind of guy who gives up easily. What if you just walk in up to your ankles, no farther?" Lu said.

He sized up the water, looked at Lu, then down at his feet, which were buried in sand. Then he surprised her by saying, "Ah, hell, you drive a hard bargain."

Lu hooked her arm in his and they walked to the edge of the wet sand. The tide was low, and the surf had dropped considerably. They stood there for a moment, then Lu took a step forward. Russi hung back.

"Just one more step," she encouraged.

His arm tensed, but he moved up so he was next to her. A small wave rolled up the beach and covered their toes in white, crackly foam, then retreated. "Did I ever tell you about my surfing escapades in Waikiki?" he asked.

"What? You've been holding out on me. You, a surfer? I don't believe it."

He held up two fingers. "Scout's honor. My buddy and I used to go before the war broke out, every chance we could. I even had my own board, a beast of a thing, but I loved it. Some of the best times of my life out there, gliding over the water without a care in the world. I took Izzy one day—she was a real natural."

"Did you surf after the war broke out?"

"Not at first. They barbed-wired-up the beaches. But after Midway, things relaxed a little. I spent every moment I could in the water. Which wasn't a whole lot. We trained constantly when we were ashore."

"What about Izzy? Was she from here?"

"No, she was navy. She'd tell you she was a secretary, but that would be a gross understatement."

"What did she do?"

"Codebreaking. Top-secret stuff."

Lu was impressed. "Women did that?"

"Hell, yeah. They were better than the men, from what I hear. But no one talks about it, it was all hush–hush. Still is, I think."

Russi was hanging in there, stiff but still breathing.

"Now that would make for a great story. Do you know where she is now?"

He shook his head. "Last I heard she was still on Oʻahu. She married soon after the war and started teaching." A wave came up and buried their feet, swirling up around their ankles. He stepped back a few feet. "When I left for China, we weren't on good terms. It was all my fault. I was dumb as a monkey back then."

"And after China?" she asked.

The scar on his face had reddened some. "After China I was in no shape to try to find her. I didn't even know my own name for a while. I'll leave it at that."

Lu let the weight of his words sink in, as ten feet offshore a small *omilu* jumped, followed by a barracuda. There was a feathery texture to the water, where a school of fish swam underneath. He watched, too. Whatever had happened to Russi, happened in China.

"So, wait, you left Hawaiʻi and never spoke to her again?" she couldn't help but say.

"That about sums it up. I wrote a bunch of letters and never sent them. Tracked down her phone number and kept it on a piece of paper under my pillow, but could not bring myself to call. And then she got married. What was the point?" he said, backing slowly up the beach.

It was so easy to picture the war happening to the nameless, faceless masses. But when you stood shoulder to shoulder with someone who had been there and been inexorably changed, and you felt the pain seeping out from their pores, you better understood the magnitude. For every human involved, war had left its residue.

She could tell he was done talking; this time she took his advice and let it go. "Well, you did it. You got your ankles wet. How do you feel?"

He looked relieved. "Survival always feels good."

"To celebrate, maybe I'll let you win at chess later," she said with a smile.

"Nope. Never. I'll get you fair and square one of these days," he said, punching her in the arm.

The old Russi was back.

After a quick breakfast of scrambled eggs and a side of papaya, Lu downed two cups of dark coffee, and went off with Sheriff Rapoza and Russi to the lava tube. A layer of gauzy clouds kept the sun at bay, and they moved along faster, now that they knew where they were going.

"Any new ideas about who this could be?" Russi asked.

"There have been a few people unaccounted for along this coastline, but most were ocean related. Fisherman, swimmers, that kind of thing," was all he said.

This time, they had two flashlights, and at the mouth of the lava tube they hunched over and entered the cool, dark tunnel. With the light, the cave felt less ominous, but the dank smell was still there. The bones were right where they'd left them. Lu had begun to wonder if maybe they'd made a mistake, maybe they were animal and not human. And maybe they were just some disturbing dream. But the minute the beam swept over them, all question evaporated.

"*Auwe,*" Rapoza said, squatting down for a closer look. "Human. And not too old."

He asked Lu to hold his flashlight, and snapped a few shots from different angles. Beneath the bones, the reddish thing was definitely material of some kind. He pulled it out with a stick and held it up. Red and white polka dots.

"A swimsuit?" Russi said.

"Looks that way. The dry air in Puako is like a preservative, especially out of the elements like this," Rapoza said.

"Can you tell if it's male or female?" Lu asked.

He lifted the skull, weighing it in his hand. "My guess is female. See how the forehead is rounded? Tends to be less so in males." He then pointed at the pelvic bone, to a curve on one side. "And the sciatic notch is usually broader in females. Like this."

"What about how long she's been here?" Russi said.

The *it* had suddenly become a *she.*

Rapoza stood up and stretched, yanking his belt up under his paunch. "That is harder to determine. Did you notice anything else when you were here?"

"It was too dark. We didn't have a flashlight," she said, looking over at Russi, who was shining his light in a crack under the bones.

He leaned over. "Give me that stick."

Rapoza handed him the stick and he started poking at something, working intently to bring something up from inside the crack.

"What is it?"

"Jewelry, maybe."

After a few tries, Russi held the stick up with a tarnished ring on its tip.

"Nice work, Russi," Rapoza said, setting the ring in his open palm.

Delicate and finely wrought, a cowrie shell in tarnished silver sat in the beam of light. Russi turned and walked over to the skylight. Something was up. He looked pale as a sheet.

Lu went to him. "What is it?"

"I know this ring."

"What do you mean?"

"You two okay over there?" Rapoza called.

"Affirmative," Russi answered. He rubbed his face. "Fuck."

Rapoza, oblivious to the new development, said, "All pau here. Let's get going."

Without a word, Russi brushed past Lu. She tried to hold on to his arm, but her hand slipped off from the sweat. "You need to tell him," she hissed.

He stopped and turned, out of Rapoza's line of sight. "I need to do something first. Promise me you won't say anything until then, okay? I just need a couple of days."

Since the bones had nothing to do with Joni, she agreed. "Fine, but only if you let me in on it. Maybe I can help."

"Not this time, kid."

30

THE INFORMATION

Hawai'i Island, July 1965

Back at the hotel, the three of them parted ways. Russi had only grunted simple yeses or nos along the way, and the glint of blue sky was hard on the eyes after being in the dark cave. They passed the third hole just in time to see Big Joe and Bobby Dean Dixon drive their golf balls across the cove and onto the green. Senator Fuchs was not so lucky. His ball splashed into the ocean.

Mr. Rapoza promised to get back to them with any information. Lu let Russi go without a fight, and went back to her room to see if Dylan had called. He hadn't.

After a quick dip to cool off, she still felt heat rising off her skin, so sided up to the Hau Tree Bar for an ice cold chocolate malt. Next to her, the senator's wife was sitting with June Cosgrove, sipping drinks with pink umbrellas. They were dressed in starchy white tennis outfits, and both had turned twelve shades darker than when they'd first arrived at the hotel. They looked like clones.

"Hello, ladies. How was your game?" she said as cheerfully as she could muster.

June smiled. "Splendid. I daresay those courts have one of the finest views in the world."

Lynette sipped her drink and said, "Hot."

"I went out for a hike this morning. Have I missed anything? Any news on Joni Diaz?" Lu asked.

"Nothing that I know of, but they're being rather tight-lipped about the whole thing," June said.

Lynette added, "It seems pretty straightforward to me. The woman was high, she went in the water—or maybe she fell in—and she drowned."

The coldness in her voice chilled Lu off right away. "No one deserves to drown, especially someone as young and vibrant as Joni," she said.

June cut in. "Oh, they're probably just crossing their *t*'s and dotting their *i*'s. When it's someone hugely famous, there's always a big to-do."

Lynette was wearing sunglasses, so it was hard to see her eyes, but her mouth seemed to droop, and the smile lines in her cheeks looked deeper. Lu noticed an ashtray full of butts in front of her.

"Has anyone said anything about being able to leave?" Lu asked.

"Mr. Rockefeller said he'd brief us all this afternoon," Lynette said.

In the room, Lu went straight to the typewriter. She typed every thought that came into her head about the hotel, about Russi, about Joni. They were each their own story, yet they were so intertwined she couldn't imagine writing one without the others. Styles would probably hate it, but she could edit it later. Just as she was about to head out looking for Russi, Dylan called.

"Any news?" he asked.

Lu told him the latest.

"Sounds like quite a morning. I wish I had more for you. John Walsh happened to be in the office and he used to cover the DC beat. He said Fuchs was known to piggyback on a few of JFK's trips. Rumors also floated that he bagged an intern or two of his own."

"Just rumors?"

"Isn't that what they always are? What woman is going to come forward and talk? Besides, that's part of the deal. They know it going in," he said.

Her feathers ruffled. "If I was that intern, there would be a front page story about it the next day."

He laughed. "Oh, yeah, that was the reason I love you. Now I remember."

"I'm serious."

"I know you are."

A lizard appeared on the glass door, big eye watching her. Seeing it made her happy. Geckos had always been good luck in her family. "The more I think about it, the more I feel like Fuchs is somehow to blame, even if it was just by toying with her heart," she said.

"If they were having an affair, someone would know about it, wouldn't they? What about the wife—isn't she there?" Dylan said.

"Yes, but wives don't stop these kinds of guys, you know that. I feel like talking more pointedly to the senator. I'll ask Russi what he thinks."

Dylan coughed. "Um. Sounds like you and Russi are pretty tight over there. Is there anything I should know about?" he asked.

Was that jealousy she heard in his voice? "Be real, Dylan. The guy is almost twice my age."

"That doesn't mean anything. It didn't stop Olivia Bell

from hanging out with him. Or Daisy Lopez. Or a dozen other high-profile women."

"I guess I'm not high-profile enough. But seriously, there has been no weirdness between us whatsoever. He feels like a cool uncle or something," she said. "Did you know he also dated Joni Diaz?" she added.

"Doesn't that make him a suspect?" Dylan said.

"It does, but that was years ago. Plus, Russi is not a killer. I know that."

"Do you?"

"Without a doubt."

"Be careful, Lu. I know you want to impress the boss. But your own safety comes first," he said.

"I'll be fine."

When Lu hung up, she walked out onto the patio and looked down on the bay. It was the perfect bird's-eye view. In the sandy middle, where the water was translucent turquoise, anything dark stood out. On the edges, lined with coral shelfs, not as much. The yellow and purple hues of coral, accented with red pencil *wana*, created a vibrant underwater palette. She scanned for any signs of a body. It was natural instinct. Part of her still in denial, the other part wanting an answer.

Joni, what happened to you?

The afternoon was shaping up to be a stunner. The royal poincianas showed off their red blossoms, bees hummed in the kiawe and the ocean sparkled. Lu fanned herself with a newspaper as she went in search of Russi. He wasn't in the bar or the lounge or even on the beach, so she went back up and knocked on his door.

A muffled voice came from inside. "I don't need anything."

"It's me, Lu," she said, resting her cheek on the cool wood and listening for footsteps.

Silence. She was about to give up on him when the door swung open. "What do you want?" he said, with no move to let her in.

"I spoke to Dylan and came by to fill you in," she said, looking up at him.

"Any dirt?" he asked.

She smelled alcohol on his breath.

"Nothing especially concrete, but plenty of rumors about Fuchs being inappropriate with interns. He was also friends with Jack Kennedy and partook in some of his so-called 'trips.' Have you heard anything?"

Russi cocked his head. "Not girl related. My source did tell me that the reason the Nazi stuff got shoved under the rug was because someone—an unknown player who could only be one of a few influential people—shut down the investigation cold. Even more interesting is that Fuchs has ties to the American Academy of Human Genetics, an organization that many believe is really a new take on eugenics."

"How can that even be possible after the Nuremberg Trials? I thought eugenics has been outlawed."

Russi poked his head out and looked up and down the hallway. "Come inside."

His room was spic and span—the bed all tucked, no clothes or papers or bikinis strewn about as in hers. There were three yellow legal pads stacked on the table, and a cold Primo beer. Next to that was a blue Lettera 22 typewriter. Of course he'd have an Olivetti. Russi was dressed in swim trunks and a tight T-shirt. He smelled of coconut suntan lotion.

"Tell me you're not naive enough to think that Nazis are gone and the world is peachy again," he said, pulling out a chair for her.

"No. But I would expect it in Germany, not here."

"Where do you think they got their ideas?" he said.

"What do you mean?"

Growing up in Hawai'i, Lu had been sheltered from much of the white supremacy theories. Dark-colored skin was considered a blessing here, and she couldn't fathom it being any other way. It wasn't until she moved to the mainland, where people thought she was Mexican and treated her differently, when she finally understood that some people did not approve of who she was simply based on her darker tone.

Russi took a swig of his beer. "You've never heard of the Eugenics Record Office, aka the ERO? They were respon sible for forced sterilizations across our fine country to improve our gene pool, get rid of those pesky Indians and poor people. They also outlawed immigration from southern and eastern Europe. Read— where the darker-skinned people are."

Lu was floored. "I had no idea."

"This was all halted in the late thirties, but evil has a slippery way of showing up again under other names. Most genetic research is for our betterment, so they say. But not all. And it may seem like a righteous cause, as I'm sure it did back then, until it gets into the hands of the wrong people," he said.

"So how is Fuchs involved?"

"By drumming up funds. Sitting on the board. It all sounds up-and-up, but there's a dark side. Make no mistake, Aryan supremacy is still espoused on our shores."

"So, we know he is a bad man. Just how bad, is the question," she said.

Russi offered her a beer and popped open another for himself. "Time will tell. Or maybe we should. What do you think? We could team up on a story, uncovering the hidden life of Senator Richard Fuchs."

"You would do that?"

He waved her off. "Aw, come on. It's no big deal."

"Do you remember how it was when you were just starting out? When you had to take the first job offered you? This is a huge deal, Russi, and you know it."

To shut her up, he handed her a box of half-melted chocolate-covered macadamia nuts and she happily savored four of them, even if every finger was brown when she finished. Russi had started jotting down a note on his yellow pad and was lost in thought for a while. The wind blew in the watery sounds of swell on rocks.

"I think I'm going to leave *Sunset*," she said, not quite sure why she was telling Russi this, of all people.

"Either you are or you aren't."

"Well, then I am."

"Why would you do that?"

"Because my heart isn't in it. You were the one who brought it to my attention the other day. My professor helped get me the job, and I'm forever grateful, but I'm just not interested in their kind of stories. Don't get me wrong, it's a great magazine, just not for me."

"Where do you see yourself? Be honest."

"Time."

To his credit he didn't laugh out loud. "You know that women at *Time* are just fact-checkers. Researchers, right? All the writers are men."

"So I've heard."

"What makes you think you'd be different?"

"Maybe if I approached them armed with some stories they can't refuse, I could get a foot in. Say, something about a corrupt senator? Or even better, a series of profiles of WWII veterans twenty years later."

"I like how you think, kid, but your chances are less than slim," he said, mouth curving up on one side. "I can't grow a mustache to save my life, but would you look at that. A girl named Lu with a chocolate mustache. That'd get you hired, stat."

Lu licked her upper lip and tasted chocolate. She ran to the bathroom, only to see two triangles of chocolate that had eluded her napkin. She tied her hair in a knot and wiped down her face with a damp washcloth.

When she came back out, Russi said, "I'll help you any way I can. But just so you know, I think where you really belong is back here in Hawai'i. New York isn't really your cuppa joe."

"But there's nothing big here."

"*Big* is not what matters. What matters is that you're doing the work that feeds your soul. Trust me, you'll be much happier and a much better writer if you write about what interests you, not what you think you should be writing to prove something to someone. Living in New York would shrivel you up and suck the life out of you."

"How do you know that?"

"Because I see the way you are. I came from New York, but you come from these islands. They're under your skin in a way that makes your eyes light up whenever you talk about anything Hawai'i. I see you in the ocean every morning, you're a fish."

She thought back to that morning on the beach. *You have Hawai'i written all over you*, he'd said.

"I can always come back later," she said.

He waved his hand around. "I know, I know. You spent all this time at your fancy school, getting your fancy job. You have your eye on the big prize. But just because you *can* do something, doesn't mean you *should*."

Lu was floored. No one had ever spoken so bluntly to her. Could it be possible that something you thought you always wanted was not at all what you wanted?

"You're wrong," she said.

The words tasted bitter on her tongue.

"Dreams change. Nothing wrong with that. Be honest with yourself. Hawai'i may be small, but what about *Paradise of the Pacific*? A great magazine."

"How do you know about *Paradise of the Pacific*?"

One of the oldest magazines in the country, and a fine one at that.

"I do my research. At least consider it, will you?"

Lu didn't answer.

"Oh, and I just checked with Rapoza. He's still trying to reach next of kin for Joni. I'm calling this into a friend at the AP. Just the facts. I'm surprised the story hasn't leaked yet," he said.

"People in Hawai'i are different. They watch out for each other," she said.

"You remind me of myself when I was just starting off. Determined, starry-eyed, green as the grass on that golf course out there," he said.

Lu blushed. "I'll take that as a compliment. Since being green is an inevitable part of life."

"As you should."

"Are you going to tell me about the ring?" she finally got the nerve to say.

His eyes dipped to the table. "The ring belonged to my friend Izzy. I would know it anywhere. Don't ask me how the fuck it got in that cave, but I need to find out."

"Maybe it's just a similar ring?" she said.

"It's not."

A moment of silence fell between them. For the first time, Lu noticed a small photo album lying on the coffee table. Leather-bound with fraying edges, it looked like it had seen a lot of use. *Walt & Izzy* was on the cover in faded handwriting.

"It seems unlikely that Izzy would be our skeleton, when

her friend was the one that drowned nearby. And if her friend drowned, why would she be all the way up there in a lava tube?"

His voice sounded strained. "*Unlikely* doesn't cut it. I need to know for sure. I've put out feelers. It's something I should have done a long time ago but was too thick-headed to figure it out. I need to find her."

31

THE PHOTOGRAPH

Hawai'i Island, July 1965

Lu placed a call to Styles. She'd been avoiding calling him as she worked through story angles in her mind. And even though this wasn't a *Sunset* story, he deserved to know about Joni from her. Before the rest of the world. She dialed his home number, and the operator put her through.

"Where the hell have you been? I've left fifty messages," was the first thing he said.

Five, not fifty. Styles had always been prone to exaggeration.

"Sorry, Mr. Styles. Rockefeller had us on a tight schedule and I was working on my story late at night, and then, well, we've had a situation unfold. The sheriff gagged us until he notified the next of kin."

She could hear him blowing out cigarette smoke over the line. "Next of kin? What kind of situation are we talking about?"

"Joni Diaz is missing and presumed dead. It looks like she may have drowned."

A glass shattered on the other end, and suddenly he was yelling into her ear. "You are shitting me. *The* Joni Diaz?"

She felt sadness at the thought that, to him, Joni was a news story, not the lost heartbeat of a woman gone far too young.

"The one and only. Saturday night was the last time anyone saw her."

His voice rose. "You've known about this since Saturday?"

"Sunday morning, but—"

"Never mind, forget about it. Give me a sec and I'll take down what you've got. I can send this along to my buddy at the *Chronicle*," he said, rattling something around in the background. "Okay, ready."

She read from the paper she'd typed out.

Singer Joni Diaz has disappeared and is presumed dead. Diaz was a guest at the Mauna Kea Beach Hotel, Laurance Rockefeller's grand new resort, when she failed to turn up for a morning swim Sunday morning. Later that day, after an extensive search, her shoes were found on the rocks near the ocean. Diaz is a competent swimmer, but on Saturday night, the surf rose quickly. Authorities believe that she may have been swept off the rocks and drowned.

Diaz had befriended the Rockefellers while at Caneel Bay Resort, another Rock Resorts property in the Virgin Islands, and was invited to be part of a VIP grand opening weekend, rubbing shoulders with the likes of Bobby Dean and Mina Dixon of *Readers Monthly*, oil magnate Big Joe Wallace, philanthropists June and Leonard Cosgrove and Senator Fuchs and his wife. Sources state that there has been no sign of foul play, but all guests at the hotel are ordered not to leave the property until authorized by the police.

Diaz was born in San Diego to Mexican parents, later moving to Los Angeles where she landed a record deal with Icon. The world fell in love with her soulful voice and never looked back—

Styles stopped her. "I'll cut it at *police*. Is there anything else you can tell me? Are they sure there was no foul play?"

She kept her hunches to herself. No use implicating anyone until she had something concrete.

"Not right now. Without a body, there's nothing to go on."

"What about the hotel story?"

She lied. "Everything is great on that front."

"You don't sound too sure about that."

"Don't worry, you'll have your story."

Everyone was on their own for dinner. Lu was relieved because the last few days had caught up to her and all she wanted to do was sit on a beach chair, watch the sunset and sip a cold drink. Not think about anything. The muscles on the right side of her neck were in knots, and her heels were blistered from the new tennis shoes she'd bought to play golf and tennis in, but instead had only worn hiking in the lava.

Jerry made her a rum-and-pineapple concoction and sent her on her way. Armed with sunglasses and a *Time* magazine, she unrolled her orange towel with the white Mauna Kea flower—everything here was stamped with it—and lay down under the beach umbrella. Her brain ached from turning over scenarios in her head. Drawing a connection between Joni and the skeleton in the lava tube was a stretch, but she couldn't help herself. Who was this Gloria woman, and more importantly, who was the man that had been with her? She felt a compulsion to tell Rapoza, but owed Russi a day or two.

A couple of teenagers were jumping off the raft anchored

offshore, doing cannonballs and belly flops, and several women stood with their legs in the shore break engrossed in conversation, but aside from them most of the guests had left the beach for the day, probably all pink and crisp, and would be readying themselves for dinner. Fancy dresses would be worn, hair would be styled and drinks would be had. When one traveled all the way to Hawai'i, you made the most of every minute.

When she opened the magazine, which she'd borrowed from the front lobby, she flipped through the pages. It was an old habit, always starting somewhere in the middle. The cover shot of air force pilot Robbie Risner had caught her attention. He was just the kind of man who intrigued her—squadron leader of the Rolling Thunder attacks in Vietnam and an ace in the Korean War. She found the article and marked the page. There were stories about Ed White's spacewalk last month, and how Lyndon Johnson wanted to ramp up US troops in Vietnam.

Further in, she came upon a photo of Senator Fuchs. He always looked so smug, as if he knew something that the rest of the world didn't. The title of the article stopped her cold: "Are There Nazis Next Door?"

The story discussed how the United States had imported German scientists and engineers, many believed to have been active members of the Nazi party during the war, to help ensure US military advantage over Russia. Not new information. More interesting, though, was the allegation that known Nazi war criminals were being allowed into the US as potential spies, and that their own intelligence had been expunging their files. For all anyone knew, they could be living next door in perfect anonymity. Fuchs name came up as someone who had been smoothing their way. When she finished the article, she closed the magazine and set it on her warm, lightly toasted thighs.

Then, as if summoned by her own mind, Fuchs came sauntering out of the water and up the beach. In swim trunks, he was the opposite of Russi. No wide shoulders and tapered waist, just a shirt tan and some dough around the middle. Lu picked up the magazine and pretended to be reading, while observing behind her shades. There was an arrogance to the way he moved, a *look at me, I'm someone important* vibe. When he passed by several beach chairs away, she noticed two long scratches on his side, running from his lats down to his hip bone. He bent over to pick up his towel. The movement was stilted, as if he were in pain. He dried off, then slung the towel over his side, covering the scratch. But Lu had seen all she needed to.

As soon as he was gone, she slurped down her drink and ran back to Russi's room. This time, he opened right away and invited her in. He was halfway through a hamburger and nursing his beer.

"Gotta love the room service here. Can I order you something?" he said.

She was famished. "Sure, I could use some sustenance."

Something about his demeanor had shifted, and he was almost giddy. He called in her order, while licking ketchup off his fingers.

When he hung up, Lu held up the magazine, open to the page on Fuchs. "Two things. First, this article. It's not flattering—have you seen it?"

"No, what does it say?"

She told him.

"People are onto him. Good. But guys like Fuchs are slippery. They cover their tracks," he said.

"Here's the interesting part. I was on the beach reading and the senator came out of the water. When he passed me, I noticed scratches along his side that easily could have been from fingernails."

Russi stopped chewing, and spoke with a mouthful. "Whoa, kid. You sure about that?"

"No, I'm not sure they're from fingernails, but I'm sure he has suspicious-looking scratches."

"We need to tell Rapoza," he said, biting off another hunk of the burger. "Sorry to eat in front of you. I'm starved."

"That's another thing. We also need to tell Rapoza about the ring belonging to your friend. I don't feel right withholding information like this," she said.

"Don't worry, I made some headway. It looks like she's still alive. I had the operator put me through to Honolulu to see if she was still living there. But get this, she's not on O'ahu," he said, face breaking out into that famous lopsided smile. "She's here."

"Here at the Mauna Kea?"

"No, Sherlock, a place called Kainaliu."

Lu's town. Kainaliu was small. She would have known someone named Izzy. "You sure? That's where I'm from."

"That's what the operator said. Isabel Cooper was her name, and then she married a guy named Hoapili."

The name took a moment to register. Lu didn't know how long she sat there, synapses in her brain pinging around, staring at the photo album on the table. The room filled with a sticky stillness. She looked at Russi, his face eager for her to say something. Her Auntie H could not be his Izzy. *Could she?*

"Say the name again," she said.

"Isabel Cooper, or Hoapili. Izzy to me."

In the beginning, Auntie H had been plain old Mrs. Hoapili. As they became closer and their lives stitched together, she'd insisted on being called Auntie H. But names had a certain inertia. Once you knew someone by a certain name, it was almost impossible to shift gears. As though their essence was wrapped up in the letters and sounds of the word. Reluctantly, Lu made the switch. Now, she racked her memory for any mention of the nickname Izzy, and came up dry. Not to mention talk of codebreaking during the war.

"I know an Isabel Hoapili, but it can't be the same person," she said.

He frowned. "How many Isabel Hoapilis could there be in your town? Or anywhere for that matter."

Lu nodded to the photo album. "Show me a picture of her."

Russi looked at the book guardedly, as though it was some precious, secret thing. Unshareable with anyone else. He reached out and slid it across the table. "This was twenty-two years ago, mind you."

Lu opened the small book to the middle. The faint smell of flowers stuck to the pages. There, standing in sunlight with a surfboard next to her and smiling into the camera, was Auntie H. *Her* Auntie H. Younger and more angular, but not too different than the last time she'd seen her. Black hair, light eyes and an ethereal beauty that leaped from the pages.

"Wow, you were right about her being a stunner. She still is," Lu said.

She turned the page, curious to see more, and still in disbelief. The next photos were taken on a white sand beach. Izzy lay on the sand with a piece of coral on her stomach, so full of peace—and grace. In another one, you felt she was looking through the lens and into the eyes of the photographer. A knowing flicker of a smile.

"So, mine and yours are the same person? You sure?" he said, shaking his head.

"Auntie H was my neighbor, the one who tutored me. The one whose husband I told you about with the night terrors. I should know what she looks like, she's like a mom to me. In Hawai'i we call it *hanāi*. It loosely means when you adopt someone into your family, like she did with me. She had no kids and I had no mom so it worked."

"What about your dad?"

"I still lived with him. But I was at her house all the time. I stayed over on weekends a lot, kind of went between the two. Girls need moms, what can I say?"

Lu could have sworn his whole body was trembling. "Tell me everything you know about her. Start from the beginning," Russi ordered.

She thought back. "From the moment I started school in kindergarten, I was terrible at it. I refused to wear shoes, I brought in stray animals constantly and I could not read or write to save my life. That went on until seventh grade, when we had new people buy the coffee farm next door. I thought I owned the whole mountain, so I used to roam around their property and pick lilikoi after school and hunt for sandalwood. One afternoon, she was at the vine, too, holding a big basket. I almost ran, but she smiled and said, 'So you're actually a real person. I was beginning to think you were just a forest nymph. What's your name?' We got to talking and before you knew it, she was showing me how to make lilikoi pie and blackberry cobbler. Somewhere along the way, she noticed I struggled with some of the words in the recipe, and she took it upon herself to fix that." Lu paused, mouth watering just thinking about the pie.

"Did she tell you about her brother, Walt?" he asked.

"I knew he was shot down when the Japanese attacked O'ahu, and I know they were close, but she rarely talked about him."

Closing her eyes, Lu saw an old photograph on the wall in Auntie H's kitchen. A young man standing with a surfboard, same as the one in the album. *Walt.*

Russi nodded. "Walt and I were like brothers. Izzy came looking for me when she got transferred to Pearl and we struck up a friendship." His hand went to his scar, and she could tell he had gone back to some old memory. His lips folded in on themselves. "I was too dumb to notice that I was falling head over heels until it was too late. Course, in good old Russi fashion, I botched the whole thing. Then they shipped me off to China and that was that."

"You loved her," she said.

It was plain as day.

He shrugged. "What wasn't to love?"

Lu knew all too well about the fine and blurry line between friendship and love. "Strange, though, she never mentioned being a codebreaker. But then she was always more of a listener than a talker, and I was a talker. I loved to tell stories, so we were a match made in heaven. Before she came along, the animals were my main audience, but she made me feel interesting. Even smart. I told you about her husband, Cliff. He was part-Hawaiian and the nicest guy. I could tell she was crushed when he left, but also relieved. Watching him go downhill had been rough on her."

"Did she remarry?"

He was holding his breath.

"No," she said.

"And she still runs the farm?" he asked.

"She loves that farm. I can't imagine her ever leaving. I worked for her in the summers and earned money for school. I picked coffee beans all morning, and in the afternoons when the clouds came in we played chess," Lu said.

Russi smirked. "Damn. No wonder you're a hotshot player."

"I never came close to playing like Auntie H—Izzy—though. You were right about her being the smartest person you know. Her brain works at lightning speed. Which is probably why I never pictured her as an Izzy. Did you come up with that?"

"Walt did. He talked about her all the time, so I just assumed that was her name." He shoved the last bite into his mouth, and started talking with his mouth full. "I read somewhere a while back that she was teaching at the university. Does she still teach?"

Lu could have spoken until she was blue in the face, and Russi would have wanted more. "Why don't you ask her yourself? Have you tried to call her?"

His eyes pinched together. "Hell, no."

"Why not?"

"This isn't something I can do on the phone, kid."

32

THE STORY

Hawai'i Island, July 1965

In the morning, Joni's disappearance was headline news. The world's most famous songstress, Rockefeller's swanky new hotel, a possible homicide. Speculation would be rampant. There was so much sadness tugging on Lu's heart. Only a small few could probably call Joni friend, and yet she was known by millions. Lu felt blessed to be among the few, a brief but deep connection.

Also on her mind was the matter of Russi and Auntie H. How would Izzy react when seeing him after all these years? Lu hoped to God she wasn't making a mistake by springing him on her unannounced after all she'd been through. There were usually two sides to a story, and Lu knew nothing of Auntie H's side. She had never once mentioned Russi.

They wrangled a truck from one of the security guards and got approval from Rapoza to leave the property for a visit home. She'd lied and said her father had come down with pneumonia and she needed to see him before flying back to the mainland.

"Why do you both need to go?" Rapoza asked.

"Moral support," Russi said.

That they both had their cameras around their necks might have tipped him off, but he was so wrapped up with the case that the whereabouts of two journalists were minor details. As they passed the front gate, several cars were parked outside, men in suits leaning on their hoods, smoking. Mr. Buttonwood was talking to them, hands flying this way and that.

"The press," she said wistfully.

"Glad that's not us right now," Russi said.

Lu teased. "We have bigger and better things to do."

She could tell he was nervous. When they'd met in the lobby, his leg was bopping around and the first thing he said was, "Am I too dressed up?"

Wearing white linen pants, a long-sleeved white button-up and a black belt, he looked stylish and swoony. And ready for a game of cricket.

"Do you have an aloha shirt?" she asked.

"I live in New York, for chrissakes, what do you think?"

"Then I think you look perfect," she'd said.

Russi had insisted on driving, and as they rode up Kawaihae Road to Waimea, the air cooled considerably. Dry parched earth gave way to chartreuse hills peppered with cattle. It seemed impossible that the land could change so dramatically, and the chilled air was heaven on her skin. But that was the Big Island for you—it had every climate under the sun.

From Waimea, they turned toward Kona at the junction. On their left, Mauna Kea took up a big swath of sky. The car had no radio, so to ease his mind along the way, Lu picked his brain about the job and how he honed his famed photography skills. A master with the nuances of light and timing, his pictures were bold and daring. Life-altering even.

When asked his secret, he took a few moments before answering. "'Embrace light. Admire it. Love it. But above all, know light. Know it for all you are worth, and you will know the key to photography.' Who said that?"

"George Eastman," Lu said, not missing a beat.

"Good. That's the best advice I've ever heard. Other than that, you have to be a keen observer. How you see things matters more than what you see, and that just comes with practice. Trusting your eye is everything. Once it's in you, you can't get rid of it. Even when I had to bail out of my plane in enemy territory, and I'd jammed my ankle and cracked my shoulder on the tail, I remember seeing this brown river snaking through the green jungle. Late-afternoon light poured out from the clouds and here I was floating down, probably gonna be captured, but it was so stinkin' beautiful. Woulda made the best photo of my life, hands down. I still see it, clear as day."

Lu sensed a window. "What happened when you landed?"

Russi took a deep breath, kept his eyes on the road. "I landed in the fricking river. Me and the parachute all tangled up. The water was mud and slime. One arm and one foot out of commission and I was drowning. I'd already swallowed gallons of water. And I thought to myself, maybe it was for the best, because if I was caught, it wouldn't be pretty. Especially if they found out what I'd done in Rabaul."

His fear of the water now locked into place.

He stopped. Lu turned toward him. "What did you do in Rabaul?"

"That's a story for another time," he said, then continued as though he needed to get this out. "Suddenly I was being yanked back up like a fish. Someone had my chute lines and I felt around for my knife so I could cut myself loose. It wasn't there, of course. When I came up, I was face-to-face with two scrawny Chinese kids who dragged me to the side of the river. One gathered up my parachute and the other shoved me into a small ravine. I was too weak to resist. Besides, I had seen the Japanese soldiers on the other side getting ready to come after me. The kids covered me with bushes, smoothed everything off and left me. I felt like I'd been buried alive.

"I heard the motor of a small boat pull up close. They were laughing as they searched for me, calling out to each other as if this was some rabbit hunt. One guy came so close he dropped his cigarette on the bush above me. And I know it sounds impossible, but I could smell them—sweat-soaked boots, body odor, fishy breath. My ankle was on fire and I was in and out of consciousness. I remember thinking that if I survived this, I could survive anything. But you know what? There's another kind of fear, manufactured by your own head, but that feels just as real. I don't know why it comes up, but it does. And every time, it flattens me. You saw me in that boat."

Lu nodded. She could feel his fear now, pulsing through the car, as the story spun out of him. She was on the rim of her seat. "What happened next?"

"Sometime later, Chinese rebel fighters came and loaded me up on a door and took me to a dilapidated house. They made me drink some bitter tea. They were using sign language to communicate, but a little while later, twins from Shanghai showed up who spoke perfect English. They told me where we were—deep in the middle of bum-fuck nowhere— and said a doctor would be coming soon. I remember crying at my good fortune. But when the doctor came in and said he wanted to put a long needle in my mangled arm to 'let the air out,' I had second thoughts. In the end, I let him because I was too weak to resist. As if that wasn't bad enough, he made me soak it in scalding water over and over and over. Then the twins told me he was going to stitch my arm and my face up using tiny needles to numb me. At that point, I was starting to wish they'd left me in the river. But it worked, and I hardly felt a thing," Russi said.

"What about your foot?"

"After a bunch of poking and prodding, he said it wasn't broken and bound it tight. Looking back, I think the man was a genius. He left me with this sack of stones to carry around until the pain got so bad I had to put it down. Each day, I was to put another stone in the sack. I did what he told me, and a couple weeks later, I could at least get around a little. Those people took such good care of me—I think about them all the time. They were putting themselves in danger by helping me."

"Most people in the world are good," Lu said.

He nodded. "Most. Not all."

"And then?"

His eyes watered, and she could tell he was trying to hold it together. "They fashioned a bamboo seat on two poles and a couple of the rebels carried me from village to camp to makeshift shelter, if you can believe it. The countryside was spectacular and covered in these delicate white flowers—when it wasn't bombed out—and the Chinese villagers welcomed me like I was some big whoop-de-do. Sometimes even setting off fireworks. Again, risky stuff back then."

He wiped his face with his sleeve, tears rolling down his face, and kept talking. "Did you know it's customary there to sing to your hosts after dinner?"

Lu resisted the urge to lean over and hug him. "No."

"Yeah, well, neither did I. But it was expected so I did it. Word must have traveled that I could sing a good tune, because in one town, as soon as we got there, they put me up on a plywood stage, along with posters of Churchill, Roosevelt and Stalin. A pile of troops gathered around and their leader insisted I sing for them. I guess I did well, because they cheered and clapped like I was the Second Coming. But then, in one town, I lost all my money to the mayor's wife in a rigged game of what she called *pokie pokie*. Didn't bother me one speck. I owed them a helluva lot more than money."

He went quiet, and Lu didn't say anything. They were passing through Puʻuanahulu, a blip of a town with her favorite little red painted church. Lava rock walls divided the area, and the cattle of Puʻuwaʻawaʻa Ranch roamed through silver oak and jacaranda trees that turned flaming yellow and purple in May. The land fell halfway between mountains and sea.

"How did you get out of China?" she asked.

"Eventually, we reached the coast, and after a two-day boat ride from hell, they got me to a US base—exactly six weeks after my plane went down. What became clear pretty quick was that after almost drowning in that river, I'd developed some weird aversion to water. A visceral thing—you saw it. And wouldn't you know it, but my family had been notified that I was dead not long after my crash. To say they were overjoyed was an understatement. But I came back a different man. At first I was just elated to be back on American soil, but the nightmares came on with a vengeance. I would wake up screaming and crying and I was having trouble remembering things. My arm was still jacked, so I saw an orthopedist and he told me that Chinese doc had saved my life. They operated and I got most of the use back. On one hand I seemed okay, but on the other I was a mess."

"What did they do for the nightmares?" Lu asked.

"Gave me some kind of intravenous bullshit that was like having a lobotomy. I tore out the needles and called my colonel to get me the hell outta there. Luckily he did," Russi said.

All at once, Lu felt the crushing weight of his memories. He had carried these for twenty years, tucked away in some dark and lonely part of his mind. The fact that he was sharing them with her now spoke volumes.

"Your story can help people," she said.

"How do you figure?"

"Because you're a well-known, well-respected journalist. If others hear your story and see that you're talking about your experience, it could inspire them to do the same. And now, we have all these guys going off to Vietnam. I think it's important for people to know the long-term effects of war and what people have to live with in the aftermath."

"How do you know some things aren't better left unsaid?"

"It's not like you'll be forcing anyone. But sharing your pain can help diffuse it. I believe that."

He chewed on that for a while, and his chest moved in and out more easily. "I have to say, it feels a little freeing. I've never told anyone that whole story—not even my ma and pa. Every time I came close, my heart would start racing and I'd get this jumpy feeling right here." He put his hand on his solar plexus. "There are a lot of other things to tell, other horrors, but I think I'm done for the day."

"I don't blame you."

Russi let out a big sigh. "Good, because I don't want to be a basket case before we even arrive."

Driving through Holulaloa, which had once been a coffee town, and later a sugar town, felt like stepping back in time. It was tiny and now seemed empty, since sugar had been on the decline. The light scent of ginger and dew came in the car windows.

Russi stuck a piece of gum in his mouth and began chewing furiously. They had switched places, Lu now driving, and she kept up the conversation, pointing out the Inaba's pink hotel, then farther on down, where the old Kona Bottling

Works used to be, and the Japanese language school that had closed down during the war.

As was usually the case in the morning here, the sky was painted blue and cloudless. That would change later, when clouds formed on the slopes of Hualālai, bringing moisture and tadpole-size rain. A perfect climate for coffee. Russi was staring out over the ocean, which from this elevation looked blue and benign. His leg started bouncing up and down.

"Are you okay? Do you want to pull over and stretch your legs?" she asked.

"Nah."

"Do you need to pee?"

"I'm fine."

He didn't look fine. He'd had at least a couple cups of coffee this morning. Looking back, she should have stopped him. The coffee at Mauna Kea was like a jolt of adrenaline.

When she turned the car off Mamalahoa Highway and up the gravel road to the farm, Russi put his hand on the dashboard, as if bracing himself. "Maybe we should just turn around. I should have called first. Showing up unannounced on her doorstep is a rookie move."

"If it makes you feel any better, I did call her. I told her I was coming by for a quick visit. So, it's not totally out of the blue."

"You didn't mention anything about me, did you?"

"Of course not."

They bumped around for about five minutes on the rutted road, then came to a fork and carved wooden sign that said Cooper Coffee Co.

"Did she tell you that before we even landed in Honolulu, Walt had decided he'd move to the Big Island and get a coffee farm? No idea where he got the notion, but he was fixated. Wanted me to partner up with him," Russi said.

"Cooper and Russi," Lu said, trying to imagine Russi living this far out in the sticks and growing coffee. She could almost see it.

"All these *coulda-beens*. It's tough, you know? You plan on your life going one way, and then it careens off on some other route altogether," he said.

"You ended up being a photojournalist like you wanted." She slowed the truck.

"And Izzy ended up living her brother's dream. Good for her. She could have done anything, and she chose this." Russi lowered his sunglasses and eyed a donkey standing in the road up ahead. "You see that animal?"

"I'm not blind."

"Is that a mule?"

Lu laughed. "It's a Kona nightingale—a donkey. They're all over the place up here. Izzy has her own little herd."

They drew close and Lu rolled to a stop. The donkey didn't budge, just stood there munching on flowers growing in the middle of the road. Its tall ears twitched, but that was it.

"Not a lot of traffic up here, I take it," he said.

"More four-legged than two."

Russi opened his door.

"What are you doing?" she asked.

"I need to get out for a minute, get some fresh air, say hi to the donkey—shit, I don't know," he said. As soon as he stood, he leaned down and looked in at her. "Wait, we don't have a lot of donkeys in New York City. Do they bite?"

Prolonging the inevitable. Lu could hardly blame him.

"They can. But these are pretty docile."

She humored him and got out, too. The donkey started nosing around Russi's pant pockets, sniffing, then nibbling. Russi jumped back. "Hey, fella, that's off-limits to you."

They rubbed the donkey for a little while, behind the ears

and on the side of his neck. Then Russi found a sweet spot on his rump that caused him to grin like a happy chimpanzee. Soon, Russi was laughing and his body loosened visibly. All that pent-up energy released into the atmosphere.

A little farther up the road, he had Lu stop to pick a few stalks of ginger. She felt nostalgic with all the coffee mountain smells—damp soil, burnt husks and clouds that hadn't formed yet. When they finally pulled up in front of the house five minutes later and turned off the car, it felt like she'd done a cross-country road trip. The house hadn't changed a bit. Red roof, green paint, giant wraparound porch. A neat row of hydrangeas skirted the front, flanked by a lawn of freshly mowed grass. Russi sat quietly, hands folded in his lap.

"Want me to go say hi and break the news?" she said.

"I think it's too late for that," he said, nodding toward a shack off to the left.

Izzy was walking toward them, taking off her gloves, waving and smiling. Completely unsuspecting. A lanky dog barked from the porch. Lu climbed out and met her in front of the steps, giving her a kiss and a big hug.

"What a treat, Luana! I wasn't expecting you until this weekend."

"I just couldn't wait," Lu said.

Izzy looked her up and down. "So grown-up and gorgeous, but still the same. I'm so proud of you."

"You look happy," Lu said.

It was true. Izzy's black hair was loose and layered and accented with a few leaf fragments. She looked hip in a pair of faded blue jeans, a man's button-up tied at the waist and rubber boots. The woman never stopped working.

Izzy held her open palms out. "Life is good. We've had a great crop this year, *and* I figured out a new way to roast the beans. I'll show you later if you have time."

"Yes!"

Izzy looked past her, toward the car. "You brought some-one with you?"

"I was going to tell you on the phone—"

Lu turned. Russi was standing with one arm on the roof of the car, clutching the flowers in his hand.

"Hello, Izzy. It's good to see you."

33

THE GUESTS

Hawai'i Island, July 1965

Isabel was up early checking on Mele, her overly pregnant donkey. When she'd bought the farm fifteen years ago, a bunch of donkeys had come along with the place. Descendants of a line of hardworking animals who ferried bags of coffee beans to the coast, her current ones were fat and lazy. They also had a talent for multiplying. Each had its own personality, and Mele was a lilikoi-loving princess who hated to be alone. She followed Isabel everywhere.

After assuring herself that Mele was okay in a small paddock behind the garage, she brewed a pot of coffee and sat on the lānai with Kolohe, her mutt, taking it all in. Mornings here never got old. When she'd first come over from O'ahu to look at land to buy, and stumbled upon this ramshackle house and struggling coffee farm, she saw right through the years of neglect and tangled vines creeping all over the railings. In her eyes, it was perfect. She could almost picture Walt standing between the trees, picking coffee beans and humming *Amazing Grace*, his favorite song.

She put in her notice at the university—she'd done her

time—and they moved in on the twentieth of July. Cliff was more excited to fish on the weekends than anything, but he was enthusiastic about a fresh start. Isabel was hopeful that the farm would give him a sense of purpose and keep him busy, but the nightmares still plagued him. Isabel ended up doing most of the work herself, getting well acquainted with a hammer and a paintbrush.

It felt like forever ago when they'd met at a victory cele-bration on Hibiscus Drive. The whole island was in a frenzy, with huge parades and fireworks and men and women kiss-ing in the streets. Izzy had given up waiting for Matteo. She'd already been through hell and back, thinking he was lost in action for six weeks, and then learning from Hudson of all people that he had shown up at a naval base in South-ern China, carried in on a bamboo throne. She kept expect-ing a letter or an apology or a knock on the door that never came. So, when Cliff asked her to dance, she held out her hand and accepted.

Twenty years ago, next month.

A family of pheasants ducked in and out of the tall grass on the other side of an old rock wall, and she watched them, allowing herself a brief walk down memory lane. Back to the war, to the Dungeon and codes, and to the months she'd spent with Matteo Russi. She'd never told a soul about those years. There was too much heartache involved. When she'd finished her coffee, Isabel brewed more for Lu and mixed up a double batch of mango bread, a few loaves for her workers and two for Lu.

She was checking on the donkey again, who was posted up behind the garage studio, when she heard an engine. Kolohe started barking as a truck pulled up. It had been almost two years since she'd seen Lu and she could barely contain her excitement. Lu hopped out and ran over to greet her. Isabel hugged her and didn't want to let go, inhaling her beachy smells and feeling her soft, curly hair. There was no one alive who she loved more than Lu. Whoever said a daughter had to be blood related?

Kolohe loved Lu, too, and greeted her with spins and twirls and whines. Lu laughed and bent down to kiss his head. Isabel noticed someone else in the car. A man stood up. A dark-haired man, backlit by the sun. For a second, she thought it was Matteo Russi. Probably because she'd just been thinking about him. One of those strange tendencies of the universe. Isabel squinted. He was holding fresh-cut yellow ginger and looking directly at her. Dark hair, dark eyes.

"You brought someone with you?"

"I was going to tell you on the phone," Lu said, turning to look at the man. "But we thought it would be better in person."

We? The man came around from the car and was walking toward her. She had a clear view of his face. He smiled. A whoosh ran through her whole body. Oh my God, it really was Matteo Russi. Same gap between the teeth, same swagger, same everything.

"Hello, Izzy, it's good to see you," he said.

Isabel found that she couldn't speak. A vibration started up in her legs and moved its way up her torso and down her arms. Out through her fingertips. She reached out to Lu to steady herself. "Matteo? What are you doing here?" she said, half whispering.

"Lu and I are on assignment at the Mauna Kea hotel and we just made the connection. About you, I mean. I asked her to bring me," he said, still holding the flowers.

"What a surprise this is."

The math was not adding up.

"I know it's a shock. We can leave if you like, come back another time."

"No, no, you just drove all the way down here. It's just the last thing I would have ever expected. To see you standing here in the flesh."

He shoved the flowers at her, as though just realizing he still held them. In the exchange their hands brushed, and they both froze. Then the moment passed. He stood there awkwardly, bouncing on one leg. "Looks like you found yourself a real slice of heaven up here. I'm happy for you."

If anyone, he knew her motivation for owning a coffee farm. "Being here was inevitable. Plus, I got Lu in the bargain, so that made it all the sweeter," she said.

Matteo Russi had just waltzed up and shoved a ginger bush in her face. As if that could make up for twenty years of silence. Twenty years of wondering what might have been. Even when she'd been happily in love with Cliff, thoughts of Matteo would rise up when she least expected. She could still see herself throwing that pillow, heart cracked in two, as he'd walked out the door. He'd hurt her badly.

"Would you two like to come up? I have some fresh mango bread," she offered, trying to appear calm and unfazed.

Lu squealed. "You didn't!"

"You know how it is with the pigs. If I don't pick them before they fall, every pig within a ten-mile radius beds up under the tree at this time of year."

The old mango tree stood at least seventy feet tall. Every season, without fail, it delivered truckloads of mangos. She made mango bread, mango chutney, mango ice cream, mango mocha, and still had tons to spare. So much so, that by August she couldn't even look at another mango.

"You sure it's not an imposition?" Matteo asked.

He seemed so hesitant.

"Positive. Come on."

She turned and walked toward the steps, Lu next to her, Matteo trailing behind. His presence was palpable, heating up her skin like it always had. He sat on the ohia log bench on the deck, while she and Lu went into the kitchen. Once there, with Matteo out of earshot, Isabel leaned back on the fridge and put her hands on her chest and let out a big, "Oh my God."

"Are you okay?" Lu asked.

"I'm not sure."

Really, she wasn't. Her hand went to her watch, as it always did in hard times. She'd replaced the band a few years back. The smooth leather felt cool against her palm.

Lu was bubbling. "It's been such a crazy week, and weirdly, we've become close. When we put two and two together, and I realized that the Izzy he'd been talking about was you, we both knew we had to come. He was freaking out on the way down. This is a big deal for him, too."

"He burned me, Lu. Did he tell you that?"

Burn was a bit of an understatement, but over the years she'd come to understand that Matteo had never belonged to her in the first place. He had been devoted to Walt, and to the war. To doing the right thing and chasing a dream. But Matteo had been right about one thing: she wouldn't have been able to handle losing him. As it was, she was still mourning what might have been.

"I should leave you two alone to talk. He has a lot to say to you," Lu said, biting her lip. "But also, we came for another reason."

"What other reason could there be?"

"Let's talk outside, with Russi."

Isabel faltered. "I'm not sure I'm ready for this."

"No one is asking you to do anything. Just listen. Would you do that? For me."

Isabel sighed and went over to slice the mango bread, while Lu poured coffee into three tall mugs. Neither spoke for a time, and Isabel finally said, "I just wish you had warned me."

It was impossible to be mad at Lu.

"I suggested it, but he was adamant. I think he was afraid you wouldn't see him."

Out on the lānai, Kolohe had joined Matteo on the bench. Isabel set everything on the table, but Matteo couldn't move because the dog's head was resting on his lap. Years back, Isabel had found Kolohe way up on the mountain, bones showing and weak with hunger. Hunting dogs often got lost up there, and if they were lucky, found their way down the mountain. In the shape he was in, Kolohe would never have made it down. Isabel had saved his life, and in turn, he'd become her most devoted friend.

"I'm stuck," Matteo said, running has hands through Kolohe's short, brindle fur.

Lu looked surprised. "I've never seen him act like this. He usually shies away from strangers."

It was true. Kolohe took a while to warm up to people, and was guarded around most men.

"Dogs always have a thing for me. Don't ask me why," Matteo said with the hint of a smile.

Strange how many of her memories from the war years had blurred, but those involving Matteo were still clear as motion pictures. Sometimes, when she closed her eyes, she could still smell the salt on his skin.

Lu handed him a plate and a mug and said, "I know you've already had your quota, but you need to try this coffee."

Isabel sat on the far end of the bench, looking out into the trees so she didn't have to look at Matteo. Close enough to touch Kolohe's foot, but far enough to feel safe. There was so much simmering beneath the surface, so much to ask and say, but more than anything, she wanted to know what had brought them here. "Lu tells me that you two came down here for a reason other than just to pop in and say hi," she said.

"Have you read the papers today?" Matteo asked.

"I don't usually read the paper until the afternoon. There's too much to do around here in the mornings."

"One of Mr. Rockefeller's guests went missing, is presumed to be drowned. You probably know of her—Joni Diaz."

"The singer?"

He nodded. "A real tragedy and everyone is torn up about it. Anyway, they did a search and ended up finding her shoes on the rocks out near the point. But not before Lu and I went off on our own to help out and came across an old skeleton in a lava tube."

He paused, rubbing Kolohe behind the ears in his favorite spot.

"Was it precontact?" Isabel asked, knowing that caves up and down the coast were full of old Hawaiian bones.

"These aren't," Lu said.

"We brought the sheriff back the next day. He examined them and thought it was a woman. Been there anywhere from ten to fifty years. And we found something else, Izzy."

Isabel was trying to see the connection between a missing singer who she'd never met, an old skeleton and herself. Why had Matteo come all this way to tell her about it? There was no discernible pattern. Or was there?

"You said this was north of the hotel? Near Spencer Beach?" she said.

"It was a ring. I recognized it right away," he said, voice low.

A lump formed in her throat. "What did it look like?"

"It was *your* ring. The one you got on the way to Goat Is-

land. I lost my mind for a few hours there, when I was trying to figure out how that ring could have ended up in some
cave in the flipping boonies, unless it was on your hand." He
turned toward her, and when she looked into his eyes, she
found she couldn't look away.

"I got two of them, remember? One for me and one for
Gloria."

He frowned. "No, I don't remember."

"It was such a fleeting moment in time. And think of what
you've been through since then. But tell me, is the cave underwater?" she asked.

"High and dry," Matteo said.

Isabel didn't like where this was headed.

"You sure about that? What about in wintertime, when
the surf gets big?"

"This was way above any high waterline," Lu said. "We
were well into the kiawe forest."

That ring had been on Gloria's hand the day she left for
the Big Island. Isabel tried to make sense of this new information. "Where's the ring now?"

"Sheriff Rapoza has it."

"How sure are you that it's the same ring?"

"I might not have remembered you getting two, but I
know the ring."

Isabel went inside and opened her little box from the windowsill, the one she put the ring in when she was out working in the yard. She brought the ring outside and held it out
for them both to see. They both spoke at once.

"That's it."

Lu spoke up. "It's the same. Only yours is shiny."

Kolohe, who sensed that something big was going down,
flipped around, and nuzzled his head into Isabel's side. She
pulled him close as that old sadness swooped in. *Sweet Gloria.*

"You think she could have been swept down the coast and somehow managed to climb out on the rocks? Was there anything else in there with her?" she asked.

"We don't know. And yeah, there was that polka-dotted piece of material, maybe a swimsuit?"

An image arose. Gloria in front of the Royal Hawaiian Hotel, looking ravishing in a red polka-dot suit, leaning on a coconut tree, knee bent and in love with the world. Even though the world was at war. She was that kind of person.

Isabel stood up and went to the railing. "She loved that suit. I helped her pick it out, and she told me I could borrow it whenever I wanted."

"You two coulda been twins. I remember that. Double trouble."

"What did Rapoza say when you told him about the ring?"

Matteo, who had been leaning with his forearms on his thighs, sat up. "He doesn't know yet. I needed to find you first."

"You realize that this changes everything, don't you? Way back when, I told the detective that I didn't trust Gloria's boyfriend, Dickie, but everyone seemed satisfied that she'd drowned. It was almost as though they couldn't be bothered to even look into him. There was too much other stuff going on."

"Why didn't you trust him?" Lu asked.

Isabel explained how Gloria had come to her after finding the letter, and then the note that she'd tossed into the trash. *I did find something curious, tell you when I get back.*

She turned to face Matteo. "You know who he is, right?"

"I hardly remember the guy. My focus was elsewhere," he said.

In the slanted sun, she could see that fine smile lines had formed on his face. If anything, they made him more distinguished. And now, he was staring into her with such force she was pinned to the post.

"At some point along the way he went back and took his birth father's name. Dickie Thompson is Senator Richard Fuchs."

34

THE MESSAGE

Hawai'i Island, July 1965

In the years following Gloria's death, Isabel had kept tabs on Dickie. He moved up in the ranks and by the time the war was over he had helped oversee the rebuilding of countless ships and submarines in the Navy Yard at Pearl. When the war ended, he left the islands and went home to Pennsylvania and married his high school sweetheart. All of this intel had been gathered through the coconut wireless.

Over time, busy with her own life, she lost track of his whereabouts, until the night she saw his face on the evening news. White teeth, tanned face, blonder hair and a different name. Yet Dickie beyond a slice of doubt. The shock had sent her into a funk for a few days, trying to arrange the pieces in place. She knew from Gloria that he'd lost his father young, and been adopted.

Isabel put the memory aside and slipped back onto her sunny porch with Matteo and Lu. They were both staring at her.

Matteo said, "He's at the hotel. Right now. Fuchs is a guest of the Rockefellers."

A cold wind blew through her mind.

One man.

Two women.

Both dead.

Matteo ran his hands through his hair. "I've met Fuchs a couple times, and never once did I ever recognize him from O'ahu. How can that be?"

"You only really met him once, though, didn't you? At the house party in Kailua. That night at the bar didn't count, when you were with Alice," Isabel said.

"You remember her name?"

She shrugged. "You aren't the only one who remembers things."

"I do know that the guy rubbed me the wrong way. He was so cocksure he was going to beat you at chess, and then you clobbered him. I wanted to hold up your hand and walk you around the place like the champ that you were. Give you a gold belt or something," Matteo said, half smiling.

"He looks different now. His hair is longer and lighter, and he got a tan. Maybe even had his teeth fixed, whitened or something," Isabel said.

"Never trust a man who dyes his hair. Journalism 101," Matteo said.

"We need to tell Rapoza," Lu said.

"Did Senator Fuchs know Joni Diaz? We know he had motive for Gloria," Isabel asked.

Lu explained what she knew, how Joni had alluded to being in love with someone and not able to tell. "But there's nothing concrete. Especially with no body. I'm afraid that it could end up being the same scenario as with Gloria. Girl missing, presumed drowned. No real questions asked."

She thought of the folded piece of paper resting patiently in a koa box in her closet. "Not if I can help it," Isabel said.

Matteo looked up. "You know something?"

"I should have brought this forward a long time ago. But I had already appealed to everyone I knew to investigate Thompson... Fuchs...whatever, and been shut down at every turn."

She went into the bedroom and came out with the box. She set it on the table and they all crowded around. Yellowed with time, the middle fold cracked through in a few spots. Isabel smoothed out the paper.

It contained a coded message that had come through in late 1944. The Japanese had recently changed additives again, and much of the message was garbled, but Isabel had sat up when the name Kuehn appeared out of the mix. *Otto Kuehn.* Father of Dickie's so-called friend. German spy.

Frustrated at the quality of the message, she nevertheless persisted at decoding it. Between the static, words emerged: *Explosions at Pearl...ships being prepared for transport... LSTs sunk, many killed and missing, 10 buildings destroyed...ammunition believed...destination Marianas... Kuehn...payment delivered... Tomimura.*

There had been a press blackout on the West Loch disaster, so how did the Japanese know about it?

The linguists believed that beyond the information about the explosion, the message referred to a town in Japan where Kuehn must have had ties, where payment would be made: Tomimura. But Kuehn was locked up, and Isabel felt strongly that there was something between the lines that they were missing. She had that tingle down her neck.

She looked at Matteo. "Does Lu know?"

"I just told her what I know, which isn't much."

Lu reached out and grabbed her hand, a reassuring gesture. "I always wondered what you were leaving out about the war years. And I'm not surprised, really."

"You realize this is all still classified, don't you? We can't be having this conversation," Isabel said.

"What conversation?" Matteo asked.

"I don't know what kind of trouble I could get in for even having this message in my possession. I made a copy of this at three a.m. while working the night shift, and kept it hidden in the hem of my bathrobe," she told them.

Matteo's leg was bouncing again, in that way it always did when he got excited. Or nervous. "Are you going to tell us what it says?"

She told them about the message, and then added the kicker. "We had a few linguists that really knew their stuff, but none agreed with my theory that *To-mi-mu-ra* was not a town but a name." Isabel pointed to the word, which she'd hashed up into syllables with a pencil. "Mura means *town*, but in some cases it can also be *son*. And when you combine the two together, you get Tomi-son, which is how the Japanese would pronounce Thompson."

Reading it now, it was so clear.

A light rain started up outside, seemingly out of the blue. This was the first time Isabel had ever told anyone outside of FRUPAC, which was where the CIU unit had relocated after the Dungeon.

Matteo and Lu exchanged glances. "Are you sure about this?" he asked.

Isabel tucked her hair behind her ears. "For a long time, I wasn't. We had a few top-notch linguists, but they weren't well versed in some of the nuances of Japanese cursive and older forms of writing. Sometimes that made it hard for them to think outside the box. At one point, I took on the job of translating a recovered diary, and had to delve deeper. But I gave in and had to trust that they knew what they were talking about. But it nagged at me."

"I'd believe you over them any day," Matteo said.

It was still hard to believe that Matteo Russi was here on her coffee farm, brown eyes looking her way. She went on, feeling more than a little disarmed. "Then, about five or six years ago, I was over at Mr. Hamada's getting some seedlings and something he said reminded me of the message. Old man Hamada was born in Japan, so I asked him what he thought. I didn't give him any details, obviously, but asked if Tomimura could be a Japanese version of an American name. He said *definitely*."

"So, let's say we have an intercepted message from Tokyo, and it ties Thompson to Kuehn—"

"We already know that Thompson worked in Kuehn's warehouse," Isabel said.

"How did the FBI miss him on the first go-around?" Matteo asked.

"Because he's smart. While Kuehn was living large on his Japanese salary, Dickie remained anonymous in the shadows. And then he joined the navy. You've seen him in a debate, haven't you? Smooth as butter," Isabel said.

"Can we take this message to Rapoza as evidence?" Lu asked.

"I need to make a call first. Lu, why don't you show Mr. Russi around. Maybe check on Mele. She's out back, ready to pop."

Isabel watched them go. Seeing the two of them together was like watching an old movie and a new one side by side. Two worlds colliding. Maybe the compass on the watch had led him here, finally swinging to its true north. Just before they reached the edge of the wall, he slowed, turned back and caught her watching. He smiled.

Ever since her conversation with Mr. Hamada, Isabel had thought about tracking down Hudson and telling her story, asking for advice. They'd left on good terms. In fact, by the time the war ended, Isabel was often the one who got handed the "hard" messages first. Last she'd heard, Hudson was living in the mountains of New Mexico, retired and raising alpacas. It always fascinated her to hear where her coworkers had settled, and what kinds of peculiar professions or hobbies they'd taken up when the war ended. The war had been a great equalizer. It was sometimes easy to forget that just like everyone had a life before the war, everyone would have a life after. *Everyone who survived.* But also, that life would never ever go back to normal. Not for them.

His wife picked up on the second ring, and Isabel strummed her fingers on her address book while waiting.

"What a pleasant surprise," he said, sounding genuinely happy to hear from her.

They made small talk for a few minutes, catching up on lives, and then Isabel told him the whole story. She'd been anxious about the part where she copied the message, but Hudson didn't bat an eye.

"Why didn't you come to me at the time with the message?" he asked.

"None of the guys agreed with me. I thought maybe I was losing my mind, or wasn't being objective. It was a particularly active time and I'd been awake for what seemed like weeks."

He chuckled. "You probably had been."

"I should have pushed it, but I had no proof of anything, and by the time I spoke with Hamada, the war had been over for fifteen years. It didn't seem like enough to come forward and point a finger at a US senator."

Isabel looked at the photo of Walt on the wall, watching over her, as always. She was doing the right thing, at long last.

"Listen, this is an unusual situation. I'll make some calls and get back to you." There was silence on the line, and then he said, "Fucking A, as Denny would say. This could get ugly."

"It already is ugly."

After hanging up with Hudson, she walked back onto the porch, glancing around for Lu and Matteo. Drizzle had given way to steamy sunshine. She walked toward the garage to see if they were with Mele. A strange grunting arose from behind the structure. She started running, and made it in time to see a foal's head slip out of Mele, who was lying on her side on the grass. Matteo and Lu were standing back, near the rock wall, watching. Lu had seen this before, but Matteo looked unsure.

When he saw Isabel, he said, "I hope you know something about how this works."

"Mele knows what to do, she doesn't need me. But I like to be here just in case."

Mele kept turning around to see the foal, encased in a bag of amniotic fluid. Its tiny perfect profile was enough to fill even a bitter heart with love. Isabel came around and stood by Lu and Matteo, keeping a healthy distance.

"Easy there, mama. We're here with you," she said.

Mele pushed. Nothing happened. The donkey then stood up and started walking in circles, as if trying to see her foal.

"Is there a problem?" Matteo asked.

"I don't think so, it just takes time."

They moved back so they were sitting on a bench under a giant jacaranda tree, letting nature run its course. Mele lay down again on her side, eyes wide, nostrils flaring. They waited a short while longer, and still the foal didn't come out. Isabel knew that the main danger was having it suck back into the birth canal and drowning. She glanced over at Matteo, and their eyes met. Even though he had no idea what he was doing, having him here felt good.

When twenty more minutes passed, Isabel began to worry. She pulled out her birthing box, with towels and antiseptic and gauze, then went over and bent down next to Mele, running her hand down the animal's back. The foal was in the correct position, head resting on its two front legs, one slightly forward of the other for easy passage.

"Push, Mele, push," Isabel said.

Mele let out a long moan. She appeared to be straining more than usual.

"I think she needs help. Lu, can you go call Dr. Greenwell and ask her to come as soon as she can? Her number is on the fridge. Matteo, I need you over here with me."

A second later, he was kneeling beside her. "Just tell me what to do."

"I'm going to break the bag, and I need you to grab the legs and gently but firmly pull." She pointed toward Mele's underbelly. "You have to pull in this direction or you could hurt the foal's back."

"Roger."

Matteo was dressed in all white and looking very stylish, but it was the worst possible attire for the job he was about to do. "You may want to take your shirt off," she said.

He looked down, then said, "Nah. I can always get a new one."

They were kneeling next to each other, shoulder to shoulder. His sureness gave her confidence.

"So as soon as I break the bag, you pull, okay?"

He nodded. All signs of nervousness had left him. Isabel broke the bag and wiped away the clear film over the foal's tiny, precious nose, and the foal took its first breath.

"Now," she said.

Matteo gripped the foal's ankles and pulled steadily in the direction she'd shown him. The foal seemed wedged in place for a moment, but once its front half was free, the rest of its little body slid out in one big whoosh. Small and wet and dark, the foal was all legs and ears.

"Now we step away," Isabel told him.

Mele took over from there. Nudging and licking and mothering. The tiny foal made a few failed attempts to get its legs under itself.

"It's a girl!" Isabel said.

Matteo's clothes were no longer dry. Or white. "Would you look at that. Never thought I'd add donkey midwife to the résumé," he said.

Again, the foal unfolded her legs and tried to push herself up. This time she succeeded in standing. Mele sat back and watched, head drooping in exhaustion.

"Probably not what you expected this morning," Isabel said quietly.

"You can say that again," he whispered. "But look at that little thing."

She snuck a look at Matteo, who was watching the foal with such tenderness he may as well have been the father. The foal was now prancing around on wobbly new legs.

"Have you ever seen a birth before? Of any kind?" she asked.

He shook his head. "I've seen men die, but never, not once, watched anything being born."

Isabel smiled. "It almost feels like each new birth helps cancel out more than its share of sadness in the world."

He seemed to be studying her, his eyes boring deep. "Some things have that effect."

35

THE BEACH

Hawaiʻi Island, July 1965

The early-afternoon onshore wind beat the water into a frenzy. Blues and whites and grays all mixed together in a mash of chaotic motion. Fresh out of the shower, towel wrapped on her head, Lu sat on the lānai and studied the moods of nature while waiting for Russi and Sheriff Rapoza. But before they arrived, Dylan called.

"I have some new information for my favorite journalist," he said, a smile in his voice.

"And I have some new information for my favorite photographer."

"Glad I still rate as your number one."

"Always," she said. "You go first."

"Soooo, I discovered that, until 1948, Fuchs went by the name Thompson. In the navy, he was known as Dickie Thompson—"

She cut him off. "I know that already. We found out this morning. Wait until you hear this story, Dylan. But you have to swear not to tell a soul. Not until we talk to the police, which we're about to do."

"Cross my heart," he said, and she pictured the way he did that, running his finger down along the contours of his face and across his chest, without ever lifting it. She told him everything they'd learned from Izzy.

When she was done, Dylan whistled. "Guys like Fuchs think they're untouchable. When I found out he changed his name, I called his office to ask why. The lady who answered said that his mother had insisted he take the name of the man she remarried, but once his mother died, he changed it back. In honor of his father."

"Sounds reasonable. Unless you're a murderer. Then it's awfully convenient," she said.

"What about Russi and your friend?"

One thing she loved about Dylan was his unabashed interest in the lives of other people. And not just because he was in the field.

"He was so nervous going down there I wasn't sure he would go through with it. And then Auntie H—Izzy—she's always so cool and collected, but I could tell she was rattled," she said.

"A meeting like that would rattle the best of us."

"It seems like the hardest part was both of them knowing what they'd let slip out of their hands."

Silence on the other end.

"What a position to be in," he finally said.

"It makes one think."

"It does."

Five seconds later, there was pounding on the door. Lu said goodbye and opened up, ushering in Russi, Rapoza and Bull. The dog must have smelled the foal on Russi, because he sniffed and slobbered all over him and would not leave his side.

"I must smell like donkey, even after a hot shower," he told Rapoza. "Long story."

"I have time."

So, Russi laid it all out for him, with Lu dropping in details here and there, like seeing the scratches on Fuchs. Rapoza kept a poker face the whole time. When they'd finished, he said, "Let me run through this again. Senator Fuchs, who once called himself Thompson, is the same man who was with Gloria Moreno when she allegedly drowned at Mauʻmae in 1943. But now Gloria's ring was found near the skeleton in the lava tube, which you believe positively IDs it. And you suspect Fuchs is responsible for killing Joni Diaz. But as of yet we have no body and no motive."

"If Gloria 'drowned,' then why is her body a hundred yards inland, deep in a cave?" Lu said.

They hadn't told him about the old Japanese message from Izzy. They still needed her approval, and they didn't want to get her in hot water.

Russi chimed in. "Oh, there's motive. The roommate maintains that she told the cops back then that Gloria had found a suspicious letter and was concerned Dickie might be a spy. The cops ignored her."

"What about Diaz? Motive?"

"When she told me about the man she was in love with, and sworn to secrecy, I got the feeling she was on the edge. Maybe she threatened to go public? Fuchs is up for reelection, and imagine what his constituents would think if they found out he was having an affair with a Mexican singer. It would ruin his career."

Rapoza jotted down a list of notes, then stood up and said, "These are serious allegations. I need to get ahold of my boss and make sure we have our ducks in a row. Then we'll talk to Fuchs."

"The sooner, the better," Lu said.

"I know that, miss. We'll be back in the morning. Meantime, don't you go saying anything to anyone. Especially Fuchs. If you're right about any of this, he's not someone you want to mess with."

Lu woke even earlier than usual, despite hardly sleeping. Clouds slung low over the bay and she smelled rain. The weather seemed unusually moody for this time of year. Her mind was still a jumble from events of the past few days. So much heartache, and yet so much hope. Funny how the two often went hand in hand.

The beach awaited, hard sand laid bare in low tide. It was dark enough so Lu could only make out shapes. The trees stood unusually quiet, and the water was tranquil as a mountain spring. She thought of Dylan again, and how things might go when or if she made it back to say goodbye. Spending time with Russi and Izzy yesterday had impressed upon her the importance of speaking your heart. What if she lost Dylan without telling him how she felt? Could she live with that?

As she neared the Kona end of the cove, a big log appeared. Depending on the currents, fallen trees from around the island or even from the west coast washed ashore on these beaches. Some over a hundred feet long, others polished smooth and worn from months at sea. When she was almost upon the log, she noticed branches coming off the trunk. They looked almost human. A faint smell of fish and decay lifted off it. She stepped closer, then went still as a fence post. This was no log or branch. This was a body.

The dead woman was lying on her side, twisted, hair splayed out like seaweed and one arm behind her at an unnatural angle. Bile rose in Lu's throat. Finding a skeleton was one thing, but a dead body something else entirely. A strange pull grounded her to the sand. A need to stand and look, to comprehend what she was seeing. *Death*. Her feet remained planted, though a part of her wanted to bolt.

"I'm sorry, sweet friend," she whispered, for there was no mistaking who this was.

Joni.

Two small black crabs climbed down the torso, scurrying toward her feet. It was too much. Lu turned to run back and report what she'd found, but someone was standing there, blocking her way.

"Is everything okay, Miss Freitas?" Senator Fuchs asked.

"No, it's not. It's Joni," she said, pointing.

He didn't say anything at first, just stood there. Didn't even try to look at the twisted form in the sand. *He doesn't know that you know*, Lu reminded herself. *Stay cool.*

"Well, I suppose it was bound to happen. Did you know that bodies usually sink first and then later float to the surface?" he said.

Her skin electrified. What a bizarre thing to say. Lu glanced past him to see if there was anyone else around. They were alone. "No, I didn't. Now, excuse me, I need to get back and tell someone."

He blocked her, then lightly grabbed below her elbow. "How about we walk to the end of the beach, in case there's anything else to see, and then we can go back and tell Mr. Rockefeller together."

When he didn't let go, Lu went along with him. Breaths became hard to find.

"I've been thinking about what you said to me the other day, about you and Matteo Russi finding something else of interest. It really made me curious. Would you care to elaborate what it was that had you so intrigued?" He tried to sound casual, but she noted a slight tremor in his voice.

"Oh, nothing. We found some really unusual petroglyphs that I'd never seen before. I used to come up here a lot, so that was really surprising to me. I'm an amateur archeologist."

"Oh? What were they of?"

Her eyes scanned the beach for any kind of weapon—branch, rock, coconut, anything. "Just unusual-looking canoes and geometric shapes, hard to describe."

"You know, something about you reminds me of Miss Diaz. Do you sing?" he asked.

This was getting weirder by the second.

"Not at all."

Fuchs forced a laugh. "Hmm. Perhaps, then, it's that you two are both dark-skinned, pretty things. What is your family background, Miss Cooper?"

"My dad is Portuguese, my mom Irish. What about you, Senator? Fuchs is a German name, isn't it?" *You Nazi motherfucker.*

His grip firmed up on her arm. "Very astute of you. You're smarter than you look, aren't you?"

"Oh, I'm smart, all right," she said, eyes locking on a piece of driftwood about twenty yards away. They were getting farther and farther from the hotel, and the pink light from earlier had been blotted out by clouds. The question of whether he was really unhinged enough to do something to her kept looping around in her brain. Each time the answer came back the same.

Probably.

"You know, I think I'll turn around now," she said.

He leaned in so his mouth was inches from her ear. "Am I making you nervous?"

A voice inside said, *Run*, but his iron grip was beginning to cut off her circulation. "Actually—"

Behind them, someone yelled. "Hey! Wait up!"

They both turned to see Russi running toward them with a towel around his neck. Senator Fuchs looked flummoxed, and Lu had never in her life been more relieved to see someone.

When he reached them, Russi's hair was askew and he leaned down with his hands on his knees to catch his breath, "There's a fucking dead body back there, did you see it?"

Lu gave him a look, but he probably wouldn't notice in the dim light. "We did."

Fuchs let her arm go, and remained cool. "We're on our way to report it to Mr. Rockefeller—just wanted to check there wasn't anything else on the rest of the beach first."

Ready to hightail it out of there, Lu grabbed Russi by the hand and pulled at him. "We'll go, Senator. You keep walking."

As they ran back to the hotel, Lu would not let go of Russi's hand. She was half-hysterical while trying to explain what had just transpired. Russi, in turn, seemed to understand and let her keep his hand. It was big and warm and comforting.

"The guy knows it's over. He's getting reckless," he said.

"I'm just happy you came when you did."

"Thought I'd work up my nerve to dip a leg in or something, without anyone around."

"Weren't we supposed to do it together?"

"You have enough on your plate."

"Russi, we had a deal."

"I think we got more important things to worry about."

Rapoza, his chief, several other detectives and the coroner showed up an hour later. Entry to the beach had been blocked off and Lu and Russi sat in the lobby drinking coffee, watching the hotel get taken over by law enforcement. Mr. Rockefeller had been gracious and helpful, but you could see the toll this was taking on him—his grand opening marred by such ugliness. They watched as Joni's body was carried out on a stretcher, under a white sheet. Stanley followed behind, ten pounds lighter than when he'd first arrived.

"Do you think they'll arrest Fuchs?" Lu asked.

"That remains to be seen. Right now, it looks like all the evidence is circumstantial. They may have to build a case first. But I'm not sure how things work here in Hawai'i."

"Just like they do anywhere else in the country. We have a court system."

It had been six years since statehood.

"Let's hope if it makes it that far, the judge isn't easily intimidated," Russi said.

"You met Judge Carlsmith. I wish it could be him."

"That won't happen."

"Someone like him, then. Not some pushover. And someone who can't be bought."

"Agreed."

What they were really waiting for was to see if Rapoza came down with Fuchs in handcuffs. Neither of them wanted to miss that. They'd given the sheriff all they could, without Izzy's message. She hoped it was enough.

"I'm gonna go see if Izzy called," Russi said, leaving her alone with two bronze statues for company.

He came back ten minutes later. She hadn't. "I tried to call, but there was no answer. You think she's avoiding me?"

"Don't be stupid. She's probably out with the foal," she

said, noticing how worked up he was. "Why don't you just go back down there?"

"You think?"

"I know."

36

THE CONVERSATION

Hawai'i Island, 1965

Isabel had spent much of the morning sitting by the phone waiting to hear from Hudson. Every now and then, she'd run outside to check on the foal, who she was now calling Pepeiao, Hawaiian for *ear*. She'd also pulled the old photo album from the top shelf in her bedroom and brought it into the kitchen to help her pass the time. Even back then, Matteo had been a natural. Harnessing light and snapping just at the right moment, freezing the expressions of his subjects in time. He was a genius at anticipating.

The photo album hadn't left the shelf in a while. Every time she looked at the pictures, it brought up emotions and memories better left behind. Bittersweet, with more bitter than sweet. When she got to the page of Goat Island, she stepped back into the photos, feeling the warm sand on her back, the wind on her skin. That was the day that everything changed. When she realized she was in up to her eyes. What a fool. She slammed the album shut. Matteo had come back not to see her, but because of the murder.

Screw him.

She heard an engine, tires crunching on gravel. Probably Dr. Greenwell. Isabel went outside to greet her, but it wasn't the doctor; it was Matteo. He was just shutting the car door, and turned to see her. This time he was dressed in jeans and an olive-colored T-shirt. Aviator glasses.

"You're back," she said, nonplussed.

He grinned, almost bashfully. "It appears that way. Can I come up?"

"Where's Lu?"

"I came alone. I was hoping we could talk."

Some moments in life are meant to be remembered. Isabel had dreamed about this encounter for twenty years—where they might be, what he'd be wearing, what he might say, what *she* would say. And now, she stood rooted on the red painted boards on her deck, mute as a piece of wood.

"Izzy? Please," he said.

"Come on up."

She led him into the kitchen, which smelled of the roasted coffee beans and akala berry scones she'd been baking. Late-morning light shone in through the panes, brightening up an old glass milk bottle with a purple agapanthus in it. The album was still on the table.

He sat down, and Isabel took her time in washing a few dishes, buttering the scones, anything to keep from sitting and facing him. Meanwhile, he told her about Joni's body washing ashore, and the weird interaction with Fuchs.

"Lu must be in shock," she said.

"Lu's a tough kid. She's handling it," Matteo said, reaching out to the album and opening it to the Goat Island page. She swore his features softened when he looked at it. "I don't know why, but I brought mine along on this trip. I made one for you and kept one for myself. All the same shots."

That took her by surprise. "You lugged it all the way to Hawai'i?"

"I think a part of me knew I was meant to find you."

She chewed on that for a while, then braved pulling out a chair to the side of him, so they weren't facing each other—that would be her undoing. "I took mine off the shelf this morning. Answer something for me, will you?"

"Anything."

"Why didn't you get in touch after China? I thought you were dead, and it nearly killed me, and then when they told me you were alive, I kept waiting to hear from you. But I never did. That wasn't fair." She said it all in one breath, in case she lost her nerve.

"Oh, but I did write to you, that's the messed-up part. I wrote you about ten different letters and they all ended up in the trash. *Dear Izzy. My Dear Isabel. Dearest Izzy.* Then I got ahold of your number and could not bring myself to call you. It was like I was paralyzed. I guess you could say I was a casualty of war, fighting my own demons and losing badly. Then later I heard you got married. And you know what?" he said.

"What?"

He took a deep breath. "That broke me."

Isabel finally turned to look at him.

One side of his mouth curved up and he was staring at her intensely. "I was crazy for you. Head over heels, mad. But I had myself convinced like some dumb piece of toast that I didn't deserve you and I was going to ruin your life. You'd already been through so much. I was young, Izzy, and I loved you."

Love. If ever there were a word she didn't expect to hear from Matteo Russi that was it. Her mind was flitting around like a honeycreeper, thinking back to that time when she'd thought he died, and then later, how she'd feverishly checked the mailbox for a letter. Waited for a call.

He reached out and took her hand. Warm, as always. Rougher than she remembered. Could this really be true?

"Say something?" he said.

Isabel squeezed his hand as a tear ran down her cheek. "Oh, Matteo. You have no idea." She got up and went to the windowsill, picking up a white coral heart and setting it down on the table in front of him. "I told myself all kinds of stories about why you never got in touch with me. And on so many occasions, I wanted to toss this back into the ocean. But I couldn't do it. You meant more to me than anyone alive, and this was the only piece of you I had."

Matteo picked up the heart and slid it next to the Goat Island photo. "Damn, you are every bit as beautiful as you were that day on the beach. Even more so."

She fought back a sob. "I loved you, too."

Love. Present tense.

He pulled a yellowed, crumpled envelope out of his pocket and held it out to her. "Here's proof."

The envelope was addressed to her home in Honolulu. It even had a three-cent stamp on it, honoring those who served in WWII. It was small and about twenty years late. She just sat there looking at it, dazed.

"Would you read it?" he asked.

Isabel took it from his hand and opened it, the seal loose but still holding. A regular old piece of lined paper, folded in half. Nothing fancy.

Dear Izzy,

It's me, Matteo. But I guess you already know that. I hope this letter finds you happy and in good health. I believe you know that I was shot down over China and got out of there by the skin of my teeth. The war is over now, but it'll never be over for me, for you, for those of us who lost loved ones. I'm going to get straight to the point here. I made a big mistake by leaving without telling you my real feelings and regret it every day. I'm only now coming out of a long recuperation and the only thing that has kept me going is the thought of flying over there and seeing you. Would that be too much to ask? I have so much to say to you, but I need to say it in person. Just say the word and I'm there.

Love always,
MR

A tear dripped onto the paper. She looked up at him and smiled. How quickly she would have said, *Yes, come.*

"I know it's no masterpiece, but hey, I was young and dumb and scared out of my wits," he said.

"It's perfect."

Matteo yanked her chair closer and pulled her into him. He held her against his chest, tight and furious. He spoke into her messy hair. "I don't expect you to say anything or answer me, but I want you to know I promised myself that if I ever found you I would do whatever I could to have you in my life. Even if it meant just being your friend. Hell, I'd be happy to come here and help pick coffee beans, or deliver baby donkeys, if that's all I could get. I want more, but I'll take whatever crumbs you give me."

He pushed back so he could look her in the eye. He hesitated, then went to kiss her lightly on the forehead. Isabel lifted her face, and instead their lips met. Suddenly, they were back on a deserted beach, a coral heart resting warmly on her stomach. This time, there was no war. *This time, she would not let him go.*

37

THE PERFECT SHOT

Hawaiʻi Island, 1965

Like any respectable journalist, Lu had remained in the lobby long after Russi left, chipping away at her story with the help of extra-hot coffee and banana bread. If they did indeed arrest the senator, she wanted to be there to witness it. She had her camera ready.

At precisely 11:55, the elevator opened and out walked Rapoza, the police chief and Fuchs——in handcuffs. He held his chin high, and wore a look on his face that seemed to say, *I'm untouchable.* Lu dropped her pencil, lifted her camera and snapped away before anyone had a chance to know what was going on. No doubt the press would be outside the gates. Word of a dead body had a way of traveling.

"Son of a bitch," she muttered under her breath.

She jumped up and trotted over to them as they made their way out across the sea-blue tiles. Fuchs instinctively went to raise his arm over his head, but they were bound behind him. "Senator Fuchs, do you have any comment?" she said.

He said nothing.

"Did you have anything to do with the deaths of Joni Diaz and Gloria Moreno?" she asked.

Still, he remained quiet. Neither of the officers seemed to mind that she was following them.

Lu ran in front, finding the perfect angle. The lobby and the ocean beyond as a backdrop. *Click*. "Is it true you were a spy for the Japanese?" *Click*. "The Nazis?"

A fury blazed in his eyes for a split second. *Click*. Then he regained his cool. Smiled. "This is all a big misunderstanding. My people will sort it out. You'll see."

She lowered the camera. "I don't think so. Not this time, Senator."

A big, juicy piece of justice would be served. Lu was sure of it.

She booked a flight out for the following morning. Russi had been gone all day, and she began to wonder if he would even come back. She took it as a good sign. Watching her final sunset, she sat beneath the beach heliotrope tree just below the hotel, baking in the warm sand. She'd already swum the bay a couple of times, burning off tension from the past several days. Her limbs felt heavy in that satisfying, well-exercised way.

How was it that she should get to be sitting here, alive and feeling the sun on her skin, when her friend had washed up dead on this very same beach this morning? The unfairness stung. She thought of Russi and how, in war, he'd dealt with the same burning question on a daily basis. And not just Russi, but millions of others.

The sun dropped behind the clouds, sending out beams of gold in all directions. So much beauty. So much pain. Lu lifted up her camera and tried to frame the shot. There was too much beach, not enough ocean, so she stood up to find a better vantage point. Dusting sand from her skirt.

"Get closer to the water," a voice behind her said.

She turned. Russi was standing there with Izzy, lit by the sun. There was so much love surrounding them you could almost see the shimmer.

"You two, get over there. Now," she said, motioning them to stand at the water's edge.

Izzy grabbed Russi by the hand and pulled him over. They stood in the wet sand, arm in arm, heads together. Ocean lapped at their feet. Russi didn't complain. Just smiled, big and wide.

Click.

In the morning, Lu got an unexpected call. It was early, before coffee. She was still in bed, one leg under the covers and one out, listening to the sound of the ocean. Amid all the chaos of the past few days, she hadn't made it to the farm yet to visit her dad. A part of her had held out hope that he and Donna would make the drive up to see her. They hadn't. Some things you just had to make peace with.

She reached out and picked up. "Hello?"

"Luana? That you?"

The most familiar voice. Crackly. Deep.

"Dad, good morning."

"Have you seen the *Tribune* yet?"

"No, but I know all about the story. Believe it or not, Joni and I had become friends before she disappeared," she said.

"The story isn't about Joni Diaz, it's about you."

Lu sat up. "What do you mean, *me*?"

"It talks about you—island girl made it big. How you went away to college and landed a job at *Sunset* and now are back to cover the Mauna Kea hotel, and how you helped with the Diaz case. It even has your picture," he said.

She was having a hard time registering this news. Surely he must be mistaken. Or maybe she was dreaming. She pinched her thigh to be sure.

"But I haven't even spoken to any reporters. Who would write a story about me of all people?" she said.

"Says here it's a special to the *Hilo Daily Tribune* by Matteo Russi. That's your buddy, isn't it, the one you took down to see Mrs. Hoapili?"

Oh, shit.

"He didn't!"

"Looks like he did."

All this time, while she'd thought she had been interviewing Russi, Russi had been studying her, taking her in. He'd flipped the table on its end, and Lu had never even suspected. As much as Russi didn't like his picture taken, Lu did not like to be written about. She was the one who did the writing. The person behind the story. Never the story.

She heard chukar birds making their distinct racket in the background. That and the distant sound of a motor. Her father took a sip of his coffee—she heard him swallow—and could picture him perfectly. Sitting on the lānai on the worn wooden bench, pulling on his work boots. Sun filtering through the banana patch. Spiderwebs and stillness.

He cleared his throat. "I know I should have said this a long time ago, but I wish I could have been a better dad to you over the years. I was so wrapped up in my own bullshit I dropped the ball. Big-time."

He paused. Lu waited for him to go on. Her dad never talked about feelings, so this was new territory.

"Then you wanted to leave for the mainland and I wanted you to stay. You thought I had no faith in you, but that wasn't it."

"What was it, then?" she asked.

"I thought if I could keep you close, on island, I wouldn't lose you. But I kinda lost you, anyway."

His words were bittersweet, and Lu felt sad for their lost past, but hopeful that this might be a turning point. He was wrong about one thing, though.

"Dad, you never lost me. I still love you, no matter what. Me leaving had nothing to do with you or the farm. It had everything to do with college and a career and experiencing life somewhere else for a while."

"You're just like your mom, you know that? She had all the brains."

"Don't sell yourself short, Dad. You are smarter than most people I know. The world needs people with knowledge of the land and the plants. Farmers are not given near enough credit as far as I'm concerned."

That got a laugh. "You never thought so when you were a teenager."

"Teenagers rebel. It's their job."

"Yeah, well, I gotta admit I'm glad you're past that stage. And I see now that you were meant for bigger things."

Bigger came out *biggah*, as all his words were tinged with pidgin.

"*Different* things, Dad, not bigger."

"Are you still coming down to visit? If not, we'll come up that side. Donna wants to see the hotel, too."

"I'll be down for a quick hello before I fly out. I leave from Kona. Nothing about this trip went as planned, and I have to get home to see someone before he leaves for Vietnam. But I'll be back soon."

Sooner than you know.

epilogue

Winter is dry season on the western slopes of Hualālai, but even then, the foliage is dense and green and plump with moisture. On this particular Tuesday, honeybees buzzed in the occasional ohia blossom, and Hawaiian hawks floated overhead. Lu felt as though she'd just been here, and yet in these last six months, so much had happened.

Joni had been laid to rest in her hometown just outside of Los Angeles, with Lu and Russi both in attendance at a private ceremony under a cluster of weeping willow trees. Hearing Joni's voice, her song, her laughter, coming out of the record player only added to the heartbreak of the day. She might have been famous all the world over, and larger than life, but she was as mortal as the rest of us.

In the United States District Court in Honolulu, the Fuchs trial wrapped up in just over a month, with convictions of two counts of murder, and conspiracy to commit espionage—in large part due to Isabel's testimony and the decoded Japanese message she had kept all those years. The FBI was also able to directly connect him with Kuehn and the passing of US secrets to the Japanese. Lu had been called to testify, as well, eager to do her part in putting him away for as long as possible. The scratches on his side also helped condemn him, as did his wife admitting he had slipped out of the room that night and later returned with wet hair. In the end, Fuchs was sentenced to life in prison without parole, and sent to Leavenworth. A small price to pay for the evil he had wrought on the world and almost gotten away with.

And in a big leap of faith, Lu had left her job at *Sunset* and written up the story on Russi, who had bared all. It was emotional and raw and real. He was a champ through the whole thing. Not only that, but she and Russi teamed up on the story about Fuchs. *Time* magazine had eagerly bought both, and they used her photo of Fuchs being taken out of the Mauna Kea in handcuffs. Since then, she'd been hired as a staff writer at *Paradise of the Pacific*. Russi had been right, after all. Hawai'i needed her, and she needed Hawai'i.

This time, as they bounced up the unpaved road to the coffee farm, Lu was with Dylan, not Russi.

"I still can't believe you grew up here. It's beautiful, but it reminds me of the jungles in 'Nam, only without Charlies hiding out in the next bush with pockets full of grenades and AK-47s ready to blow you to smithereens," he said.

Lu glanced over at him. "Nope, these forests are safe. The only thing you really need to worry about is Hualālai erupting, but who knows when that will be next. Maybe another thousand years." She reached over and grabbed his hand. "I'm glad you're here."

He seemed twenty years older.

"You think you're glad," he said, slowly shaking his head.

The timing had worked out perfectly. Dylan had called late one night from his little apartment in Saigon and told her he was coming home, by way of Hawai'i. Every minute that he was away, there'd been a silent ticking clock in her head. He called when he could, telling her how he'd hitched a ride on a chopper to the front lines at the Delta in the morning, jumped into the trenches with the grunts and made it back to Saigon by nightfall to telex his story. About the soldier who'd fallen on a mine, not thirty feet ahead. And that maybe being a war correspondent wasn't his thing.

In July, after leaving the Mauna Kea, she'd made it to San Francisco in time to see him for one hour before they had to leave for the airport. He had a duffel bag bulging with camera gear and a backpack larger than him waiting patiently by the door. Lu knew it was now or possibly never to let him know how she felt. On the plane ride, she'd been rehearsing what to say, and imagining the particular facial expressions her words would elicit.

Dylan, I need to tell you something.

I think I might like you more than just friends.

Please don't go.

And he would say, *I have to.*

As it turned out, she didn't need to say anything at all. The minute she stepped in the door, he swept her into his arms and pulled her close. She smelled Ivory soap on his skin and beer on his breath. He messed up her hair with his big hands, which for some reason made her want to cry. Her ear fit in the depression just below his clavicle—he was that tall—and she could hear his heartbeat. A strong reminder that he was alive, at least for the moment.

"I've been thinking a lot about us since I got the call. We've known each other for how long now? And you know what the crazy thing is?" he said.

She could hardly breathe. "What?"

"I only just now realized how much I love you. Like, really love you."

He spoke as though it were the most natural thing in the world. No hesitancy, no nervousness, just God's honest truth. When she didn't answer, he pried her from his chest and looked into her eyes. "Say something?"

Lu felt wingbeats beneath her ribs. "I know. I love you, too. Always have."

Later, she watched him walk out onto the tarmac, jeans a little too loose, arms a little too long. But those arms were the finest arms she knew. And they loved her. And she loved them. And now they were going off to cover a war that no one was really sure about. Men were dying on both sides in alarming numbers. Innocent people were being shot in the streets. Vietcong were *cracking the sky* and *shaking the earth*, and Americans were caught in the middle. So, when he called to say he was coming home, she knew what she had to do.

Isabel had left the truck for them at the airport that morning, and Lu and Dylan had flown over together from Honolulu, holding hands the entire way. Every chance he could, he touched her. Hand on her back, leg up against hers. Elbows bumping.

Now, they pulled up to the house. When Lu shut the engine, quiet settled in, under the seats, between her shoulder blades, all around them. She felt home in a way she never had before. Which made her think, *Home is a feeling, not a place.*

"You sure she doesn't mind me tagging along with you?" he asked.

"She's going to love you, come on."

While they were rustling around in the back, grabbing bags, Isabel appeared on the porch. She was holding a jug full of something orange, hopefully lilikoi juice. She set the jug on the table and ran down the stairs. Lu introduced her to

Dylan, who she hugged as though he were her own son coming home from war. A good sign, because Isabel could come off a little aloof at times. Not if you were her inner circle, though. Those lucky few were loved fiercely and they knew it.

"I was starting to worry you wouldn't get here while it was still light," Isabel said.

"I wouldn't miss this for the world," Lu said.

Isabel took them up back to the *paniolo* cabin, a little red-and-white house that was half fireplace, half deck. Every nook and cranny was covered in cowboy paraphernalia—hats, ropes, horseshoes, spurs, old black-and-white photos of cattle drives down the coast where the interisland steamer waited. Isabel loved antique hunting and had a nose for it. When Lu was lucky, she'd get to tag along. Her favorite find was an old leather saddle from Samuel Parker himself. Never mind that she had no horse to put it on. *There's always some-day*, Isabel had said.

After a quick freshen-up, they found Isabel sitting on the porch swing, holding a glass of red wine. She wasn't alone. Matteo Russi was by her side, Primo beer in hand. Her head rested on his shoulder as though it had always belonged there. One of his arms was slung around her. The swing lightly moved back and forth.

Click.

Russi smiled wide. "Would you look at what the cat dragged in."

Lu rushed up. "I can't believe you're here!"

"Believe it, kid. I bought a one-way."

Isabel glowed from the inside out. "He did."

Dylan stood, mouth agape, then regained his composure and stuck out his hand. "Mr. Russi, I'm a big fan."

Russi pulled him in for a half hug. "I hear you took one for the team. My hat's off to you for going over there, man."

"It's the least I could do."

Isabel steered them down the steps. "We'll have plenty of time to talk later, but I'd like to get this done while we still have sunlight."

They followed her across the driveway, through a hole in the rock wall and into a newly mowed area. There was a long wooden bench, cut out of a massive ohia trunk. Someone had left two shovels, two sets of gloves and a bunch of young coffee trees in burlap, ready for planting. Russi whistled and, a moment later, Mele and a little donkey came trotting down the driveway and into the clearing.

"Pepeiao, look how big you've gotten!" Lu said.

Pepeiao made a beeline toward Russi.

Isabel laughed. "You should see these two. She follows him around like an imprinted duckling. He slips her guavas when he thinks I'm not watching."

While Mele seemed only mildly interested in the group, Pepeiao rubbed her neck against Russi, and sniffed his pockets. Russi produced a few small apple cubes in his palm and shrugged. "What can I say? Love is love."

Lu watched Isabel watch Russi. The way her smile lines deepened, and how her eyes lingered long after he'd finished speaking. It was as though she had to make up for all that time apart. Years of longing finally quenched.

They were here to plant a small grove of special coffee trees in honor of Walt. *Walter Grove.* A living legacy that would always remind them of the loving, kind and idealistic man that he was. Big brother, best friend, gone too young on this same day, twenty-four years ago. Walt had now been dead almost as long as he'd been alive.

Russi and Isabel took the shovels and got to work. Lu and Dylan carefully placed a sapling in each hole, covering them back up and adding fresh mulch and mac-nut shells. It felt good to get her hands back in the dirt. Hear the sound of honeycreeper wings whirring through the forest. Sweat well earned. There was a strong feeling that all was right in the world.

After the last sapling went in, Isabel pulled out an old crumpled envelope with a letter. Russi put his arm around her waist, protectively. Tenderly. She began to read.

Dear Sis,

I do believe I've fallen in love, and her name is Hawai'i. I am smitten with everything about her. There is no other place I'd rather be stationed on the whole of this planet. The water is warm, the air is sweet and you can walk around in shorts all year 'round. At least that's what they tell me. By they, I mean the locals, who are as friendly as they come and are constantly offering to teach us new things. How to do the hula, play the ukulele or surf on the rollers outside of Waikiki.

My partner in crime is a guy named Matteo Russi, a real firecracker from New York City. He flies circles around me, but I don't mind. It's good to have guys like that on your team. Russi and I have been surfing a couple of times and been bit by the bug. It's like flying, only on water. You would love it. And come to think of it, you'd love him. We already have plans to move over to a place called Kona and start a coffee farm when this blows over.

I sometimes forget why we're really here, that overseas there are wars going on, but that forgetting goes away as soon as we go out for training, and practice landings on a tiny strip in the dark. The skies out here are black as hell. You could have filled a whole bucket with the sweat off my brow. For the meantime, I'm going to enjoy every beautiful day in this place. You need to come visit, or maybe even get yourself stationed here, too. I'm sure they could use you. Miss you to the stars and back.

From Hawai'i, with love,
Walt

That night, sitting around the firepit, they drank a little too much wine and told stories about the war. The old war and the new war. Dylan and Russi hit it off splendidly, and once the two of them started talking cameras, Lu moved close to Isabel. They sat arm in arm.

She could feel Walt's presence all around, even though she had never met him. He so clearly lived on. Not only in their hearts, but in every tree and every flower. In the donkeys that carried the coffee beans. The clouds that watered the land. The soil. The starry sky. Maybe that was the secret to dying—to live a life with so much heart that, when you go, you are never really gone.

★ ★ ★ ★ ★

author note

While this novel is purely fictional, and the characters and story arose out of my imagination, there are places, people and events in this book that are inspired by real places, people and events. Certain facts have been tweaked for the sake of story.

In the 1943 story line, the Dungeon, also known as Station Hypo, was a real place where highly classified work was done. It was here—and at a few other key places like Washington, DC, and the Philippines—where enemy messages were decrypted that helped the Allies win the war. This was where Joe Rochefort worked, and he and his men were instrumental in winning the battle of Midway. Though there were no women in the Dungeon (to my knowledge), over ten thousand women worked tirelessly on cracking German and Japanese ciphers and codes throughout the war. These women were our secret superpower, and they did everything from breaking major codes to translating messages to traffic analysis. I was inspired by a few particular women, especially those who worked on the Japanese cipher machine Purple (what I call Magenta, though Purple was actually solved much earlier) and JN-25, the Japanese naval code.

Operation Vengeance and the shooting down of Admiral Yamamoto's plane was a pivotal part of the war in the Pacific, and a major blow to Japan. It was a daring feat with terrible odds of success, but succeed they did. I found the book *Lightning Strike: The Secret Mission to Kill Admiral Yamamoto and Avenge Pearl Harbor* by Donald A. Davis to be highly informative as well as a fascinating read. The real pilots who made up the "killer" flight to actually take down Yamamoto's plane were Captain Thomas G. Lanphier Jr., Lieutenant Rex T. Barber, Lieutenant Besby F. Holmes and Lieutenant Raymond K. Hine. And the pilots chosen to cover the "killer" pilots and provide backup were Major John Mitchell, Lieutenant William Smith, Lieutenant Gordon Whittiker, Lieutenant Roger Ames, Captain Louis Kittel, Lieutenant Lawrence Graebner, Lieutenant Doug Canning, Lieutenant Delton Goerke, Lieutenant Julius Jacobson, Lieutenant Eldon Stratton, Lieutenant Albert Long and Lieutenant Everett Anglin.

Otto Kuehne (full name Bernard Julius Otto Kuehn) was a German national convicted in Hawai'i as a spy in early 1942. He used his family to help gather information on American forces and sent it to Japanese consulates. Otto was sentenced to death by firing squad, but after the war he was deported to Germany. Regarding the Tomimura message that helps prove Fuchs was a spy, there really was a navy yeoman named Harry Thompson, who was recruited by the Japanese in the 1930s to board ships and provide engineering, tactical and gunnery info about the US Pacific Fleet in San Diego. Famed cryptanalyst Agnes Meyer Driscoll had a hand in deciphering an intercepted message that helped nail him. The real Thompson was convicted and sentenced to fifteen years in prison, though had it been wartime, he would have most likely received the death penalty.

In the 1965 story line, the Mauna Kea Beach Hotel is indeed a real place, and I tried to stick to the facts as much as possible regarding the hotel itself and Laurance Rockefeller. In July of 1965 the hotel opened with big fanfare, and there was a VIP weekend with Mr. Rockefeller's special guests. However, the characters in this novel are my own creations, as was the story line—there was no murder on the opening weekend. My grandparents were at the opening of the hotel. They lived in Waimea in the 1970s, and whenever we went to visit them, they'd take us to brunch and then set us free on the beach. It was always a highlight of our trips and I have fond memories. Also, since then, I've spent countless hours swimming, snorkeling, paddling, hiking, sailing and surfing in Kauna'oa Bay and up and down the Kohala Coast, so I know the hotel and the area well. It truly is a magical and special place, and I hope I've done it justice in my descriptions.

I can't even believe that I have five books out in the world now and a bunch more stewing in my brain. Being an author is a dream come true for me! I am grateful to everyone who helped me give birth to this novel. My wonderful agent, Elaine Spencer, who helps guide me every step of the way. My talented and extraordinarily insightful editor, Margot Mallinson, who has such skill for drastically improving my stories, and the whole team at MIRA, who have all been great champions of my work. It really does take a village to put a book out into the world, and I feel blessed to have such a fabulous village. Also, it takes a patient man to live with me when I am writing and have my head in the clouds much of the time—forgetting to screw on the lid to the peanut butter or rinse the sand off my feet—so thank you to my loving boyfriend, Todd Clark. I'm also very thankful for the sharp eye of William Hochman, aka Bulldog 6, who helped me with technical and WWII details, as well as just being a huge support overall. And to all my friends who help me brainstorm and come up with book ideas and mull things over with me and read early copies, you know who you are. Malia and Dolan Eversole helped me plot this one—thanks guys. It truly has been an honor to write these WWII Hawai'i stories, and I thank each and every one of you for reading them. *Mahalo nui loa!*